SINFUL SECRETS OMNIBUS

A Pride & Prejudice Variation

EMMA EAST

Copyright © 2022 by Emma East

All rights reserved.

No part of this book may be reproduced in any form or by any electronic or mechanical means, including information storage and retrieval systems, without written permission from the author, except for the use of brief quotations in a book review.

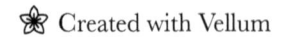

❀ Created with Vellum

FOUND BY DARCY
BOOK ONE

I

SHE HATED DARCY.

No. That wasn't the whole of it, wasn't strong enough. She *loathed* Darcy. Despised him and his smug airs and the sneer he held for the people beneath him—which was nearly everyone in his scornful eyes. Her vocabulary was not capable of adequately painting the picture of her loathing, but if she tried, she would verbally paint the picture of a man trapped inside a house and a bucket of water sitting untouched at her side.

And why did she loathe Darcy? Charlotte would call her silly. *Do not defend the poor man with no prospects and anger an esteemed man like Fitzwilliam Darcy.* But as couples swirled around them, heedless of the glares Darcy and Elizabeth exchanged, the clashing of two powerful wills, Elizabeth was not predisposed to follow her friend's advice.

"Then you would admit you treated a man who should have been like family to you in such a loathsome way?"

"I did not admit to that," Darcy said.

"But you didn't answer, and your silence speaks volumes, sir."

There was so much venom in his eyes that surely she would die right there in the middle of Netherfield ballroom. The dance continued, emotions absent, rehearsed, both stiff with rage. When the dance forced them to touch, he ripped his hands back as soon as he could, as if the temptation to strangle her meant he couldn't touch her beyond a few moments.

As he moved back a couple paces, mimicking her steps, he said, "If you are so keen to defend Wickham, then you must have proof of these salacious stories of his."

"The proof lies in his condition," she snapped.

A muscle in Darcy's cheek jumped. "I see. You rely only on his word, then. A man who can hardly be called a gentleman."

Her eyes widened. *Further* proof of his vicious bias against Wickham. "Unlike you, I don't care if his father was a steward."

Darcy's expression flickered, and she tilted her chin high because *of course* Darcy would be surprised a young lady like herself wouldn't care for the trappings of title and wealth. He would expect her and everyone else to think exactly as he did.

"I see," Darcy said, and they joined together in the dance, walking sedately down the line, her fingertips barely touching the sleeve of his arm though she should have been clasping his hand. His tone gritty, hard, he said, "Then I do not see what else we have to say to one another."

They reached the end of the line. His eyes flashed as she glared at him. "That might be the first time we agree."

"Very well," he said. And he did not speak another word for the length of the dance.

The way his eyes gleamed with danger made several people glance nervously at him as they passed down the line. With his dark curls, broad shoulders leading down to a tapered waist, and strong, athletic thighs, many of these glances lingered in admiration. But Darcy had none of it, his stern expression rebuffing any who might wish to get close.

Not Elizabeth. She did not wish to get close, and not all the smiles in the world would change her mind. The muscles in her jaw ached from clenching her teeth for so long. Elizabeth loved dancing, but tonight she wished she had broken her leg.

"Why did he even ask me to dance?" she asked Charlotte whenever she could finally escape and sought refuge in the arms of her friend. Darcy had not even looked at her when he bowed at the end!

Charlotte was peering over her shoulder. "I don't know, since now he is glaring so fiercely I suspect he wants to throw you out of Netherfield."

"I wish he would," she snapped, feeling heat climbing the back of her neck. "Without Lt. Wickham here, there's nothing to look forward to."

"You could always dance with your cousin again. He came by looking for you."

She scowled. "I hope you told him I jumped from the balcony."

"He said he would look for you after the set ended. Lizzy, what *are* you doing? You anger Mr. Darcy, you spurn the attention of your cousin, all for a soldier in the regiment who could not trouble himself to come to Netherfield as promised."

"Because he wishes to avoid a scene with Mr. Darcy," Elizabeth insisted. "It is *his* fault he is not here. As for my cousin, I would rather eat flies than look at him. Did you know he set his sights on Jane before Mama told him Jane had a suitor? Then—and I tell you, I watched this play out in our sitting room—he looked about the room at my other sisters and then settled on *me*. Now he expects me to be grateful for his attention because I am not the loveliest, and yesterday he recited a list of the traits he requires in his wife."

Charlotte's expression grew increasingly amused as Elizabeth continued, and now her eyes glittered with mirth. "And what was on this list, pray?"

"The usual tenets to obey and be bored to death, as you can imagine, with the added requirement to be a humble supplicant under her husband's tutelage in all matters." Charlotte made an indelicate noise. "Exactly my thoughts."

Charlotte opened her mouth and then paused at the sight of something behind Elizabeth. Elizabeth knew that look all too well, and clamped her mouth closed.

"There you are!"

Elizabeth grimaced at Charlotte at her mother's screech, delivered directly by Elizabeth's left ear. Charlotte beat a hasty retreat after a sympathetic look at her friend's predicament. Elizabeth watched her friend leave and wished she could escape too.

"You silly girl, *what* could induce you to hide and ignore your cousin, Mr. Collins?"

Elizabeth mentally braced herself as she faced her mother. People started turning their heads, only causing the stinging in Elizabeth's cheeks to grow worse.

"Mama, not here," she said, or tried to say. Her mother was having none of it.

"He told me you ran off directly after your dance and didn't even share a drink with him. What kind of game are you playing, spurring the man who could kick us out of our home when your poor father is gone?"

She looked around helplessly. "Mama, you're attracting attention."

"Good! Perhaps the scrutiny of our neighbors will force you to behave for once in your life. Reckless, bold, proud. You'll see us on the streets, and for what? For your little scribblings? You spend more time with ink on your hands in those worlds you imagine than you do seeing the world you live in, the world where we need your help."

Anger flushed her cheeks now. Her mother did not like Elizabeth's hobby, though her stories and poetry did no one any harm. But any way she could dig at Elizabeth's confidence, Mrs. Bennet would take, and painting a picture of Elizabeth's scribblings being the cause of their eventual destitution pleased her mother's flair for the dramatics.

"Of course I won't choose writing over our family," Elizabeth tried. "I was dancing."

Her mother, naturally, did not listen. She grabbed Elizabeth's arm, grip pinching her as she turned her toward the far wall. "Now I am marching you over to Mr. Collins right now, so you might make a good impression on him. Stop with this proud attitude, Lizzy. No other man has shown an inclination for you, so you may as well help your family by encouraging Mr. Collins."

"I don't *want* to encourage Mr. Collins. You've encouraged him enough for the both of us," she protested, and managed to extricate herself from her mother's grip. As her mother spluttered behind her, Elizabeth slipped into the crowd, her only goal was to get away.

Once far enough away from her mother, she slowed her steps and corrected her carriage to one of confidence, though her insides jittered with various anxieties. Her mother would do anything to secure her future and the future of Longbourn, but she had never thought that might mean forcing Elizabeth to encourage Mr. Collins. Elizabeth would speak to her father as soon as she could. Mrs. Bennet would surely listen to him, and realize Elizabeth would never marry the odious parson.

Searching the room for a friendly face, she caught the eye of the man in question. His face lit up, and he gestured her over, spilling half of his punch on the floor as he did so. Elizabeth grimaced and ducked behind another guest, using their bulk to search for Charlotte or Jane.

Jane was in the line of dancers with the gregarious Mr. Bingley. Elizabeth envied her for a moment, wishing someone would look at *her* with utter devotion, and then she slipped away through the crowd in the opposite direction. She would look for Charlotte in one of the other rooms.

But as she darted into the hallway, Mr. Collins called out for her attention, and she realized with mounting dread that she had not lost him at all.

Where to go? Where to go? Let Mr. Collins corner her and he would undoubtedly bore her to tears for the rest of the night. She glanced behind her, fearful to realize he was following at a good speed, though right then he stopped to apologize profusely to a gentleman whose toes he'd stomped on.

A distraction. Elizabeth put it to good use, and hurried forward, slipping between guests, using her size to her advantage as she escaped further into the crowded hallway. Mr. Collins' alarmed cry far behind her made her grin.

But where to go from here?

Guests pressed up against her, the space so tight here in the hall she could barely breathe. The entranceways to the sitting room and dining room were similarly crowded. The

Bingleys had invited the whole county and nearly the entire regiment here tonight, and no one had turned down the invitation.

Except Wickham, she thought with a scowl.

A loud, braying laugh caught her attention. Lydia was on the stairs with Kitty and a few of the soldiers. While the stairs were occupied with so many people, the balcony appeared empty. If she could slip up there, maybe she could tuck herself away into a room somewhere for the remainder of the night. It meant a boring evening, but at least she could escape Mr. Collins and her mother couldn't harangue her anymore.

A flash of black in the corner of her eye made her choice for her. She hurried forward and up the stairs, not daring to look back and catch the eye of the parson. People parted for her and Lydia said something as she passed, her glittering eyes speaking to the amount of punch she had imbibed, but Elizabeth went on without answering. She slipped around the corner and out of sight.

Elizabeth remembered the layout of the upstairs from her unfortunate visit here while Jane recuperated under Mr. Bingley's care. She scurried to the study, found it empty, and closed the door behind her.

A few minutes passed with her ear pressed to the door. It didn't sound as if he followed her. She sighed and straightened away from the door.

If she had to hide away for the evening, there was no better place to spend it. A wall of shelves held at least a hundred books, all of them bound in rich leather. She approached the bookcase, grazing the lip of a shelf with her fingers as she walked down the wall, admiring the works of dozens, if not hundreds, of authors.

All male. For now, that was what society expected. Great

works were written by men while women were resigned to penny tales. Elizabeth wanted to change that. She wanted to have her name bound in leather with expensive gold leaf and foil.

"I'll be here among you one day," she said, picking up a volume at random.

If only people could *see* that. If her mother would stop haranguing her to become a wife, if she gave Elizabeth a chance instead of stifling her every creative thought, maybe…

It would never happen. Her mother, so set in her ways, had a little mind, and the thoughts on that mind were centered around protecting Longbourn. Elizabeth didn't want to lose her home, but it wasn't fair to make Elizabeth shoulder the burden either. She spent all her life second to her other sisters, prettier and more talented. Couldn't she have one thing—her life—to herself? Her father had promised she need never marry against her inclinations, but now that he was sick…

"What are you doing?"

Elizabeth spun, the book clutched to her chest. "You!"

One serious eyebrow lifted. "Indeed, it is I. A guest of this home. Unlike you, Miss Elizabeth."

Darcy might examine her like a bug waiting to be stomped under his heel, but she would not act like one. She lifted her chin. "Mr. Bingley said I was free to borrow any book I wished."

That eyebrow again. "During a party?"

She could be haughty, too. "I didn't find enough entertainment. I suppose the guest list was lacking in that area, likely through no fault of Miss Bingley's."

That irked him. The flash in his eyes said she had scored a point.

The irritation smoothed away, not a ripple giving away his displeasure. He took a step into the room, the door falling shut behind him with a click of hardware. Elizabeth tensed. There was something to Darcy that reminded her of etchings of hunting wolves. A sleek, savage beauty that could trick a person into forgetting the fangs hidden away. He stepped away from the door and prowled closer to her.

"You take inordinate pleasure in the company of a soldier, but do you truly know anything about him?"

Whatever she'd expected, that was not it. "I know enough," she said, squaring her shoulders.

Darcy's lips quirked at this response. The lamb bleating angrily at the lion. She scowled.

"Do you imagine he is giving you the same thought as you do him? That he holds a tender place in his heart for you?"

Closer, closer, but nevermind that. Her cheeks burned at his insinuation. To bring up something like that so blatantly... surely, he meant to obtain a rise out of her in retaliation for pricking his pride.

"I don't expect anything from the gentleman. He is a friend of mine and my family's."

"Is he now... with five young, handsome daughters? I imagine he's paid particular attention to your family."

"What do you insinuate?"

"I *insinuate* that his interests have less to do with making your acquaintance than finding a willing partner to his particular... past times."

Elizabeth's lips parted. He was closer now, feet away and coming closer, but she paid no mind as she instinctively rejected his statement. "Lieutenant Wickham has only *ever* been proper—"

"Yes, proper, to spill the supposed intimate details of his

life to an acquaintance. Unless you are particularly close?" He cocked his head, narrowed eyes assessing her every twitch. She couldn't imagine what he might mean, though a creeping suspicion unfurled uneasily in her stomach. His expression cleared. "I thought not. Therefore, Miss Elizabeth, you must ask yourself why he sought to gain your trust so quickly."

"I..." This line of discussion confused her greatly. She shook her head. "He sought-sought to warn me about you."

A hard glint in his eye. "A regular saint is he, George Wickham. What, pray, did he warn you of?"

It was all confused. His manner intimidated her, and she didn't know whether to attribute that to their privacy or his cool, predatory stare. The lamb had lost her bleat, and her shoulders hit the shelves behind her. Her voice shook when she said, "Your character was the main discussion. What you stripped from him was awful."

"What I stripped from him." He repeated it in a flat tone. "What *I* took from *him*."

And then he was upon her, flush against her with nothing but a book and a sliver of air between them.

Her eyes widened. "What are you doing?"

"Showing you what your beloved Wickham wants with you."

He kissed her. A savage, brutal kiss that held no love, only a need to impart a searing flame, to dominate. His grip squeezed the breath out of her, and she gasped against his mouth, helpless as he squeezed her to him. The fire of it.

The *fury*.

Like a man possessed, possessed by her, Elizabeth, seeing *her* like no one else ever could. Meeting her with a passion she didn't know existed outside her own soul. This was raw, not tempered by polite society expectations, but heat and fire and his tongue twining around hers as if he might die without it.

Elizabeth had two choices. She could yell and shriek and bring down the study with accusations—or she could do what she did, which was meet him with every ounce of fury held within her soul. Fury of having nothing of her own, desire to strike out. Their wills clashed and Darcy groaned into her mouth and buried his fingers in her hair, scattering pins over the floor with a clatter.

The noise made him jerk back. The study echoed with their gasps. He stared at her, fire still blazing bright in his eyes, and then his expression shifted and his arms fell from her sides. Elizabeth, chest heaving, stunned into silence, could only watch as he gave her one last furious look before he stormed out of the study.

2

Elizabeth didn't like to say vulgar words, but for Darcy, she would think them.

Irritating.

Awful.

Derisive.

Proud.

Amazing kisser.

A more despised human could not exist in Elizabeth's mind. It did not matter how handsome he was. How his generous mouth curved in an almost smile when something amused him. The curl to his hair that seemed so playful compared to his stern mien.

The way his large hands framed her face as he kissed her.

She shook the memory away. No. It was not right to think of Darcy in such a way. As if she had *wanted* to be kissed by a man who claimed to loathe her with every look. The firmness to his lips, the way he speared through her mouth in a provocative manner—how could one want such a thing?

Elizabeth left the thoughts out into the hall as she crept into her father's study. Due to his condition, the doctor advised them to keep Mr. Bennet downstairs for the time being. He refused to be anywhere other than his study, and a bed was placed there despite all of Mrs. Bennet's nervous sensibilities of such an action. It meant her father was comfortable in his favorite room in the house, and Elizabeth did not resent him for whatever small comfort it provided.

The room was dark, the curtains pulled tightly against the autumn chill. Slices of light interrupted the dark wood walls and cast gloomy shadows. The carpet absorbed her footsteps as she crossed the room to her father's bedside. Soft breaths puffed out of his thin lips. Elizabeth wrapped her hands around the bedpost and watched him for a long moment.

He used to be the first one up. The mornings they would spend walking around the estate, viewing the majesty of the morning before everyone came awake, remained her fondest memories. *What I would give to see you like that again, Papa...*

Her father had read to her stories about magic words and fairy godmothers. Some of her sisters focused on the parts of the story with the handsome prince. Elizabeth had always focused on the turns of phrase, the broad strokes of a pen painting a portrait easy to see in one's mind. How one told a story was more important than the story itself in her eyes.

Mr. Bennet had cultivated this unique viewpoint in his daughter, encouraged her interest despite Mrs. Bennet's horror of how she would turn out. An educated daughter was better than a married one, he would say, sending his wife into fits. Every time Mrs. Bennet insisted on a new dress, a pretty bonnet, Mr. Bennet was there in the background with a new book to study.

She looked at her father's weak body for a time, not daring to disturb his rest. *If only I could find a story to bring you back to us.*

The door closing behind her as she left her father's room had a finality she didn't want to confront. She loved her father more than anything, and the thought of him leaving her pierced her heart. Closing her eyes, she took a moment outside her father's room to push down the tears prickling behind her eyes.

"Dear cousin Lizzy. There you are."

Elizabeth jerked. After Darcy left the study, Elizabeth had remained upstairs in a daze until she saw the carriages pulling to the front of Netherfield Hall. Only then did she hurry downstairs and pretend to be part of the throng for her mother's benefit. Mr. Collins had expressed his displeasure over how little he had seen his dearest cousin over the course of the night, and she'd ignored the rest of his natter while they loaded into the carriage and said their goodnights. Her attention was too preoccupied by the dour visage of Darcy as he watched their party leave.

Mr. Collins smiled, revealing his crooked and misshapen teeth in a smarmy smile that made her light breakfast roil in her stomach. Her reprieve was over.

"Mr. Collins."

The curtness in her tone would have revealed her disinterest to a less tone-deaf man. However, Mr. Collins dazzled her with his stupidity. "Visiting your father, I see. You are a dutiful daughter, indeed. It is a compliment to your dear parents' rearing. How is your father this morning? I knocked earlier but heard no response."

"He seems—"

"In good spirits, I hope," he said with another sickening smile. "It is partly that which made me seek you out this morning."

Her head began to shake. "Mr. Collins—"

"I assure you your dear mother has given us the use of the front sitting room for this joyful occasion," he said, and Elizabeth was struck anew by how dreadful he was. As if she desired the attention of a man who reminded her of a pig in a parson's hat. A poorly dressed man, at that.

"I can walk on my own," she said, jerking her elbow away when he tried to grab her.

His smile returned as he grabbed her, his grip pinching and unyielding. "An independent spirit is not something to thumb one's nose at, of course, but there is a time and place, dearest cousin."

Jerking her arm back did nothing as he tightened his grip. She turned her head as he marched her toward the front of the house, desperate to find an excuse, an interruption to the dreadful event she suspected Mr. Collins would force her to suffer.

Her eye caught a shape in the doorway of the darkened dining room. "Mama," she said, recognizing her mother's distinctive cap. Imploring her didn't help, however. Mrs. Bennet merely slid deeper into the gloom.

There would be no help from that quarter. Quite the opposite. Her mood darkened and then turned to pain as Mr. Collins used his grip on her arm to shove her into the sitting room.

"Ow!"

She rubbed her arm, shooting an uneasy glance at Mr. Collins as she faced him. He did not look repentant. "I apologize for the need to handle you with more force than you are used to, my cousin. I assure you, it is meant kindly, only to assist you in meeting your mother's expectations that we might have a serious discussion today. You have a knack for being occupied right when I wish to speak to you!"

He wagged his finger at her like a naughty girl, but her attention focused on the door closing behind him.

Alone. With Mr. Collins.

"Mr. Collins, whatever you wish to say, I would preface it by kindly asking you to reconsider. I've no desire to disappoint you—"

"As well it should be for a compliant young lady as yourself." Mr. Collins' smile turned her stomach. She took a step back as he stepped away from the door. This time, unlike Darcy, she was not frozen with intimidation, but hasty in her disgust. The contrast between the two struck her for a moment, and then she stumbled over the rug and needed to pay attention to the moment. Mr. Collins shook his head. "You should be careful, cousin Elizabeth. Perhaps you should sit."

"I will stand," she said. Not so compliant, after all.

He gave her a patronizing smile. "I commend your spirit, cousin Elizabeth. I will dare to say that your uncommon spirit is one of your characteristics which drew me from the first time I stepped foot into Longbourn."

"Mr. Collins—" She debated fainting. Would it truly stop this madness, or would he propose to her unconscious body? Bile thickened in the back of her throat.

"I'm sure you are wondering the reason I brought you here this morning."

"I'm not, I assure you—"

He clasped his hands in front of him. "Upon my decision to journey to Longbourn, preceded by the noble Lady Catherine de Bourgh's insistence that I might come and make peace with your father after the acrimonious relationship he shared with my own father, I decided to choose amongst my no doubt lovely cousins to ensure the estate remained in the hands of family. Another peace-making gesture, of course, as I've no wish to hurt my dear family."

"I fear I must go," Elizabeth said, and made to draw around him. The tension inside her had grown too much to bear, and it was either escape or throw herself out the window.

"Cousin Elizabeth!" His eyes flared as he grabbed her elbow, stopping her hasty retreat, but Elizabeth was quick enough to jerk away in time. She hurried to the door and grabbed the door handle as he came after her. "Your mother has given me leave of your time this morning—"

A perfect excuse. She yanked open the door and escaped, calling over her shoulder, "My mother did not inform me of this. Good day, Mr. Collins!"

She did not get far before her mother caught up to her. "What happened? Has he offered? What did you say?"

"I dared not give him a chance to embarrass himself with my refusal," she said, trying to sidestep her mother. Angry tears threatened to fall over her eyelids. Her mother. Her own mother had given her permission despite knowing Elizabeth's desires. Her own mother now stared at Elizabeth as if Elizabeth had spit on her corpse.

She snatched Elizabeth's wrist before she could go far, cheeks turning red and her eyes furious.

"You shall get back in there and accept his *very* generous offer before he believes you to be ungrateful."

Elizabeth jerked her arm out of her mother's grasp and pushed past her. "I won't, I *won't!*"

Mrs. Bennet made an *oomph* as Elizabeth's reckless escape caused her to bump into the wall. Her voice was furious as she turned and called at her. "Lizzy, get back here! Elizabeth, do your duty to this house—"

"I won't!"

SHE RAN until she couldn't, and then she walked, leaving Longbourn in the distance. There was nowhere to go, though. It was hopeless. If she went to the village, her aunt would tell her to listen to her mother. Secure their future. But the image of Mr. Collins leading her into his bedroom made her stomach threaten to spill her meager breakfast.

No. Anything but that.

Elizabeth walked toward the village anyway, despite the anticipated lackluster welcome from her aunt. The forest on one side was thinned, their leaves stolen by the passing seasons. The sunrise filtered through the bare branches, casting pale light on the road and the fields which had seen its last crop harvested. She rubbed her hands over her arms, wishing she had something thicker than her shawl to protect her from the cold.

A rider in the distance surprised her. It was so early in the morning, dawn still shaping up in the sky as the rider approached down the lane. Elizabeth often walked at this hour because she wasn't likely to see another soul.

Her disappointment turned to bitter ash when she realized the rider was Darcy.

He did not slow his approach or show any reaction to seeing her. She forced herself forward. Maybe he would ride past her and they could pretend they didn't see each other at all. But as they got within feet of each other, Darcy did slow, his black gelding lifting its head as Darcy tightened the reins.

"Miss Bennet." His expression gave nothing away. He

could be speaking to a dog for as much emotion as he showed.

Her lips thinned. "Mr. Darcy."

"Where is your coat?"

As if he had a right to comment upon her wardrobe. She narrowed her eyes and lifted her chin. "The walk is invigorating enough to warm the blood."

He snorted. "It must not be so invigorating today. You are shivering."

Elizabeth hastily stepped backward as Darcy dismounted his horse. A cold burn brushed her cheeks as his muscled, strong thighs outlined by his doeskin breeches caught her attention. Pulling her shawl tighter, she cleared her throat and pretended the sight of his tight backside did nothing to her.

Darcy faced her, his sheer height surprising her. It seemed overnight every one of his physical traits appeared amplified in her mind. The cleft in his chin. The lock of hair curling across his forehead. She couldn't stop looking at him and finding something new to admire, something she hadn't given any thought to twenty-four hours ago.

Darcy gazed at her, and he did not seem equally captured by her physical beauty. "We need to speak."

"Then speak." She folded her arms, tucking her hands into the warmth of her body heat. Shivering, ha! She was perfectly fine.

"Not here." Darcy's gaze flicked over the deserted lane before he nodded at the trees. "There."

"Do we need that much privacy? Do you expect the road to tell your secrets?"

He strode away without a backward glance, his horse following sedately. Elizabeth groaned under her breath and followed, casting a wary look over her shoulder. Longbourn was in the distance, and it didn't appear as if anyone was chasing after her. What could it harm?

They entered the privacy the trees provided and then further, deeper, past the treeline. She wished she'd pulled on thicker socks before leaving home and she stifled a shiver as Darcy apparently found enough privacy for them and faced her.

"I won't marry you."

She drew up short as, disregarded now, Darcy's horse bent to mouth at the dying grass. "I didn't ask."

Darcy draped the reins over a low, dead branch before folding his arms and giving her a narrowed look. "Oh, yes, because after last night it would not be preying on your mind."

"Maybe it preyed on yours, but I was not so unfortunate," she said, the rush of seeing the truth on his expression warm and addicting. She smirked. "Suffice to say, I have better things to think of than *you*, Mr. Darcy."

His eyebrow lifted. "Is that so?"

"I don't want anything to do with you. The last thing I wish to do is marry you."

A point. Another brief rush, petty though their verbal sparring was. She bit back a smile, seeing his narrowed eyes. "So you say. Your mouth has a habit of contradicting your body, does it not?"

Her smile died. "My lips and my body are on the same page."

Challenge flared in those dark eyes. *Caution, Lizzy.* She straightened her shoulders as he took a step forward.

"Shall we test the veracity of that?"

Curiosity prickled under her skin. Leaving was her best option, but she wasn't one to leave a question unanswered, even if it was in her best interest to get as far away from

Darcy as she could. Besides, she couldn't deny the warm feeling his attention stirred in her middle. She didn't want to leave the heat and go back to the cold of not knowing.

"Why would you want to? It's *you* who said you don't want to marry me."

Expression impassive, he stepped toward her, leaves crunching under his boots as he closed the distance between them. "Call me inquisitive. I see before me a woman who would argue about the color of the sky with me. Is it because I spurned you?"

A laugh burst free from her, her eyes widening. "Spurned? I see the way you look at me. That is not a man who's successfully spurned a woman."

Darcy's brows drew down, that spark of irritation telling her she had scored another point. He made it too easy. But the realization that she was right was overshadowed by Darcy bearing down on her.

She stumbled backward, but she'd forgotten her surroundings. The breath whooshed out of her when her back hit a hard tree trunk. Darcy's dark eyes grew bigger, the blacks in them growing to blot out the color. Trapped with nowhere to go.

"Tell me how I look at you, Miss Elizabeth Bennet," he said, his voice a croon that slid down her spine like a lover's caress. A curl fell over his eye as he dipped his head, so close his warm breath washed over her cheek. "Tell me why you're looking so hard."

"Darcy…"

His hand came up and cupped her throat, the barest pressure hiding a dangerous threat. "Could it be that you enjoyed what happened last night? Could it be you pine for a repeat demonstration?" His gaze dropped to her lips, his eyes two black pools now, and she dared not breathe, her lungs burning.

Darcy crushed his mouth against hers.

Alive. Golden light poured through Elizabeth, blazed through her anxieties and burned them away as Darcy bore her back. Her hands came up, clinging to him as her knees buckled.

The question of how he did this to her was considered and discarded. What mattered was the now, the rush of his hands grabbing her sides and dragging her to him. She wasn't wearing as much underneath her dress either, meaning that when he cupped her breasts, she could feel it like nothing she ever had before.

"Is this what you want?" he growled. She whimpered, alive under his touch like she'd never thought she could be. Melting into him, she gloried in his touch, him plucking and twisting her nipples until she was gasping and whining under his touch.

He nipped her bottom lip, the rush of pain a complement to the need burning inside her. A need for something she didn't understand, didn't know how to articulate beyond pointing to the growing fire through her middle.

"Darcy…"

"Is this what you want? Tell me." His voice, roughened with desire, tugged at that feeling in her center. His tongue parted her lips the next instant, swallowing her cry, and she burned so hot she expected steam to rise off her skin. He pulled away, and then bit her lip when she chased after him. *"Tell me."*

"Yes, yes!" Her nails scored his cravat, ruining the perfect lines of it as he ruined her. "Please!"

With a frustrated noise, he pulled back and her back hit the tree as he scrabbled at her skirts, exposing her to the cold air. She grabbed at his shoulders, not knowing why she was pulling at him, and then his hand dived between her thighs. Two crows in the trees overhead flew off at her cry.

"You're slick for me," Darcy said, voice washed away, as if he couldn't believe she'd given him such a precious gift. Then his mouth slanted over hers with a fury he'd so far reserved solely for her, and she clung to him as he speared her with both tongue and finger. The pressure was tight, not wholly comfortable, her nerves sizzling with his touch as he parted her lower lips and thrust deep into her. "Fuck, you're on fire," he groaned, and the obscenity was almost as arousing as the hand between her legs.

He thrust against her, the outline of his erection against her hip giving her a little thrill each time he rubbed it against her. But it was his hand between her legs that sent her gasping and clutching at his jacket. The way his palm spread open her lower lips, pressing against something that made her whole body go *zing*, was pure magic.

She came with another cry, loud and clear, bursting from her lips until Darcy smothered it with his mouth and tongue. He soaked her up as she clenched around him, pressing and rubbing until she was a limp mess, held up only by his hips and his hand.

Darcy took everything, stealing it away with vicious satisfaction. And when she was left panting for breath, he pulled back and held her gaze as he sucked his wet fingers into his mouth.

Elizabeth returned to Earth, never knowing something as obscene as Darcy licking her dew off his fingers could be so arousing. His dark eyes never left hers, a challenge she was both afraid to meet and excited to chase. She leaned back against the tree, catching her breath.

Darcy dropped his hand to his side, his gaze raking over

her disheveled form with evident satisfaction. "Clean yourself up," he said, and turned away.

Watching him go, unable to move on her weak legs, she at least didn't have to worry about the cold weather anymore. Darcy had rid her of her shivers, perhaps permanently.

3

"Do you know what we need to improve our miserable moods?"

Darcy's furrowed brow did not smooth out at Miss Bingley's question behind him, the cheer in her voice too forceful, calculated to pique his interest. "Yes?" he said, because polite manners dictated he respond to an outright question. Although Miss Bingley certainly needed no encouragement, Darcy felt it prudent to respond or else risk her poking at his temper all night.

He stared out the window, the cold and dreary day reflected in the landscape. Greyness had settled to camp over Netherfield and the surrounding countryside, and it put a shiver in his bones. The trees were bare or were almost there, and his gaze continuously turned in the direction of a certain house of a certain family with a certain daughter who intrigued him.

"Mr. Darcy, I believe you're gathering wool while I'm attempting to speak to you." Over his shoulder, Miss Bingley pouted.

He withheld a sigh. "What were you saying?"

"I should hardly tell you if you are not paying attention. Pray, perhaps *you'll* tell *me* what has caught your attention. You've been so moody the last couple days."

What right Caroline Bingley thought she had to monitor his moods, he did not wish to investigate. "The weather."

A simple, curt answer, and Miss Bingley's shoulders dipped as she realized that was the only answer she would get from him. She rallied in the next instant, a spark flaring in her eyes, her cool determination burning fiercely.

"It's this place," she said. "What I think we need to get us out of all these horrible moods, is to return to London. The weather may not be much better, but the entertainments are, I daresay."

Mrs. Hurst, sitting beside the fire, snorted at the understatement.

"What I propose," Miss Bingley said, drawing across the sitting room to stand beside Darcy, though she shivered a little away from the fire, "is we leave in the morning and go after my brother. Surely, the both of us together can convince him to stay a little while longer before we return here to this dreadful situation."

The way she sneered at the room was hardly called for, especially after her extensive re-decorating prior to the ball. The walls were freshly wallpapered, the floors shone, the drapes were thick and elegant. But perhaps she sneered at the way her brother-in-law's mouth hung open as he slept on the settee by the wall.

He flicked his gaze to her. "Charles said he would be back in a few days."

"It will take us half a day to be in London tomorrow, and another hour to convince him to stay for a week or two longer. He won't mind one bit."

The way she waved her hand so airily spoke to her confidence. Darcy believed her. Charles was an amenable sort and agreeable to all of his friends' plans. His only strife came when two friends disagreed about what activity to do. Then he usually demurred to whoever's opinion was fiercest, or to Darcy's opinion, if available. Which was understandable given the nature of their relationship, the amount of service Darcy had provided Charles over the years since his parents' passing. If Darcy had a brother, he would wish for one as well intentioned as Bingley, if not so uncertain in his own desires.

Mrs. Hurst's bracelets jingled as she twisted them around her wrist. "While we're there, we can talk to Charles about Miss Bennet."

Miss Bingley simpered as if it was a topic that wasn't clearly in the air between them. "She's a lovely girl, of course," she started.

"But her connections…"

"Or lack thereof, you mean."

Ah. Darcy saw it now as Caroline gave him a beseeching look. He pretended not to see it as he turned to the window.

"I'm willing to stay at Netherfield for a few days. I'm expecting a package, and it would be a hardship on my time to have it rerouted to London."

"I can surely give instructions—"

"I desired to come to Netherfield to get out of town, Miss Bingley. I'll stay here with a skeleton crew and await your brother's return. If he decides not to return, then I'll join the party in a week."

He said it as if Miss Bingley had any say in the matter, and Caroline Bingley, so desirous of a claim on Darcy's time, leapt on the opportunity to manage him.

"But only for a week, you understand? I'm sure you'll be

dreadfully bored with no company," she said with a little laugh.

He looked at the window, past his reflection and into the distance. "I'll find some way to cope."

THAT NIGHT, Darcy coped, in part, by a healthy amount of whisky. Enough to make Miss Bingley's smirking, catty presence tolerable.

Miss Bingley was a handsome woman, there was no mistake. Fine cheekbones, flawless skin, and an elegant manner. Miss Bingley was known to turn heads in a public setting, and she was favored in many circles for her excellent manners. She simply did nothing for him. Every third drink of her tea was slurped. The way she wrinkled her nose instinctively at an afternoon reading repulsed him. She believed her prestigious schooling took the place of true esteem. Given her faults, Darcy found no reason to be impressed by the time she devoted to showing herself off to advantage to him.

He made it through dinner wondering when her presence had shifted from tolerable to insufferable. As his friend's sister, he'd never protested her presence. Her quest for his attention was easily ignored... until they came here to Netherfield and Elizabeth Bennet entered his orbit.

Could Miss Bingley have noticed the way she drew my eye, before I even did?

Elizabeth Bennet of Longbourn should not have outshone a woman like Caroline Bingley. Yet, she did in every way. Her grace, her bearing, her temperament... the juxtaposition of her innocence and naivete combined with a natural cynicism of the human spirit made it impossible not to notice her.

Not so innocent now… No, he'd made sure of that today, hadn't he? Memories returned to him, so vivid it was as if they were back in that wood again. Her fingers digging into his arm, her cries muffled into his mouth, her eyes burning for *more, more.* Surrounded by trees, nature hushed around them. His own world within which to torture her until her cheeks flushed and her tongue begged.

"Mr. Darcy?" Miss Bingley gave him a coy smile. "You were staring quite pointedly at me."

"I was?"

"Just now." Her sister, occupied by the contents of her wine glass, didn't look up as Miss Bingley batted her eyelashes. "Pray, what subject is on your mind to make your eyes twinkle so? Whatever daydream it was, it appeared a pleasing one."

Only Elizabeth Bennet spreading her thighs on a bed of silk for him, but he was certain the topic would be taboo at the dinner table.

Down the table, Mr. Hurst mumbled around a piece of chicken. Miss Bingley's expression flickered with annoyance. "What was that, Hugh?"

"I *said*, the old boy's probably thinking about how far Anderson's fallen since the venture soured." Mr. Hurst smiled nastily. "I read they found a few pieces of wood floating in the ocean and not much more. Anderson will eat his shirt on that venture."

"Hugh," Mrs. Hurst said, but it was no use. Her husband had spent the effort to gather steam about this and he would not let it go to waste. Miss Bingley's shoulders fell when she realized the topic was irreversibly changed with her brother-in-law's loud guffaw.

"Can you believe the ship containing over two thousand pounds for these so-named mercantile explorations ended up on the bottom of the ocean? What will those fish spend it on, do you imagine? Kelp?" He laughed and smacked the edge of the table, his flabby face turning red. "I hope old Anderson is kicking himself for not listening to you. A waste of two thousand to foot that mad scheme. You must've laughed yourself silly—well, if you had a sense of humor."

Darcy set down his fork. "Thirty souls were lost on board."

Mr. Hurst waved it away with a roll of his eyes. "There goes your sense of humor again. You can't say you don't find some churlish amusement in the news. He spent all this time nagging you about not investing, spreading your name across that paper of his as another of those fools without business insight, and look what happened."

"I didn't invest because I didn't believe in the product, not because I think he is a bad investor."

Miss Bingley looked uneasily between them and tried to save the evening. "Save your business discussion for after dinner or you'll put us all off our meals," she said with a titter.

Darcy didn't have any intention of continuing the discussion, but he appreciated Miss Bingley's diverting her brother-in-law. Mr. Hurst grunted and Darcy gave her a brief nod when Mr. Hurst returned to terrorizing his dinner.

"Will you see us off in the morning?" Miss Bingley kept him at the bottom of the stairs after dinner when he would've gone immediately to his room, for he'd claimed to need to send correspondence to London with them. Miss Bingley had stopped him rushing off, however, by simply blocking the stairs with her body. Now a demure smile played around her mouth, a much younger, more fragile woman staring at him from under dark eyelashes.

Darcy was instantly wary. The foyer was empty, not even a servant to serve as witness. He made sure to keep ample space between them. "I don't think it's necessary, no."

"Oh." She pouted. "What a shame since it'll be at least a week before we see each other again. You're a cold man to not even offer a warm farewell."

The coy flutter of her eyelashes would make a lesser man resent the nice dinner he'd just enjoyed.

"Farewell, Miss Bingley."

He left her on the stairs and closed himself in his room. His unfinished letters called to him, but at the moment he didn't wish to waste a candle.

He was glad for the dark as he stepped up to his window. He feared what his reflection would look like in the glass.

Darcy would've taken that woman today. Elizabeth Bennet. The bane of his thoughts for weeks now. Digging for control didn't work when it came to her. He would've taken her over the desk in Bingley's study if she let him.

Look at me now, Father. An innocent. He'd broken his moral code. Cruelly introduced her to the world of romance by a man too cowardly to do the right thing by her.

And by heaven, the next morning he was on his horse, pacing the area where he'd last seen her, watching the road for the woman who kept haunting his dreams. Foolishly, desperately hoping for a sight of her.

Darcy didn't say goodbye to the party leaving for town, probably causing the opposite effect he desired on the incorrigible Miss Bingley. With his luck, she would believe it endearing. His inattention this time didn't come from deliberate insult, but one of focus. He'd been awake to watch their carriage roll down the drive, anxious to see them off before he dared to go to the stables for his horse.

Seeing *her* again was his only need.

Infectious. Poisoning him as surely as if she dropped arsenic straight into his mind. Where was his intellect, his logic and reason? Why was he shivering in the cold at the crack of dawn when he should be bundled in a warm bed?

Elizabeth Bennet had infected him.

A half hour passed. Darcy dismounted and released his pent up energy pacing and stomping his feet to be rid of the cold. Disappointment made the situation worse. It had been a vague hope. He had other strategies to see her available to him, but he'd hoped he wouldn't need to employ them.

A puff of fog shielded his vision for a moment, and when it disappeared, he made a noise. In the distance, a pale shape was revealed out of the morning mist as a woman in a white gown and a familiar blue coat.

Madness. Witchcraft and spells. No woman had bewitched him or muddled his senses like she did.

"You came."

She stood before him like the mistress of the land, hands folded demurely, her lips pressed together. Darcy was but a bug under her heel. A glimmer of excitement ran through him. Only he had the key to make her cry out in pleasure. She might hide behind her stern expression, but Darcy would not forget the wild, passionate creature underneath.

"You speak as if we arranged this meeting. I walk every morning." She folded her arms, her energy nervous, gaze darting around as if she expected someone to walk upon them in an instant though hers was the only face he'd seen so far.

"There was no arrangement, true. Maybe it was my... hope that you answered, rather than any summons."

"Hope?"

Her eyebrows lifted toward her hairline, something of his imperious aunt echoed in her narrowed eyes. He stifled the urge to fidget, pulling on his training to remain cold and controlled. Being nervous was a choice.

"Perhaps it's also why you took the same path that led here to this place. In all the directions you could've gone once you left your front door, your feet led you here." A pink flush was spreading up her neck toward her throat and he knew he had her, so he let a hint of cockiness enter his tone. "You wanted to see me again."

"And if I say I always walk this way, will you argue that with no proof I am simply avoiding admitting you are correct?"

An eyebrow lifted. "Do you always walk this way?"

"No," she said, and her stare challenged him to make her change her mind. But Darcy was no fool. The admission, vague though it was, implied she did come here for him, and that set fire to his senses.

"Then we are two people who have coincidentally met twice in as many days," he said. "Perhaps, however, you would walk in the opposite direction tomorrow, to Netherfield."

She crossed her arms over her middle, eyeing him warily. "Why would I do such a thing?"

They were alone. No one nearby for miles. He took the chance, pleased by the surprise in Elizabeth's expression as he stepped up to her, how her wariness dropped away as anticipation tightened her features and widened her beautiful eyes.

For she was beautiful, the handsomest woman of his acquaintance, and he wanted her in his bed. Couldn't stop thinking about it. Dreaming of it. Since their first kiss when she burned with such passion for a man she supposedly despised, he'd been lost. And now he was taking another step down a road of moral uncertainty, of sinful pleasure, and he could not stop himself if the Archbishop of York showed up himself to lambast him.

"Lizzy," he said, dropping his voice, thrilled to discover how his very voice made her pupils widen, black spreading over the rich color. Her breath shuddered out of her when he clasped her elbow, but she didn't pull away. "Come to Netherfield. The Hursts and Miss Bingley left today. I'm the only one left. I can arrange for the house to be empty for the full morning."

"I… why?" Her gaze dropped to his lips. "I'm - I'm not sure—"

"Shall I remind you?"

He would've taken any excuse, this was just the simplest one. She stiffened as he curled his arm around her back, the next moment melting into him, her eyes soft and yielding as he dipped his head.

Kissing her was the perfect storm. A light touch of lips, turned to a steady, persistent drizzle as she softened and leaned into him, deepening to a roaring gale as her lips parted to his tongue and she unleashed the fury of her passion. The fury, the stinging winds of it. He could only clasp her tighter and struggle to survive.

Darcy wanted her more than any woman in the world.

The way she yielded and trusted him was a heady aphrodisiac. Tasting tea on her lips, holding her trembling form, hours could have passed spent drowning himself in her. It took everything in his power to listen to the strain of his lungs and pull away and they shared mingled breaths as they both filled their lungs with the other. Her dark lashes trembled before they lifted and she met his gaze.

"I'm not experienced with this," she whispered, looking away as if ashamed of her inexperience.

Thrilling heat flared through him and it took everything in his power not to sweep her up again and bring her directly to Netherfield.

"I don't think that will be an issue after tomorrow. It is your choice, Lizzy. Always your choice."

She would choose to come to him, or she wouldn't. He would accept either, though he'd struggle with grace. If she turned him down, he wasn't certain whether he could restrain the urge to hunt her down and ravish her. *Not* something he'd like to explain to her father.

Her fingers spasmed on his coat as if she debated drawing him down to her again. Hope surged in his chest as her eyes spoke of her acceptance, and a moment later she nodded.

"Tomorrow morning, then. I trust you to arrange the details."

Wild promises sprang to his lips. How he would pleasure her for hours. How she'd beg for him to take her maidenhead. How he'd take her to the heights of passion she would never know again. He kept his lips pressed together, nodding once before he reluctantly released her. Darcy was a man of action, not words. He would make no promises, only show her exactly what he intended.

And for Elizabeth Bennet, Darcy intended to give her everything he wanted.

4

"What is it, my dear? You have a dark look about you."

"I'm sorry, Papa." She'd been thinking about the moment after dinner when Mr. Collins suggested they go for a walk, notably staring at Elizabeth when he made the suggestion. Her disgust for the idea must have shown on her face, because her mother had taken her aside and scolded her soundly for letting down the family and continuing to be a disappointment.

What of your sisters? What of Jane? If you do not begin showing Mr. Collins the proper respect, he'll surely throw us all out on the street when your father dies. He'll spit on your father's grave because of you!

The most beautiful spirit in the world could not match Jane's. She deserved everything she wanted and more. But must that mean Elizabeth should sacrifice her life and happiness for her? Jane was already blessed with so much…

Feeling a twinge of unease in her chest for the unkind thought, Elizabeth focused on her father. It was a rare opportunity nowadays to have his attention in a long moment of clarity.

"Papa, have you spoken to my mother about Mr. Collins? She apparently gave him permission to apply to me and it was a Herculean effort to escape before he could do the terrible deed."

"I have, and I do not agree. But your mother is insistent that it is a fine match. Say, tell me, is he as ridiculous outside this room as he is inside? He reads the most soul-deadening literature to me. Even Fordyce, if you can stomach the name."

"We've had to stomach much more than that," she said. "He tries to read the sermons to us nightly. It sends Lydia into fits of yawning and so our mother will have to remove her from the room before Mr. Collins grows irritated."

Mr. Bennet released a gusty sigh and folded his knobbly hands on top of the blanket on his lap. "If it was my choice, you would never have to marry. Unfortunately, I don't have the capability to stop your mother's schemes."

"So you know."

"In detail," Mr. Bennet said, grimacing. "I've forbidden it and threatened to throw her out into the wilderness, but your mother knows me too well. She has cared for me for many years. The only threat she faces is what will happen when I pass."

"If," she said.

He gave a wan smile. "You'll find we all die, it's simply a matter of time."

"But you won't die anytime soon," she insisted, knowing it was important to make this point with her father. "And you're finding a way around the entail with Mr. Laurence, so my mother won't need to worry."

"If only it could be so simple."

"Oh, Papa, you must have more confidence. It will be resolved. Then we might return Mr. Collins to his wonderful patroness and not darken our doorstep any further."

"Indeed, that is my very wish. In the meantime, Lizzy my dear, respect your mother."

A leaden ball of fear dropped into her stomach. "You don't mean…"

"I don't mean marry Mr. Collins, of course. But perhaps you should find reason to be out of the house more often. Go and meet those officers I hear Kitty and Lydia giggling about. If you find your husband among them, your mother cannot fault you."

Her stomach soured after the conversation, so Elizabeth went straight to her bedroom after slipping out of her father's room. She'd lost the ability to remain calm while Mr. Collins expounded on the wonders of a house with a shelf in a closet and Lady Catherine de Bourgh. Much better to sit in her room with a single candle to chase away the gloom and think about what she'd agreed to that morning.

Go find a husband within the regiment. Or should I find one that's nearly peerage, Papa?

She laughed to herself. No, she did not plan to take Darcy's offer. Their kisses, wild and furious, lit her up from within, yes, but a few kisses were nothing. Turning onto her back on the bed, her hand drifted down her stomach in a gentle caress, her mind occupied remembering the feel of him between her legs. How large his hand was, how he knew her body better than she ever did. She had never known there was a button down there to be plucked and pressed until her whole body shook.

How had he known? The only answer was that he was a seducer, accustomed to women throwing themselves underneath him at every opportunity. Elizabeth would not be one of those women to stroke his ego and hope for a marriage contract.

Her eyes drifted closed. *Is this what you want?*

How she thrilled to be held down by him. She'd never imagined something so exciting, and a curious part of her wanted to know more. The ease in which she lost herself within it, forget about all the responsibilities weighing on her shoulders, the burdens that she did not want. Forgotten in a haze of pleasure and lust. And Darcy did not expect marriage, had no ulterior motive of her time or her heart.

If she wished for an escape, however temporary, he was perfect.

But she couldn't do that to her father.

"Lizzy? Lizzy, wake up. Whatever possessed you to go to sleep so early? You must wake up at once."

"What?" she said, blearily peering about the dim room, her mother's figure only a shadow at the edge of her bed. "What is it, Mama?" she asked as she sat up. "Is my father—"

"Your father is fine, I've only just come from his bedside," Mrs Bennet said with a huffy attitude at her daughter's question. She waved it away and sat on the edge of the bed, the mattress dipping at her weight. "It's Mr. Collins I've come to speak to you about. He's generously decided to give you another chance."

"Joy," Elizabeth muttered.

"What was that?" Her mother's voice was a whip.

"Nothing, Mama."

She sniffed. "Anyway, he is willing to give you another chance, but you must make yourself available to him. Kitty and Lydia declared they would walk to the village if the weather remains fine, and Mr. Collins *graciously* agreed to accompany them. I expect you to keep him company and accommodate him like a daughter who respects her parents. Understood?"

Each word made the knot of worry and fear and anger in her chest grow bigger and bigger. A tangle snarling and spitting and she wasn't sure what would come out of her mouth if she tried to respond right then. Accusation, fury?

Respect your mother. Respect your parents.

She swallowed back the bitter words, let it explode on her tongue instead. Her neck bent. "Yes, Mama. I'll walk with them to the village tomorrow."

Mrs Bennet leaned back and opened and closed her mouth as if she had expected to browbeat Elizabeth. But Elizabeth understood that Mrs Bennet must have spoken to Mr. Bennet, or else why remind Elizabeth to respect her parents? Her father must've approved this, and Elizabeth would not go against him.

"Good," Mrs Bennet said. "You'll be on your very best behavior, correct?"

"I will," she whispered, and the world tilted around her as her mother left, satisfied. The miserable future expanded in front of her, devoid of hope and happiness.

In the morning, she dressed in the first rays of the sunrise filtered through the lace sheers. She kept to the side of the staircase where the boards did not creak and picked up her walking boots in the vestibule to put on outside.

"Lizzy? Where are you going?"

Elizabeth caught her breath, putting her hand to her racing heart. "Jane. I didn't expect you to be awake."

Jane stood in her white gown, curiosity furrowing her brow. "Are you going walking?"

A minor damper on her plans, she tried to keep her face neutral. "All the way to Oakham Mount. Did you wish to come with me?"

Jane's expression softened into a smile. "You will madden our mother with your independence," she said with an amused shake of her head. "I'll distract her when she figures it out."

She hurried across the entryway on stocking feet to kiss her sister upon the cheek. "Thank you, Jane dear."

There was a reason Jane was her favorite, and Elizabeth smiled to herself as she crossed the courtyard and jumped the stile to the field beyond, pointing herself in the direction of Netherfield. Though Jane might not appreciate Elizabeth's true destination, or the motivations behind it, what she didn't know wouldn't hurt her.

She did wish briefly that her sister might have inquired why Elizabeth had retired to bed so early, or wished to be out of doors instead of enjoying the time with their family. Jane wouldn't understand Elizabeth's answer, though. If not for Bingley, Jane would have gladly done what her mother asked in regard to Mr. Collins, no matter how gruesome the prospect. Jane had no desire to buck against their parents' orders—after all, would she not risk illness by traveling in the rain at her mother's insistence? Whereas Elizabeth would've put her foot down at such nonsense, Jane had no such ability.

Jane would certainly not understand Elizabeth's desire now. To grasp hold of something of her own, something solely for her benefit. To do something *sinful*.

Elizabeth looked toward Netherfield and took control of her future.

5

He saw her approach from the front sitting room where he'd taken his tea after a bite of breakfast. He had no appetite.

Netherfield was empty except for a woman in the kitchen and a servant in the stables. He'd excused his valet for the day and dressed himself.

Elizabeth approached on foot, coming out of the mist like a goddess of earth and air, her cape flowing around her ankles, her cheeks flushed with exertion and her hair loose around her shoulders.

It brought him forcefully back to when she walked to Netherfield for her sister. Now, she journeyed to him.

The sitting room had a door to the front gardens, thrown open during parties to let in fresh air. He rose and swiftly opened it to her, noting with pleasure how she, despite an initial shyness, bravely smiled.

"Tea, coffee?" he asked as she slipped past him, careful to check her walking boots for mud.

"Tea would be nice."

"A long journey requires refreshment," he said as he defied ritual and poured for her. She took hers with barely any milk, which he dutifully included. "There are sandwiches, too."

"Maybe later," she said, thrilling him. Later would come and she would be here. Her fingers grazed his when she took the cup and they shared a moment.

He wondered what she saw in him. A man who barely slept for the excitement of this moment? A man going against all his rules to taste her?

Standing opposite each other, she finished her tea. He took the cup, set it aside. He took her hand, drew her away, and she came. Their footsteps whispered on the stairs, down the long hall to his room.

The estate was empty. He turned the key in the lock, anyway.

It was the right thing to do. The subtle stiffness in Elizabeth's shoulders didn't exactly relax, but it did smooth out some, her hunted expression fading. It was replaced with a faint lost expression, reminding him how young she was.

"So." She blew out her cheeks. "I assume there are preliminaries."

An involuntary smile tugged at his lips. "Less formal than that, I assure you."

"Right."

He heard her throat click, ignored it as he approached her. Slowly, like a faun found in the woods.

"Would it be less intimidating if I undressed?"

"Less?" she blurted, and he laughed. At her injured look, he tamped down his smile. "You are in a rare mood, Mr. Darcy."

She didn't resist as he took her hand, covered her

knuckles with his palm. "I have a beautiful young woman in my bedroom."

Elizabeth studied his face and said, in a manner Darcy couldn't tell was a joke or not, "If that's all it takes to put a smile on your face, maybe you should partake more often."

"Why do you say so?"

Now a hint of a blush teased its way up her neck. He couldn't keep his gaze away from it. "Your smile makes you uncommonly attractive."

"Oh?" This pleased him. *Uncommonly* attractive, even. "I suspected it was my charming personality."

She tugged her hand out of his with a frown. "What has possessed you? I fear being melodramatic, but this simply isn't like you."

"Easy," he said, taking hold of her shoulders and turning her so her back pressed against his chest. For all her distrust, she leaned into his touch. He hid his smile. "I thought to relax you with smiles and laughs. Obviously, the wrong course for a creature such as yourself. You desire a hand to make you yield. *That* is what will relax you."

His hand smoothed down her arm, breath ruffling her hair. His lips curved as he heard her shaky exhale. With his winning hand, he was emboldened, and he drew back to pull her cape from her shoulders. It dropped to the floor in a flutter of velvet.

"Today, you came to escape," he whispered, sliding his hand through those thick curls down her back, sweeping them over her shoulder to reveal her smooth, pale nape. He rubbed his thumb over the bone at the base of her neck. Goosebumps grew around his touch, but she didn't weaken. Brave woman. He leaned down and replaced his thumb with his mouth. "I'll allow it."

"What next?"

"What next? What do you expect will happen today?"

"I expected, er, more…"

"Me jumping on you and rutting like some barnyard animal?"

Her sharp breath cut through the room. She faced him. "I didn't mean—"

"Don't worry," he said. "I understand."

She bit her lip. "How many times have you…?"

"Once, and my father thrashed me soundly when he found out the girl lighting my fires was teaching me the carnal arts. She had a good severance, and there were no bastards, and now I think I'm going to take off your dress."

She flushed but didn't stop him as he turned her away again and plucked at the ribbons of her dress, loosely tied, perhaps by her own hands. The ribbons fell free, leaving the heavy linen to sag away from her petite frame. The thin shift underneath was practically translucent.

She breathed shakily and though he listened for one, no protests came from her lips as he pushed the sleeves of her dress down. Soon it caught at her hips, and he hooked his thumb in the material, teasing himself with the feel of her now under only one thin layer, before he shoved the fabric to land at her feet. She stepped daintily out of the dress and picked it up, conscientious hand smoothing out the wrinkles before she laid it over the chair.

"My apologies."

"No harm done." He missed the woman who would stare boldly at him from across the ballroom, not this stranger staring at him like a shy girl at her first assembly.

Then she dug her hands into her shift and tugged it over her head.

He had no time to prepare. He went from half-hard to full-mast in a painful instant. Dusky pink nipples made his spit thicken. A thatch of enticing curls between her thighs. Soft curves combined with an athletic figure that made his hair stand on end with need.

"Get on the bed," he rasped.

She stood there, left ankle tucked behind the other, dark eyelashes trembling as she stared at him. But the burn of his desire couldn't stand another moment, and he took her by the elbow and led her to the end of the bed, sitting her there on the edge.

"Darcy—" she said in mounting alarm.

"Stay there," he said, and dropped to his knees.

Her scent as he wedged her thighs apart with his shoulders lit his nerves on fire. Sweet and welcoming, inviting him to lick and suck and drink his fill.

And he did.

Elizabeth threw herself flat on the bed, gasping to the heavens. "What–Darcy… oh!"

She may have been naïve to the ways of lovers, but her hips knew the instinctual rituals. They moved, and he followed, soaking up her dew with quick strikes of his tongue, eager to have all of her.

Did all women taste as good as her? He couldn't imagine it. Sweet nectar fell from her lips and she sighed her pleasure above. Her thighs shook as he lapped it up, his cock pressing like an iron rod against his trousers.

"Darcy!" she cried.

"Be still," he growled, grabbing her thighs. He was ravenous as he fell on her, as her cries rang in his ears, as he feasted and she trembled.

Finally, he was sated, and he loomed over her while Elizabeth gazed up at him with eyelashes wet from her tender emotions. She looked exhausted, and a wicked smile came over him. He would do so much more to this innocent.

"Turn over." He didn't recognize the voice that escaped him. A vicious growl. The feral beast she pulled out of him, which escaped him whenever she was nearby. A man that only wished to ravish and ravage.

Elizabeth obeyed.

"Toward the mirror," he said, moving off the bed, stripping down as quickly as he could. He wanted his skin against hers, and as he watched she moved crossways across the bed, her reflection looking back at him in the gilt-edged mirror he'd set against the wall for this purpose.

She looked scared, aroused, amused—all manner of emotions flitted across her face, a woman bared before her man in every way imaginable.

The bed dipped as he set a knee on it, then the other. Her reflected eyes grew large as he molded himself against her back, her gasping at the first touch of his hot flesh to hers.

"This doesn't feel real," she whispered. "It feels like a dream."

He pressed a kiss to her shoulder, watched her reflection tremble. "A pleasurable one, I hope."

Her satisfied hum reassured him. "Oh, yes." She tilted her head, not content with the reflection of him, and pinned him with a single dark eye. "*Why* is there a mirror facing your bed, Mr. Darcy?"

He lifted up, hand and eye following the curve of her arse. "So that I may not miss a moment," he said. "And you might have a show as well, if you wish."

"How thoughtful."

"I thought so."

Her response was a gasp as his hand slipped between her thighs and he soaked his fingers in her heat. "Does-does all lovemaking happen like this?"

"Like this?"

"With the woman upon her stomach?"

"No," he said, fitting himself to her, watching with heat when she arched into him as if she too could not wait for him to be inside her. "Sometimes the woman may be upon her knees, or her back, or riding astride her gentleman."

"Your girl who lit the fires was very skilled."

He huffed. "Now, Elizabeth, I must ask something very important of you."

Her head bobbed. "Go on."

It was torture to fit the head of his cock in her heat and not yet be able to sink home. "You are allowed to say two words and only two words. Do you wish to know what they are?"

"Mm-hm." She looked at him over her shoulder. "That was me obeying, by the way."

He uttered a tiny growl as he sank a little deeper into her. "I appreciate that. Now about those two words…"

"Yes?" She sounded as out of breath as he felt.

"Two words," he repeated, licking his lips, watching his cock disappear into the tightest, hottest heat of his life. "Two words… repeat after me, Lizzy. Fuck…"

"Fuck," she gasped.

"Me."

"… You."

He huffed a laugh and saw the hint of her smile reflected back at him. "Touche."

But neither of them was laughing when he sank home deep within her. Her hiss was almost drowned out by his belly deep groan as he struggled not to spill right then and there. His mind sputtered to a stop. Hot. Tight. *Lizzy*.

"Darcy!" Her gasp cut through his euphoria like a knife

through butter. He came to, finding her flushed, arching under his ministrations, lovelier by far than he'd ever seen.

He leaned down, rubbed his cheek against her shoulder. "How do you feel?" he asked, aware of his power here, of what role he needed to play for this innocent woman even though she gripped his cock in a way that made his world tilt.

"Fine," she whispered, the comforter clenched in her tiny fists. Her eyes were closed, the thin lids moving as her eyes did underneath. "Full. I didn't know I'd feel so…"

"Good?"

"Joined," she finished, brow furrowing. "Joined to you."

His teeth skimmed her shoulder, a flick of his tongue providing him a hint of salt to cherish. "It's only just begun, Lizzy dear."

"I thought it would hurt more," she said as he made his way to the nape of her neck, her voice growing thin as he kissed and nipped at her skin. "But it feels…"

She was shifting, even if she did not know it. Subconsciously moving against him, desiring the same friction that burned at the edges of his control. The outer edges of his vision blurred when he moved, her silk heat clutching all along his length when he thrust home. She muffled her cries in the comforter, and he could think of no finer picture than Elizabeth Bennet prone beneath him, thick hair fanned out around her, her cries the greatest music to his ears.

The burn was building in his chest, in the base of his cock and the seed in his sac. For years, he lived in a fog. A fog of duty, of living to the memory of his father, of being the parental figure his sister needed. A fog of responsibility with emotions and spontaneity tamped down, deep down underneath frozen earth.

Elizabeth was water, was chaos. She broke through the

shell and struck the heart of him, her heat blinding, bursting through his defenses with innocent naivete. He gripped her, their bodies moving in tandem, watching their mirrored reflections when she came undone around him, anchored to this reality of burning heat like the heart of a hearth.

Arching against him, her expression tightened as she sought her pleasure. It was coming to him in sticky waves, and he fought against them as he strove to reach her, to bring her under at the same time as him. Although the likelihood of that was growing slimmer with each passing second as his sac drew tight.

He drew up, peeling their sticky flesh apart, their gasps and the sound of their bodies meeting a symphony to his senses. The view of his cock disappearing between her thighs, glistening with her dew, was nearly too much to bear.

He'd planned so much for their time together, crafted eroticisms that would leave her nipples hard on her deathbed, and now she'd stolen away his senses. He grit his teeth, a vicious snarl cutting across his face as he willed himself to last.

Together, together. A chant erupted in his mind as he gripped the beautiful globes of her arse, sinking in as deep as he could go. Her name spilled from his lips, followed by a whine from hers as she rocked back onto him. The thin sunlight stretching across their bodies was fading at the edges of his vision, shifting colors of blue and gold creating a kaleidoscope behind his eyelids.

He didn't want this to end. But with her high, breathy cry, it did.

She clutched, her core rolling over him and squeezing him from base to tip. This woman who started their acquaintance fighting him at every turn now yielded completely.

He came. Fingers digging into her flesh, the bed creaking

underneath them, *more* and *need* and greedy pain-pleasure sucking the breath from his lungs.

Finally, he sank onto her back.

They lay together for a time, their panting breaths mingled, her unruly hair in their faces and making him uncomfortably warm.

"Mr. Darcy?"

"Mm?"

"A lovely winter's day, isn't it?"

He shifted, and the extra sensitivity made his vision explode in stars. "A very fine day," he agreed when he caught his breath. He withdrew despite the loss this engendered in his breast and collapsed to her side. "Why do you ask?"

She rolled onto her side, her wide smile taking his breath for other reasons entirely. "Now we've discussed the weather. So when I say I came across Mr. Darcy upon my morning walk and exchanged boring pleasantries, I will not lie."

He reached over and cupped one lovely breast, feeling a tinge of regret that he had not worshiped their beauty in more than a cursory way. "I am in your service, Miss Bennet. I'm available to exchange boring pleasantries all day."

"How noble."

He admired the curve of her lips. "It is a pain I'm willing to bear."

6

A NEW WOMAN LEFT NETHERFIELD. A NEW WOMAN WITH A new spine.

The sun seemed different as she stepped out underneath it. Sweet air caressed her skin, escorting her all the way to Longbourn. A whole new world stretched out before her. The fingers that adjusted her cape around her shoulders were strange and new.

A new woman.

I'm a woman now. No longer a girl, I've taken my first step to independence. She grinned. *A huge step!*

To think, only a short time ago she loathed Darcy. Now her thighs ached because of him.

And all of it because of Lt. Wickham. She'd hardly given the officer any thought since the Netherfield ball, so confused were her thoughts by everything that occurred during and afterward. It made her a poor friend, but her mother would say she had been a poor daughter for some time, so at least there was symmetry.

She reached Longbourn while the morning sun still

dominated the sky. Exchanging her walking boots for slippers, she headed for the stairs. She intended to clean up a little, almost afraid one of her father's hounds might sense the change within her, or her mother's sharp senses detect her daughter's deflowering.

"Lizzy. There you are."

She stopped at the bottom of the stairs with a grimace before turning to her mother. Warily, she watched her mother bustle out of the front sitting room, knowing her mother's cheerful tone was only a ploy for their guest's sake.

"Good morning, Mama."

"Have you been out walking? Hopefully you are not too tired. Your sisters have only just decided to go to town." While her mother's voice was all that was pleasant and loving, her eyes warned Elizabeth to say the right thing. "Mr. Collins will be escorting them to town and surely you wouldn't want to miss the chance to go."

"I'm not tired," she said, shoulders slumping.

"Good, dear." She patted Elizabeth's arm before she turned to the sitting room and called, "Lydia, Kitty! Elizabeth is ready if you are."

"Finally!" Lydia exclaimed that she came out, pulling on her gloves, her bonnet already tied under her chin.

"Is Jane not going?" Elizabeth asked with rising dismay. If her sister didn't go, this truly would be a horrendous journey to the village.

"Jane has some correspondence to write for your father," Mrs Bennet said.

Mr. Collins followed Kitty out of the sitting room and gave them his best supercilious smile as he folded his arms in front of him. "Yes, your sister is a most dutiful daughter to devote herself to her father's interests."

"All my daughters know the value of duty," Mrs Bennet

said as if assuring him that, of course, all of her daughters were just as good as Jane—even though not as pretty.

He turned his smile upon Elizabeth whose stomach turned. "Duty and sunshine, isn't that right, my dear cousin Elizabeth? I understand you were walking early this morning as is a habit for you. Truly, there is nothing more worthwhile than enjoying God's great splendor—although, I will inform you, my cousin, Lady Catherine does not look fondly upon walking *too* much out of doors as it can freckle the skin. She has adamant views against excessive walking."

She gave a wide and happy smile. "I should have taken her advice years ago then, for I'm afraid my skin hardly suffers the sun's effects anymore. I'm just about all freckle."

Mrs Bennet issued an uneasy chuckle. "Oh, what a funny girl she is, don't you think? You hardly have a few," Mrs Bennet rushed to say as Mr. Collins frowned at this bold and unrepentant statement. He looked at her cheeks and nose with unhappy scrutiny. With a glance at Elizabeth to warn her against further impertinence, Mrs Bennet ushered Mr. Collins and Elizabeth to the vestibule where Kitty and Lydia waited with unconcealed impatience.

Elizabeth hardly understood her mother's objections. She wasn't beautiful and knew it was one of the reasons why the cultured society women of Netherfield looked down on her. A smug smile curled at her lips as they walked down the lane, her sisters loudly flattering Mr. Collins for agreeing to escort them to the village while they were still within their mother's earshot. Miss Bingley may have found a new appreciation for freckles if it could have led her to Mr. Darcy's bed. As a new woman, her *own* woman, Elizabeth smiled and waved to her mother watching from the sitting room window.

"THIS IS QUITE a warm day for autumn," Mr. Collins said, fumbling his handkerchief from his pocket and mopping the sweat dripping from his brow.

Elizabeth pulled her lips between her teeth to stop her smile. "I find it refreshing," she said.

Kitty and Lydia did not hide their giggles when they looked over their shoulders and saw the state of their cousin. "Mr. Collins, perhaps you might need a rest. We're only halfway there!" The two girls burst into muffled giggles.

"I think," Mr. Collins panted, "I can," more panting, "manage, thank you."

"It's no trouble to stop," Elizabeth said, trying to maintain a sympathetic mein. It was only a few miles. "Though I fear you might have to sit on the grass."

"Unfortunately, my allergies prevent…" He gave up the attempt to speak.

"Are you allergic to grass?"

Kitty and Lydia were both fascinated and gawked at the profusely sweating parson. Lydia, ever the dramatic, contemplated this as if he was allergic to sunshine. "How queer! So you don't enjoy a picnic?"

"Or fishing?" Kitty said with a touch of horror. The sport was the only time she truly enjoyed being out of doors.

Her teasing tone went well over his head. "It is a bane I must bear, I'm afraid. Truly, there is nothing that can be enjoyed out of doors that cannot be enjoyed when one is comfortable in front of the fire."

"I don't think it is possible to fish indoors," Kitty said.

"Nevermind that. All one truly needs to live a fulfilled life is His word. Is that not right, my dear cousin?" He directed an exhausted smile towards Elizabeth as he stuck his sopping handkerchief into his pocket.

"And a good pair of walking boots," she said, to his displeasure and her sisters' amusement.

They reached the village of Meryton eventually, their pace dampened by Mr. Collins' poor stamina. He was shaking and pale when they entered the shadow of the church which marked the entrance of the village. However, his spirits soon lifted as he admired every nook and cranny of the village, declaring it was a decent, picturesque place, and went into such raptures about the cobblestone and the hedges and even an unwitting bird flying overhead that Elizabeth felt she had exhausted her ability to hear for the rest of the decade.

With a similar irritation, Kitty and Lydia could not bear the delay when there were officers to flirt with, and her sisters strained to leave the sightseeing behind for the streets closer to the shops and their aunt's home. Uniformed men off-duty routinely loitered in the area as they searched for amusement, and today was no exception, to her sisters' mutual pleasure.

"—find that the village of Hunsford near Rosings Park where my humble abode is situated contains almost as nearly a striking cobblestone as—"

Her cousin's prattle continued as her sisters met with officers. The men met their cousin with poorly concealed amusement and Elizabeth and her sisters with more enthusiasm. However much she tried, Mr. Collins was determined to put himself forth in every conversation, and eventually they moved to their aunt Mrs. Phillips' home so that he might prattle at *her* instead.

Thankfully, her aunt seemed willing to listen to her cousin. Even if she did look on in bemusement as he carried on about the fireplace bricks for nearly half an hour. The pudgy little man found a steadfast listener as they started their cards and Mr. Collins immediately lost the first game.

"It must be because of his profession that he is able to speak so long."

"Yet he says so little."

Across the table, Lt. Wickham shared a smirk with her.

Elizabeth's aunt had invited over some of the officers at her nieces' prompting and Lt. Wickham had been part of that contingent. The tables were set out as soon as possible for a jovial midafternoon of games. Somehow Elizabeth was spared sitting with Mr. Collins as her cousin regaled Mrs Phillips with compliments. Indeed, Lt. Wickham had made a point of sitting with Elizabeth and they paid attention to the games halfheartedly as they chatted near the window.

The urge to broach the topic of Darcy sat behind her teeth. Should she? She decided she would leave it, understanding that in her naivete she might reveal more than she wished if Darcy was broached in conversation.

However, Lt. Wickham soon brought him up. "I understand his party left for London recently."

"Indeed."

"We can only hope they do not return as quickly as they left." He gave her an indulgent smile. "We might even be lucky enough not to meet the esteemed Mr. Darcy again. I for one would not be opposed to the idea, knowing what I know about him."

"Oh, but Mr. Darcy did not go with his friends."

"He didn't? How do you know?"

I just spent the morning in bed with him.

"I ran into him on a walk the other day," she said, staring hard at her cards.

"Did you? Was he walking near Longbourn? I suppose

he is not used to the leisure of country living and was looking for excitement."

She tried to make a joke. "Excitement at Longbourn?"

"I find Longbourn exceedingly pleasant," Lt. Wickham said with a gleam in his eyes as he looked at her. She dutifully let her gaze drop and Wickham seemed pleased with himself as he returned to the original subject. "Did you speak with him for long? He was never one to linger with those he considered beneath him."

"Erm… There was very little conversation." *Very little indeed.*

Thankfully, the topic moved on. Elizabeth refrained from bringing up what Darcy said about Lt. Wickham to him. She was not so much worried about horribly offending her acquaintance, but whether Lt. Wickham would question why Darcy had confided in her as much as he had. Explaining to him that somehow a kiss had extracted Darcy's confidence was impossible.

"Miss Lizzy?"

She looked up, flustered, and found Lt. Wickham smiling. "Yes?"

His gaze dropped to her mouth. "You're touching your lips."

She quickly clasped her hands in her lap and gave an uneasy laugh. "Oh. I was lost in thought. It's my turn, isn't it?"

After spending a pleasurable time playing cards and games, it was decided they would leave her aunt's house and visit the attractions that window shopping could provide. This was not a surprise to Elizabeth. Lydia couldn't stand to have pin money sitting idle in her purse when it could be invested in a new ribbon or trimmings.

They walked as a group toward the square and its shops.

Elizabeth managed to escape walking beside Mr. Collins by the simple expedient of walking too quickly for him to catch up. Instead, it was Lt. Wickham who linked their arms together.

They had just reached the square when Kitty exclaimed, "Oh my, there is Mr. Darcy!"

"What a horrible man, I thought he was long gone from here," Lydia said, not bothering to tone down her voice. Elizabeth held her tongue but cast a sharp look at her sister which was promptly ignored.

Mr. Collins then had to put in a nasally word to this insult. "Mr. Darcy is esteemed throughout the community and the favored nephew of my patroness, my cousin. You should not speak thusly of him."

Lydia also ignored him. "La, is he coming over?"

Elizabeth felt Lt. Wickham's arm tense under her hand. She glanced at his face and saw a degree of fright in his eyes. Darcy's glare was more ferocious than ever, but now it was all reserved for the gentleman at her side. Even from this distance she could see his jaw clenching as he observed the group.

Lydia was right. He was coming over.

"Good day," he said when he reached them. He flicked a glance at Lt. Wickham, but it was only to signify how completely he ignored him otherwise. His stare was now on Elizabeth, potent and focused. She flushed as she curtsied, feeling as if she were an experiment under a spyglass.

"I'm afraid we must be off." She hadn't noticed Lt. Wickham sharing glances with his friends, but now Lt. Wickham made his goodbyes.

"But I thought you were off duty for the day!" Lydia complained.

This made color rise to Lt. Wickham's pale cheeks. "Yes,

but it's grown late in the day, and it's better for us to get along before we get chastised."

"Lydia," Elizabeth murmured as Lydia again tried to protest. Lydia and Kitty pouted as their friends, including the admirable Denny, pulled away with a regretful look. Without further ado, Lt. Wickham left with his friends, She could already hear Lydia complaining to their mother later about the inconvenience of Darcy showing up.

Darcy's manner was subdued when he turned away from watching the officers leave. "Might I ask where you were going?"

"Nowhere in particular," Elizabeth said.

"To the hat shop, actually," Lydia said with a sour look at Elizabeth.

Darcy rocked back on his heels as he considered them. A beat later, after he seemed to come to some decision, he said, "Since I have scared away a portion of your escort, I would offer my own services. May I join you?"

He held out his arm to Elizabeth and, shockingly, the other to Lydia.

This was a turn in fortunes. Even Lydia could not turn down the honor of being escorted by the richest man of their acquaintance. Lydia could find no fault with the gentleman's manners and she even lifted her chin like some haughty socialite as they walked across the square three abreast. Lydia broke character soon enough, however. "Poor Kitty that you do not have a third arm, Mr. Darcy! She must walk with Mr. Collins."

"Lydia!"

"Well, it's true," she said with a giggle.

Darcy did not just escort them to the shop. He lingered even though Mr. Collins did a passable job of acting like a fly buzzing around his ears, attempting to impress him with his most pompous airs. Darcy persevered, taking a place near the window to watch outside while Mr. Collins buzzed around him. Besides a small group of officers, Elizabeth couldn't tell why he kept such a vigilant lookout.

As for herself, Elizabeth darted glances at him from where she pretended to admire the lace on display. Had it been as Darcy said? Had Lt. Wickham run away in fright?

Lt. Wickham had always been steadfast in stating how he had nothing to fear from Darcy, and yet he could not be in Darcy's presence for longer than a moment. There was a history there that couldn't have been explained properly, because Elizabeth couldn't understand. It was very curious, and she found herself unable to stop thinking about Lt. Wickham's pale face.

Neither could she stop her mind lingering on how intensely Darcy had gazed at her.

Abruptly, Darcy left the window. Mr. Collins spoke to thin air for several moments before he realized Darcy had abandoned him. He ducked his head and looked around for the closest distraction while Elizabeth quickly pretended to be admiring the lace.

Darcy slid into the empty space beside her and frowned at the array of lace before them. "Can you come tomorrow?" His voice was a low timbre that drew down her spine like his caress had that morning.

"That's risky," she said out of the corner of her mouth. "Once was enough, wasn't it? We should not be greedy." Yet the temptation…

"Tomorrow," he said. "Same time."

"Mr. Darcy, I see you have noticed the lovely lace my cousin has selected. What small frivolity is this that entertains the young ladies, yes? I myself see no harm in indulging if one has the pin money. I find lace can be put to several industrious uses. Not only bonnets and fripperies, but the stylings of the home are not complete without little feminine touches such as these, don't you think? Lady Catherine, your aunt, has told me recently that she believes such feminine touches upon my little abode near Rosings would do quite well to refreshing the place, and while I have no former complaints about the décor of the prior parson, may God rest his soul—"

Darcy's frown grew, but it was Elizabeth who grew truly uneasy by Mr. Collins' significant glances at her. There was no doubt in his mind *who* would be providing the feminine touches he lacked.

She caught Darcy's eye as Mr. Collins prattled on. His gaze darkened and her body responded, stomach tightening and heat creeping up her cheeks.

Tomorrow.

7

He was struck breathless when he saw her in the village. Struck, and angry.

Something had to be done about Wickham.

Why would she even still associate with him? He told her Wickham was no good. The irony was not lost on him that *he* was as morally repugnant as his old acquaintance, and that burned him even more.

He returned to Netherfield. Empty Netherfield. His footsteps echoed in the halls. The rooms loomed large, his presence a tiny speck compared to its emptiness. He ate dinner at the long table by himself, feeling a fool surrounded by the vacant place settings.

"Tomorrow."

What power did she have to make him want? She was right. Extending this dalliance was a risk. Every moment together increased the chance of being caught, of ruining his reputation. He should be happy with what he had and appreciate the fond memory of taking Elizabeth Bennet's maidenhead.

But Darcy was not happy with what he had. Darcy sat at the empty table with its emptiness a physical presence all on its own, sat and stewed and ruminated on why *Wickham*, Wickham of all people, with no honor and no recommendations, got everything he wanted.

Seeing her on Wickham's arm made him feel like he stood on quicksand. Floundering. Messy. Fighting to take back control.

He would ruin Elizabeth for him. After Darcy, Elizabeth Bennet would never want another, and certainly *Wickham* would never turn her head.

He'd had her body. Now he would take her future.

"Come," he said when she stepped inside Netherfield through the garden door.

She followed, his hand engulfing hers, their illicit presence noted by portraits and gilded mirrors as he led her upstairs.

"This cannot happen again," she said as soon as he locked the bedroom door behind him. The familiarity of his bedroom to her now was a quiet thrill. He took her cape off her shoulders, pressed in at her back. "The risks are too great. We shouldn't—"

"Hush," he said, and put his mouth to her throat.

Words escaped her as fire raced through his touch. He cupped her breasts, thumbs rubbing over her nipples until they grew hard with aching for him. The heat of his body at her back chased away the morning chill left in her bones, chased away reason and logic, until the Elizabeth left behind was a wanton, needy creature and Darcy her creator.

"I hope you're not pressed for time," he said, the first

thing he'd said of any note, his hips thrusting his growing bulge against her arse. "We're going to try those other positions today."

Other positions… what…?

By the time the memory returned, it was too late. Darcy stripped her to her underthings, shrugged off his morning jacket to the floor, and lifted her up in his arms. He threw her down to the mattress and she bounced only a moment before he was on her.

No, on his *knees* before her.

She had an instant to tense and then he wrapped her thighs around his shoulders. Ecstasy struck her like a physical blow when he put his mouth to her and her cries rang through the room. He didn't let her flinch away, didn't let her escape as fire raked over her like living claws. She clenched his hair, his shoulders—nothing could budge him until all that remained of her was a limp, sweaty mess.

"Please, please…" He lifted his head, mouth shining with her release. Even his breath on her tortured flesh made her tremble. "You're trying to kill me, aren't you?"

"Never that," he said with a wicked smile. Then he rose to his full height, silhouetted by the morning light from the window, a great dragon looming over the town he meant to savage.

Elizabeth held her breath.

"You know what sweetness this is, seeing you like this?" His hands covered her stomach, caressed her ribs, cupped her breasts. "If I were a master artist, I might still capture only a tenth of your glory."

"You already have me in bed, Darcy. The time for flattery may be past, but do continue…"

"Oh, I will," he said, notching his cock at her entrance. "Like the gratification of being the only man to see you like this, how tight you are"—they hissed together as he stretched her around him—"of why I ever have to leave this heaven."

Her lips parted on a moan that rattled her chest. He filled her until they were flush, her legs shaking around his hips, his hair falling over his eyes in a rakish way. Filled to the brim, bringing with it sticky, beautiful pressure. *This* was the moment she'd paint, a moment pure in its wickedness.

Darcy leaned down and wrapped his lips around her nipple, striking through her a double pleasure that left her grasping the back of his head as if to trap him there forever. He didn't appear to mind, licking and nibbling and sucking until she grew weak—before transferring his attentions to the other. Again and again as his hips drew back and returned with aching languidness.

Heaven, he said. At this moment, teetering on the brink of ecstasy, her blood burning, she would call it purgatory.

"Darcy!" she cried, sinking her nails into the fleshy meat of his arse.

Darcy growled and slammed forward. The heavy wood bed rocked under them with each thrust, Darcy rising up and holding her hips as he fucked her, eyes black with lust. Wild creatures possessed them both, primal need driving them onward, and she howled when she crested into a fizzling, fiery sensation.

"There you are." His throat sounded like it was filled with gravel. He gripped the base of his cock and withdrew. Her body spasmed, core clutching, the loss of his presence hitting her dearly.

"What are you doing?" she asked, pathetically reaching out to him, bereft and aching for a fulfillment she couldn't name. "You didn't…"

"I didn't," he agreed, the bed dipping as he climbed into the bed beside her, "but I promised to treat you to different positions, and I always meet my obligations. Now climb into my lap, Lizzy."

He sat back against the headboard, his legs stretched out, and his cock pointing straight up. She held her tongue on how playful it looked, as stiffly proud as Darcy at a ball, and rolled over and did as she was told. "Curiosity and the cat," she said.

No amount of preparation could have braced her for what sliding down on him felt like. The most important change was her participation. No longer was she the prone woman waiting for her lover's embrace. Now it was Darcy looking up at her when she gripped his shoulders and slid down his length. Controlling their speed, dominating their connection. She led, she possessed, and there was no headier feeling than the power she stole back from him. *This is how the heart of a storm feels.*

Darcy's tortured groan as she lifted up would be her fondest memory. She waited for him to take control, to speed things up. Her pace grew slower in anticipation, as if daring him to yank back this precious, sweet control. That didn't happen. His head fell back, the veins in his throat bulging as he let her master him with her hips.

Elizabeth could not take the teasing, not after that. Nails digging into his shoulders, she rode him, the tingling warmth of an impending climax building in her midsection with each joining of their bodies. Built and built, urged on when Darcy's used his talented tongue to torture her poor nipples, her body no longer under her control as she rode him to heights they'd never reached before.

She slammed into that peak with the force of a runaway carriage. Blinded, a buzzing drone in her ears of her own cries. She shook and curled into him, clutching at his shoulders the same way her core clutched at his cock.

"Lizzy!"

Darcy stiffened against her, and his arms banded around her back. She tumbled and careened from a great height, and he held her, buffeted by the same storms that pinned her. He filled her with heat as fiery as the blood pounding through their veins.

Slowly, she regained her breath, gulping a lungful of sex-filled air. Sweat rolled over her lower lip and she licked it off and brushed her fingers through Darcy's dampened curls, affectionate in an absentminded, gentle way.

"That was…" She stopped, smiled and cleared her throat. She'd lost her voice sometime in their lovemaking.

Darcy's head fell back. He looked as if he'd returned from a two year vacation in Bath. She'd never seen him so relaxed or soft.

"Are you alright, sir?" she asked, knees brushing his ribs as she squeezed him.

He returned it with languid strokes up and down her back. "Alright? I suppose I am. The girl who did the fires never did that."

"Oh, really? Then I am unique."

That rather pleased her. If one thing in their affair made her self-conscious, it was that she was unlearned and inexperienced compared to him. She had no doubt, given his dopey expression, that she'd surpassed his expectations, which were undoubtedly high.

She shifted, bracing herself on his thigh. "Stay," he said, making her pause. His dark eyelashes fluttered against sun-kissed cheeks. "Give me but a moment to catch my breath."

Her cheeks pulled into a grin. "You sound older than your years, Mr. Darcy."

With a grunt, he shifted, clasping her to his chest and rolling them in one smooth movement. She landed on the mattress underneath him, his weight atop her a comfortable suffocation. Her legs wrapped around his hips, carnal instincts taking control of her muscles. She blinked and stared up at Darcy, the curl of his mouth creating a frisson of lightning delight down her spine.

She'd once loathed this man. Now she knew their wicked natures matched.

He dipped his head, nipping at her jaw. "How much of your morning do I have, Miss Bennet? Because I feel quite up to meeting the challenge you just issued."

And with a twist of his hips that forced a moan from her throat, he proved himself correct indeed.

"I have some time, I think."

8

How virile he felt! Though he was still in his prime, she gifted him the energy of a man ten years younger.

He took her in every position he could think of, amazed anew each moment he spent with this sighing, gasping creature underneath him. The grip of her small hands on his back, his arse. Her sweet cry as she shook around him. Not to mention the heat of her, unending, pure.

He relished stealing this from Wickham, from any man who hoped to introduce her to the pleasures of the flesh one day. She had given her firsts to him, and he snatched at them greedily.

"My good sir, I don't think I have a muscle that isn't sore now," she said, pushing on his shoulders, her tiny frame situated perfectly in his lap.

Perhaps it was the way her eyes danced. Perhaps it was the thought of his bed being empty without her. Perhaps it was madness.

In the next moment, he said something horrifyingly stupid.

He laughed and reached out to tuck a damp curl behind her ear. "Come to me tonight."

"Tonight?" Her lips parted, and he knew he'd said the wrong thing. She drew back. "I can't leave—!"

"Don't tell me you've never walked out of doors at night," he said, laughing, trying to hastily cover up the error with a lackadaisical attitude. His lonely bed loomed behind her, the sheets rumpled, smelling like her. He imagined the hell that awaited him if she left and he had nothing to cling to except pillows, no warmth except the memory of her. She was so alive, so radiant, he had to have her in his bed again.

Her eyebrows lifted toward her hairline. "Very rarely, and never so far as Netherfield! I would break my ankle, and while our boudoir activities may be a worthwhile pursuit in the daytime, I hardly see the need to risk life and limb for them at night."

He chuckled and brushed his knuckles over her dewy cheek. "Then I haven't convinced you well enough. Come outside tonight if you dare. I'll be waiting for you on the lane."

Curiosity, always with her insatiable curiosity. It lit her eyes now, made them gleam in a way that made his cock twitch inside of her. Despite how equally worn out he was, he would find another burst of energy if she kept looking as tempting as she did.

"And what will happen on the lane? I can't imagine anything except the bitter cold and too many thorn bushes."

"Hmm, I'll have my carriage, so we might escape the thorns at least. As for the bitter cold..."

Her gaze dropped to his mouth, hypnotized, her lips parted as she waited. "Yes?"

She looked at him as a woman should look at her man, her lover, and his chest swelled with pride.

"I'm certain we can find a way to combat it."

He kissed her, silencing any objections she could think of before they could form. Darcy would have her again, again and again. Her body, her soul, those curious, wicked eyes - they would all be his. For Darcy was a greedy creature and, once decided, he did not easily give up what was his.

"Tonight," he told her, and it was done.

Only as she walked away from Netherfield, her slight form a distant figure on the plains, did he wonder what spell she wove around him. He'd given her his seed, and what had she given him except this yawning hole he'd never realized lacked for filling? It was as if her presence in his arms shone a brilliant ray of sunshine into the darkest corners of his soul, and without her warm embrace, he did not like the chilly feeling left behind.

Darcy had thought to steal her away from Wickham, but he hadn't expected a mark to be left on *him*.

Tonight. Tonight he would figure out Miss Elizabeth Bennet.

9

The *hmpfh* she received from her mother when Mrs Bennet saw her slipping out of the kitchen was as much recrimination as she could give at the time with Mr. Collins on her heels. Elizabeth, frozen in the doorway, had little time to brace before her odious cousin parted ways from her mother's company to approach.

"My dear cousin, Elizabeth—my goodness, you appear out of sorts! Did you run into, erm, any issues upon your walk?"

Elizabeth looked down at herself while her mother hurried forward to interject, thus saving what little reputation her daughter had in Mr. Collins' eyes. "A few wrinkles, I suppose, but Lizzy, you must remember to make the girl press your dresses before you go traipsing about!"

"Sorry, Mama," she said, though she hated to place the blame on their girl. Those wrinkles were well earned on the floor of Darcy's room. Besides, Mr. Collins was not worried about her rumpled clothes, but looked at her as if she had just rolled out of a thorn bush in front of him. She gave a wan smile and self consciously touched her wild hair. "I should go to my room and refresh myself."

"It is as I said about walking being the pastime one should enjoy in short bursts, not hours," Mr. Collins said, moving out of her way and continuing to speak to Mrs Bennet as Elizabeth hurried to the stairs. "I do believe she had more *freckles*, too," he added in a horrified half-whisper. Mrs Bennet stuttered out a reply while Elizabeth escaped up the stairs to her bedroom.

Jane looked up from writing a letter at the desk beside the window and took in Elizabeth's appearance with widening eyes. "Lizzy, goodness, whatever has become of your dress?"

She glanced down and laughed at her poor appearance. "I didn't see how many wrinkles it had before stepping out this morning, I suppose. Who are you writing to?"

Always talk about others. That was the key to making self-absorbed people forget about your issues. Though Jane gave her a look of reproof for the redirection, she answered readily enough. "It is to our Aunt and Uncle Gardiner. I wanted to express my thanks for the treats they sent along with their last letter. Really, Lizzy, tell me you did *something* to your hair this morning. You look like a ruffian!"

Of course, that was the problem with Jane. She *wasn't* self-absorbed. More, she loved Elizabeth like a staunch friend, so deceiving her as she did her other sisters and mother was difficult. *But not impossible,* she thought, and mentally girded herself to lie to her dearest sister.

She gave an aggrieved sigh. "I knew you would be angry… but I went to Oakham Mount on my own, and the wind gave me a good deal of grief for my trouble…"

"You walked all the way there? And did you hurt yourself?" She hurried across the room to her and grabbed her wrists, turning over her arms so she could check for damage. "The last time you went by yourself, you were savaged by thorn bushes. We were picking leaves out of your hair for weeks!"

"You exaggerate," she said with an uneasy laugh. "See? I'm fine."

Jane dropped Elizabeth's arms with a sniff of doubt. "You seem to be fine. What I'm most surprised by is that you did not return with ink all over your fingers. Did you not bring your book?"

Elizabeth's eyes flicked to her writing desk, her manuscript neatly put away and untouched for several days now. It was unusual for Elizabeth not to devote some attention to her current manuscript, a book she had been writing for a six-month now. "I've not been in the mood to write, I suppose."

Jane's eyebrows lifted high. "Coming from my sister who said 'one does not wait for lightning to strike, but creates the lightning'?"

"I must have been suffering a bout of optimism. I should leave that to you, dearest."

"Lizzy, you do make fun. I could never do as you do with your witticisms and turns of phrase. How you describe the landscape and the people around you... I await the day I can read your story in whole rather than in the snippets you tease me with!"

"Someday soon, I hope, but right now I cannot seem to be either witty or artistic. It is the awful Mr. Collins who does this to me! I cannot function with him hovering about like a fly. Mama is sure to be angry if I smash the little insect, but if he does not leave the house in a week, I will scream! Do you happen to know when he will leave?"

"He has not given a timeframe, unfortunately," Jane said

with a soothing squeeze of Elizabeth's arm. She returned to the writing desk and sat, primly tucking her skirt underneath her. "Our mother is also eager for him to leave. Our father is growing in poorer spirits by the day."

"He is a cloud hanging over all of us," Elizabeth said solemnly as she followed her sister. Standing beside the window, she frowned out at the nice day. "I have this awful fear Mama is pushing Mr. Collins to propose today."

"You would be right."

Elizabeth's gaze spun back toward her sister, now unhappy and pale, her lips pressed together. "She said something?"

"I heard her in the hall this morning. He came straightaway to await you, I believe, but you had already left. They were both cross and, well, I couldn't help but overhear." Her sister's discomfort admitting her eavesdropping, while normally amusing, only turned her stomach now.

She looked toward the door, biting her lip. "I think I need to go speak with our mother."

Jane turned to her, her hands twisting together in her lap. Worry knitted her brows. "I won't try to speak against you for I know your feelings, Lizzy, but I fear our mother will resist you. She has high hopes that a marriage will protect our home if… if…"

When their father passed.

Silence descended over the sisters. The grim future held no hope, no happiness. Elizabeth blinked back the prickling sensation behind her eyes, and she wished, of all things, to be back with Darcy. Back in bed where she did not have to think of such things, back in his arms which was an escape from this grey world.

"I need to speak to Mama," she said, and hurried to find her mother.

"I won't marry him."

Her mother's gasp was nearly loud enough to draw out anyone listening from the corridor outside the back sitting room. Her mother used this room in the afternoon to find a release from the relentless heat of the sun. The song in the next room paused for an instant before Mary continued her piano practice.

Mrs Bennet threw her fan down on the side table. "You will lower your voice, young woman, before Mr. Collins hears how insolent you are toward your mother!"

"I would obey anything except this!" she exclaimed. "Nothing you say can convince me to accept him."

"Even your father's health? Our family's ruin when Mr. Collins can throw us out into the street any moment he pleases once your father passes? Why? For your worthless scribblings? Can you not scribble in Hunsford as much as you do here?"

"I know you will never respect my passions, but must you attempt to force me to go against every inclination?"

Mrs Bennet's anger made her draw herself up in her chair. "I will do anything in my power to protect our family! You will accept Mr. Collins–who has shown great willingness to overlook your many flaws, I must point out."

"My flaws?" Her disgust, combined with a glowing certainty that she would never convince her mother, made her issue her final salvo. "I wouldn't marry my cousin if he were the last man on Earth."

Mrs Bennet threw her arms into the air. "Spite. Spite is all this is! This is what I'm owed by an ungrateful daughter!" Mrs Bennet threw herself with enthusiasm into her opportunity to bemoan her circumstances. "What have I done to raise such a terrible creature? You would throw away our futures for your selfishness!"

She lifted her chin. "Yes, perhaps I am a terrible daughter, and I've come by it honestly since you have never had an *ounce* of maternal sentiment towards me."

"Ahem."

The two women straightened at the interruption, though they did not stop glaring at the other. Mr. Collins offered a stomach churning smile when they reluctantly turned to him.

"If I may interrupt this scene of family discord and provide some reassurance and perspective," he said, stepping into the room. He straightened and cleared his throat with a tiny *hem hem*. "My cousin Elizabeth. You need not fear an address from me. After the shocking events of this morning, of note your disarray and your continued resistance to Godly advice about excessive exercise, not to mention the disharmony sowed between your loving mother, I do not wish to elevate you beyond cousin. It would suit neither your temperament nor, most importantly, mine, to subject myself to your brash behavior. My reputation—"

"Oh no!" Mrs Bennet sobbed. "But, Mr. Collins, you must!"

He grew louder in reply, nearly shouting over the sobbing Mrs Bennet. "—will not be besmirched by a young lady who shuns a humble, simple life in the country for the trappings found in activities beyond unsuitable for a respectable young lady." He paused while Elizabeth's face turned ashen. "Your so-called novels, cousin, do you no credit. A sonnet or poetry might be acceptable, even admired by those of the upper classes, but *novels*, cousin? I do not think it appropriate, and only your father's health bids me to stay my tongue on bringing to him the most severe censure.

"I believe the best thing I can do for you, my dear cousin, and the kindest way to set you on the right path, is to discourage this pursuit of novelty and the dissent into godlessness. Our feet are firmly grounded on God's green earth, and there is a reason our heads do not reach the clouds." With that rendering Elizabeth speechless, he turned to Mrs Bennet and issued a curt bow. "I do not blame you for Elizabeth's deficits. It is a lack of firm leadership within this household that has caused it, and for that I cannot hold you to blame. Hopefully, there will come a time when all your daughters will bow their heads not to imagination, but to humble faith."

The mantelpiece clock ticking away complemented Mr. Collins footsteps down the hall as he departed. Elizabeth opened her mouth, shut it. There was nothing she could say. No defense against her pompous cousin's assertions. What utter ridiculousness. However, foreboding prickled at her arms and up her neck and culminated in an icy trickle down her spine when she looked at her mother's expression.

"You–you—"

Beyond words, Mrs Bennet grabbed hold of Elizabeth's wrist and yanked her toward the door. Mary and Kitty stuck their heads out of the music room door as Mrs Bennet marched them by. They saw their mother's expression and quickly darted back inside the music room and closed the door. Mrs Bennet marched Elizabeth straight to her father's study.

Her father's bed was lit by the midafternoon sun, and he puffed away soundly in his sleep until Mrs Bennet roused him by grabbing and shaking his covered foot.

"Mama! We shouldn't bother—"

"Mr. Bennet! Mr. Bennet, wake up at once and know what your daughter has done!"

Mr. Bennet roused, smacking his lips, his thick brows wrinkling and then drawing into a straight line when he saw Mrs Bennet holding onto Elizabeth while she tried to struggle out of her iron grip. "What is going on here?"

"Your daughter!" Mrs Bennet, chest rising and plunging as if she had run a mile, her cheeks blustering red, let Elizabeth tear free before she pointed a finger at her daughter's chest. "Your daughter has just thrown our lives away and now Mr. Collins is resolved to never have her, and he has promised me we will be under his thumb for the rest of our lives."

It is better than in his bed, she thought, and snapped her mouth shut on the comment when she saw her father's eyes flash.

"Elizabeth? Is this true?"

"Of course it is true," Mrs Bennet said. "She offered him the highest insult, making her voice heard all over the house when she declared she would not have him, and so he came in and said *he* would not have *her*, and now we will be destitute! Thrown upon the streets for the vultures to feast upon our flesh as I wither, *wither*—"

"Mrs Bennet." Her father's voice rarely grew loud anymore, but now it did, stern and angry as he stared at his wife.

Mrs Bennet, simmering, settled and sniffed. "Well. What shall you do about this? We've no hope, none whatsoever—"

"I will never do anything if you do not cease your interruptions," Mr. Bennet said. Mrs Bennet gasped, but did as her husband bid with bad grace, folding her arms over her ample bosom. Mr. Bennet ignored this and turned to Elizabeth.

The weariness in his eyes made her own sting. "Papa, I—"

"I will say the same to you, young lady." His severe tone made her close her mouth with a clack of teeth. Mr. Bennet waited a moment, but when neither mother nor daughter tried to interrupt him, he spoke. "I believe I asked you to respect your mother, Elizabeth."

Elizabeth could not hold her tongue then. "You said nothing about *marrying* him! You expressly said not to!"

"Mr. Bennet!" her mother gasped.

"Yet I did tell you to find a marriage outside this house if you did not wish to marry Mr. Collins," Mr. Bennet said. "You have not done so, I take it?"

Darcy flitted across her mind, but she buried it quickly. "No, in the two days since our conversation, I have not found a husband, Papa."

"You need to speak respectfully to—"

Mr. Bennet waved his wife away with a humored gleam in his eyes. However, his tone was dreadfully serious when he said, "Mr. Collins is the future of this household, though I am sorry to admit it. It behooves you to keep him happy. If you choose not to, what compunction does he have to treat you and your family well? In the unfortunate event Mr. Bingley chooses not to apply to me for Jane's hand before I pass, he could deny her the happiness she deserves. He could even ask her hand, and will she muster up the courage to deny him like you have?"

"She would be a good girl," Mrs Bennet said, sniffling into her handkerchief.

He watched Elizabeth while she struggled to push down the salty sting in the back of her throat. "But must I give up everything, Papa?"

"We must all give something," he said. "You have deluded yourself to think that your life will not change very much, for you do not believe I will pass. I *will* pass, Lizzy, and

Mr. Laurence will not find a loophole to extricate us from this unfortunate future. You *will* face it. You will all sacrifice to it. It is your decision whether you will choose family or yourself."

"Now go," he said with a heavy sigh, sinking back into his pillows. His eyes closed. "I feel tired. Mrs Bennet?"

Mrs Bennet went to her husband's side, her eyes shining. "Yes, dear?"

He reached out and touched her hand. "Sit with me a while?"

Her smile was tremulous when she sat at the chair by her husband's bedside. "Of course," she said while Elizabeth quietly closed the door behind her.

"What's the matter?" Jane asked when she came to their bedroom later, finding Elizabeth abed, her face buried in the pillows. "You haven't eaten all day. Whatever is the matter?"

"I do not wish to speak of it," she whispered, her throat raw with tears. "Please do not make me speak it."

"Oh, Lizzy," Jane said, sitting beside her and smoothing a hand over her hair. "I will not press you, but may I stay and be with you?"

"Yes," she whispered, and the two sisters remained in silence for some time.

10

Her aching stomach woke her some hours later. Jane was gone, likely called downstairs. Sunset stretched across the horizon outside her windows, the last beauty before a darkness and gloom she could already feel pressing in on her.

Papa is right. I'll only hurt my family if I continue like this.

She mustn't be selfish. Her father was correct—she did not wish to admit that his passing would come sooner rather than later. Each day brought them closer to the very hour he would pass from this world. Elizabeth might close her eyes and her ears to all the signs, but deep down she knew death's icy claws neared.

At the same time, must she be the only one who sacrificed for their family? Tears pricked her eyes, a burn building in the back of her throat. Jane would be happy with Mr. Bingley. Lydia and Kitty could do what they wished, their mother permissive and lax with their care, and Mary did not put herself forth except to play piano and sing. Her mother instead put it all on Elizabeth, and it wasn't fair.

She had never liked Elizabeth. She was not fair like Jane

nor robust and flirtatious like Lydia. Officers did not interest her above all things, and gossip was not top of her mind. She read too much, wrote nonsensical stories, walked too often, and favored 'mousy Charlotte' over the prettier, popular girls in Meryton.

Mrs Bennet suffered Elizabeth's presence. To Elizabeth, she only wished to escape Mrs Bennet's presence.

If only Mr. Collins was not so loathsome and ridiculous, Elizabeth might be tempted.

She turned on her back, resting her hands upon her stomach and staring at the canopy above her bed. Her hunger pains had lessened, and she had no wish to go downstairs and join the meal. No, what she wished was to find a way to please her father.

If only Mr. Collins took to one of my sisters instead.

She chewed her lower lip. Perhaps that was the key. If Mr. Collins would not marry *her*, he could instead find the wife he wanted in her sisters. An image of Mr. Collins listening to Lydia's yawning during his sermons came to mind, and she giggled. No, Lydia would not do, but perhaps Kitty or Mary would better suit his *humble* life.

In the morning, Elizabeth would plant the seed. After all, her sisters were keen to sacrifice *her* to Mr. Collins. They should be happy to make the choice themselves, and her father would not be disappointed if she had a plan to regain Mr. Collins' good opinion.

SHE WOKE sometime in the night. She could hear Jane softly puffing in her sleep. Jane had not closed the hangings so the faint moonlight allowed Elizabeth to see her sister curled up on her side of the bed.

Darcy.

She winced. With everything that happened, she'd forgotten about Darcy. It was so late in the night, he'd probably already returned to Netherfield. What Elizabeth should do was close her eyes and try to return to dreamland.

It would be the safest choice. The choice least likely to disappoint her father.

But of all the people in her life, it was Darcy she could forget with. *His* arms could comfort her.

Not that I will tell him so, she thought as she pulled on her dress and re-plaited her hair down her back. Sliding her cloak over her shoulders, she looked to her sister's sleeping form, knowing it would not be only her father disappointed if anyone found out where she went tonight.

But go she must.

Compelled, drawn, she slipped downstairs on her stocking clad feet. Longbourn at night seemed abandoned though she knew the doors she passed upstairs hid sleeping figures behind them. The moonlight created ample light to see by for a woman who had grown up in these halls, but still created enough shadows to make the flesh on the back of her neck prickle.

She reached the front corridor and paused by the vestibule to put on her walking boots. A click from further down the hall made her freeze. No, no one should be awake at this hour…!

The light of a candle proved her wrong, however. Someone was up, coming from her father's study, and before she could do more than straighten, Mr. Collins came into sight.

They stared at one another. Both of them up far later than they should be, yet Mr. Collins the one who held all the power. She swallowed.

"Mr. Collins."

His eyes darted down the hall, then to her attire, obviously suited for the outdoors. "Cousin. You are not where you should be."

Her pride pricked her. "Neither are you."

Mr. Collins stood taller, his expression trying to remain unaffected. "It is my prerogative to be out of my room at night."

"With my father's books?"

She pursed her lips while Mr. Collins stiffened. He had two of her fathers books tucked against his side, but the spines were familiar to one who had run her hands along her father's bookshelves for many a year.

Her father never allowed one of his books to leave his study. Their inheritance, he sometimes said, and cautioned Mrs Bennet to keep a close record of all the titles with the help of Mr. Laurence.

Now Mr. Collins had two of them, and while she might've been sneaking out, his expression said his intentions were much more sinister than hers.

"Your father has allowed me to borrow these," he said, eyes narrowing.

"In the dead of night," she said.

"What agreements exist between your father and myself is none of your concern. But where my erstwhile cousin sneaks off to in the dead of night *is* my concern," he said with an unearthly golden gleam in his eye from his candle. Elizabeth found herself taking a step back, her shoulder bumping against the vestibule wall. "Where do you run off to, cousin? An illicit lover, perhaps? Have your morals left you so low as to potentially elope? But I see no luggage, so perhaps not…"

Mr. Collins may have been short and squat, but he had

the advantage of surprise on Elizabeth, and when he shot forward and pressed her to the wall, she found her head snapping back and hitting the plaster. The books scattered on the floor, one of them landing heavily on her foot. She struggled, hands coming up to ward him off, but he was ready, grabbing her wrists and forcing her still. The candle's heat burned her shoulder before he drew it away, setting it aside on a nearby table before returning to glare into her eyes.

Time slowed. The world grew blurry, her eyes burning with unshed tears. Mr. Collins' squeezed her wrist and her mouth opened on a gasp when pain shot up her arm.

"If you are kind to me, dear cousin, I could find it in my heart to forgive you these sins against your family." She felt his breath on her cheek, hot and stinking. "But first you must prove you are not as cold as you seem…"

"Get off me!"

He struggled with her wrists while his other hand tried to find the opening of her cape. "A young woman should not be so loose with her affections—"

"I said, get *off*!" Her wrist screamed in his grip, but though she managed to tear free, he kept her pinned to the wall.

He was breathing hard, and it was not all from their struggles. He was excited, and she could feel said excitement against her leg. "Your mother would cry in joy if she knew how you came to me, came to be guided back to the path of light as my yielding wife."

Her hand scrabbled to the side. Caught on the heavy candleholder. It was heavy and her sweaty hand almost lost its grip, but she managed to close her palm around it and she swung it at Mr. Collins' head. Hot wax splattered over her hand, burning her knuckles, and Mr. Collins' head whipped to the side when the candlestick connected with his temple.

He stumbled back. That was what mattered.

Elizabeth pushed past him and found herself free. Free, gasping with the horror of it all, stumbling over the spilled books toward the door. "Impertinent wretch!" Mr. Collins snarled behind her, and she spurred her legs to move and fled out the front door.

11

Where the hell was she?

He rubbed the tops of his knees, the friction creating a pleasant warmth for his numb hands. Darcy laughed to himself. Elizabeth's premonition that they may simply shiver together might come true if it took her much longer to arrive. All his hot bricks would be for naught.

Darcy didn't resent her for the time, however. They'd set a vague timeframe, one molded by how late her family took to their beds. He did not have a house full of family to sneak around, as she did, so he tempered any ill feelings when they tried to rise.

That was not to say Elizabeth courted the most suspicion tonight. His own activities this evening had raised eyebrows in the stables. It was not often a gentleman demanded a carriage packed with hot bricks and blankets, but no driver. He'd made certain provisions for the stablemen's silence on the matter, but raised eyebrows would eventually mean whispers in the village, whispers that might one day reach Bingley's ears.

A sudden boost in energy overcame him and the only outlet was bouncing his legs. He felt like a boy again! How had she managed to do this to him? It had been impossible to focus on a single task today. His correspondence was a mess. But knowing he would soon have her bountiful curves under his hands again had distracted him completely. He wished this feeling, this anticipation and schoolboy giddiness, would last forever.

And it would. He'd made the decision today. An apartment in London. An income. A bed lush with furs and silks. A life *together*.

His cheeks warm, he smiled to himself. Weeks ago he would've scorned those who took such efforts, but now he understood. When you found happiness, *this* blissful sort of happiness, you took it by whatever means necessary and damn the rumors and consequences. Elizabeth was his woman and no one's opinion would sway him. Better yet, *no one* including that no-good Wickham, would be able to touch her.

The crunch of footsteps outside stiffened his shoulders. He had no time to brace before the latch on the carriage door opened and moonlight and icy air spilled inside, followed by the silhouette of a head.

"Mr. Darcy?"

He smiled. "What would you have done if it wasn't?"

"Screamed and ran," Elizabeth said, the carriage suspension groaning as she hoisted herself into the carriage and pulled the door closed behind her.

"Then it is good that it is me. Here, I have blankets for us." He slid over and pulled her into his arms, sharing the warmth of his blanket. She hissed in pleasure as she leaned against him, the touch of cold air seeping through his clothes.

His mouth found hers, swallowed her little relieved sigh when she melted into him. He could not wait to return to Netherfield and press his face against his pillows, smelling her scent lingering there. But first he would have her. Feel her shiver and shudder against him, buck up into her core.

He wanted to erase her chill, and his roaming hands traced her through her clothes, pulling more sighs from her as he imparted his warmth. "Your cheeks are cold," he murmured.

"I am Lizzy no more, but one big ice cube," she said.

Playing out fantasies in his head all day had led him here to her yielding and loving in his arms. Laughing, he grabbed her wrist and meant to draw her arm around him. Elizabeth hissed and jerked back.

"Ow!"

"What is it?" he asked, damning the lack of light.

"Nothing, it's nothing—"

He pulled back and ran his thumb over her wrist. Her mew of discomfort said it *wasn't* nothing. "Are you hurt?" he asked. "What happened?"

"I - my wrist, um—"

"I've never known you to be speechless. What happened?" A grim fear grabbed his chest and by the thin light coming through the window he could see her wince. "Did someone hurt you?"

Her breathless reply didn't reassure him. "It's nothing, really."

"Your father did this to you?"

Elizabeth tried to jerk away, groaning as she did so. "No," she snapped, voice thin with pain. "My father, even if he had his health, could never."

Yet her reply confirmed his suspicions. "Then who?" He flipped through the people inside of Longbourn and certainty settled in his chest. "That parson. Lizzy. Look at me. Did Collins do this?"

His vision, adjusted to the darkness, saw the hazy shape of her nod. "Yes," she ground out, and then her shoulders crumpled. "Yes, he did. He wanted—my mother wants us to marry—"

Marry that odious man! He nearly didn't hear the rest of what she said because of the buzzing in his ears.

"—and I refused and then this evening he caught me sneaking out and I think he was stealing some of my father's books and the things he *said*! Oh, it was horrible!"

"What happened?" His tone echoed the murderous urge in his hands.

She released a shaky, tearful sob. "I hit him with a candlestick. I didn't know how else to get him off me. And now I am here and I never wish to go back there again!"

"Why didn't you say something at once? No, nevermind that." He took her into his arms again, relieved when she let herself relax into him. Smoothing his hand over her shoulder, hating the tears he felt against his collar, he thought of his plan. Some alterations were necessary. "I'm taking you to London straightaway in the morning."

She stiffened. "What—I can't—"

"I won't have you abused by your relations," he said as she pulled out of his embrace.

"You'll do no such thing! I cannot *leave*!"

He sighed and pinched the bridge of his nose. "This is not how I wished to make the proposal"—her surprised breath nearly derailed him, but he went on—"but I feel expediting this is prudent now. Return to London with me, Lizzy. There are very nice apartments for sale near Marylebone, a fashionable neighborhood in reasonable distance to my own townhouse—"

Her scathing voice interrupted him. "You may buy an apartment wherever you wish, but I will not step foot in it." The heat of her reply scalded him. "I will never go to London with you!"

"Then you will stay here and be pawed at by that odious…!" He took a deep breath. She was a contrary creature, and he needed the reminder. "You need protection, and I want to care for you. I want you close to me."

There. Now it was out in the open between them.

She was shaking her head. "Whatever am I doing here?" she said, muttering to herself. "This is madness, utter madness. I have let this go on too far—"

She threw the blankets off her lap and went for the door.

"Lizzy!" He reached out for her, but she slipped from the carriage before he could untangle the blankets from his legs. He freed himself with a curse and climbed out after her, dismayed to find her already ten paces ahead on the lane back to Longbourn. "Lizzy!" he said, chasing after her.

She spun with him when he clamped his hand on her shoulder. "No, Darcy! No, I will not. Your *proposal* is denied with extreme prejudice!" She swiped his hand off her shoulder as he stepped back from her fury. "You no longer have leave to use my Christian name."

The horses were whinnying, stomping and nervous. He glanced back and found the wood blocks dislodged. "Wait!" he snapped at her and ran back to the carriage as the horses started pulling. He kicked the blocks back in place, snarling and red-faced when he looked back and found her striding away. "Damnit, Lizzy, just wait!"

The horses, skittish, stomped and skittered, and he had no choice but to go forward and soothe them, watching Elizabeth disappear into the dark with bitterness churning in his gut.

Damn.

12

She simply didn't understand. Darcy told himself that as he tossed and turned in the sheets, her scent captured in the fabric and by turns tempting and infuriating him every time he caught a hint. She didn't give him a chance to explain correctly and, in the morning, he would explain again. In the light of day, in a more reasonable state, she would understand his offer.

But was she bloody infuriating!

His temper was no better in the morning. He took his coffee by the window, a piece of him hoping... But no, she would not make the journey to Netherfield.

He itched to hop astride his horse and ride to Longbourn straightaway, but he mustered patience and stayed inside. A respectable hour would be better.

Darcy's opinion had not changed. He wanted Elizabeth. Wanted the feel of her skin against his. Wanted the pull and tug in his chest as they embraced. Wanted to be rid of every mile between them and keep her in silks and furs, tangled up in him as much as she tangled him up in her. There were oceans between Netherfield and Longbourn and this was his ship to bring her back.

He wanted permanence. To know when he reached for her, she would be there. He wouldn't lose her over something so silly. Let her shout and kick all the way to London as long as she *went*. She was his mistress in spirit already, and he refused to return without her.

But before the clock struck ten o'clock, the house broke into a flurry of activity. He looked up from his musings and found a carriage coming up the lane. Muttering a curse under his breath, he prepared himself for the arrival of Bingley and company.

"We left London frightfully early!" Caroline complained when the party had all settled in the dining room for a late breakfast, fastidiously hiding a yawn behind her fan. She shot a perturbed glare at her brother. "He could not be persuaded otherwise."

Whether Caroline meant being persuaded from the early trip or from returning at all, Darcy didn't have to guess. From both sisters, the resentment was palpable. They could all guess the reason behind the light shining in Bingley's eyes, and he confirmed it to Darcy moments later.

"I would not waste a minute longer in London after my business was done. Darcy, you should know I have come to a decision—I will ask Miss Bennet to marry me. While I was in London, do you know what I realized?"

"What is that?" Darcy asked.

Bingley's smile shone, not even realizing his sisters were sharing dark looks. "My heart remained here in Hertfordshire and that, my friend, that was when I knew nothing would make me happier."

Darcy had to force himself not to grimace. "I wish you much happiness. That is, of course, if she accepts."

Miss Bingley scoffed while Mr. Hurst chortled, nearly choking on his pastry. "We all know how joyous those in Longbourn will be."

"I go this very afternoon to lay my heart down at her feet—"

"Oh, please, won't you wait one day?" Mrs Hurst said and Miss Bingley frantically nodded. "It will not hurt to have one more day to think before starting down this path."

Bingley lifted a hand. "I've thought enough. I could not spend one second *more* thinking when I know what I want."

"You will look desperate!" Miss Bingley said. "Surely, Miss Bennet won't look kindly on the offer if you apply to her at once. You look - look like you're out of options," she said, striking out while her brother's expression faltered. "Please," she said, reaching over to cover his hand. "One more day. She will be there tomorrow and you can refresh yourself from the journey. You must be presentable, after all."

Bingley nodded slowly, his brow furrowed. "I don't want her to feel insulted. She's cautioned me at least once about rushing in without thought. You're right. She will appreciate that I've given it proper consideration." He frowned. "I think. Maybe. Oh, I do not know! Darcy, let us go for a ride and let the outdoors sort me out!"

Darcy agreed. While Bingley told the servants to have their horses ready, Miss Bingley leaned over and confided in him. "Do what you can, *please,* Mr. Darcy. He uttered such nonsense the whole time in London!"

But Darcy could not find it within himself to burst Bingley's happiness. After all, his own happiness rested at Longbourn too. It would be some kind of karmic curse to warn Bingley away from the Bennets when he hoped the next day would settle his future.

He rode with Bingley over the estate, idly checking fences, mostly enjoying the sunshine.

"Anderson asked about you, Darcy," Bingley said, his breath pluming in the air. "He said you sent a letter of condolence after the loss of that ship. Very sincere, he said."

"It was a terrible tragedy. Despite our differences of opinion, he's a good man, and I knew he would be blaming himself for it."

"He thinks the world of you," Bingley said as they paused on a hilltop, looking at the expanse of land that would soon become Bingley's permanently. "I know he's searching for something that you'd eagerly invest in."

"If he would stick to what he is good at, he would see none of these issues. He does not have an eye for anything outside of publishing. Just like I do not try to source fabrics for the latest fashions when my expertise is mainly agricultural."

"You've *some* interest outside of farming and sheep," Bingley said.

"Yes, but I invest in those who know about fabrics and milling and whatever else. Anderson is not an expert in anything except publishing, and until he focuses on publishing only, I will not invest in him."

"Those circulating libraries of his do a nice turnabout. I know I've received value for my subscription. Anyway, Anderson asked when you would return to London as he had some other ventures to discuss with you. Do you know when? I couldn't give him an answer. Honestly, it surprised me that you sought to stay here instead of returning with us."

"I needed the quiet," Darcy said, ruffling the mane of his horse while she bent to chew on a clump of brown grass.

"But I may return sooner rather than later. I am too old to go here and there without a rest."

"You? Too old?" Bingley laughed. "Might you even think of settling down for good, Darcy? If you find a bride quickly, we might even manage a double wedding."

He snorted. "I am not in the market for a bride. There is no one my equal that I could suffer to share my life with in that respect."

As to settling down… He had different views on that point.

"When do you go to Longbourn?"

Bingley tossed his head. "I figure about nine o'clock. Then Caroline will be asleep and cannot stop me. Why?"

"I'm thinking of joining you. I want to… be the first to congratulate you."

Bingley smirked at him, his horse pawing at the ground. "Really? I almost imagined you might have your eye on one of Miss Bennet's sisters. A certain one with fine dark eyes?"

"Brown eyes," he said. "And no," he said, turning his horse away and starting down the hill. "I will return to London *without* a bride."

But, he hoped, something far better.

13

They left Netherfield at nine o'clock on the dot. It was another restless night for Darcy. He resolved that once they were settled in London, he would stay at Elizabeth's apartment for at least a week in order to improve the bad temper that two nights of poor rest gave him.

They were accepted through Longbourn's front door at once, and they spent the moment removing hat and gloves in the vestibule. Darcy expected to be led to the sitting room and could not temper his excitement. To see Lizzy again, to know if her mind had changed, to find some way to speak with her by herself. He had so much to say to her.

However, Mrs Bennet met them by the vestibule, her smile tremulous and eyes swollen. She gave them both a warm greeting, her smile turning genuine with Mr. Bingley's enthusiastic greeting.

"Is everything well?" Mr. Bingley inquired, his brow furrowing.

"Ah, a small household matter. Nothing to concern yourself over. Now that you have come to visit us, the day seems much brighter!" She turned to Darcy. "Mr. Darcy, when Mr. Bennet heard you were here, he asked that you meet him in his study."

He exchanged a surprised look with Bingley. "Yes, of course," he said and Mrs Bennet directed Mr. Bingley toward the front sitting room before guiding Mr. Darcy further into Longbourn. He could not imagine what Mr. Bennet might want with him.

Elizabeth wouldn't have *said*… surely Mrs Bennet would greet Darcy far differently if she knew he debauched her daughter?

Mrs Bennet led him down the hall, darting nervous glances at him that only increased his nerves, especially with her red-rimmed eyes. "I caution you that my husband is a sick man. Not contagious, mind you," she added quickly as if that would be top of his mind. She wrung her hands when they stopped before a door near the back of Longbourn. "So his appearance may be startling."

He inclined his head. He knew this from Bingley's interactions with the gentleman. "I understand, Mrs Bennet."

With a deep breath, she pushed open the door. The study was clothed in dark woods and lush fabrics. A clinical, indecipherable scent filled the air and tickled his nose.

"Mr. Darcy."

A large four poster bed dominated the room where a desk would normally be. He approached, the thick carpets softening his footsteps, and bowed near the foot of Mr. Bennet's bed. "Mr. Bennet. It is a pleasure to make your acquaintance finally."

Mr. Bennet was a thin man, gaunt in the grey light of morning coming in through the windows, and the bruises under his eyes showed long periods of unrest and unease.

What affliction he suffered, Darcy didn't know, however it must have impacted him most severely over the years.

Despite this however, Mr. Bennet did not appear weak, but stern as he gave Darcy's appearance the same consideration. His steely gaze found Darcy wanting. "You seem to be more polite than what I was led to believe."

Darcy didn't know how to respond to that, so settled for, "I've been accused of being standoffish during public events, yes, if that is what you refer to. I prefer smaller groups, truthfully."

"Yes, a man like yourself would prefer a more *intimate* environment. That way you can give individuals your personal attention."

"Yes, I suppose…"

Darcy furrowed his brows, not understanding where Mr. Bennet meant to lead this conversation. He'd heard from the neighborhood that Mr. Bennet could be odd at times, with a cutting sense of humor, but this was unexpected still. Even now Elizabeth would be in the sitting room with her sisters and he hoped to use Bingley's distraction to speak to her privately. He thought that was more important than Mr. Bennet making infuriatingly veiled remarks to try to make him uncomfortable.

Mr. Bennet saw Darcy's confusion, the hint of frustration, and thankfully put him out of his misery. "You wonder why I asked for you, I take it? Well to me, it is a wonder that you have to guess. Mr. Darcy you are not welcome within Longbourn. Do not even come within her shadow, because you are not welcome there either. My Elizabeth has told me how you've persisted in your attentions toward her despite every rebuff on her part. Elizabeth is not a stranger to unwanted attention, but she said yours has unnerved her, and yesterday she showed me a bruise from your hand, sir."

Cold. Icy wind stung his cheeks, ripped talons through his chest. He stared at Mr. Bennet with that wind so loud he had to fight to comprehend each strike of the hammer Mr. Bennet laid down. Elizabeth had said… persisted… bruised by his hand…

"That is not true," he said, a whisper in the howling gale of Mr. Bennet's pale, unflinching gaze. He forced strength into his voice. "No. Bring"—*Lizzy*—"Miss Elizabeth here and we will come to the truth of this. I did no such thing."

She came to me. I did not—does she really believe that?

No, it can't be. A lie. She lied to her family.

Mr. Bennet glared at him like a slug on a prized rose-bush. He folded his knobby hands atop his blankets and looked down his pointed nose at Darcy.

"I sent Elizabeth away to relatives. She left yesterday. It was the only way to restore some peace of mind to her after the state your attentions left her in. You can no longer bother her, sir, and now I ask that you leave. Leave Longbourn. Leave Hertfordshire. Only my daughter's reputation keeps my lips sealed from the rest of my family and my neighbors, but if you try to linger in my neighborhood for one half hour longer than it takes you to pack, I will spread the tale of your wickedness in every ear that will bend my way." His thin lips lifted in a faint smile. "With your standoffish attitude in public so far, I imagine many ears will bend my way."

Each promise was another sharpened icicle through his chest. All he could manage when Mr. Bennet finished was a wooden bow. "I assure you I will get to the bottom of this. There has been some grievous misunderstanding, and I encourage you to look closer to home for the troubles your daughter suffers."

Mr. Bennet's eyes narrowed. "I may be sick, but I am not stupid. See to your own character, Mr. Darcy, before you instruct others how to manage their homes. Now..." He coughed then, a wracking cough that rattled in his lungs. However, he was not diminished when he lifted his gaze back to meet Darcy's, as severe as a snake defending its nest. "Did I not tell you to leave my home?"

Darcy left.

He left behind no greetings, and did not go to congratulate Bingley if the happy deed was done. He stopped outside and let the winter's bite sting his cheeks.

"Sir? Sir!"

Who but exited Longbourn after him except for Mr. Collins. Truly, a gift. The man who deserved Mr. Bennet's ire and censure. Not only annoying, but a cruel villain who would assault a woman in her father's home.

He was chattering in his whinging prattle as he came down the steps before Darcy could fully turn his head. "I hope you will provide your noble aunt a satisfactory report of my progress when you next write to her. Though I have not secured a wife as I had yet planned—*ah!*"

Darcy snatched Mr. Collins hand and twisted, bearing down all his weight on the parson's wrist. A dark pleasure as vicious as poison simmered in his blood when Mr. Collins' eyes bulged in fear.

"You will leave this house and never return, understand? I know what you did," he growled, relishing the fear in Collins' watering eyes while bones creaked under his grip. "You tried to take that which is not *yours*. I will take great pleasure ensuring my aunt is well versed on the moral fiber of her clergyman."

Mine, he wanted to say. *You tried to take what is mine.*

Mr. Collins whined pathetically. "B-but nothing—I did nothing but try to stop my cousin! I-I assure you, my-my-my intentions were... were..."

He leaned down until they were nose to nose. "Leave Longbourn today and go fast, Mr. Collins. Go fast and pray you can beat the post."

With Mr. Collins whimpering behind him, Darcy left Longbourn.

Elizabeth would pay.

CAUGHT BY DARCY

BOOK TWO

I

It was one of those spring days that made Elizabeth long for the countryside. A finer day could not be had traversing the hills and plains of Hertfordshire where the sky stretched as far as the eye could see. Where she could lift her arms and spin in dizzying circles until she fell, laughing, to the ground with no one the wiser of what a fool she was underneath her poised exterior.

Instead Elizabeth sat in a park in the heart of London, listening to the joyful shouts of her niece and nephew while they played. Trying to spin in a circle here would see her flailing into some innocent passerby and they would undoubtedly fine her or at least ban her from the park if she acted in such a manner.

London was full of people. It was a crowded place in general, the streets dotted with women window-shopping and gentlemen in their hats and walking sticks. Urchins would stand on street corners, shouting about their wares, and the stench of horse flesh was thick with all the carriages for hire on the nicer streets. The park was supposedly a reprieve from all the madness outside the thick hedges and gates; however, most everyone was attempting to escape the riff-raff and commotion, so they ended up bringing it with them when they flocked into the park. Buggies passed by with gentleman and ladies wanting to see, and more initially, be seen. Vendors called out to passerby to see their wares and foodstuffs. Deeper inside the park were performers, musicians, and not a moment of simple *peace*.

Elizabeth looked about from her spot on a bench in all this commotion, wondering how many of her neighbors on the other benches were dreaming about their homes. Surely, all of these people were not from London? It seemed impossible to be from here. London was not a home, but a destination.

How many of them could never go back home?

Never will you step foot in my home if you do this, Elizabeth! Never!

Even all these months later, her mother's disappointment rang in her ears. Nightly, her mind spun over those last moments in Longbourn. Her father's study door closed. Her pale-faced sisters in shock and disarray. Mr. Collins hiding away in the house somewhere, licking his wounds.

And Elizabeth's lips sealed about what happened, what truly happened, because she could not bear to know her mother would marry her to a man like that knowing what a despicable fiend he was. Let that be one thing she never found out about her mother, because as much as she hated her mother's actions to see her married off, she loved her mother with a daughter's ferocity, and she couldn't bear a world where her mother betrayed her like that.

A shout rang out, distracting her from her musings. A faint smile came to her lips at the sight of her niece and nephew playing with ribbon and sticks by the pond's edge. It was a rare day she didn't think about home, but today the memories were more bittersweet than most.

"Drat! Deary me, the wind's caught it now!"

Unbound pages flew past her, skittering along the grass. Elizabeth shot up and, along with a harried and harassed gentleman, scrambled to pick them up before they could plummet to a watery death in the pond.

"I have them!" Elizabeth called, crushing the papers in her hasty scramble to grab three at once. She put them in some semblance of order and turned to find the gentleman chasing after a final rogue page. Elizabeth walked back to the man's bench, smoothing out the papers the best she could.

The gentleman returned, puffing and carrying a dozen wrinkled pages. She grimaced at the page in her hand, a mess of ink barely discernible under the wrinkles.

"I'm afraid this one may be beyond me."

"It's enough you tried, young lady. Thank you for your assistance." The gentleman wiped at his sweaty forehead with his handkerchief, his big, round belly stretching his fine vest and jacket. "It's all a mess now."

"I'm sure it's salvageable," she said, applying herself to putting the pages back in order. "Oh, I think whoever proofed this missed an error. It should be 'whom', not 'who'." He peered over her shoulder and she pointed to the offense. "See?"

"You saw that in a moment. You read uncommonly fast."

"I don't know whether it's uncommon," she said, confused by his interest. "It's just the speed I read."

"Do you like to read, then?"

"Of course."

"Then I imagine you subscribe to one of the circulating libraries. Anderson's is the best." His chest swelled. While she debated telling him that she had little income to subscribe to one of the libraries, he went on, "So you like to read and you can spot mistakes at a glance. Tell me, do you write as well?"

"I've actually submitted to Anderson's publishing house before, but I never heard back."

"Our backlog is enormous. So you do right. Romance, I imagine?"

"The vagaries of love have made an appearance in my work," she said, a blush stinging her cheeks at the way he scrutinized her. "But I prefer to think my work captures the essence of humanity's passions and follies."

He looked over her with a narrow, considering look. "Hmph. A lot of money to be made telling fanciful stories about the vagaries of love. Frankly, Anderson's needs more girls like you. A quick read, a discerning eye for errors… are you looking for employment?"

"I… are you doing this for a lark?" She looked about for anyone who might be watching and giggling, but everyone seemed to be ignoring the two strangers huddled over a stack of papers. "I say I'm a writer and now you're asking—"

"For an assistant," he said, picking up his papers, disheveled though they were, and pushing them into a canvas bound portfolio. "Bring your work tomorrow, and I'll look at it. If it's marketable, if I can get subscribers, if if if… what I need, however, is someone to edit. There's a boom in publishing, dear woman, and not near enough people to put books in the hands of the hungry masses! Here's my card. Arrive at nine o'clock sharp. Or don't," he added, seeing her expression.

She laughed to hide how flustered she was. "You don't even know my name!"

He puffed out his chest. "What is it then?"

"Elizabeth Bennet."

"Well, I am Gregory Davies, and now we are acquainted. Come to the publishing house tomorrow and we'll see if you are a good fit. And bring your novel, too, if you're so inclined, but I make no promises. Now I must be off or else the missus will claim I'm dallying."

Watching the odd Mr. Davies hurry down the path, mopping his brow with his handkerchief while he clung to his portfolio with the other hand, Elizabeth felt like she watched the moment from outside herself. What a strange encounter. What an even stranger gentleman.

Elizabeth took her niece and nephew back home in an odd mood. She helped the children bathe and eat, and by the time her aunt returned from visiting friends, she had picked up and put down the card so often that the edges of the card were bent and curling from the oils on her fingertips.

"What is it?"

"It's… well…" Elizabeth explained in halting tones, not sure why she brought it up at all and aware of the way her aunt stared at her in rapt attention. "An amusing encounter, but it couldn't be real, could it?"

Her aunt leaned forward, eyes sparkling as they so often did with Elizabeth. "I think it could be very real. He makes a good point about publishing. It is all my friends talk about nowadays, and I've debated a subscription before with your uncle. It does make reading so much more accessible and I understand some of the circulating libraries will hold raffles and teas for their members." She looked at Elizabeth, looked at her in a way her mother never had. "You should do it."

"But *employment*?"

"Think of it as pin money."

"My mother—"

"Your uncle will be thrilled, just you watch," Mrs.

Gardiner said, and at dinner time, she proved correct. Mr. Gardiner went beet red with pride and toasted to his niece, the newest author to come to society.

Elizabeth hurried to set his expectations. "Mr. Davies wants an assistant. He only said he would read my novels and if they're good, he'll consider taking them on."

At least, that was her understanding when she left the park. It was all a blur now. A hurried rush to grab papers, an invitation, and offer of employment… was this real?

Mr. Gardiner put down his glass and shook his finger at her. "When this Davies reads your work and loves every word, I want you to come fetch me at once to read the contract he puts in front of you."

Elizabeth took to bed in a queer mood. Her post had been left in the hall and she brought it with her, a bubble of disappointment in her throat when she didn't see the familiar hand of her father on any of the letters. He'd written once since her arrival to make sure she was settled, and since then had been silence. Her mother had written once as well, and she kept the letter in her writing desk to take out and reread when she got too homesick.

You are never allowed into Longbourn again as long as you continue resisting your parents' wishes.

Tonight, she ignored the temptation to read her mother's letter again and instead opened her sister's most recent letter. Their correspondence was weekly and Elizabeth diligently kept it alive, not only because it kept her abreast of the latest happenings in her sister's marriage to Mr. Bingley, but it remained her only connection to Longbourn now. Her other sisters wrote sporadically or not at all, and Elizabeth had finally given up writing them regularly. Jane, however, eagerly returned her letters and Elizabeth imagined the postman hardly received any rest between the two of them alone.

Today's missive was a thick one, detailing plans to hold a spring games day for the neighborhood, new renovations to the bedroom suites, and even the possibility of an indoor water system that confused Elizabeth but seemed to greatly excite Mr. Bingley, and thus Jane. Elizabeth read it by the dying light coming through her window and lit a candle to respond and relay her own news. She demurred on the invitation to visit Netherfield for the games and stay for several weeks, but she was happy to discuss the strange encounter at the park.

Chewing her lip, she penned that she would send an update after she met Mr. Davies again at the publishing house. Then she leaned back and stared at her bold script, the slight shake of her pen at the end of the sentence…

She was wary, but that was no reason to run, was it?

She finished off the letter and set it to the side to finish the next day.

She dressed for bed, humming to herself. Having not felt this level of optimism in some time, it took her a moment to realize she was actually smiling when she pulled the covers up.

However, her thoughts soon turned to far less happier topics as soon as her head hit the pillow.

Late at night when she was left with only her thoughts and dreams… her mind drifted to those moments better left forgotten. Those hours alone with Darcy, in his bed, in the morning sunlight when the world was still and his touch left her shivering and simmering.

Rolling over, Elizabeth resolved never to think of it again. A common resolution, broken every night.

What would Darcy think if she was employed? Her

industrious relatives might be pleased, but he certainly wouldn't be, she decided. No, he had thought she had better ways to spend her time…

I want you, he'd once said to the young woman she'd once been.

I am no longer that woman, and it's far past time to care about what he thinks of me, in the unlikely event he still does.

And so resolved, she went to sleep that was for once filled with happy dreams instead of dreams of sheets twisting in her grip or a mouth pressing searing kisses to her collarbone.

2

"As you can see, we're nearly at capacity. We'll have to tear that wall open for more presses by the end of the season, mark my words."

Mr. Davies waved lackadaisically to the far east wall which shuddered every few moments with the terrific noise of the printing press behind it, each *thump* of the press sending little pieces of plaster and dust to the ground behind the rows of makeshift desks stitched together for the binders. "Mr. Anderson has already purchased the warehouse across the street for future expansion, but we'll need all the room we can before he can retrofit it to our needs. And here are my editors, the lousy lot of them."

This time he directed her attention to the row of men and women, though mostly young men with serious little beards, diligently scratching and marking various stacks of papers Elizabeth assumed were manuscripts. A woman about Elizabeth's age stuck her tongue out at Mr. Davies, who had the grace to ignore it as he passed. She winked at Elizabeth as she followed along behind him.

"This would be where I, erm, work, then?"

"These novels have been approved for publication—yes, I knew you would be shocked! A busy time it is, and so many libraries to keep stocked! No, no, you will be here."

He led her through the row of editors and to a small office. A large desk dominated it, covered in a mess of papers it would take ages to sort through. To the side, by the door, was a smaller, cramped desk, and to this Mr. Davies pointed.

"Are you a yappy dog?"

"Erm…"

"Because I need one!" he boomed. "A yappy dog to guard my desk from the dreck and trash—mind you, a lot of it is trash, but there are nuggets of gold in there, and we'll find out yet if you can separate the two!"

"The nuggets or the dreck," she said, uncertain whether to be offended or not when a muffled *"yip yip"* reached her through the doorway.

"You are not my first assistant nor will you be the last. I'll give us a week to sort out whether you have any talent or not. What's that in your hand, girl?"

Girl. That will become tiring.

If she had any sense, she would turn on her heel, return to Gracechurch Street, and wipe her hands of the whole adventure. Instead, she handed over her painstakingly copied novel.

"It's my latest novel."

He took it with a considerate frown and hefted it in one hand. "Big enough to split into three."

She gave him a shocked look. "But it's not three."

"Start writing in threes then!" His bark made her jump, but it only seemed to be a habit for him to talk loud enough to be heard over the oppressive noise of the printing presses. "Three novels is what our readers want, though they all claim to want one. The numbers do not lie. Cliffhangers! Mystery! Intrigue!"

"You'll publish it?"

"If I like it, *if* enough subscribers sign up, if if if." He waved to the cramped desk with its stack of manuscripts. "For now, that is what is most pressing. The vagaries of love can wait until the slush is cleared."

Mr. Davies laid her book on his desk where she imagined a paper tongue might come out of the overflowing stacks of papers and swallow her novel whole. However, it did not, and the desk held the extra load with no issue.

He looked at her. She stared back. "Well?" he barked.

She jumped and scrambled to her spot.

Yip yip, indeed.

Her first few days as Mr. Davies' assistant were the most harrowing of her life.

The most *fun*, too.

Her fingers were sore from marking, circling, and sometimes slashing out full manuscript pages. "Though if the author has paid to publish their work, it is likely to go through the barest minimum of editing before we send it to the press," she told her aunt the evening of her third day while she rubbed warm rose oil over her tired, aching hand. "It is only the novels we publish for their merits which go through the more rigorous process. Mr. Davies says this is the busy season, though Miss Brown says it is always the busy season."

Mrs. Gardiner observed Elizabeth with a smile on her lips. "You enjoy it, don't you?"

"I do," she admitted with an embarrassed blush. "The

work is interesting and, although my book still sits unread on his desk and he doesn't appear to have any intention of picking it up, Mr. Davies is not a terrible overseer. After I proved I could sort through the drivel and the gold, he's allowed me enormous discretion."

"I wonder why that is," Mrs. Gardiner said. "A gentleman is normally loath to give away freedoms so. Does he have other responsibilities? You say he leaves the publishing house early most days. Perhaps he gives you freedom so he can enjoy other pursuits."

"I think Mr. Davies would live at the publishing house if he could," she said. "I've never seen a man so joyous to begin his day or reluctant to leave in the afternoon. Not even my uncle," she added to her aunt's amusement. "No, I start to think Miss Brown is correct when she says there are troubles at home for Mr. Davies."

"Hmm. It could be simple gossip. You trust this Miss Brown?"

"She's an amiable sort of person and she's done me a great favor introducing me to everyone and seeing me settled in. She doesn't intimate Mr. Davies' home trouble in a malicious way that I can detect. She seems fairly concerned for him for the most part."

"Best not to speak of it then, until Mr. Davies does himself," Mrs. Gardiner said. "I'm glad you're finding friends, and an occupation. It sounds like a good way to spend your day, reading books and discussing the merits of story and style. Except I believe I will keep only to the library instead as I don't believe these old hands could withstand the joy of it," she said with a glance at Elizabeth's ink-stained hands.

"So you subscribed?"

"Yes. Of course, only one of Mr. Anderson's libraries

would do," she said, making Elizabeth smile at the loyalty, "and I may bring a guest any time I wish. Will you have a day off soon to join me?"

"If Mr. Davies doesn't like my assistance by the end of the week, I will be at your disposal," Elizabeth said.

Mrs. Gardiner pushed herself to her feet. "Don't tease, Lizzy. We both know this suits you more than corralling two rambunctious children all day. Besides, how will you ever find a husband if you are tied to this house all day?"

With a smirk and a swish of her skirts, she left.

Elizabeth finished up her trial week and, to the surprise of no one, Mr. Davies determined she was a passable goldminer. He paid her for the week—less than she deserved but more than she expected—and told her to return the next day. Elizabeth debated only a few seconds before agreeing.

So the days went by. Breakfast at home or a muffin in a napkin before she walked the blocks to the printing press, a surprisingly short distance away. The sun would be rising fully when she sat down at her desk to start the day's work.

Her desk evolved with time. One day cleared of all but two manuscripts, the next day filled anew in a transformation that seemed never-ending. Reading speed and comprehension was one of the quirks her mother used to sigh over, a sign of a too educated young woman who would never find a husband, but here, she was among her people. Not only Miss Brown and the young ladies, but the male editors, all of them happy to join in this publishing business as apprentices. One day, these young men with their serious beards hoped to aspire to a role like Mr. Davies, collecting authors under their belt like trophies, or even higher.

Some of the young ladies who worked at the press resembled Elizabeth and Miss Brown—too poor to care about being respectable—but the ladies who bound the books were less advantaged than they, and they arrived in the dregs of sunrise and worked until after the sun went down. Elizabeth found them good company though, and frequently struck up conversations on the intricate process their small hands could accomplish more efficiently than a man's.

Another week passed, then a month with Elizabeth barely noticing, so busy was she. Each time she entered Mr. Davies' office, she looked to the spot where her manuscript still sat and over time her nerves stopped jittering and her disappointment faded when she saw it still unread. She had too much work to do to give it more than a passing glance.

Eventually, one day she left the publishing house early and, using her earnings, hired someone to drive her to the offices of Mr. Laurence.

The Bennet's solicitor worked in a part of London bursting with respectable legal offices. She felt quite out of place on the street alone with ink on her hands, serious looking people passing her by with stern expressions. The sounds of carriages rolling past was pleasant to the ear after a day in the press. Preoccupied by her nerves and the stream of people she needed to weave around, Elizabeth walked up the steps into Mr. Laurence's office. A kindly young man escorted her in front of Mr. Laurence's desk with a subdued, "Your ten o'clock, sir."

Mr. Laurence was an elderly gentleman above her father in years. A shock of white hair topped his head and his hands were knobby and gnarled with age. He peered at Elizabeth over his spectacles and it reminded her so vividly of her father that she instinctively smiled.

That smile seemed to melt Mr. Laurence's stern expression, and his pointed face relaxed. "How may I assist you today, Miss Bennet?"

Right to the quick. She liked that.

"The entail upon Longbourn, sir. I've come to replenish your retainer. It is not a lot, mind you, but I can make a deposit weekly if you'll continue to look into my father's estate."

He glanced at the few pounds she sat on his dark wood desk. "Surely it's better spent on hats and ribbons?"

"My income is better spent here."

He sat back in his chair, the wood squeaking under him. "Your father's retainer has been depleted, with little return on investment. I'm loathe to give you any kind of assurance that your money will not be wasted in a fruitless endeavor."

She had expected this, though it sunk her heart to hear it. "My sister recently married. My hope is that, even if the estate could not be given to my mother or to Jane, it could be transferred to my brother-in-law."

A thin-lipped smile. "Not to you?"

She shook her head. "I don't desire it for my own. Only for my family."

He peered at her a moment more before releasing a gusty sigh. "This is a new avenue. It could bear fruit, but again—"

"You cannot guarantee anything. I understand. I simply want to ensure that all possibilities are investigated."

He scrutinized her for several long moments, and she straightened her shoulders, trying to impart a strong appearance. She was no silly girl to be intimidated by a stern expression.

"Does your father know you are here with your pin money?"

"My father likely thinks it's as fruitless as you do, but it is *my* pin money to spend how I see fit."

He took in her raised eyebrow, her confidence, and if he thought she was a little girl fighting a dragon with a stick, at least he did not condescend to her. "Very well," he said with a deep nod. "I will continue with this information you've brought me. Mr. Bingley is the gentleman in question, correct? I believe I remember the announcement."

The tension fell from her shoulders. "It is. Thank you, Mr. Laurence."

"Miss Elizabeth Bennet, I present to you the esteemed Mr. Anderson, our patron and owner."

Elizabeth nodded to the handsome gentleman who stood in the doorway of Mr. Davies' office. He wore a fine jacket and overall looked better suited to a drawing room than in the publishing house. But he didn't seem to mind the terrible thumping constantly coming from the next room and seemed immune to the mess in the office. Elizabeth hoped she didn't have ink on her nose.

"Good day, sir, and well met."

Mr. Anderson's left cheek dimpled when he smiled. "This is the new assistant, then? I have you to thank for Mr. Davies' good mood."

"He has good moods?" Elizabeth responded with a teasing smile at Mr. Davies, who blustered convincingly. "Shall I make tea?"

This was another of her duties, only performed when Mr. Davies hosted various gentlemen in his cramped office. She stood and used a handkerchief to discreetly wipe the ink off her hands.

"Mr. Anderson never takes tea—"

Mr. Anderson was staring at her, a tilt to his mouth. "Today, I will submit to the torture," he said, turning toward Mr. Davies but keeping her in his sights. "I have quarterlies to go over with you. We can speak about the future direction of the schedule."

Elizabeth squeezed past Mr. Anderson in the doorway and hurried to the small kitchen. The schedule. It was what they all worked toward. But Mr. Anderson sounded ominous. Would they be changing direction? Moving from romance—the majority of which came across her desk—to some other topic? Would she lose her publishing house position so soon? She thought of her meeting with Mr. Laurence only last week and grimaced.

Mr. Anderson was seated in the only remaining chair in the office when she returned with the tea tray. Mr. Davies had cleared a passable space on his desk for the moment and her eye was immediately drawn to the spot where her manuscript still sat on the corner, untouched. She placed the tray, careful of her feet so she didn't knock over the many stacks of manuscripts now on the floor.

"You must not judge us harshly for our mess, Miss Elizabeth," Mr. Anderson said as she arranged the cups and poured. "No milk, please."

"I would judge the mess more harshly if there was not order within it," Elizabeth said. "Mr. Davies has his own system of filing that defies all filing cabinets."

"I wonder if you'd be so complimentary if Mr. Davies wasn't present."

She handed him the tea, aware in the way a lady was when her fingers brushed his. With a face like his, he must be accustomed to young ladies blushing in his presence, so she determined not to.

"Fortunately for Mr. Davies, he won't know either way," she said, and Mr. Anderson's gaze twinkled with bemusement. She turned to Mr. Davies and handed him his tea. "Shall I take notes?"

She would've offered to leave, but her curiosity demanded she make the effort to listen in.

"Stay," Mr. Anderson said. "But don't take notes. I will do so myself." He lifted a small bound book, worn with use, and a fresh quill pen.

Elizabeth glanced at Mr. Davies, found him satisfied, and sat at her desk, adjusting her chair to face the two gentlemen.

"It concerns the Blue Coat series."

Mr. Davies sat back in his chair, clasping his hands over his enormous belly. "Ah, that one. It practically flew off the press. We had two printing runs before we said *enough*."

Mr. Anderson looked to Elizabeth. "Are you aware of the novels in question?"

"I wasn't here when those were processed, but Mr. Davies had me read them as an example of the type of manuscripts we wanted to pursue."

"Ah, right. Well, the issue is the young lady in the novel. This Emily character begins as the daughter of a respectable family and improves her station to the wife of a duke. Not an issue in itself, but her *path* to her new station has created some ripples within the reading community. The fact that it is questionable whether she was married before… erm, notable events took place," he said, the tips of his ears turning dark.

"She was married prior to any lovemaking," Mr. Davies said, confused, completely ignoring the way Mr. Anderson began to cough, the tops of his ears reddening.

Elizabeth wasn't phased. The contents in the manuscripts had ceased to make her blush some time ago.

"That is not explicit, however, with how often Emily met the Duke prior to their marriage. There are some passages—"

"Those imply kissing, perhaps light petting," she said at

once. Mr. Anderson watched her and heat raced up the chest, the precursor to a full blush, when she realized how unaffectedly she spoke of such things. So went her resolve to not blush in his presence. This was not the publishing house editors discussing the merits of a scene, but the wealthy owner of the house, a gentleman several times over by dent of his business ventures.

However, Mr. Anderson turned in his chair, including her in the conversation, and if he had any thoughts about her impropriety, his expression did not voice it. "Yet the very ambiguity of the passages is the trouble at hand. At various functions in the last week alone, I have fielded concerns from four mamas about the scenes, leading to whispers that we are printing mere smut for the populace."

"Smut! That is nothing," Mr. Davies said with a snort. Elizabeth nodded. There were far more explicit scenes in some of the manuscripts in this very room.

Mr. Anderson lifted his shoulder. "The scandal of this forbidden romance has threatened to turn many away from their subscriptions… scandal is one thing, but if it affects subscriptions, I'm afraid I will have to err on the side of caution."

"What do you think, Miss Lizzy?"

Girl, she noted, was not used in Mr. Anderson's presence. Hiding her smile, she tilted her head. "About whether we should continue publishing these forbidden romance tales as is? Do we have proof other than whispers of scandal that subscriptions would be canceled?"

"Whispers can soon turn to cries of outrage," Mr. Davies said.

"But it has not, as of yet, impacted sales, no," Mr. Anderson said. "Tell me your perspective as a young lady whose family might be outraged by these offenses. Should we pull these types of work for editing? Deny them entirely?"

"I believe," Elizabeth spoke slowly, choosing her words carefully, "respectable young ladies may speak the right words publicly, but many will still flock to these types of tales. The forbidden appeal of it will bring them."

"But do we not have a responsibility to maintain the moral fibre of the populace?"

Elizabeth laughed lightly. "Simply because I read about a highway robbery does not make me likely to go out onto the road on my own. Similarly, a tale about forbidden trysts does not make me likely to yield to one. When I open a book, I enter a world where it is safe to indulge in my fantasies. It is a… release, of a sort. Whilst I am within it, I may experience that which I never will, and then I may close the book and return to my world a little happier to have lived a life forbidden to me in a way that did no damage to me or mine."

His eyes lit at that and he turned to Mr. Davies. "I shall steal her for my own if you aren't careful. She's wasted on the slush."

A stranger compliment she had never had, nor one she cherished so much. Elizabeth tucked away her smile, all too aware of him not as her boss, but as a man with a slow, full lipped smile.

She looked down at her lap, wishing she'd had the foresight to take notes anyway to have something to do with her hands.

The conversation shifted to the rest of the quarterly schedule and the various strategies they had in place to ensure the circulating libraries' shelves were always full. Mr. Anderson did not make meaningful conversation beyond that, and rose to leave soon afterwards, casting a look at Elizabeth. "Mr. Davies, do you mind if Miss Elizabeth walks me out?"

"Do not go stealing her away. The slush needs her touch a little longer."

"I won't," Mr. Anderson promised and Elizabeth rose and walked with him through the editors, giving Miss Brown a small smile when the younger woman raised her eyebrows at Elizabeth.

Mr. Anderson asked how she enjoyed the publishing house so far, how far away she lived from the house, and whether she could see herself continuing on with the house. He seemed satisfied by her answers, and nodded when she mentioned Gracechurch Street, as if he knew the place himself, though he didn't cast aspersions like someone of his position could very well have. That put her at ease about his character.

They stopped at the open doors of the press, the thump of the huge machine sending a little wave of dust down into their hair.

"I have something to ask, Miss Lizzy—pardon me, may I call you Miss Lizzy as Mr. Davies does?"

"Of course. What can I do for you?"

"It is not what you can do for me, but something I wish to do with you," he said, making her eyebrows fly straight to her hairline. "Might I call upon you this Thursday afternoon?"

"Call upon me?" The words didn't make sense. Mr. Anderson wanted a social visit with his employee's assistant?

Mr. Anderson tucked his notebook under his elbow and looked at her from underneath a lock of blond hair almost shyly. "Will your parents object?"

Elizabeth found her tongue—and her senses. She

colored. "I live with my aunt and uncle. I don't think they would object if you visited…"

Though she dearly wished to ask *why*, she held back. Mr. Anderson made her tongue tie in a way she hadn't anticipated, and now he beamed at her.

"Good. I will see you Thursday, then. Good morning, Miss Lizzy." Donning his hat, headless of the dust on it, he strolled off down the street and Elizabeth caught herself staring.

Maybe it was nothing. A business opportunity. A job offer. He seemed so impressed with her today, it was likely.

But while she watched his tall frame leaving through the people on the street, her chest twinged with anticipation that had nothing to do with the publishing house.

3

THURSDAY CAME. ELIZABETH WOKE AND ATTEMPTED TO GO about her day in a normal manner. Breakfast, publishing house, manuscripts, tea, an argument with Mr. Davies about an author's treatise on libertarianism cunningly seeded into a manuscript about the war.

After she escaped the publishing house early in the afternoon, she realized that by pushing aside thoughts of her social call with Mr. Anderson, she had completely failed to erase her nerves.

Was it because he was so handsome? No. She was no stranger to handsome men, and her mind turned to Darcy pinning her to a tree, burning gaze searing through her.

Her shoulders hunched, and she hurried with renewed quickness to her aunt and uncle's home. She wouldn't let *him* enter her daylight thoughts. In the past few weeks, she'd actually managed to entirely forget about his part in her past.

Her aunt had not gone calling this morning. Upon hearing that Mr. Anderson—yes, *that* Mr. Anderson wanted to call upon them—Mrs. Gardiner had turned into a cleaning and decorating dervish. She hired two more girls for the moment to straighten the whole house, refreshed the draperies in the front with new fabrics from her husband's business, and even rolled up her sleeves herself to give Elizabeth's cousins a fresh haircut—*just in case*, she told Elizabeth, which still made her laugh. Was Mr. Anderson going to call out her cousins from the nursery and inspect them?

The house on Gracechurch Street gleamed when Elizabeth stepped in the front door. The furniture polish stink had faded, thankfully, and the scent of fresh lavender instead permeated the rooms. Her footsteps swallowed by the rugs, she searched through the front rooms for her aunt and found her preoccupied in the kitchen downstairs at a table loaded down underneath two sets of china.

Elizabeth put her hand to her chest and stared at the beautiful glassware. "Please tell me you did not buy new Wedgwood ware for what's bound to be a ten minute social visit!"

Mrs. Gardiner waved off her concerns. "Our serving tray was cracked and there were various chips on some of the saucers. It happens over time, and this was as good an excuse as any to replace them. But now I'm struggling to decide which one I like better. This one with the peonies or this one with the little roses?"

Elizabeth barely needed to glance at them. "The peonies, if I must choose. They're both lovely."

Mrs. Gardiner nodded. "So it shall be. I'll wrap up this set and send it to your mother. Do you think she'd like that?"

Her aunt was always too kind. She offered a smile. "I think she'd find the roses beautiful."

"Then that's settled. Lizzy, tell me that isn't what you're wearing?"

She understood her aunt's wrinkled nose immediately and laughed. "No! I must go upstairs and change now."

"And wipe the ink off your cheek," Mrs Gardiner said with a little smile and a twinkle in her eye. "Unless you think Mr. Anderson would appreciate it. Gentlemen have funny ways, you know. I met my husband with flour on my cheeks, and see where we are now."

"I'm sure it's nothing like that," Elizabeth said with a nervous smile. "There must be something he simply didn't want to discuss in front of Mr. Davies. Maybe he is trying to poach me for another position within the house, as Mr. Davies feared. It is an underhanded way to do business, surely, and I've already determined I won't stand for it."

"Unless he offers you more wages," Mrs. Gardiner pointed out practically.

She grimaced. "Well, it is only pin money. But now I must go or else I'll be unpresentable."

"You'll find a new dress at the end of your bed."

"You shouldn't have!" she exclaimed.

"It's only a little thing, but I've been so appreciative of your time here." Mrs. Gardiner rounded the table and squeezed Elizabeth's elbow, her eyes crinkled with warmth. "You expect this has something to do with the publishing house, but I foresee something else entirely. Please humor me, and we can see which one of us wins this little wager."

"Well, now that you have made it a competition, you are putting yourself ahead already with this new dress."

Her eyes twinkled. "When one is in a competition, one seeks advantage."

Elizabeth pinched her lips together but could not hold her composure long and laughed. "Thank you, really. I've loved every minute here and I'm so thankful you were willing to take me in—"

Mrs. Gardiner clucked her tongue, chastising in her good-natured way. "You are not a stray on the streets. You are our favorite niece, and might I say you take after your uncle more than most, so it's no wonder we get along so well. Now shoo and make yourself presentable."

The dress was beautiful. A soft lavender linen made her gasp at first sight—it must've been one of her uncle's most expensive fabrics—and it looked beautiful against her skin. But she almost feared the image looking back at her in the mirror. What if Mr. Anderson only wished to offer her a job? This could easily make him believe she desired to put herself forth. It could put him off entirely.

Then it is what it is. I'd be a fool not to wear this when my aunt made it especially for me.

She nodded. Mr. Anderson and those of his ilk would come and go. Family was more important. She would wear this and please her aunt.

Mrs. Gardiner glowed when Elizabeth returned and Mrs. Gardiner caught sight of her. "Perfect," she said, just as a knock at the door sounded. "Let Mrs. Potts get it. You come sit. Oh, you've gotten all the ink off your hands. Both cheeks are clean? Perfection."

They settled onto the settee and the chair in front of the open window, the gentle fragrance of spring flowers a pleasant fragrance in the air. Vague noises of Mrs. Potts welcoming Mr. Anderson and taking his hat reached them and then she brought him through to the sitting room. "Mr. Anderson, ma'am."

Elizabeth soothed her nerves and started with introductions. "Mr. Anderson, might I present my aunt to you."

"And I am charmed to meet you, Mr. Anderson. My husband has some dealings with your mercantile productions and he speaks very highly of you."

His pleased smile broadened. "I thought I recognized the name. Yes, Mr. Gardiner is a boon to London, I'll have you know. Is he here today?"

"I'm afraid not. With the season coming upon us, we might not see him at home until long after supper. He enjoys it so much I find it hard to call him home." She provided a small smile towards Elizabeth. "His niece is just the same when it comes to industriousness. They can hardly keep still for wanting something to do. That was why we encouraged Elizabeth to work with Mr. Davies when the opportunity fell into her lap."

Mr. Anderson's smile towards her lit her up from within. He spoke to Mrs. Gardiner, his gaze squarely upon Elizabeth. "I assure you, the pleasure is all mine. She's a credit to you all."

Mr. Anderson gladly sat on the settee when Mrs. Gardiner offered. By the way his ears reddened, Elizabeth suspected he liked her dress too. He chivalrously included Mrs Gardiner in conversation throughout the visit, but he couldn't stop darting tiny peeks at Elizabeth when it was her aunt's turn to reply. Elizabeth could see her aunt noting that with particular pleasure.

The flutters in Elizabeth's stomach only grew.

Over tea, he told them that his parents had passed some time ago and since then he had been responsible for the vast empire his father left behind. It was nothing the newspapers hadn't told them already, but he flavored it with tales of his father that made her smile. There was a vast amount of love there for his family, and regret that he was the only one left.

His manner was so open and sincere that Elizabeth found it hard not to be charmed by him. *I'm in grave trouble of developing a crush.*

The thought came to her: what would Darcy think of

her aunt and uncle? Would he approve, even though they were merchants? He'd been unimpressed by the spectacle of her mother—heavens, he'd thought Elizabeth was only good enough to be his bedwarmer, not a wife he respected. She could not imagine him charming her aunt as Mr. Anderson was, nor in a manner so effortlessly ingratiating.

She shook away the intrusive thoughts. It didn't matter. She would never have anything to do with Darcy again.

Elizabeth needed to focus on the gentleman in front of her. A gentleman whose visit had nothing to do with offering her new employment. There had to be some flaw to him, right? She decided to probe at Mr. Anderson's future, trying to determine whether this perfect gentleman was truly who he said he was.

"Where do you see the publishing house in time, Mr. Anderson? Do you ever feel you'll focus on your own pursuits at some point?"

"Do you mean, will you ever have to find new employment at a competitor?" Mr. Anderson laughed at Elizabeth's expression, a warm and pleasant sound that tickled her awareness of him seated next to her. He leaned back, considering the question and giving it its full weight. "I'm fully aware of the privilege I've been handed, and I want to see my father's legacy continue. But no, I'm never one to rest on my laurels."

Elizabeth smiled and took a sip of her tea. "I think that's an understatement based on what we've read about you in the papers."

"You know there's nothing true in those papers, and I say that from experience." Mr. Anderson gave a rueful smile. "It's true that I have other investments running. None have fully taken off to the extent I desire, but it's diversified my interests, and for that I can only be grateful. The business of news and publishing can be fraught with some tension from the public, as you became aware of the other day, Miss Lizzy."

Elizabeth turned to her aunt. "Oh, he's speaking about those novels. The ones with the Duke."

Her aunt's expression cleared in understanding. "Ah. Those."

"Have you read them, Mrs. Gardiner? Your niece believes we should continue to keep them and those novels containing similar characteristics on our shelves. Do you share a similar opinion?"

Mrs. Gardiner's reply was measured—and a surprise to Elizabeth. "Many do not like the fact that women can read in the first place. My own father, for instance, felt it was inappropriate and claimed poets put too many ideas in my head, though he had many kind opinions about women's abilities in other areas. Not to sound too much like a radical, but is restricting what's on the shelves just one more effort to set women back in the world?"

Elizabeth tutted as she took up her tea. "I would say these novels are a far cry from notable poetry. Nay, should not even share a room with them, much less a shelf."

"He did not ask about my *preference* for these books," Mrs. Gardiner said with a teasing huff. "Elitism festers in you, Lizzy."

"If it helps any matters, I do not believe *my* novels should be on the same shelf either," Elizabeth said with a smile.

"A novel opinion about the education and upbringing of society's young women!" Mr. Anderson seemed happy about the straightforward reply, his expression relaxing into a smile. "I will admit it was one of the thoughts on my mind too. If I had a sister, I don't see what harm these books could do. It's not as if these novels encourage readers to go against king or country."

"Some would say a lady who thinks too much is trouble on her own," Elizabeth said, recalling her mother.

"Ha! I would've liked to see someone tell that to my mother. She was one of his first editors when my father started out, you know. The first defender of the slush pile, as you are now, Miss Lizzy."

Elizabeth chuckled. "I hope she took more care not to get ink on her face."

There the conversation transitioned into one about the merits of the slush and the types of novels in the publishing queue which they looked forward to. Once the plate of finger sandwiches were emptied, Mr. Anderson soon after announced his impending departure. But before he stood, he turned to Elizabeth.

"I've been invited to a friend's party next month, one of the first of the season I'll be attending, and I secured an invitation to bring a friend. Would you consent to join me, along with your dear aunt as chaperone, of course?" he added with a respectful look at Mrs. Gardiner. Mrs. Gardiner beamed, and then quickly shielded it and looked to Elizabeth.

Elizabeth smiled demurely, looking down. "I would, thank you."

Afterwards, her aunt didn't even gloat about their wager, only smiled and hummed more than usual as they went about their business. Elizabeth found herself smiling, too.

OVER THE NEXT MONTH, Mr. Anderson saw fit to visit the publishing house several times to see Mr. Davies and, she suspected, Elizabeth. He did not linger, all too cognizant of the greedy press's mouth they had to fill every day, but Elizabeth was distracted the rest of the day on the days he visited, regardless. Mr. Davies seemed to suspect something, but though he hummed and gave Elizabeth curious looks, he said nothing, for which Elizabeth was grateful.

Mr. Gardiner was shocked by the news that, not only had Mr. Anderson *not* signed up Elizabeth's novel, but seemed to only want a social call. However, he deemed Mr. Anderson a great man, a brilliant investor, and insisted Elizabeth go to his warehouse and select any fabric she wanted for a new dress for the occasion.

"My wardrobe is plentiful already," Elizabeth tried, but he would have none of it.

"No, no. In fact, tomorrow, I will send you over to a dressmaker I know. They owe me a favor and I've been attempting to figure out how to call it in. This is a perfect excuse."

"I don't have the funds for that kind of dress."

"As I said, they owe me a favor."

And that was that. Elizabeth went to the dressmaker with a letter from her uncle clutched in her sweating hand. It was the nicest dressmaker's shop Elizabeth had ever been inside. The proprietor read the letter with a frown that soon cleared up. He would be delighted to see to Mr. Gardiner's niece, and the rest of the appointment was spent on measuring, fitting, and selecting fabrics.

"This is fresh from your uncle's warehouses, the newest sensation among the ladies in town." He held out a beautiful blue that made Elizabeth's mouth dry.

"It's beautiful," she whispered.

The proprietor showed off large, square teeth. "Upon you, magnificent."

The flattery aside, the next week Elizabeth had a dress

befitting, if not the queen, at least someone who attended court. She dedicated extra time to preparing for the event, obtaining approval from Mr. Davies to skip the day while she focused on ensuring her hair was shiny and fragrant with rosewater and her skin lustrous from oils.

Her extra effort was rewarded by Mr. Anderson's shock when he saw her. Pleasure suffused his features and her cheeks warmed under his attention.

Mrs. Gardiner waited at the bottom of the stairs beside the gentleman. She spoke up when Elizabeth reached them. "I must go upstairs quickly. Silly me, I forgot my gloves." Giving Elizabeth a significant look, Mrs. Gardiner hurried upstairs.

Knowing very well that her aunt's gloves were safely stored in her clutch, Elizabeth repressed a smile and turned to Mr. Anderson. Pleasantries were on her tongue, but Mr. Anderson was quicker.

"While we have a moment… thank you for accepting the invitation." He lowered his head, looking at her with bright sincerity in his blue eyes. "I must have you know how much I've looked forward to spending the evening with you."

Elizabeth's stomach fluttered. "You have?"

His tiny smile, almost shy, did nothing to improve her growing blush. "Very much so. It's nearly been impossible to stay away from the publishing house."

"You haven't stayed away at all," she pointed out, raising her brows. "You've been by every week."

"It would've been every day." Mr. Anderson stepped back when Mrs. Gardiner appeared in the hall, her gloves securely in her grip, and Elizabeth turned away, knowing her blush would give away this breathless feeling that had overtaken her.

Mr. Anderson escorted them into his carriage, a fine

conveyance with beautiful, silk black horses, and cushioned seats which helped protect them when the carriage rolled over the rough cobbles of Gracechurch Street.

Elizabeth composed herself. So Mr. Anderson appeared to enjoy her company. She must not place importance on it until there was some discussion of more substance—no matter Mrs. Gardiner's sly smirks to the contrary.

Mr. Anderson helped maintain an energetic conversation nearly the whole way into the heart of London. Then he sprung a surprise on Elizabeth.

"You know, I hadn't thought about it. Are you related to the Bennets of Hertfordshire?"

"That is where I hail from, yes."

"Then you will know the gentleman hosting this party. Our mutual friend married a young woman with the last name Bennet from Hertfordshire and Darcy spent some time there late last year."

All the air went out of her. "Mr. Darcy?"

"Yes, do you know him?"

A curious ringing sound overtook her senses. Her vision blurred. She couldn't feel her cheeks, her hands, the pumping of her heart. Vaguely, she heard her aunt's reply.

"I believe you wrote about a gentleman by that name once before. Don't you remember, dear?" Mrs. Gardiner turned to Mr. Anderson. "My eldest niece married Mr. Bingley, actually, if that's who you're speaking of. We were overjoyed to hear the news."

"So you've met. What a happy coincidence! Mr. Bingley is a dear acquaintance, and I'm overjoyed he found happiness. As for Mr. Darcy, he is the finest of them all. I've been looking forward to this all season—it's not often he holds parties, but his younger sister has recently come out, and I assume she's husband shopping. Not to be crass about it," he added with a sheepish look at them both.

Elizabeth forced her mouth to open. "What otherwise occupies young ladies?" Her companions laughed, but her heart was no longer in the conversation. No, her whole mind was overtaken by thoughts of *him*.

Calm. She would be calm. And if she told herself that enough, she might be capable of it. Elizabeth looked down at her lap, her knuckles white where she clenched her fan. Various strategies to escape rushed through her thoughts. Sickness. Claiming she broke her ankle. *Really* breaking her ankle when she jumped from the carriage mid-ride.

But her aunt looked so happy, and Mr. Anderson had looked forward to this night, and her uncle had extended himself to offer the fine fabrics for this beautiful new dress.

Elizabeth did not have the heart to disappoint any of them.

Why hadn't she asked who would be their host?

4

"I say the white. Purity, chastity, it is timeless and effortless."

His sister's voice could be faintly heard down the hall through the open door of the study where he read. "While I'm not opposed to the white, I think I prefer this green…"

Ms. Chapman, the widowed companion he hired for his sister, clucked her tongue. It was a common tic of hers to pronounce judgment, to express disapproval, and to utterly pluck Darcy's temper. "It is your coming out, dear, not a public festival. It's not suitable. *White* is suitable."

Ms. Chapman also had *views* on what was suitable and not, and since Darcy had arrived at the townhouse in London, he'd learned that most things in Ms. Chapman's opinion were the latter.

Georgianna's dismay was unheard, but he could imagine his sister's expression perfectly. He lowered his book, frowning intently at the wall while he listened to what transpired in the sitting room.

"This fabric and this one. Wholly unsuitable for a young

lady like yourself. You do not have the figure for this style either, I don't know what the seamstress was thinking to send it—"

Georgianna would come out in a month's time. Darcy knew little about this process beforehand, but he made his sister's life his sole priority, and thus he had become educated in the particulars. In every single way, his knowledge of the marriage market was as sharp as any doting mother's would be.

He rose from his chair and strode to the sitting room.

"Mr. Darcy!" Ms. Chapman was flustered to see him appear in the sitting room doorway, smoothing her hand over her skirts and offering him a pursed smile. "We are in the midst of designing your sister's new wardrobe."

"I see that." An array of hats and fabrics and ribbons were strewn about and an order he could not decipher at first glance. His sister sat in the middle of it all, drinking her tea and looking dolefully at a green velvet.

Ms. Chapman continued to chatter. "It has been a fraught process, I'll tell you. Over half of these fabrics are—"

"Unsuitable. Yes, I heard." He looked at his sister. Georgianna lifted her eyes almost reluctantly, the tips of her ears pink in the way that told him that although she was frustrated, she was embarrassed more. Her smile was wan and her eyes gleamed more than they should. "What do you think?"

"I..." Her gaze flicked to Ms. Chapman and then lowered to her lap. "Certainly there are designs I do not like."

"*Many* of them," Ms. Chapman said. "I hardly know if we'll have the time to request new fabrics."

He ignored her, staring at his sister. "The green in your hands. What do you think of that?"

"It is—"

"Ms. Chapman, I was speaking to my sister."

Ms. Chapman's teeth cracked as she closed her mouth. Her expression shriveled into something resembling a cat's behind. "Very well. Georgianna."

He withheld a tut. It sounded like she was giving *permission* to his sister to speak.

Georgianna's shoulders drew in toward her ears at Ms. Chapman's clipped tone. She licked her lips, gaze flitting from Darcy to her stiff companion and back. Darcy kept his composure, expression neutral, knowing it was important to give his sister the options without pressure.

"The green is what I want for my party." Her shoulders curled inward when Ms. Chapman's cheeks reddened. "I think."

"Very well, the green it is. I think it's a fine choice." He turned on his heel. "Ms. Chapman, a word."

The chill fell from Ms. Chapman like fog from an ice house when she joined him in the hall. He closed the pocket doors to the drawing room, shutting out Georgianna's face just as she nervously bit her lip. He turned to his sister's companion, his face stony, and her mouth was already open.

"It isn't how these things are done. Your sister must make choices and you must listen—"

He kept his voice steady even though a good shake to the woman sounded reasonable. "I am listening to my sister. Are you? If her choices are reasonable, then I have no strong opinion about her choice in fabric. I hope you will bear that in mind."

She puffed herself up like a toad in its hole. "You engaged me to become a moral compass for your sister. This is not only in respect to her choices as a young woman, but down to the very choice of her style of dress and manner!"

At least she could stand up to him, even if the subject was utterly ridiculous. He could not understand why this mattered so much. It was fabric! Ms. Chapman was the type of woman who preferred her opinions above all.

"Are the fabrics going to open my sister up to criticism by the larger populace? I see dresses in these fabrics and styles and sitting rooms and events constantly. There's nothing wrong with them. I engaged you to help steer my sister and to protect her from undue influence. I did not engage you as a warden. If we allow her no choice at all, what kind of woman does she become then? Allow Georgianna her discretion in this."

She threw back her shoulders. "And if I object?"

Then I shall show you out with pleasure. But he held his tongue on that thought. Georgianna would not like it if he dismissed Ms. Chapman. He did not understand that either, but he did not need to understand.

"Your objection is noted. Would you like to say something in return?"

Ms. Chapman needed the income this position supplied. Her father struggled at home and her own husband had passed after a long illness, leading to some debts while he convalesced. He could see the fight behind her eyes, a struggle between getting her way and allowing a much younger woman hers. Eventually, her reason prevailed, and her shoulders slumped. She nodded. "Then I defer to your opinion, Mr. Darcy."

He looked down his nose at her, once again proven correct about her sensibility and lack thereof. "You defer to my sister's opinion. Now. I must leave on some business. I expect the dresses to be ordered by the end of the day at the latest. I would like to speak privately to my sister before I go."

Georgianna's grimace marred her sweet face when he returned to the sitting room. She'd lain aside the green velvet and looked at him under a troubled brow.

"Did I offend her terribly? I suppose I saw this beautiful fabric, the same as Miss Barnes', and I did not think it was inappropriate if she wore it—I may have argued too much."

"You didn't argue enough." He expected her surprise and wished he could tell her of the world—and he wished she would believe it. Instead, he focused on what he could conceivably influence. "Assert yourself and do not be ashamed of it, sister. You have worked mightily on this brain of yours, I would hate to see it wasted bending to people like Ms. Chapman."

Her smile was tremulous, as if she almost didn't believe Darcy's words. But he realized that her smile was more the devious sort when she said, "So if I asserted that I would like to see you dance at my coming out, you would say…?"

"I will take a turn as expected of the host."

"Fitzwilliam. That's not what I mean."

He repressed a smile and straightened the cuff on his jacket. "I know very well what you meant."

Her eyes were as blue as their mother's and could see right through his tactics. "I want you to be happy, brother. You've been so quiet since you returned to London."

"That does not mean I require a woman to nag me. You are the only one allowed to do so." He tweaked her ear for old time's sake.

She laughed and batted him away, but he could tell she wasn't fully satisfied. Her gaze grew distant, her smile fond. "I want to see you settled. Our parents had a lovely marriage and I think back to how they laughed together and I want that for you. Someone to make you smile."

Yes, theirs was the happiest marriage he knew. One he would never find himself.

"Let us see to this before you start matchmaking. Please, I beg of you." He leaned over and kissed the top of his sister's head. "I have some business to conduct. I've told Ms. Chapman that the dresses shall be ordered at the end of the day, and I expect you to hold that. We have a timeline and we can't see you in last season's dresses at your coming out."

She settled back in her seat with an unhappy sigh. "I promise. One day you will find a young woman who deserves you, you know. I promise you that, too."

It was impossible not to see the gangly girl of eight before him in her pout. He touched her hair briefly, removing his hand before he could muss her hair. "Until then, I'll take care of you."

He left in a subdued mood, unhappy that his sister obviously worried for him. He wished she wouldn't.

His carriage waited for him outside the townhome, and he nodded to the driver before climbing in. The streets of London were quiet here, but grew louder when they drew into the heart of town. Darcy stared out the window, preoccupied by the feeling of something missing that his sister's comments inspired. He was happy, wasn't he? The average person looking in on his life would scoff in derision if Darcy claimed otherwise.

An advantaged background, a comfortable life, a loving family… he needed nothing more.

He especially did not need to bind himself to another soul simply to fit a mold of what a gentleman did. *That* was a ticket to unhappiness and regret, and Darcy lived with too much regret already to actively add more. After all, he'd once trusted Wickham like a brother, despite his poor judgment, and thus left his sister defenseless to Wickham's villainy. It had nearly killed him to see his sister so broken. Now that she was finally blooming into happiness again, the last thing he wished was to give someone the power to hurt her—and through her, him—again.

These women like Miss Bingley and Ms. Chapman who could not stand another woman in the room were not *isolated* characters. No, these jealousies hid in every woman's heart. It did not matter that she was his sister—no, that made it worse. Miss Bingley's attempts to ingratiate herself with Georgianna would undoubtedly disappear, along with her friendship, if Miss Bingley ever realized Darcy would not marry her. It would crush Georgianna's spirit if it ever happened. In what ways would a wife hurt Georgianna if she ever understood she came second in his affection for his sister?

Darcy shared with Georgianna not only their two loving, loyal parents, but a bond built by years spent under the scrutiny of the public and their relatives after their parents passed. He remembered the false words of comfort and watchful eyes quite clearly even ten years later. The expectation, the wait, for Darcy to fail his father's memory. For Georgianna's spoiling and ruination under the relaxed care of her brother and cousin. *They all thought we would fail, every single one of those whispering gossips in the tea rooms and private assemblies and clubs, and we didn't.*

He couldn't see how any woman would ever surpass Georgianna in his heart.

Not to say he despised the thought of a bed warmer, though. A woman with whom to spend his nights, to dip into the pleasures of the flesh—he was not opposed to that in the least.

The pleasant thought made his mind turn to the puzzle of Elizabeth Bennet. The woman he'd once chosen for the privilege. Where had she gone? After she ran him out of Hertfordshire, she'd done a masterful job of hiding herself. It was almost amusing. Like she *feared* him.

And well she should. He did not appreciate being chased out of Hertfordshire by her father's threats, nor the fact that he'd disappointed Bingley by not being able to attend his wedding for the same reason. His friend had been cruelly hurt, and it now took Bingley many weeks to respond to Darcy's letters. Bingley had even declined the invitation to attend Georgianna's coming out party, claiming renovations kept him in Hertfordshire—when they all knew that renovations was exactly the excuse one needed to come to town.

For what pain her actions caused Bingley, if nothing else, Darcy would see Elizabeth pay.

Yet Darcy could find no hint of her relations, and not knowing their surname put him at a disadvantage. But persistence was a skill he had in abundance, and a niggling issue like the mystery of her relations would not stop him. Today, he hoped his efforts would bear fruit to solve this puzzle.

A lone figure standing outside on the street made his head snap around, his temple slamming against the side of the carriage. White heat burned away his thoughts. His shoulders and back stiffened, his hand clenched into a fist. The upturned face, seen only in profile, looked exactly like Elizabeth.

Ridiculous. Here? Under his nose? On a street of solicitors? He thought her relations were *merchants*.

"Stop! I say, stop the coach!"

He used his fist to thump the roof of the carriage and

slammed open the door before he could think past the blur of excitement racing through him. He had her now—

He raced down the street, weaving around serious looking men with their leather cases and frowning at him under their silk hats. Darcy did not give them the time of day while his feet pounded on the cobblestone, searching, searching.

She wasn't there. He turned in a circle where he thought he'd seen her standing. His mouth opened. *A woman, did you see a woman standing just here with brown hair—* It was on his lips, but failed to reach past them.

He frustrated huff escaped him. Why would she even be here?

Perhaps she was brought by his thoughts, his mind imposing the lines of her face on some stranger. Whoever the woman, she was not here now, and he had no idea which building, if any, she'd disappeared into.

His driver, cap crushed in his hand, stumbled to a stop beside him. "Sir? Sir, are you looking for someone? How may I help?"

Darcy looked up to the buildings, scowling, then back to the street where the bedamned woman failed to materialize at his glare. "Let's go before we cause any road delays. I'm done."

Done for today. But this moment was something Darcy would remember later. Had he seen her? Or had he wanted to see Elizabeth so badly that he created her ghost?

STEPPING inside the dingy investigator's offices was nearly as bad as stepping into some of the back rooms of an assembly. Smoke lingered thickly at the ceiling, so potent he could taste its bitterness on the air. Wallpaper peeled away from baseboards and molding, succumbing to the weight of years' worth of nicotine. What was once an attractive office had become, under the care of this lot of investigators, neglected and filthy. He understood they had a girl come in daily to clean, and they did not pay her nearly enough.

But they were the best money could buy, and so Darcy tried not to grimace when Mr. Larson showed him to a seat in his office.

"I've compiled a list of the particulars of the individuals you asked me to perform a background on, Mr. Darcy. You can find all the information here in this folder. Please let me know if you need any more clarification on any of the topics I've listed. There are a number that I've left to the end that have less objectionable backgrounds, or insufficient information available to gather from their acquaintances and friends for me to determine their character."

"This is all of them? I didn't expect you to get through the list so soon."

"I was fortunate enough to collaborate with some of my partners who shared what information they had from other investigations. Those I am not privy to communicate to you, of course," he added with a fastidious tug on his cravat.

"Of course." If Darcy shelled out for the information, he was sure that attitude would change, but he would read the file before testing that theory. "As to the other matter?"

"Oh, yes. The young lady. Miss Elizabeth Bennet." Larson shuffled around in his desk drawers before, muttering a curse, moved to the filing cabinet. He found a file and opened it before returning to the desk, squinting as he read. "Bennet, Bennet… I've been able to track down her father, of course, but her mother's maiden name has proved a little more elusive. I suppose her marriage was not prominently displayed in the papers."

"Nor her sister's? Mrs. Phillips in Meryton."

"I'm looking for her too. Not knowing a year has proved a challenge, but I have a person working through the archives now. It would be much easier if they were based in London so I could find acquaintances."

A muscle in his jaw twitched. "Do you say it's impossible?"

"Not impossible, not at all," Larson said with the confidence of long years in this field. "It will just take longer."

Darcy pinched the bridge of his nose. "This is starting to irritate me. I'm seeing the woman on the street outside and yet there's nothing to suggest she's here."

Mr. Larson put his hands on the desk and leaned toward him. "You saw her?"

Darcy dropped his hand, disgusted with himself. "Yes. Or no. I don't know anymore."

Mr. Larson sat back in his chair, keen eyes taking in Darcy's irritation with an unreadable expression. "Mr. Darcy, if I may be so bold to ask… have you been sleeping well?" His glare answered. Larson raised his hands in surrender. "This takes time, I'm afraid. But we will find her for you."

The question was in his eyes, the tip of his tongue. He could see Larson struggling with it and it only made his disgust grow.

Why was he chasing a woman who didn't want to be found? A woman whose relations were so lowly their marriages didn't merit prominent display in the newspaper?

"I will give you your time then," he said, pushing to his feet. "Contact me at once when you have a lead."

PATIENCE WAS a strong suit of his, and though Elizabeth Bennet tested his, he spent the next few weeks while Larson worked ignoring the issue and focusing on Georgianna's debut.

He was aware, in a way he hadn't been for some time, how much his sister wanted for a motherly figure in her life. Someone to guide her through these types of affairs without judgment or belittlement. While Ms. Chapman toned down her opinions on Georgianna's wardrobe, he found her opinions lacked compassion and sympathy for the motherless young woman. However, he could not fight all his sister's battles for her.

The townhome was being transformed for the party. New wallpapers and fresh rugs were some of the surface changes. Other changes upstairs inconvenienced him greatly, but the continuous interruptions downstairs plagued his nerves.

He took a break from the constant stream of people in and out of his house by taking advantage of his club membership. Without Bingley, he felt odd mingling with the other fellows from society. He lacked the easy buffer of Bingley's presence. Whereas his friend took Darcy's silences as permission to go on, others often assumed standoffish and proud motives drove Darcy.

In some cases, that was undoubtedly true. There was no lack of so-called gentlemen Darcy would turn his back on because of their incessant gambling or bad behavior. A few of those gentlemen also held memberships at his club. Avoiding them was impossible to some extent, inviting scrutiny if Darcy became obvious about it.

Luckily, today the club lacked many of the worst offenders, and Darcy found himself settled at a card table with three other gentlemen, all of them landed and in similar situations to Darcy: unmarried and resisting the attempts from various relatives to become so.

"My mother is pushing it, of course," Hastings said, folding down the edges of his cards with his thumbnail as he always did in a nervous attempt to hide a bad hand. His mother, widowed, and sister and her husband lived with him not too far from Darcy's townhome. His aggrieved face showed how little he liked such an arrangement, especially after Mr. Barnes approached him about his eligible daughter. "Mother wants grandchildren more than anything, and now that my sister has given her babies to dote on, she's greedy for more. She doesn't care that Barnes has only two thousand pounds to offer. Mother *must* have babies."

With much eye rolling and good-natured laughter from the group at large, Hastings looked to his left.

"What do you think, Anderson? Would you turn up your nose to a moneyless young lady?"

Anderson, like Darcy, was not a gambler and was ignoring his cards in favor of a thin cigar and glass of scotch. He kicked his feet out before him and rolled his neck, considering the question.

"Naturally, I prefer a woman with a war chest, but at the same time I shudder to think of wasting her father's money over mine. A true investor does not invest more than he can afford to lose, my father said, and he never plays with other people's money."

"Better hers than mine," Gains said beside Darcy.

Darcy and Anderson both ignored this, though Darcy made careful note not to allow Georgianna near Gains. "Your father was a wise man."

Anderson smirked. "That he was. I still remember how a single tear shone in his eye when I came back with the money I was supposed to spend on chocolate, and he found I had traded it away for a box of jacks. That is the first lesson of investing, gentleman. Do not buy consumables when you can buy jacks."

"Ridiculous," Darcy said, unable to help but smile while the others laughed.

"Speaking of ridiculous, I have a new venture that you might like, Darcy. A whole line of illicit romance," he said with a grandiose wave of his hands. "The mamas are all a'rage to shun me for corrupting the poor souls of their daughters. Old Mrs. Shimwell nearly gave me the cut on the street an hour ago as I walked in."

He raised an eyebrow. "I take it you're not reconsidering your publishing line?"

"I can hardly keep a book on the shelf. I bet two pounds that old Mrs. Shimwell will be the first in line to read whatever novel lands next, just so she can have something to terrorize me about. The books sell!"

"Imagine her in an illicit love affair," Gains said, causing several shudders to go through the group.

Hastings wrinkled his nose. "What kind of books are these? It sounds like smut."

"It sounds like fun," Gains said.

Anderson waved the smoke away from his face. "Oh, harmless little books. A kiss out of wedlock, hands brushing, the like." A slow smile came over his face, his eyes twinkling. "But I've been told by a quite knowledgeable young woman that these are indulgences ladies desire to read, and not the gateway to damnation their mamas foretell. And the numbers don't lie either, gentlemen. So whichever of you want to invest in the next round of publishing, you know where to find me."

"I think I will finally take your advice, Anderson, and

avoid investing in consumables," Darcy said to much amusement, including a sheepish grin from Anderson.

It was an enjoyable afternoon and Darcy appreciated the occupation, for the most part. However, it occurred to Darcy how often women were brought up by the gentleman of his acquaintance. Was it merely because it was the marriage season? But Darcy often overheard similar conversations, protestations of matrimony, of desiring to settle down, intermingled with a nearly childlike yearning for companionship. So often when a gentleman brushed off a conversation about a particular lady, Darcy found them listening keenly whenever her name was brought up again.

Ladies were like fishing nets. Gentlemen may not wish to be caught up in them, but once they were firmly within the netting, it was easy to let oneself be drawn up.

Better them than me.

But Hastings' annoyance at his mother earlier had also hurt Darcy, though he repressed it as much as he could. If Darcy had the chance to ask his mother, would she be satisfied with where Darcy was in life?

These topics were gloomy enough to drive Darcy out of the club, away from the smoke-filled rooms and into the light of day. Banishing these kind of thoughts were imperative before they could take root and make him grim.

In the front room, he happened upon Anderson putting on his coat when Darcy went for his. Anderson smiled when he saw him.

"Darcy! I hoped to see you again before I left, but you seemed preoccupied, so I didn't want to bother you."

"I would have welcomed the interruption, honestly."

"You aren't rushing off anywhere now?"

"All I have in my immediate future is planning my sister's party, so please, distract me."

"And I thank you very much for the invitation, by the way. I look forward to meeting your sister." He ruffled his hair in a manner Darcy knew was a precursor to being pitched. It was not the first time, nor would it be the last, Anderson would pitch him on some new venture.

Although Anderson had enough wealth that he could sit back and let the income from his publishing house roll in, he was always searching for something outside of the business his father built. Despite the progress and advances he had made to the publishing house and various associated newspapers since his father's death, he seemed possessed by the idea of striking out on his own into something new and different. The elusive white diamond. Mercantile from India. Locomotives. The uncharted territory of the Americas. Darcy, whose wealth was built on a strong foundation of common investments in safe stocks, the land, and agriculture year after year, looked upon these ventures as highly suspect.

Darcy was not wrong.

"Have you ever heard of Campton-on-Sea?"

They'd taken a table by the window in the front of the club, less occupied by others and facing the street, removing their jackets for the moment while he listened to Anderson's pitch. He searched his memory. "I don't believe so."

"Well, that may be because it is on the very cusp of growth. Seaside town in the south, predominantly fishing and sheep for the most part at the moment, and a sizeable portion of land fronting the sea that will see large growth in the future. The immediate future," he said with a large grin, "and that is where I would like *your* help reaching that vision."

"You're creating a seaside town."

"Not creating it, the town is already there. However, I'm maximizing its potential. So much potential, Darcy! The residents are lovely and welcoming and I say with the utmost sincerity that it's the most beautiful place I've ever seen. It will *astound* you. Sweeping views Londoners will flock to, huge cliffs straight from a painting. Not to mention the waters. Perfect for sea bathing and taking in the minerals. I think, in time, we can even give Bath a run for its money."

"Oh, can we?" His mouth curled. Anderson's enthusiasm had caught up many an investor—sometimes to their success, sometimes not. Darcy tried to avoid losing money. "I don't recall agreeing. What other investors do you have on board?"

"None, at the time. You are the first I've approached and hopefully the last. I have enough by myself to create my vision of a resplendent, homely seaside resort."

"Then I fail to see how you need my investment."

"I would not come to you if I *needed* investment." His eyes burned with the vision of his future. "I know that together we can build it up to be great. Let me take you down there next month and I've no doubt you will see the same potential that I have."

"Next month? That's unnecessary pressure on Georgianna's debut. My obligations—"

"Then bring her too. Or come down this summer, it is not as if the town will move."

"I will have to think on this."

"In the meantime, I can send you the particulars and the plans that I've had drawn up. I would appreciate your input, if nothing else."

He sat back, smiling at the investor. So much younger, but he could be great if he simply *focused*. Still, he was willing to humor him. "I believe this is the first pitch from you where you haven't asked for an immediate investment."

"This is too good of an opportunity to move quickly. Do

I expect overnight success? No. But you've long told me, Darcy, the importance of slow growth. This time you'll see that I've taken it to heart."

"And are you going to write about my participation in your newspapers?"

Anderson grinned ruefully. "I've learned from my mistakes. Only when it's a success will I ever mention your name."

"I can make no promises, but I will glance at whatever you send. My sister takes precedence, currently."

"Understood. But you will see, Darcy." He tapped the heavy wood table with his knuckles. "This one, it's too perfect an opportunity for even *you* to pass up."

He scoffed, amused by the younger man's confidence. "Do I look like a man enthralled by a sea-bathing paradise?"

"You will be, and if you aren't, I'll eat my hat."

"*That* I would invest in."

"I thought so."

5

"That woman is an utter"—Fitzwilliam stopped in the act of closing Darcy's study, looked around the room, and relaxed while he shut the door—"utter menace."

"So you've met Ms. Chapman."

"What a bore!" Fitzwilliam stomped to the desk and threw himself down in the chair across from it. "Told Georgianna that service awards were nothing to be impressed by —*within my hearing*, mind you. I'd like to ask how many services she's provided that have been recognized by the king."

"Georgianna insists she's fond of the lady, though I fear I'll need to disappoint her soon. There was no lack of criticism of the new decorations while they were in process."

"I noticed the spit shine. It looks good."

"Thank you."

"Why was she criticizing it, though?"

"Well, she didn't say it to my face"—the woman would be idiotic to do so—"but I imagine she was offended I prevented my future wife of the joy of it."

Fitzwilliam scoffed. "I imagine she'd complain if the queen herself decorated your house. Face it, you've engaged a woman who breathes complaints."

Darcy shook his head. "She won't last long, and I'll survive Georgianna's disappointment. She must have some redeemable qualities, but with every passing day I begin to doubt that."

"So what are you doing sequestered in here? Hiding from her?"

"Partially," Darcy said to Fitzwilliam's answering snort. "But I have some pressing correspondence to go through. Here, I'd appreciate your assistance since it has to do with you as well."

Darcy held a letter out to him. Fitzwilliam recognized their aunt's handwriting at once and took it with a slight frown. "I assume she's still complaining you don't plan to visit this year?"

"I told her she's welcome to come, but she's insisted on setting up introductions to her acquaintances for Georgianna. I did the due diligence on their backgrounds—"

"Did you now? That's forward thinking of you."

"When have you known me not to think of the future?"

"Silly me. So, what did your digging reveal?"

"Some debts. A few who frequent the gaming hells too frequently. But there is one gentleman in this list I'd like you to investigate tonight."

"Oh, this sounds very cloak and dagger." He looked up from the letter to search Darcy's expression. "Shouldn't we let Georgianna investigate the fellow? I assume it is for her benefit."

"It's our responsibility to make the best match for her."

"Yes, well, I may not share Georgianna's sensibilities and

what she'd find suitable in a husband. Not playing that field myself and all..."

Darcy refrained from muttering about his cousin's playful nature. "I prefer to vet them all before the question ever arises. If any of them fail to impress Georgianna, that is her prerogative, of course."

"So you don't plan to force a match." Some tension in Fitzwilliam's shoulders relaxed. "Good. I'm happy to waylay the man with some discussion, see how he reacts to some pressure. But I assume I'll be busy most of the night, as you will be dancing."

"Beyond opening the dance, I plan to abstain. It might reflect poorly on me, but people will understand I need to watch out for Georgianna."

Both of Fitzwilliam's eyebrows lifted toward his hairline. "And how will you watch out for her better than the woman you engaged to do that very activity?"

Darcy scoffed. "Please. I'll need to be around just to ensure Ms. Chapman doesn't scare them all away."

"A fair point. Who else is on the guest list? Any young ladies of particular note?"

"All the—to use Miss Chapman's phrasing—acceptable ones, of course." He looked up and caught Fitzwilliam's eye. "What?"

"Nothing."

"You were giving me a look. I know you and your looks. What are you thinking?"

Fitzwilliam lifted one shoulder in a lazy shrug. "Only, I had some thought this would be the perfect opportunity to find a young lady yourself as your sister shops for a husband."

"Not you too." He scowled over his desk at his cousin.

"No, to answer your question, tonight is solely dedicated to Georgianna."

"I've taken a gander at the guest list. There are some good families there."

He didn't trust Fitzwilliam's innocent expression at all. "Yes, many of them with eligible bachelors."

Fitzwilliam sighed and gave up on the matter. "I saw some familiar names. There's Anderson, of course."

Darcy snorted. "He would likely spend Georgianna's fortune in the seaside. He sent me this big plan of his to build a new tourist destination. Some potential, true, but it is riding on the waves of popularity. The seaside will not always be popular."

"That, I will disagree with you on. Plans, huh? Has he asked you to invest?"

"He has, though I don't plan to. Nor do I plan to let Georgianna waste her money on the venture either. Besides, the point is moot. I understand Anderson has entered the marriage market himself. He requested an invitation for a young lady of his acquaintance tonight."

"The cheek!"

He lifted his shoulders. "It's a small matter, there's plenty enough room."

"Pity. I like the old boy. A good sort, you never hear about him except when his investments explode like that mercantile ship did last autumn. Nasty business, that. I wonder who he'll show up with tonight. Perhaps Ms. Chapman has a lovely sister."

He snorted at that, and Darcy was grateful he could avoid the irritating woman for the time being. The hour to get ready soon came upon them and Darcy retreated to his rooms to dress.

The bustle of the streets never ended outside and the

open window in his room allowed him to hear carriages roll past over the cobblestones and various conversations down on the street below. Once Georgianna was happily settled, he hoped to leave the townhome to her care while he retired to Pemberley. He was tired of the noise, the bustle. A long stretch of land to race his horse over was exactly what he desired. Space to spread out, to stretch his arms and never touch another person. Peace from society and its expectations, something he would never get in London.

One day soon, he hoped he could return to Pemberley for good.

Naturally, the Hursts and Miss Bingley were one of the firsts to arrive and he cut short his daydreaming to begin greeting his guests. Miss Bingley approached him like a stray dog circling garbage discarded on the streets. Bracing himself against the flirtatious glitter in her eyes, he gave her a nod when she stepped in front of him in the line.

"What a sight for sore eyes you are. We missed you at Mrs. Davenport's ball last week."

Mrs Davenport over-inflated her importance. Miss Bingley would wait quite a bit before she saw him at any of her functions. "Yes, I've been busy."

"And what fruit your efforts have borne," she exclaimed, beaming as she looked about the front hall. "It is simply beautiful here. I assume you and Miss Georgianna designed all the improvements yourselves." She didn't wait for his reply. "I know several people who will be quite jealous of these new parquet floors."

"Whether they are jealous or not, it's not my concern. Pardon me, I must welcome Mr. and Mrs. Elkton."

The indignity of being waylaid thus irritated his nerves, he pushed it down, resolving to pay better attendance on the other guests. He couldn't afford to let Miss Bingley monopolize his time as she usually did at his first hosted ball.

"Nervous?" Fitzwilliam kept his comment low as Darcy joined them in the receiving line next to Georgianna.

He shot his cousin a stiff look. "No."

The doors were thrown open to the front path and narrow garden in front of his townhome. The streets were clogged with carriages, footmen bearing torches for light, and guests making their way inside. The chaos set his nerves on edge. This was why he chose to arrive late to most public events, to avoid this madness. But now he was the center of the madness and it couldn't be helped.

Georgianna best marry quickly so I never need do this again.

Though, of course, he wouldn't *push*… but encouragement certainly was not out of place.

"This is a lot of people, Darcy," Fitzwilliam muttered from the corner of his mouth. There had been a little time to converse in between the constant guests. "Certain there's enough room inside?"

Darcy finished shaking the hand of Mr. Hugh, watching his eldest son who had moon eyes for Georgianna. "Positive." Though he was certain his face would cramp if he had to force out one more smile.

Fitzwilliam looked bleakly down the line of people waiting. "I'm not sure if I share your optimism…"

There was a break though, after that first initial rush of people. Long enough to quickly refresh himself and return, happy to let Fitzwilliam use his gracious manners to charm the guests. Miss Bingley presented another effort to distract him and insert herself into the receiving line as if she had some importance. Darcy shared a look with his cousin and Fitzwilliam took the challenge, distracting Miss Bingley and leading her away before she had time to comprehend the deception hiding behind the charm.

Darcy released a relieved sigh.

Beside him, Georgianna smiled up at him. "It's a wonderful night. All my friends have shown up, too."

That had niggled at his sister's insecurities, Darcy knew. After spending so much time in Ramsgate, she worried none of her acquaintances in town would remember her, or would wish to attend tonight. "Of course they did. You are a Darcy. You have friends in many places who will support you."

Her gentle manner, her ingrained grace—he had no doubt she was society's most admired woman. Even without her dowry, she would have friends and admirers galore.

He shook a few more hands and his face failed to cramp, the flood of guests slowing. Darcy looked up at one of the last carriages and gave Anderson a tight smile as the gentleman caught his eye before turning to hold out his hand to his guest.

The light was low but the full moon allowed him to see a beauty step out of the carriage, taking Anderson's hand with a small smile. Darcy stared. The features didn't make sense at first. He shook his head to clear his vision, but the image of the woman remained the same.

Rooted to the spot, his face frozen, he could only watch as Anderson led two women up the path, one young and beautiful and the other older but poised and graceful.

Anderson beamed when they met, turning an admiring eye to his guest. "Mr. Darcy, I understand I don't have to introduce Miss Elizabeth Bennet to you, but I would introduce her lovely aunt, Mrs. Gardiner."

"A pleasure, Mr. Darcy. Your home is beautiful."

He barely heard the woman's words. He unclenched his

jaw and jerked his head at his sister. "My sister, Georgianna Darcy."

"It's lovely to meet you." It was the first she spoke and his memory had not captured how melodious her voice was, a pleasing husky melody that conjured up images of secret amusements. She did not look at him, only Georgianna who was smiling at the introduction.

Darcy issued a slight bow. "Pardon me, I must go."

His legs led him inside. Chatter and laughter and the calls of people seeing their friends rushed at him from every side. He closed his ears to it and went to the refreshment table, where he grabbed a wine glass and filled it to the rim. Thoughts rushed to fill his head, but he silenced them with an iron will and took a long drink.

It did not help.

"Mr. Darcy, I understand the musicians are ready when you are."

He finished the wine. "Fine." He didn't know to whom he spoke and when he turned around, they had disappeared into the crowd.

Anger was growing inside him. The *gall*. To step inside his home after everything as if she had any right.

There were so many people in the house, there was no possibility his eye should have landed on her when he turned around. Instead, the waters of the crowd parted and allowed him an unimpeded view of her standing in the doorway of the ballroom. Hundreds of candles highlighted the shine of her hair, and there was a glow in her skin, accentuated by the curve of her delicate neck and decolletage, that no other woman could imitate with hundreds of oils.

He needed more wine.

"Thrilled to be here, Mr. Darcy! What lovely changes you've made—this wallpaper is new, isn't it?"

"Yes, it matches with the…" He watched Anderson point to the line of dancers beginning to form and Darcy drew off at Elizabeth's smile. The two broke away from Mrs. Gardiner, who beamed at their backs while they moved to the line of dancers forming. Elizabeth's smile was one of eager delight.

His lips pressed tight together. So.

"I must go." He did not tone down his abruptness, leaving the guest mid-sentence. He strolled toward the line of dancers, losing sight of Elizabeth and Anderson when he joined at the top of the line as the host.

"I almost didn't think you would make it." Mrs. Elton beamed at him from across the line. As the lady of the highest rank in the room, she was delighted to take his invitation to open the ball.

Darcy returned her relieved smile with a stiff one. "I apologize for the delay."

From beside him in line, Georgianna across from him, Fitzwilliam nudged his shoulder. "If you keep up like this, you'll have much to apologize for tonight. What took you?"

He caught Georgianna's eye, the glow of happiness surrounding her. "Nothing," he muttered back.

He did not allow his attention to roam during the dance. The line was long enough he couldn't see far enough anyway except when the dancers travelled down the line. Then he was forced to look upon Elizabeth, who did not look at him once, and had her head turned away when he danced down the line with Mrs. Elton.

He would not have enjoyed the dance anyway, he told himself. But Elizabeth had no right to smile like that.

Darcy performed the dance by rote. Mrs. Elton's enthusiasm seemed sour as he walked her back to her husband with a few words after the dance. No doubt there would be talk. Another log landed on the bonfires of his displeasure.

"What a wonderful opening dance." Miss Bingley took the opportunity while he refreshed his wine to cling to his side. She sighed sadly while she idly flapped her fan, sending stifling rosewater scent toward him. "I'm only sorry my brother could not be here to enjoy this. You know how dearly I hoped for a closer relationship with Georgianna."

How insulted Bingley would be if he heard this. But his sister ignored Darcy's furious silence and went on. "I couldn't bear to stay in Hertfordshire when there is so little to *do* there, no intelligent discussion to be had anywhere. I'm sure my brother would be happier in town too, but he insists on remaining near Jane's family."

Now Darcy reminded himself why he made himself scarce when Miss Bingley visited Georgianna. He pursed his lips with a glance at the new line of dancers. Only Anderson' back was visible where he stood, but as the dance begun, the press of bodies parted enough to allow a glimpse of Elizabeth's elegant posture wrapped in luxurious velvet.

Had Anderson brought her that? He scanned the crowd and found Mrs. Gardiner dressed with a understated flair, though well put together. She did not look like she could put her niece in those kinds of fabrics.

"—a certain young lady with *fine eyes*, if you care to know."

He blinked and turned to frown at Miss Bingley. "Pardon?"

She smirked, fully aware she now had Darcy's full attention. "I suppose you haven't heard. No, it's not something my brother would wish to speak of…" The gleam in her eyes when she leaned towards him, added to her hushed voice, spoke to the scandal. "There's a rumor her mother won't have her back at Longbourn. If Mrs. Bennet was *my* mother, I would consider it a boon, but apparently Miss Eliza did something *dreadful*. One of the youngest ones, whatever their names are, said it had to do with a *gentleman*." Her raised eyebrows when she leaned back spoke volumes. "If they are to be believed, she's nursing her reputation with her Cheapside relatives."

Cheapside! Blast it!

Darcy could shake himself. Bitterness burned his tongue, unable to be washed away with the most expensive wine in London. Miss Bingley. To think, Miss Bingley held the answers he needed all along. If his stupidity were a pool, he'd drown in it.

At least he had some advance knowledge to soothe his wounded pride.

"I would suggest you not spread such a tale," he said, the chilliness in his voice making her lean away from him, eyes wide. "The lady in question is a guest here tonight and even now dances with Mr. Anderson, whom I'm certain would not take kindly to hearing such unsubstantiated rumors."

Miss Bingley turned an unbecoming shade of red. Her fan forgotten, she stared at him. "Here? I did not even see her." She peered at the dance line until she found the two dancers. Her eyes widened while she took them in, and her mouth pulled in a nasty frown as she no doubt envied Elizabeth's beautiful dress. She glanced at Darcy and cleared her expression quickly. "Mr. Darcy, I'm surprised you kept up the acquaintance."

He wouldn't speak to that. "Again, I caution you against repeating these rumors."

Rumors of Elizabeth Bennet running away from a scandal with a gentleman. Rumors spread by her own sisters.

He wished suddenly he hadn't chosen such a tight cravat. It strangled him now.

His only consolation was that Miss Bingley didn't seem to know a name.

Darcy turned back to the dancers, twisted ire thick as thorned vines around his chest. Elizabeth's father had broken his promise. Ruined his daughter's own reputation to hurt Darcy.

What kind of monster would do such a thing?

And what arrangement did Elizabeth have now with dopey eyed Anderson?

6

AFTER THAT FIRST UNCOMFORTABLE MOMENT WHEN DIZZINESS swamped her and she had to lean on Mr. Anderson, the ball became almost bearable. She danced twice with Mr. Anderson and laughed so much she had to fan herself as he led her back to Mrs. Gardiner.

"You are hard to keep up with, Miss Lizzy!" he said, laughing. "Let me go get refreshments for us. Mrs. Gardiner? A refill?"

"Please," Mrs. Gardiner said, her cheeks rosy. Mr. Anderson's charming smile had that effect.

Mr. Anderson looked once more at Elizabeth before departing, slipping into the crowd. He even had a nice back, she decided, which was odd to think of a man. But he looked very fine in his blue coat.

"You're staring." Mrs. Gardiner laughed when Elizabeth startled, a young woman's laugh. "I'm assuming the interest is returned?"

Her lips twitched. "Marginally."

"He's a fine, young fellow. You two have much in common, and he's gone out of his way to court you—"

"I wouldn't go that far," Elizabeth said.

Mrs. Gardiner failed to hide her smile. "After seeing his face tonight, I would go farther."

Elizabeth pulled her top lip between her teeth, trying to bite down the giddiness rising through her like champagne bubbles. She tamped it down. Something too good to be true often was.

Mr. Anderson returned managing three glasses despite being delayed three times by various conversations with—Elizabeth noted with amusement—lovely young ladies and their mothers. Many wanted a hand in the Anderson fortune, and with a noteworthy, handsome gentleman, to boot.

"A lovely crowd, isn't it? I'd love to introduce you both—there's Mrs. Dankworth who I think *you'll* find particularly interesting."

Elizabeth smiled around the rim of her wine glass. "You certainly know how to stir my curiosity."

"I hoped so!"

A looming shadow appeared behind Mr. Anderson, growing larger, a man in stark black and starched white. Elizabeth's widening eyes alerted Mr. Anderson, and he drew off, turning around to see what caught her attention.

Her dress restricted her breathing. That was what she blamed for the way her lungs strained to function while under Darcy's burning glare.

"Darcy! You should hold more parties. I've never had so much fun." Mr. Anderson stepped back and clapped Darcy on the shoulder. Darcy barely moved, and neither did his expression despite Mr. Anderson's cheerful greeting.

"I'm glad you think so." He turned a half inch toward

Elizabeth and bowed. "I request the next two dances, if you are amenable."

Elizabeth white-knuckled her fan so hard it creaked.

Mr. Anderson's lips parted. The significance of not one, but *two* dances was not lost on anyone in the group. A pale flush made its way up Mr. Anderson's cheeks. But he turned to Elizabeth and the weight of his and her aunt's stares burned her skin.

Refusal choked her for a moment, but when Darcy's gaze slid to her aunt, the refusal died on her tongue.

She curtsied. "Thank you, Mr. Darcy."

Darcy inclined his head and turned around, departing as quickly as he arrived. His dour mood lingered, though.

Mrs. Gardiner took a drink of her wine. "He's very… to the point."

Mr. Anderson checked behind him, brow furrowed. "That he is. Quite a surprise for me. I expected him to sit out as he normally does at these events." He shifted, peering at Elizabeth. "Did you socialize with him much in Hertfordshire?"

"Not very much," she said around her numb tongue. "A few dinners, the ball at Netherfield. I wouldn't say we socialized much."

Awareness of Mrs. Gardiner's prying gaze made her skin prickle. She had no idea how well she kept her distress off her expression. Sweat beaded at her temples. That, at least, she could blame that on the hundreds of candles in the room.

Giving Mr. Anderson an eager, manic smile, she said, "So. This Mrs. Dankworth? I appear to have some time before I'm obliged to Mr. Darcy."

"Right. Right." He did a poor job of hiding his discomposure, but he made a valiant effort and held his arm out to

Elizabeth. "She's a wonderful woman, but I'll let you come to your own conclusions beyond that."

"Are you afraid to prejudice me?"

They walked away, Elizabeth smoothing away the rough edges of her worry and trying to cultivate the gay air of before. Mrs. Dankworth was indeed a wonderful woman who spent her days not socializing writing poetry and short novels for the publishing house under a pseudonym that was poorly hidden. "With my husband's full, if slightly confused, permission. He says it is infinitely more rewarding than the flower arrangements I used to put together. Prettier, too. I'm terrible with flowers. Allergies, you know. I can't see for the tears streaming down my face. Words are easier to put together."

Elizabeth liked her company very much, and they had a lovely conversation with Mrs. Gardiner which ended with an invitation the next week to visit Mrs. Dankworth's townhome. Mrs. Dankworth deemed Elizabeth charming and turned to Mr. Anderson, tapping her nose. "Don't let this one get away."

His smile spread and the way he looked at Elizabeth then gave no doubt to his thoughts. "Oh, I won't. Miss Lizzy is an exceptional member of our team."

Unfortunately, the pleasant evening could not last. The dance ended and Elizabeth's shoulders drew up while she searched the crowd. Darcy would be out there. Watching. Waiting.

If she were affected by the wine, it would've burned away when her gaze met Darcy's.

He was not too far away which worried her. Had he been listening in to their conversation? At least nothing negative had passed between them regarding the Darcys, so he would have no complaint there.

You stepped foot in his home after running away from him. He will have plenty of complaints.

The wintry night still burned in her mind. How much her wrist hurt from Mr. Collins gripping her. The way Darcy yelled when she exited the carriage. How she felt his hot breath on her neck while she ran all the way back to Longbourn, to be found weeping at the steps by her mother.

"What have you done, girl? What have you done*?"*

What had she done except deny a powerful man? And now she felt the weight of his power as he came to collect his due.

"Try not to charm her too much," Mr. Anderson said with a laugh while she placed her hand on Darcy's outstretched one.

"I make no promises," Darcy said. It should have been funny. However, lacking inflection in his tone, Elizabeth was further unnerved. Likewise, Mr. Anderson didn't seem to know how to respond, so he only dipped his head and backed away.

"Quite the protector you have," Darcy muttered when they put their backs to Mr. Anderson.

Elizabeth bit down her reply. Better to wait and see how this panned out. It was what one did while blind and deaf inside a bear's den.

"No pithy reply? No warning me away from your lover?"

Elizabeth stiffened. "I thought to save my pithy replies for when you ever have something interesting to say."

He made a noise, one of both amusement and displeasure. "I've never not entertained you before."

"If that's what you think."

They reached the line and Darcy seeded them within the middle of it. Like when they were at Netherfield, she encountered surprise on their neighbor's faces when they recognized Darcy among the line of dancers. Certainly many of them, like Mr. Anderson, expected him to sit most of the night out.

Instead he was here with this relatively unknown young woman, and she willed her cheeks not to give away her unease. Already she could hear someone behind her asking, "Who is that young lady lining up with Mr. Darcy?"

It's no one, she wanted to say. *Forget I am even here.*

She lifted her gaze to Darcy's which remained pinned to her, forbidding any discussion. One person would not forget she was here. He would never forget her insult.

Or forgive, his glittering eyes said.

But she had not come here looking for forgiveness from him. This was all a ridiculous mistake, a comedy of errors no sane author could have imagined.

She bent her neck to him as the dance opened. Then he advanced, and she had to take his hand and pretend as if her skin did not buzz under his touch.

They walked the length of the line, other couples laughing and clapping along with the music, but their small bubble remained silent, overwhelmingly so.

"You once informed me that couples commonly converse while dancing."

Elizabeth forced a sweet smile. "The weather is fine, don't you think? And there are a pleasing number of couples in the dance." The smile died. "There. I have conversed."

"What scintillating conversation," he said while they walked the line again. "I once heard you were famed for your wit."

"It has eluded me tonight."

He smirked in her periphery. "A pity. You were quite the conversationalist with Anderson. I've never seen him laugh so much. As for myself, I think I would enjoy a laugh."

They took each other's hands. She had no choice but to stare into his cold face as they performed. "So would I. It appears we'll both be disappointed."

"That is your aunt, correct? Mrs. Gardiner." Her aunt watched them from her spot by the wall, her brow furrowed. How Darcy had noticed her in the crowd was beyond her. "She's taking quite the interest in watching us."

"She's a good chaperone."

"Yes, something you've lacked in the past. I wonder why she seems so worried." They turned in the dance, far at first then brought closer than ever before, so close she could see every single one of Darcy's thick eyelashes. The flecks of gold in his eyes were large enough to swim in as he leaned towards her, voice pitched low. "Do you think she'd object if I took you upstairs right now?"

She did not stumble. That was what she remembered later, though at the time all the breath rushed out of her. Anger blurred her vision and constricted her lungs, but not enough to silence her. "Don't *say* such stupid things."

He sneered. "Then don't *play* stupid."

The dance broke them apart. Elizabeth could feel her flush but could not use her awareness to tamp down her anger. "And what way do I play stupid, Mr. Darcy? What is this farce?"

"You know very well what you did, stepping into my home as if you had any right." The way he glanced down her body erased the glow from her beautiful dress, made her feel dirty and slimy. "What are your plans?"

He came unnervingly close. Part of the dance, yes, and she abruptly despised this dance and how it required Darcy's hand to close around her elbow like a lover's.

His breath touched the side of her cheek. "Is it blackmail you wish?"

"I want nothing of you, except to see this dance end."

"And the next. You're obliged for two."

"I'd be obliged if you released me," she said.

His smirk dissolved into a hard line. "Why? Can I not torment you like you do me?"

"I don't seek to do anything, and if there's been any torment, I apologize. It was not my intent." Explaining didn't feel right. No doubt Darcy would accuse her of lying. *Why* hadn't she asked who hosted tonight's ball? She couldn't believe it herself.

"I'm sure your intent was wholly innocent," he said, lip curling. But his expression didn't seem so severe, his brow furrowed. "How is your father?"

Elizabeth swallowed. The sting at the corners of her eyes irritated her, and she looked away. "My sister says he's doing well, considering."

"And when do you plan to go back?"

"I don't." His expression didn't even shift, leading her to think he knew that already. Who told him? Mr. Bingley?

He must have. Why else would he look at me with such pity?

"What I wonder…"

Darcy was forced to stop as the dance ended. Elizabeth stepped back into the line and clapped halfheartedly, her focus on the man across from her. *Do I really torment him? How?*

Perhaps she wasn't the only one dreaming of sweat-soaked bodies and twisted sheets.

He stepped forward, the other dancers leaving or moving further up the line while the musicians rested before the next soon. He bent towards her while the room buzzed with activity, hiding them for a brief time in the crowd. "What is it you desire, Lizzy? Because I cannot imagine you would come here with no ulterior motive… unless it is just to see me."

She burned at the implication in his dark eyes and curling mouth. As if she had nothing to do but *pine* for him. Her jaw cramped from biting down so hard on what she wanted to say, which was where he could put his assumptions.

"No motive except an invitation from a friend," she said. "Why you insist I must have some ulterior motive confuses me. I'm here simply to dance, Darcy."

"You would be a fool to believe I wouldn't suspect something after your father—"

She shook her head. "My father?"

A whirlwind of green appeared beside them, forcing them to break apart. Georgianna Darcy was a beautiful young woman and from her expression she cherished her brother and this chance to tease him. "Thank goodness you came along, Miss Bennet. I feared my brother might not dance at all tonight." Her eyes twinkled as she looked between them, obviously suspecting ulterior motives of her own.

She forced herself to smile, to pretend Georgianna's brother wasn't glaring at the side of her head. "That would be a shame. Your brother is a fine dancer."

"Tolerable," Darcy said. He inclined his head as a gentleman took the spot across from Georgianna. "Mr. Anderson."

Elizabeth stiffened for a second when Mr. Anderson stepped up. However, he didn't seem to suspect anything between them. Instead, he settled in line next across from Georgianna and gave Elizabeth a cheeky wink. "I can't imagine people leaving before dawn, Darcy!"

Georgianna captured Elizabeth's attention. "How do you know my brother?"

It was impossible not to answer Georgianna's sweet smile. "My sister married his friend this autumn."

"Oh, Mr. Bingley—how happy I was about the news! He deserves all the joy and I believe I've heard a little about you," she said with a giggle that made Elizabeth's stomach twist and Anderson perk up, looking between Elizabeth and Darcy. "Fitzwilliam wrote about his time there. He said you were an admirable sparring partner."

Elizabeth cast a questioning glance at Darcy. "I never knew you to exaggerate."

Darcy's expression was stern. "I didn't."

Darcy took her hand and guided her back into line. Anderson noted this, coloring slightly.

Elizabeth nibbled the inside of her lip and knew that whatever expectations she might have had after tonight, Darcy was burning them up in flames.

"You play your part so well," Darcy said bending down so his breath brushed her ear, inappropriate yet thrilling.

But he didn't seem to care.

Elizabeth burned brightly not only because of their neighbors' curious stares, but because Darcy had a way of speaking that brought her back to when he would whisper sweet nothings against her bare shoulder.

She could almost feel his hand sliding down her naked spine now, though he barely touched her. "Does Anderson know who you really are when this polished veneer falls away?"

"What was that, Darcy?"

Darcy straightened and gave Anderson a smirk while sweat popped up on Elizabeth's brow.

"Miss Bennet was about to tell me how you two met."

Anderson's expression broke into a smile, but the dance started then. With Anderson and Georgianna dancing next to them, Elizabeth remained quiet. Despite what Darcy thought, she had no intention of creating any rumors.

In fact, it was *his* actions tonight that would spread any rumors.

He came close to her, his fingers brushed the middle of her waist and she inhaled something woodsy and bitter like a blown out match. "I'm all agog, Miss Bennet," he murmured, and it was unfair how attractive he was, how he made butterflies spawn in her stomach to distraction.

7

"I took employment at Mr. Anderson's publishing house. As an assistant."

Darcy leaned back, his shock plain, censure following half a second later. "Employment? You—what of your aunt and uncle? Can they not provide for you?"

Though he took care to keep his voice low—thank Heavens he did so!—her humiliation truly was complete. But what right did he have to degrade her life and accomplishments? She *liked* the publishing house. She liked Mr. Davies and Miss Brown and the other editors and one day *Elizabeth's* name would be on the shelves in gold lettering. And to bring her aunt and uncle into it as if they failed her because she took employment—the audacity!

If the dance hadn't necessitated them changing partners right then, she would have given him a dressing down to last a lifetime. However, after she regained her composure dancing with Mr. Anderson, a very fine dancer, she faced Darcy's scowl with aplomb.

"My relations are excellent. I won't hear a negative word spoken about them."

"I don't see why not. They've put you to *work*. You, a daughter—"

"Of a poor family with little connections," Elizabeth said, keeping her chin high. She even managed a smile. "I could imagine worse than reading books all day. Besides, it was my choice. My aunt asked me to be governess, but I realized how little patience I have for that sort of thing."

The dance allowed Mr. Anderson to interrupt them then, and he did so, Georgianna looking on with pleased interest while he beamed at Darcy. "Did Miss Lizzy tell you that my mother was an editor for the press at one point? The very same position she now holds."

"How nostalgic," Darcy said with a curl of his lip as if Mr. Anderson was a bad smell haunting him.

Mr. Anderson laughed; meanwhile, the dance took him and Georgianna down the line, leaving Elizabeth alone when Darcy's scowl returned to her.

"So that's why you took employment. To find a husband."

Elizabeth snorted. It was no ladylike snort, holding nothing but contempt. "I thank you for the compliment and your optimism about my prospects, but I must disappoint you. It is merely a way to spend my time."

"I'm certain there are other pursuits a young lady might engage in without demeaning yourself."

"Really, because the only other opportunities I've been presented were *quite* demeaning."

For the first time, Darcy actually seemed as if he had the ability to be embarrassed, though his expression shut down the next instant. "A guaranteed income, a home, independence from… anyway." They parted briefly, and the lingering hint of bitterness faded by the time they joined again. "I'm not certain that you and I will agree on this."

"I guarantee we won't." The dance was coming to an end and she couldn't be more grateful. It had not been so horrible, though it was nothing she wished to repeat. When they bowed to each other to close the dance, Elizabeth released a pent up breath.

"Would you care for a walk around the room?"

"I wouldn't impose—"

He grabbed her hand before she could step away and placed it on his. "I won't snub you in front of your aunt. There. She's smiling at us."

Forced to follow along or stumble stupidly, she cast a backward glance and found Anderson looking after her, though the next moment Georgianna caught his attention. At least he was distracted.

She looked up at Darcy while they crossed to the far wall and found him scowling at her. "You accuse me of playing games, but I find your actions exceedingly confusing. What are you doing?"

He seemed utterly blasé about all the whispers following them and set a sedate pace. "We have unfinished business."

She faced forward, smoothing out the irritation in her voice. "You wanted something. I didn't. There's no further business." It was funny, perhaps shocking, how much of a private conversation one could hold in a ballroom of people. Though people might stare and watch them, they spoke too low for anyone to hear more than a muttered snippet.

"On the contrary, we are nowhere near finished. Your father had words for me."

Elizabeth craned her neck to look at him, her brow furrowed as sternly as his. "What do you mean, my father?"

"What did you tell your father before you left for town?"

She shook her head. Instinctively, she found it hard to believe, but the thought of Darcy lying about this similarly flummoxed her. "I- I told him I wanted to leave and why."

"Because of me?"

She snorted. Not a lady-like sound, but Darcy knew she was hardly a proper lady. "You flatter yourself. You, I could avoid. But I couldn't be in the house one more second with *him*. Somehow, my father agreed, though I dared not tell him how that despicable man—" She stopped, bile in the back of her throat. Those memories were always on the cusp of her mind and now the memories rushed back like an exasperating neighbor you couldn't get rid of come dinnertime. Forcing down the bile, the bitterness still didn't leave her voice. "My mother thought I would beg to come back, but I haven't."

"Many would have." He sounded subdued. It took her a moment to realize he meant her current situation, as if reading books all day was a hardship.

That made her lips soften into a smile. "Why? I'm happy here. My aunt and uncle are wonderful. And despite what you think, I don't mind the employment. It helps me not feel like a burden on them."

"You, a burden…?" He shook his head and drew off, gaze distant as he looked about the room. Several people skittered away from his dark gaze and several ladies whipped out their fans so they could whisper behind them. He seemed to see nothing of them, and Elizabeth let the spectators fade from her mind as she looked up at his troubled face.

"If I told you your father named me directly as the reason you left Longbourn, what would you say?"

It took several moments to speak. "I would call that far-fetched. Is this true?"

"I went to Longbourn two days after we last met. Your

father requested a private interview. He had all manner of accusations ready, including the bruises on your wrists," he said with a glance toward her arm.

She flinched. "No, I never— I was afraid to name my cousin, yes, but I never substituted your name. Oh, no wonder you've been furious! No, Mr. Darcy, I'm not sure why my father said that."

"Why are you coming in so early, Lizzy? Are you crying? What happened to your arms?"

She shook her head. "It didn't come from me."

His face was creased in dark thoughts. "Perhaps your cousin saw us meet. He would have mentioned it to my aunt, though, and I've heard nothing about it. What of your sisters?"

She jumped. "Jane would never—"

"Your younger sisters have spread a tale that your mother sent you away to London to avoid a scandal with a gentleman." When her eyes widened, he explained, "If you haven't noticed, Miss Bingley is here, and she claims she heard it from their lips. You didn't mention it to them, did you?"

She drew herself up at the accusation in his eyes. "I'd sooner trust a stranger with my life than my youngest sisters with a secret. I don't know what Lydia and Kitty are doing besides trying to make themselves look scandalous. Idiot girls. The last I heard, they were obsessed with scandals they read in the papers. I'm sure they hope to share in some glory themselves by spreading that tale." She shook her head. "As for my mother sending me away, no. My father agreed to let me come to London. And now my mother will not have me back unless I marry Mr. Collins—I'm terribly sorry. I didn't intend to unleash all of this on you."

It was almost a relief to speak. He was the only person who knew everything. Strange, to have begun the night afraid of him, and now confiding in him the self-same thoughts that kept her up at night.

"Lizzy, why was mother yelling at you?"

Darcy proceeded slowly, his brow furrowed, his gaze distant as if he didn't see the crowd around them. "All this time, I've been furious at you. I'm still not sure whether to believe you or not."

She sighed. "I wouldn't begrudge you that. Your name should never have come up to my father."

That earned her a quick, grateful glance. "I caution you against writing to him about this. Bringing it up may spur him to greater action."

He was right. Her father knew how to be a thorough man. If he set his mind to destroying Darcy, he would make every attempt possible. Poisoning his name in Hertfordshire would be easy.

"I doubt my father reads my correspondence anyway, so it's no use. He's become a terrible correspondent since I left."

"But you talk to your sister, Mrs. Bingley."

"Yes, weekly."

"Could you not—" He stopped, shook his head.

"What?" she asked, and a piece of her wondered at how easily they walked together, how she could speak and he *heard* her, losing his hostility for something that sounded like concern. Not that she needed his concern, or his negative views on her employment, but she appreciated the thought, regardless.

Darcy frowned as if he regretted bringing it up. "I wondered if you might stay with them if Longbourn isn't open to you, but then I changed my mind against asking."

She smiled. "Well, now I'm curious. Why did you change your mind?"

Darcy's expression went soft when he glanced down at

her, touched by the gentleness she recalled from the autumn. It made her stomach flip. "You've tolerated my poor behavior tonight better than I had any right to expect. Does that not speak to some compatibility of spirit between us? I don't want you at Netherfield, Lizzy. I want you here."

8

"I've given you my answer. No."

His response had taken her breath away, and she was still reeling, but she knew this truth as indisputable: she would not, could not, be his mistress.

"You won't always be so happy with your employment," he said, and she bit down on the inside of her cheek, using the pinch to distract her from the outrage his sneering reply incited.

Well, not entirely distracted. "It's honest," she said, clipped and gritting her teeth. "I'm not compromising my reputation or my family—"

"A family who has all but abandoned you!" His low tone of voice hummed along the back of her spine, chilly and cold. His jaw clenched and he glowered ahead, causing several guests to scuttle out of their path without him appearing to take any note. "If they could have indentured you to that cowardly parson, they would have in an instant. What do you owe them?"

"I love my family and I won't debate this with you. I've given my answer, please respect me enough to *listen*."

Love. Couldn't he understand the concept? But no, her refusal went against his desires and he could not understand anything except that she'd been taken away, like she was some dolly he could no longer play with. She couldn't stand another moment. Not his touch, not his gaze, not the sneering disregard he had for her life and happiness. Breaking, decorum, she dropped Darcy's arm and hurried forward, hearing him scoff behind her. She crossed the rest of the distance between them and her aunt alone, keeping her head high despite the curious glances her way.

She did not turn around to see how Darcy reacted to this.

Mrs. Gardiner greeted her with a worried smile. "What was that?"

Elizabeth thanked a servant passing out iced punch from a tray. "Sorry?" she asked her aunt, the cold glass making her fingertips tingle.

"You were having quite the conversation," Mrs. Gardiner said. It wasn't like her to pry this much, but Elizabeth supposed the dramatics of Elizabeth's departure necessitated an outright question.

She looked about, adopting a blasé air, interrupting several gossips staring at her from over their fans while they whispered. She stared long enough to make them fumble their fans and turn their backs on her. "He was asking about what all has happened at Netherfield since he departed." She spotted Darcy weaving through the crowd, thankfully toward the ballroom doors. Turning to her aunt, she said, "I'm awfully tired—"

The supper bell rang.

Mrs. Gardiner perked up. "A little early, but that's no matter. I'm famished."

Elizabeth, who had been about to suggest they take their leave for the evening, buried her disappointment and returned her aunt's happy smile. "I wonder what's on the menu."

Mrs. Gardiner patted her hand. "You would know better than I, considering your acquaintance. You do seem well acquainted with Mr. Darcy."

Her smile fell. "No, I wouldn't say that," she said. "Simply a friend to my brother-in-law."

Mr. Anderson appeared at Elizabeth's shoulder, his eyes sparkling over a new round of punch. "You're free! Goodness, Mr. Darcy walks slow, doesn't he? Ha! I will tell him so next I see him. In the meantime, I heard the supper bell. Might I have the honor of escorting the most charming women in London through?"

Elizabeth laughed and the two women allowed Mr. Anderson to escort them through to the dining room. No less than sixty plates were being served this evening, and despite how the night's events had left her in turmoil, Elizabeth found herself salivating at the smells of roast duck and white soup. Though Mr. Anderson looked at her oddly once or twice, he did not pry or seem concerned about Darcy's unusual actions, and she relaxed. She resolved to survive the night with no further encounters with Darcy, which thankfully was not put to the test.

After dinner, Darcy seemed happy to leave well enough alone, and stayed out of the ballroom, and Elizabeth sat out the dances for the rest of the night, seeing there was no shortage of young women putting themselves on display tonight. Mr. Anderson danced once more with a daughter of his friend, but he too seemed content to watch the dancers beside Mrs. Gardiner and Elizabeth, and Mrs. Gardiner shared several speculative glances with Elizabeth about this turn of events.

It was almost as if, by Darcy leaving the ballroom, he agreed they should put the past behind them. It was time to return to normality and away from scandal. This was all Elizabeth had wanted.

Yet at one point in the night, she looked up at Mr. Anderson and her smile faltered. For some reason, she had expected a pair of burning, dark eyes, not Mr. Anderson's sparkling eyes. He smiled and the little flutter that often accompanied his smiles was absent.

Darcy had poisoned her.

This was further reinforced as they left, the candles burning low, the beginnings of dawn streaking the sky. In the midst of dozens of guests departing and in various states of disarray—yawning, their hair falling out of their updos, their shirts untucked after a night of playing cards—Darcy stood out for his sober posture and polished ensemble. He was impeccable, and simply seeing him there in the low light coming in from the open door made Elizabeth gulp.

Darcy bowed low to Mrs. Gardiner when they met him in the doorway, ready to depart. "It was a pleasure to make your acquaintance, and to renew an old one," he said, turning to Elizabeth for this last. "I hope we will be able to visit again soon while you are in town, Miss Bennet."

He took her hand for a moment, warmth seeping through her glove, and his finger brushed over her pulse. He couldn't have felt the way her heartbeat jumped. She told herself that all the way home while Mr. Anderson yawned and Mrs. Gardiner dozed lightly. He couldn't have. *Yet why had he looked so pleased with himself?*

"Make sure you take the day off," Mr. Anderson said

when he helped them from the carriage. Mrs. Gardiner shuffled into the house while Mr. Anderson and Elizabeth lingered at the door. "I'll tell Mr. Davies not to expect you."

"Thank you so much," she said. "I had a lovely time."

"As did I." His gaze searched hers and she held her breath. He looked so handsome in the dawn light—so why did she feel nothing right now? Mr. Anderson glanced toward the open door and then back to her. "Would it be acceptable to you if I called tomorrow?"

There they were. The flutters returned, her cheeks warmed, and she laughed, relieved ten times over. Teasingly, she said, "If I never go into the publishing house, Mr. Davies will have no guard dog to protect him from the slush pile."

He chuckled. "Very well, but only as soon as you tame the slush again, all right?"

She curtsied, pleased to see him admiring her form when she straightened. "I'll endeavor to be quick."

Standing on the bottom step of her aunt's home, she waved as Mr. Anderson's coach departed and then followed her aunt inside. Mrs. Gardiner was asleep on her feet, standing at the bottom of the staircase weaving slightly, eyes closed. Elizabeth took her aunt's arm and helped her upstairs and into her uncle's bemused care.

"I take it you had a lovely time?" he asked while Mrs. Gardiner shuffled to her dressing table, murmuring something about pins.

Elizabeth smiled. "Very much so."

"Good. And shall I throw the window open for your aunt or keep them shut?"

"I would urge you to keep them shut for the time being," Elizabeth said, rousing her uncle to chuckle. "Good morning. I'll be closing *my* curtains tight, too."

Elizabeth did not feel impaired, despite her good-natured

remarks to her uncle. She was aware of being tired, but it lingered on the edge of her consciousness, not quite overwhelming enough to send her straight to bed. So despite the urge to fall into bed fully clothed, she took her time releasing the pins from her hair, staring at the reflection of the woman in the mirror while she sat at her small desk. Dark circles under her eyes. Frizzy hair no longer elegantly tamed. Her cheeks pale.

It was not a face that should incite desire.

And yet she could close her eyes and remember in vivid detail how Darcy's mouth curled when he took her hand and how a part of her had thought—*hoped*—he might tug her into his chest and wrap his arms around her.

Elizabeth scoffed and rose. "Don't be silly, Lizzy," she said, and closed the blinds, erasing the light from her room and the reflection of the simmering desire in her eyes as she thought of *him*.

9

Those lingering, dream-like feelings faded with time. The next day, she resumed her role as publishing house mistress with a full heart. Dressed before the sky could lighten fully, Elizabeth left and hurried toward the publishing house.

It was a short, invigorating walk at a time of day before the balminess of the season could infect the air. The streets were quiet, those few stepping out of doors on errands and important work. Elizabeth kept her head down and hurried to her destination. Without an escort, she couldn't afford to draw any attention, not if she wanted to convince her uncle not to force William, one of the servants, to accompany her forever after. He had far more important things to do, and it was only a few streets.

However, this morning, having William by her side would have made the carriage following her a lot more palatable.

Elizabeth glanced over her shoulder. No, she wasn't mistaken. The same carriage had been parked down the street from her house on Gracechurch Street. She hadn't thought much of it at the time; however, it wasn't a coincidence that it was now drawing up behind her, closing in with each clip clop of the horses' hooves.

She drew her bag close to her chest. Living inside the world of fiction literature meant she was no stranger to tales of kidnappings and other morbid evildoings. But that could not happen to *her* on a street like this—could it?

The carriage drew in and Elizabeth's shoulders rose toward her ears. Should she look? If she caught the eye of the driver, perhaps it would turn out to be a misunderstanding. A silly fancy of hers. She would giggle over this later with Miss Brown.

But what if she turned her head and the driver turned out to be a villain? She could imagine his face now. A slash above his eye from a gloomy fight he barely won. Teeth missing in a horrible, mocking smile.

Elizabeth shuddered. An imagination was a terrible thing.

No. No, she couldn't let fear dissolve her senses. Steeling herself, she glanced over her shoulder at the carriage. A face at the darkened window shocked her.

A familiar face.

"Mr. D-Darcy?" she exclaimed, stumbling to a stop. She looked about, but there were few people out on this misty morning. She almost wished there were more people, for who could expect to see Fitzwilliam Darcy here, of all places? It would be a blessing to have someone nearby to say that, yes, the carriage drawing to a stop beside her held the esteemed gentleman, and her eyes did not deceive her.

Darcy opened the door before the carriage rolled to a stop. He stepped out, lightly tugging on the lapels of his fine coat. Piercing eyes assessed everything about her in an instant.

"What are you doing out here alone?"

Elizabeth cleared her throat and decided she would save her questions. "I'm going to the publishing house. It's only a few streets away."

Somehow, she thought he knew that already. Watching his expression take this in without a single flicker of surprise made her certain of it.

"Don't you know the dangers of this neighborhood? It's not a place to walk alone."

"If it's so dangerous here, what are you doing alone?"

Darcy raised a brow and gestured to the carriage. "I'm not. Like a sensible person, I have my driver. You don't even have a footman escorting you."

"Because it's not dangerous. Believe me, I've walked this path several weeks and have only been accosted once." He smirked in satisfaction at making his point. With a frown, she crossed her arms. "Today. By *you*."

"Don't be ridiculous. If you see a friendly meeting upon the street as an accosting, I hardly know what to think of you."

"I have my doubts about how friendly this is. Forgive me for misconstruing when, after all, all you've done is interrogate me."

He issued a short bow, but nothing about his laughing eyes suggested contrition. "Forgive the impudence. I'm merely looking out for your safety." He straightened and gallantly waved to the carriage. "Since we are both here, though, perhaps you'd like to ride together to Anderson's publishing house."

She laughed. "It's only a few streets away!"

"A quick ride, then," Darcy said with a hint of a smile. "Come, Lizzy. For old time's sake."

Elizabeth warmed hearing her name from his lips. A lover's caress that reached to the heart of her. He did look mightily handsome this morning, further adding to the temptation. His curls were arranged almost artlessly, as if he'd run his hand through his hair several times. The contrast of his blue jacket and starched whites made him look striking and bold.

And she couldn't forget his eyes. Those dark eyes with his thick eyelashes which had starred in a number of her dreams the past nights.

She bit her lip, searching the street. The driver was already opening the door for them and lowering the steps. There was no one about to see them, especially none of her uncle's friends who resided on this street, all instructed to ensure she made no detours and encountered no issues.

Would it be so terrible?

Yes! You know what temptation he offers!

Her lip went numb between her teeth. Yes, it would be terrible. But even more terrible would be the regret and emptiness that would eat her up for the rest of the week if she didn't chase it now.

Darcy touched her arm, and she succumbed, letting him lead her to the carriage door.

"Don't make me regret this," she said while the driver handed her into the carriage.

Darcy followed and shut the door. With a smile in his voice, he said, "Have you ever regretted a moment with me?"

"Plenty," she said, settling on the bench. And just as she suspected, Darcy settled down next to her, leaving the other bench free. Her breath caught when he turned to face her, thigh brushing hers.

"You regret all the wrong things," he said. "It's the time we've been apart I've regretted." Her head tilted back as he cupped her jaw, thumb sliding over her cheek. He watched her and she watched him. Two opponents meeting for the first time after a long hiatus, and the knot in her throat made it impossible to breathe. "Think of how long we could have enjoyed one another if not for this inconsequential misunderstanding between us?"

"I misunderstood nothing." She pulled away and Darcy let her, licking his lips while she cleared her throat. "You asked. I gave my response."

Darcy closed the distance between them, using his finger on her chin to turn her gaze back to him. "And you gave me no time to persuade you." He could sound so sweet when he wanted to, which for some reason made her melt for him.

Her gut was all tangled up in him. "Darcy—"

"So you don't wish to be my mistress. Fine." Her reluctance stuttered when he dipped down, pressing his lips against hers. The barest touch, all too brief. His breath tingled against her lips. "But allow us a chance to say a true goodbye, the one we didn't get in the autumn."

She forced strength into her throat, pulling away only enough to meet his gaze. "Here? In your carriage? When there's only a few minutes?"

"No, that does not seem appropriate," he said, brushing his lips over hers again. She twisted her fingers in her lap, trying to retain some measure of dignity as he sought to unwind her reluctance. He pulled back, watching her with unrestrained hunger. "A taste for now. Then I can arrange a long detour another day, or… or I can arrange a house for a longer assignation."

"It's not wise. I was lucky not to conceive over the autumn, Darcy." Now she understood, thanks to a circumspect query to her aunt and a few enlightening passages in recent manuscripts, how dangerous their affair was. He might be able to afford a bastard—she could never recover.

"What is one more time?" He saw her expression and drew his hand over her cheek, eyes softening. "However, if it offends you, I will not fill your precious womb with my seed. It is, as always, your choice."

Was it ever a choice with him? Elizabeth sometimes thought she was merely the puppet, with Darcy in control of her strings. He could turn her this way and that and she would say *thank you* when he had her all tangled and twisted.

"A taste first," she whispered. "Then I'll decide."

"*Yes,*" he growled. He snatched his walking stick and hit the roof. "To Harefields Street."

She grabbed his arm. "The one beyond, Four Lane. I'll walk back so no one sees us together."

"To Four Lane Street!"

The driver's acknowledgement came muffled through the roof and Darcy dropped his walking stick and ripped off his jacket. Elizabeth giggled.

"You look maddened."

Darcy's eyes lit as he threw his jacket to the bench and fell to his knees on the carriage floor in front of her. "I am. Maddened for you, sweet Lizzy, and with only a short time to slake my thirst." He placed his hands on her knees, a devilish look in his eyes. "Now spread your thighs for me."

"There's no room in here," she said, a laugh pulled out of her as he lifted her skirts.

He grinned wolfishly. "Room enough."

There decidedly *wasn't* enough room, but her breathless laugh abruptly stopped when he yanked her thighs apart and wedged himself between her knees. There was enough room to contort himself and press his mouth to her mound. It instantly lit her up, her back arching off the cushion, her hand coming down hard in Darcy's hair. Darcy's groan echoed in the small carriage, louder than the wooden wheels on the cobblestone, reverberating through her body.

This was so wrong, and yet nothing ever felt more right.

"Look at me." Darcy straightened, dipping his fingers inside her, watching her lips part as she fluttered around him. He ate up her expression, thrusting harder, curling his fingers to send her even higher. "You've missed this. Say it."

Her nails dug into the bench seat. "I-I missed you."

"Oh, *did* you?" His grin made her rethink the last couple seconds and she closed her eyes in mortification. He laughed, utter delight lighting up his expression. "For that truth, I'll reward you, sweet Lizzy."

He bent his head and did just that, and she slapped her hand over her mouth to muffle her cries. The carriage rocked along and Darcy sent her past pleasure into burning ecstasy. Right, wrong, it all flew out of her head. What mattered was the release, the real world erased and Darcy the only true thing in the world.

Then it was too much, much too much, and Darcy drew back when she slapped at his shoulders. He leaned back, one curl falling into his eyes as he admired her, and licked his shiny lips.

"Watching you quake is the greatest pleasure in the world."

"You're terrible," she said, pushing down her dress.

"In the best ways." He got up and took the seat beside her. His satisfied smirk should've irritated her. After that, she wasn't sure any irritation could touch her. *Terrible man. I cannot even be annoyed properly.*

The carriage drew to a stop. The driver's muffled voice came through. "Four Lane Street, sir."

Darcy caressed her arm. He had a very prodigious bulge in his breeches. "Are you certain you have to cut this short?"

"Very." Yet she didn't move, only turned to lean across his chest and kiss him. A true kiss, eager to taste him, to feel him again. He groaned and embraced her, tongue imparting desire and need into her being.

She finally found the urge to draw back when her lungs started to ache.

His eyelids were heavy while he watched her gasp. "For what it's worth, I've missed you too. Very much."

"That's worth a lot to me," she whispered. One more second to linger, to memorize his face, his dark eyes and the intensity of his focus, and then she drew back. "Thank you for the ride, Mr. Darcy."

"My pleasure."

He kept hold of her hand till the very last moment when she descended from the carriage, and she held that warmth to her chest all the way back to Harefields Street. Right up until she saw Mr. Anderson standing at the door to the publishing house.

"Mr. Anderson. I didn't expect to see you this morning."

He turned, a smile forming already, though it faltered for a moment. "I didn't expect to see you coming from this direction."

"I, um, wanted to do some window shopping."

"Oh." His brow furrowed before he smiled. "It must be Grinwold's shop, yes?"

A black carriage returning down the street drew her eye. "Um, yes…" she said, blinking. Was that Darcy's carriage? She couldn't see into it, but it looked remarkably similar.

She looked up at Mr. Anderson and found him frowning

at the coach. The hairs on the back of her neck stood up. The familiarity of it was striking. She swallowed and pitched a hopefully innocent question at her companion.

"What is it?"

"Nothing. I thought I recognized that carriage is all." With a shake of his head, he appeared to put the thought behind him and held out his arm to Elizabeth. "Shall we head inside?"

The carriage reached the end of the street. Elizabeth tore her eyes away and smiled up at Mr. Anderson. "Yes, we shall."

He led her inside. "I think Grinwold's shop is that way, actually, now that I remember."

"Oh, you're right… I wasn't really paying attention, but I didn't realize I would be quizzed about it." He laughed and the moment smoothed over. Elizabeth threw one more look behind her, but Darcy's carriage was gone.

10

ANDERSON.

Darcy faced forward, though the image of Elizabeth and Anderson didn't leave his mind so easily. What luck he'd decided to circle back to make sure she reached the publishing house, only to find Anderson homing in on Elizabeth's time.

Or perhaps it was an arranged meeting.

Darcy rolled his tongue over his teeth. Her flavor still lingered, and initially he only wanted to refresh it, but now...

"Crayton!"

"Sir?" The driver's muffled answer reached him.

A visit to the leasing agent was in order. Darcy gave the name of the street to his driver as he thought about what he needed. The tidy, elegant home. A full staff. The finest dresses and lace and whatever else a woman needed to live comfortably. And never again would Anderson cross her mind.

Georgianna was in the foyer, taking off her gloves, by the time he returned to the townhome.

He kissed the top of her head. "Productive day?"

"Visiting all morning with thank you cards. Oh, I didn't get to ask before you left. Miss Elizabeth Bennet? Do you know where she lives? I thought you might write Mr. Anderson—"

"No, I know where she lives. Gracechurch Street."

He'd been busy since the ball. With a name, Larson had quickly pulled the information Darcy needed. Mr. Gardiner was a fabric merchant in London, the source for most of the high shops and most sought-after tailors and seamstresses. A rising man in business, respectable.

He glanced at Georgianna. "Put on your gloves. Crayton should still be ready. We can go give our thanks to Miss Bennet now."

Ms. Chapman stepped away from the dining room where she'd been about to enter. "It's been a busy morning. We were about to have lunch—"

"You've no need to trouble yourself. I will go with Georgianna."

Ms. Chapman opened her mouth, but Darcy was already ushering Georgianna to the door. "Goodbye, Ms. Chapman."

"It's lovely to have an outing together."

He returned his sister's smile and blew on his tea. "It is, isn't it?"

They sat in a small tea shop near his club after an enlightening half hour on Gracechurch Street without Elizabeth. He was quite pleased with how the social call turned out. His assumptions about Mrs. Gardiner were not wrong; she was an elegant, educated woman of taste. He had even managed to catch Mr. Gardiner on a rare midday break. Darcy found himself pleased by their fine discourse and manners over a half hour visit. A pity some of Elizabeth's Hertfordshire relatives lacked the same refinement.

"Will you be doing the rest of my calls with me?"

Georgianna's teasing grin made him shuffle in his seat. "Probably not."

The grin grew. "I see."

"And what is it you see?"

"Only that you were keen to visit one, but will avoid all others." She tapped her finger against her chin. "I wonder what the difference might be."

"Don't make a spectacle," he said with a snort.

Her eyes twinkled. "Oh, no spectacle. I'm sure it's none of my business. It's only... a number of the people I already visited spoke up about a strange occurrence at the ball. The sight of a surly bachelor managing to dance not once but thrice. Everyone's talking about it, wondering what may have caused such a happy event."

"Georgianna." He took a sip of his tea and found it wanting for milk. His sister once feared him in the way a child fears her father and wants his blessing. He didn't know what to think about this smiling creature in front of him, obviously planning something sinister.

"I like her," Georgianna said, straightening, her smile softening. "I hope you don't mind that I left a note asking for her to visit."

"You did?" He hadn't even seen the exchange of the note. He peered at his sister with a furrowed brow. "To Mrs. Gardiner? When will she—" He stopped and cleared his throat. "When did you invite her?"

"Next Thursday. I plan to start a book club. Mr. Anderson said Miss Bennet enjoys those sorts of things."

Anderson again. Darcy scowled.

"You shouldn't listen to Anderson. His wild ideas have given him nothing but grief."

Georgianna pursed her lips thoughtfully while she stared into her tea. "He seems kind."

"Yes, *kind*. A gentleman who sees a bored young lady and puts her to work in his publishing house for a pittance."

She blinked at him. "What?"

His scowl grew while the proprietor returned to their table with their sandwiches. He'd entered hungry, now he was only angry. He waited for the man to leave before he told Georgianna, "Stay away from Anderson. More money than sense in that one."

"Miss Bennet likes him too," Georgianna said. His eyes snapped up to hers to find her smile had turned into a concerned frown. "If you admire Miss Bennet, I don't think you should wait. She's lovely and interesting and even Miss Bingley admits she has a certain manner that draws in the people around her. I don't know much about her besides what you shared in your letters, but the truth is, Fitzwilliam, I don't recall you *ever* writing to me about a woman before her. Why did you write to me about her last autumn?"

He bristled, though he tamped it down a moment later, not wishing to hurt his sister's feelings. "I shared the events happening in my life at the time while we were apart. What does it matter what I wrote?"

"How many times have you written to me about a woman before?"

"I've written about several women before. My companions at the time, Miss Bingley and Mrs. Hurst, were routinely included in my letters. Why aren't you asking about them?"

"Because you described what they said or did, but you did not describe *them*. I remember how eloquently you wrote about her wit in a conversation, pulling in direct quotes from her. I remember even then remarking to Ms. Chapman that you'd never done so before. You cared about her words and about what she said. That speaks volumes to me, and it should speak volumes to you."

I cared about getting into her bed. That is all.
Yet at one point I did care about her, didn't I?

He frowned and spoke more to his sister than himself. "You have romantic ideas."

"I think my ideas are rather sensible. Smart, too. Did you know Miss Bingley remarked to several ladies of her acquaintance already how Miss Bennet seemed put out to dance with you?"

Put out. Darcy glared at the table. "I'm not having this conversation with you. My life is my own. Miss Bennet is a friend. We shared a serious conversation, one she couldn't have had with Anderson with his focus on the mundane. Anderson has nothing to offer her," he said, before he could fully think over the words. Miss Bingley needed to stop spreading rumors. *Put out* to dance with *him*?

"I'm not sure I can agree with you, brother." She sighed and placed her hand against his briefly. "Drop by on Thursday."

"Are you match-making? You should worry about yourself, sister."

Georgianna offered him a sweet smile. "You do enough for the both of us. Now it's time I think of your happiness, especially because you refuse to."

11

"You mustn't keep doing this!"

Darcy caught Elizabeth's waist as soon as the door closed behind her and tugged her into his lap. Her breath went out of her when he buried his face in her cleavage. "*You* are the one who climbed into my carriage. I simply stopped here."

"I couldn't very well have you follow me all the way to the publishing house like a stray."

He lifted his head. "A stray? I should have you over my knee for that comment." He grabbed his walking stick and tapped the roof of the carriage. The carriage rolled forward and sent her falling into Darcy's chest. She pushed herself up with a huff.

"If you are worried about the dangers of my commute, you shouldn't. I've taken this route nearly every day and no harm has come to me."

"You should at least bring a servant with you," he said.

"I really don't need the escort," she said. After the first couple days, she had done away with the servant Mr.

Gardiner sent with her, knowing they had more important duties than to escort her around on a perfectly safe route.

"An escort would have stopped you from jumping into my carriage these past two mornings." He gripped her waist before his hand slid down and caressed her bottom. "They certainly wouldn't allow this," he said while her skin grew warm.

She wiggled on his lap. "All the more reason not to have an escort, don't you think?"

He clasped her tighter. "This wicked logic of yours is one of my favorite things about you."

"And what are your other favorite things about me?"

"You're desperate for flattery now?" When she spluttered, he laughed, showing off the dimple in his cheek. "You still surprise me, Lizzy."

Hearing her name on his lips never failed to charm her. Leaning forward, she brushed her lips against his. "We don't have much time before we get to the publishing house," she murmured.

"On the contrary…"

She leaned back to stare at his sneaky expression. "What?"

"I'm stealing you for the day," he said with a sly twist of his mouth. She huffed a laugh, still staying, not certain whether he was teasing or not. But she knew he was deadly serious when his grin turned cheeky. "See the benefits of having a chaperone?"

"Where are we?"

She let go of Darcy's hand as her feet met the cobblestones beside a smart little townhouse. Climbing vines reached up the walls, spreading the light scent that tickled her nose pleasantly. Flowers were in abundance around the two storey townhome, with overflowing window boxes and winding up the path to the door. It was out of the way, a little off the street, elegant in an unremarkable way, with an attractive view of the garden from any of the front windows.

His satisfied expression met hers and he held out his hand. "Come. I'll show you."

Something was off, but she couldn't resist the pleased glint in his eye. *Curiosity and the cat, they say.*

He led her inside and the dusty scent of a house left to wilt with the doors and windows closed assaulted her senses. She breathed past it, glad someone had thought to open the windows before their arrival. Darcy kept hold of her hand and led her through the foyer.

"The agent said the last tenant was an author who moved to the seaside last winter." He smiled when he caught sight of her expression. "I imagined that might pique your interest. Anyway, a study is back here, but the fireplace needs a good cleaning. Kitchen and servants' dwellings are through there behind the stairs. The front sitting room and dining room needs something done—the last tenant didn't improve much on the decor—but it's serviceable and both are well situated for morning light."

Elizabeth, looking through the doorway into the sitting room with wide eyes, could hardly comprehend. "Darcy, what…?"

"Here, come upstairs." Taking her hand, he led her up the stairs, the space so narrow their shoulders brushed the walls when climbing side by side. "To the right here is a small bedroom with modest furnishings, facing the back lawn. Then here is the main bedroom's sitting room, and then beyond——"

"I see."

The small sitting room opened up to a modest bedroom dressed in threadbare rugs and a gauzy curtain letting in the light streaming in through the tree outside the window.

Darcy led her forward and she followed automatically, the tight feeling in her chest weighing her down. Only when he stopped beside the four-poster bed did it lighten with the soft look in his eyes as he faced her.

"Shall we try it out?"

She stumbled a step backwards, knocking into an end table. "Try it out?"

He followed, closing the gap between them. "How else are we to know if the bed is to our liking?"

The look in his eyes made her blush. The heavy weight that had squeezed her chest ever since she followed him inside the townhouse throbbed painfully. "Darcy, why have you brought me here? What is the meaning of this?"

His fingers grazed her cheek. "This is where we can be together. Isn't it perfect?"

"Together?"

"No more brief, unfilling assignations. This is a permanent place for us, a comfortable home for you where you'll want for nothing."

Together. Another painful squeeze of her heart, so hard she could feel heat building behind her eyes. She blinked it away and took a deep breath, tasting the dust on the air. This was exactly what she didn't want.

"What about when you go to Derbyshire? What will you do with me then?"

"Do? You act as if I'll stick you in a closet somewhere."

She gestured to the room around them and a small portion of the acidic burn in her chest escaped in her voice. "Isn't that what this is?"

"You're ridiculous," he said, brushing back her hair. "I have trustworthy people at Pemberley, and most of my affairs can be managed remotely. I might have to return once or twice a year." Darcy dipped his head, warm breath caressing her lips. "I will not linger where you are not, Lizzy."

She closed her eyes. "I can't."

"You can," he said, straightening. "You will. Protection, security… all the dresses and pin money you desire—"

Elizabeth flinched. "Do you think that's all I want?" She stared into his eyes, the face that appeared so often in her dreams, somebody who knew her body better than she did. Did he really think so little of her? After repeatedly telling him she would not suffer this humiliation?

He grabbed her hand and pressed it to his cheek, his eyes closing as if this simple touch was heaven on earth. "I need you, Lizzy. I can admit that much. Why can't you admit that you need me too?"

I thought I did, she thought, snatching her hand away. But how could she need someone who thought of her so shallowly? For a moment she had believed…

I'm so stupid.

Darcy watched her with a growing frown. "What is this? Do you think you'll lack for anything because you are not my wife? I can guarantee you won't."

"You don't have to worry about that. I have no desire to marry you." Someone who thought she only wanted pin money and ribbons. Bitterness flooded her mouth.

"Good," he said, leaning forward.

She placed her hand over his lips. "I don't desire this

either," she said, something in her breaking at his expression. "I-I have to go."

"Lizzy!" He caught her before she could take two steps away. "What is the meaning of this? The house can be changed, whatever renovation you want—"

"I don't want you."

The words hung there between them. Stretched in the silence of their stillness. Her heartbeat thudded in her ears and she wondered how the man in her dreams could be so different from the one who stood before her now, why his smiles only made her sick, why his touch felt suffocating.

Darcy's glare made her feel two inches tall. A muscle in his jaw twitched. "It's Anderson, isn't it? What can he give you that I can't?"

Her eyes burned but her reply was vicious.

"Respect. He can give me respect."

A harsh noise escaped him. "Respect!"

"At least he treats me like a human, not like something disgusting you have to hide away." His eyes widened and the words bubbling in her throat, unable to be contained. "I've never been so insulted in my life."

His laugh scraped like sandpaper over her bruised and battered skin. The grip on her wrist tightened while he stepped forward, looming over her. "Anderson is nothing. He has pretty words, but nothing else. You belong with me, by my side. Why is that an insult?"

She laughed, raw and bitter. "Beside you? Look at where you've brought me, Darcy. You obviously think I'm only good enough to be under you." She ripped her hand out of his and turned away. "Bring me back to Gracechurch Street. Now."

Before I do something I regret.

She swiped at her eyes after Darcy stormed past her, the echo of his boots stomping down the stairs ringing through the empty house. She cast one last disgusted look at the bedroom, at this abandoned, dusty home, and followed, her eyes itching.

12

"Miss Lizzy? Is something the matter?"

Elizabeth jolted. She'd been staring at a knot in the wood on the top of the desk, the rhythmic thumping of the presses sending her into a hypnotic state. She tried on a trembling smile for Miss Brown, who watched from the doorway of Mr. Davies' office. "I'm fine, thank you. Lost in thought over this mess."

Miss Brown leaned against the doorframe. "Hard to untangle the good and the bad?"

Elizabeth looked down at the stack of papers before her, hardly touched. "Is there anything good?" she murmured. *Is there anything worth saving?*

She hadn't known what the totality of ripping her way out of Darcy's life would be. She hadn't known it would feel like the printing press clamping its giant jaws around her and squeezing until she couldn't breathe. The enormity of this emptiness inside her was mind boggling.

Elizabeth's mother wanted her to compromise her values for security, no matter how unhappy it made her. Her father, while sympathetic, didn't even try to stop her mother. The one spot of happiness she had, the one bit of joy, illicit though it was, turned out to be another compromise. Another jail within which she should rot whilst happiness flitted away on the other side of the bars.

Darcy was but another warden, another villain locking her away for her own good.

Elizabeth had no false notions that she would be a good wife, especially not to someone like Darcy. But did he have to humiliate her? With that dark, empty house where she would undoubtedly end up just like it, dusty and forgotten?

The agony inside her wouldn't fade. If only he had not come back into her life, she could've gone on oblivious, but happy. But no, he had to ruin her memories as well, corrode them with this knowledge that she was nothing but a pretty pet to him.

"How do I go on from here?" she asked the page in front of her.

Miss Brown put her hand on her shoulder, surprising Elizabeth, who'd forgotten her presence. She smiled down at Elizabeth, eyes crinkled at the corners as she squeezed Elizabeth's shoulder. "I like to go one page at a time."

Elizabeth conjured a smile. "You're very wise."

Miss Brown stepped away, her farewell of a cheerful sort. "I say nothing can be so terrible it cannot be whipped into shape with my pen, and your pen is even better, Miss Lizzy, so you shouldn't fret."

"If only that were true," Elizabeth muttered, but the younger girl's words had lifted her spirits in some way, and she picked up her pen with a new determination. She would forget Darcy and cease this melancholy. It was enough that she was still free to live life as she chose. No more would she think about meddling family *or* men.

Elizabeth managed to get through approximately a quarter of the manuscript, which wasn't in as bad of shape as she first believed, before Mr. Davies entered in his usual flurry.

"What a wonderful day, isn't it, Miss Lizzy? I'll even forgive you for being late."

"I'm sorry, again," she started, but Mr. Davies held up his hands to forestall her. Mr. Davies looked too mischievous for her to believe all was forgiven.

"Don't you want to know *why* I'm in a forgiving mood?" he asked while he sat, the chair groaning under his large backside.

"I hardly dare to guess."

"You of all people should know. Very well, I shall shelve my disappointment. You know I cannot stand it when you look at me with your brow raised so menacingly. My own solicitor does not look at me so suspiciously. It has to do with this, Miss Lizzy." He tapped the empty corner of his desk, and then looked surprised. "Where the hell is the thing?"

"What thing?" Elizabeth said with a huff of laughter.

"Your book! The very surprise! Don't tell me... ah, here it is." Mr. Davies plucked a manuscript from the untidy pile and held it up. Elizabeth recognized her tidy print on the front page. "With a few words from me, we've had a clamor for your book. I marked natural stopping points for a set of three books to be created from this single tome, and Mr. Anderson said we'll have it at the front of the queue as soon as you approve it."

Elizabeth felt like she'd been dropped off a cliff and hadn't seen the bottom yet.

"Mr. Davies! Is this true? With a few words—you must be teasing me."

Mr. Davies leaned back with a look of supreme pleasure. "I assure you it is very much true."

Her mouth opened and closed. She felt very much like a fish plucked from the fishing net and thrown back into the cold sea. Instant shock, trying hard to gulp down sweet air—and overwhelming, impossible joy.

Mr. Davies' lips curled up. "I believe I've made you speechless."

She put her hand on her stomach, still in freefall from this news. "Mr. Davies, if you are playing a prank upon me—"

"How horrible do you believe I am?"

"Very horrible if this is a joke."

"Then you'll be happy to hear I am not such an evildoer. I don't have a prankster bone in my body, to tell you the truth. Your book shall be published as soon as this week for an initial run of one hundred copies."

One hundred copies! She could hardly believe her ears. For an unknown author to receive an initial run of one hundred copies was unheard of outside of financial backing, but Mr. Davies merely smiled at her astounded, open-mouthed stare.

"But the merits—"

"It is your book, Miss Lizzy. You should know already how it compares to the drivel found in the slush. Your book overshadows them all!"

"Now I really think you are teasing me," she said.

He pulled out a stack of papers and tapped the front page. "I have a contract here that says I am not. I'll be trying to swindle you, actually. What do you say, then? Are you ready to draw up your contract?"

"Yes!" she exclaimed, making the gentleman chuckle.

"Very well then, pull up your chair. We shall go over the

contract details and you can browbeat me into something equitable."

Elizabeth's mood was radically transformed by the time she left work that afternoon. The contract was rolled up and ready for her uncle's review and her head was filled with what she would write to her father and Jane that night.

However, her good mood was interrupted whenever she pushed through the doors of the publishing house and found herself running smack dab into another person.

"Mr. Anderson!"

"What a way to crash into one another," Mr. Anderson said as she jumped backwards. He looked as elegant as ever except for the now crushed bouquet of flowers he carried.

"Oh, your poor bouquet! I'm ever so sorry—"

"It's nothing, I hope. I should've bought one that could withstand young authors." He beamed at her as he held it out. "For your success, Miss Lizzy."

"You are too kind," she said, accepting them. "Thank you for the opportunity—"

"There're no thanks needed on my part. I have the feeling you'll be making me quite popular in the salons and libraries in the near future."

"I'm sure you say the same to all the authors signed with you, but it makes me no less pleased to hear it."

"I can assure you that you are the very first I've brought flowers to, at least," he said, making her smile grow. "I actually came to see if I could walk you home? Your uncle may have questions about the contract, and I thought I'd address any concerns he has before we broker the deal."

"That's very generous of you."

He held out his arm to her. "Then shall we?"

She tucked her arm through his and they set off, a merry couple. Even the streets seemed cleaner and prettier than they usually did. The smile on her face wouldn't leave soon.

"I was in a very sour mood this morning, but this has completely turned me around."

"A sour mood? Who would dare put you through such a thing?"

"My own follies, I'm afraid." She waved away the thought with the bouquet, smiling at the flowers as the petals shivered in the wind. "Nevermind that, though. I feel on top of the world now."

"And there you shall remain," he said. "Now when can I start pestering you to see what else you've created?"

"A week," she said, grinning.

"I'll put a note in my diary directly."

Mr. Laurence's attitude changed drastically the next time Elizabeth came into his office holding a more substantial sum than her previous deposits.

"I've been offered an advance on sales for a book I sold to Mr. Anderson's publishing house."

"I thought you were merely employed there," the solicitor said, peering over his spectacles with the soft wrinkles around his lips conveying his admonishment. "I would expect to see such a contract before it's signed, as your family's solicitor."

"My uncle found the terms fair," she said. Besides, as Mr. Gardiner told her while they went over the contract, the important thing was to ensure they had enough room to ask for more in the future, and the contract only applied to the one book—or serial, as it was now called.

Mr. Laurence didn't seem assured. "Very well," he said as if withholding dire warnings. His wrinkled face lightened as he turned to other matters. "I do, in fact, have a favorable report for your father—as well as this for you." From his desk, he retrieved an envelope and handed it over. Her father's handwriting. Her hands shook as she took it.

"So what is the news of the entail?"

"The best hope is that your sister will produce a son who will then become heir of Longbourn with your father's blessing," he said. "The second hope is that we can entreat the courts to keep the home in the direct line with an investment from Mr. Bingley, if he is willing to purchase the inheritance from Mr. Collins, but that will take an agreement by the courts. I am waiting on a reply from your father and Mr. Bingley before proceeding further, but I have made discreet inquiries into similar situations and found there is sufficient case law to support either action."

"That does seem promising, thank you." She had little hope that Mr. Collins would be willing to agree to the proposal. He'd taken far too much pleasure practically counting the teacups and spoons and finding himself 'very satisfied' by what he found, to her mother's horror.

"With this, I'll be able to continue researching the best path forward. Again, Miss Bennet, I commend you on your efforts on behalf of your family. It is not often I see a young woman spend her pin money—and more—on such an endeavor."

"I'm only doing what I should to repay my family."

Repaying her mother for turning down the foul Mr. Collins. Repaying her father for abandoning him when he was sick during what may even be his final months. It was not enough, but it was all Elizabeth could do.

With her changed fortunes, modest though it was, Elizabeth even found it within her heart to attend the book club hosted by Georgianna Darcy. As expected, Darcy did not show his face, even in passing—a woman's book club was far too frivolous for the straight-laced gentleman—and Elizabeth and Mrs. Gardiner left the townhome with new friends and acquaintances.

"I believe Miss Darcy seemed a little wistful that her brother could not visit," Mrs. Gardiner said on the ride back to Cheapside.

"I was glad myself," Elizabeth replied, looking out the window.

"Really? I thought you liked the gentleman."

"He is my brother-in-law's close friend, and that is the breadth of our relationship. Though who knows for how long that will last," she added darkly. "Mr. Darcy has a talent for alienating the people around him."

Mrs. Gardiner tugged her gloves off and gave Elizabeth a wry look. "Careful or you may sound bitter."

"Perhaps I am," she muttered.

"What was that?"

"Nothing." Elizabeth tucked a stray hair behind her ear and looked out the window, hiding away her discontent behind a placid expression. No matter what, she wouldn't let her bad memories color her mood. Life was changing for the better—thinking of Darcy only made her heart pound for all the wrong reasons.

To think how I almost made a fool of myself by wishing for something more—

Elizabeth closed her eyes, glad her aunt could not read the mournful thoughts spinning across her mind. She resolved to lock the thoughts away somewhere dark and out of the way. Only a masochist dwelled on things like this, and she had far better things to think of than Fitzwilliam Darcy.

Mrs. Gardiner was still thinking about the young Miss Darcy. "I hope he can make time for his sister in the future. Once a young lady experiences her debut, a brother is the most important friend a young lady can have. Especially in the Darcy family's case. I believe they lost both their parents when Miss Darcy was rather young, and her brother has been responsible for her ever since. A bond closer than most siblings would be bound to form in that sort of situation."

"Hm."

Elizabeth thought back to the few times he had mentioned his sister, namely in response to Miss Bingley's direct questions about the girl. He answered in his close, guarded way, but that didn't mean he loved her any less, it was simply his nature to put up walls around people like Miss Bingley. The memories of Georgianna's debut only reinforced her opinion that Darcy cared dearly for his younger sister, and vice versa. Their interactions together were sprinkled with fondness, and Georgianna's questions for Elizabeth contained an air of sisterly concern.

Her lips twisted. Darcy would never let his sister entertain the kind of offer he'd made to Elizabeth. No, he would destroy the man that would dare, which only showed how poorly he thought of Elizabeth. Elizabeth, a woman with little prospects, was but a bothersome wart to hide, not a jewel to be shown off.

I am worthless to him.

She wished she could dig her fingertips into her head and rip these thoughts out of her mind like the invasive vines they were. The only thing she had done wrong was allow herself to pretend he had deeper feelings for her than he did. She should've trusted the evidence, not her foolish heart, and the evidence frankly showed that there were very few people who could ever love someone like Elizabeth.

"Lizzy?"

Elizabeth pulled herself out of her thoughts and found Mrs. Gardiner smiling faintly. She gestured to the door which was open, one of the Gardiner's servants waiting beyond it for them. "You must be tired, my dear. You didn't seem to notice we arrived. Go ahead and descend first."

Her face warmed. "Oh, um, thank you."

It was only another reason she shouldn't let Darcy occupy her thoughts.

Mr. Anderson caught them the next week while Elizabeth and her aunt enjoyed some quiet time in the sitting room. Mrs. Gardiner read while Elizabeth, who surprisingly didn't want to read on her day off, had started on a handkerchief for her uncle. But their companionable silence was broken when a servant announced Mr. Anderson.

Mrs. Gardiner took one look at Mr. Anderson and smiled.

"You must be here to discuss business, Mr. Anderson. I recognize your expression as one my husband commonly wears."

"You've caught me," Anderson replied, making Mrs. Gardiner laugh while he settled on the sofa next to Elizabeth. "There are a few ways to spread word of mouth before the release and I'd like to discuss them with Miss Lizzy, if you don't mind the interruption."

"Not at all." Mrs. Gardiner glanced at the clock on the

mantlepiece. "I do need to check on dinner, actually. Do you mind, Lizzy? I'll send tea in while I'm at it."

Mr. Anderson waved that away. "You don't need to trouble yourself on my account."

"If you're sure?" Mrs. Gardiner asked.

"I'm already interrupting your afternoon together, so I wouldn't go so far as to be impolite and request tea."

"Very well, but it's no trouble."

"We'll talk in here, then," Elizabeth said agreeably.

Mr. Anderson dove into the matter before Mrs. Gardiner reached the doorway. With a smile at Elizabeth, Mrs. Gardiner left them to it.

Elizabeth was accustomed to working on the product itself, not the actual sales and marketing that occurred for the books that passed through the publishing house. Now she realized that sales did not simply come because one printed the books. You had to make an effort to put them in a reader's hands. Anderson led her through a dizzying array of marketing ideas that he claimed were opportunities, including book clubs and even small advertisements in the paper. Elizabeth strove to pay attention, but her efforts were stymied by Anderson's clear enthusiasm for the project which resulted in him speaking as quickly as a runaway carriage.

Finally, Elizabeth raised her hand to stop him in the flow of his newest opportunity:

"Mr. Anderson, I'm afraid I don't understand. I don't even know Mrs. Dankworth well, but she's hosting a party in my honor?"

Anderson beamed. "Isn't it ideal? Your accomplishment is the talk of the town."

"It's been a week since our contract! How many people have you told?"

"All of them," he said and grinned when Elizabeth

laughed. He took her hands and squeezed, his earnest expression tickling her heart strings. "Please consider it for the sake of sales, if nothing else. Mrs. Dankworth's parties are well known. We'll provide a few advance copies bound in pretty leather to let the ladies feel all the more important."

"Oh, you shouldn't," she said. The bindings would cost a significant amount since they were more difficult to fashion.

Anderson's thumb swept over her knuckles, reminding her they were still holding hands. Blue eyes searched her face, his expression softening. "A woman deserves to be doted on as if she is the most important person in the world, isn't that right?"

The most important woman in the world…

Do you think you'll lack for anything because you are not my wife? I can guarantee you won't.

Elizabeth demurred, muttering something satisfactory in response while she pulled her hands away from Anderson. This was a dangerous path to walk, and she needed to keep her eyes open if she insisted on putting a foot down on the path. Letting the ghost of Darcy distract her wouldn't help matters.

She looked down at her lap. "Mr. Anderson?"

"Yes, Miss Lizzy?"

"The merits of the book mattered the most to you, right?"

"I'm sorry?"

Forcing herself to look up, she flinched away from his forthright, shining gaze. Her tongue was thick and fumbled under her control. "The reason you offered for it was the merits of the book, isn't that right?"

Please, please, be true, she thought, searching his face. *Please don't make me a fool twice over.*

"Thankfully, personal and business interests aligned this

time, Miss Lizzy. I cannot say that will always be the case." His smile was a little forced. "Don't tell me you thought I was humoring you?"

His dark blond hair, naturally curled and grazing the edge of his collar, made her itch to muss it even further. And a gentleman, too, one who would never ask her to join his bed before marriage.

One who would never offer for her to become his mistress and expect her to be *grateful*.

He is everything light in ways Darcy cannot be. How can the two compare?

"It came to mind," she said and scrubbed her hands over her cheeks. "Please ignore me."

"I couldn't do that," he said with a gentle smile. "But I'll forgive you as long as you agree to come to Mrs. Dankworth's party and distribute gifts to all the ladies."

Her lips pulled into a smile. "Somehow I feel you could talk me into anything."

He put his hand to his heart. "I shall swear to use this newfound power for good."

Was this how it felt to be swept away? Mr. Anderson had thrown Elizabeth into the river and now she was tossed from current to current at the whims of society. Yet, beyond her apprehension was a seed of happiness, faint and fragile. A dream she never imagined could be realized was actually coming true.

Her aunt returned then, having provided them plenty of private discussion, and she watched them lean away from one another with a fond expression that piqued Elizabeth's curiosity.

"Do you trust me that much?" Elizabeth asked later after Mr. Anderson gave his goodbyes and they sat for a late tea, probing at the subject like one might an untidy but difficult knot.

"What do you mean, dear? I trust you very much."

Elizabeth struggled to piece together her thoughts while Mrs. Gardiner watched quizzically over her teacup. Memories of Darcy's persistence and her mother's neglect tangled in her mind. She had managed not to ruin herself or the Bennet family, but it was only coincidence. Tarnishing their reputation irreparably would take one misstep and Elizabeth had walked the tightrope with both her eyes covered. And so recently she'd been willing to step back onto that tightrope, drawn by immoral desires and a delusion of—

She shuddered. No. Better not to dwell.

Mrs. Gardiner leaned forward and put her hand over Elizabeth's. "Is something on your mind?"

"No," she said, forcing her lips into a smile. "It might be nerves. I think I'll go take a nap."

Her aunt offered a smile. "Get some rest. I'll tell your uncle about the party. I'm sure he'll be excited. A party in honor of our niece! Be sure to write to Jane about this."

"I will." Elizabeth stood and walked to the doorway.

"Oh! I forgot to tell you. Miss Darcy is hosting a dinner next week and invited us. We're becoming very popular—"

Elizabeth froze in the doorway, her aunt's chatter washing over her. Her stomach dropped to the floor and then further. A dinner at the Darcy's.

"Very well, I look forward to it," she said, the words coming from somewhere far away. One dinner. It would be fine, right?

"WHAT DO YOU WANT?"

Darcy stood before her in the dark room. His lips moved, but the words came late to her ears and muffled, as if her ears were muffled by cotton.

"What do you want?"

Want? What did she want? Her heartbeat thundered in her chest, her limbs trembled under his dark stare. This feeling in her, like someone was pouring sand down her throat, strangled her. What did she want?

Darcy swooped down and picked her up, broad shoulders flexing under her hands as she embraced him. Time slowed, moved, drifted in a gentle wind. The sheets were warmed by the sunlight now arching over them and so were his eyes when he looked down at her, laid out on the bed underneath him.

He traced his knuckles over her cheek and her eyes fluttered. "You look more beautiful here than in my dreams. How is that, Lizzy?"

Something in his eyes made it impossible to look away from him. Despite her reluctance, despite knowing this is the wrong thing to do, she arched into his touch and let him undress her, stroking each bit of skin he revealed. Gentle, sweet, his loving gaze devoted solely to her while his hands drew forth sighs from her mouth. It was insanity, but a blissful one when they were both bare, the sheets tangled under them as Darcy's thigh pressed between her legs. She was wet, slick with longing, eager when he slid his cock against her.

He braced himself above Elizabeth. His eyes remained two dark, waiting holes. The devotion faded, light faded. Emptiness. "What do you want?"

"I want—"

Elizabeth woke with a cry. Her room was dark and her gasps filled the empty bedroom. She sat up, burying her face in her knees, wrapping her arms tightly against her. The air from her open window was chilly, kissing away the sweat clinging to her bare arms.

That was… She tried to calm herself down. It was only a dream. "It didn't mean anything," she muttered.

Her body said otherwise. It ached not from exercise, but from want. His touch lingered, his caresses, his kisses. The awful truth made her shudder.

Darcy had branded her and there would be no escape.

"This isn't fair! Why must I suffer like this when he-he—"

She slumped back to her pillows and stared at the dark canopy overhead.

What did she want?

"I'll leave," she whispered. "I'll leave and never, *ever*, see him again."

She didn't sleep anymore that night, afraid the Darcy in her dreams had heard her and would stop her somehow. Trap her in an embrace she couldn't escape as soon as she closed her eyes.

One thing was clear: Darcy was haunting her.

13

The Darcy townhome was once again lit up and visible from down the street. Happily, however, there lacked a crush of visitors on their way inside, though it was still a more sizeable dinner party than anyone would plan in Hertfordshire. Elizabeth estimated at least twenty families were in attendance, including the Gardiners and Elizabeth.

Mr. Gardiner pulled at the edges of his jacket when their hired coach stopped before the gates. "I'm overjoyed I could attend tonight."

"Especially when Miss Darcy's invitation asked so prettily that you did so," Mrs. Gardiner said. "She seems really keen on becoming friends with our Lizzy."

Elizabeth was thankful for the servant stepping up to help them out then, knowing her aunt's sly glance meant matchmaking was in her thoughts. She had no wish for her aunt to know that attracting Darcy's attention was the last thing on her mind. She quickly took the servant's hand and left the carriage.

Once on the ground, she waited while her aunt and

uncle descended, the tidy garden holding her attention. Sounds of chatter and the tinkle of someone playing the piano drifted out the townhome's open door.

Darcy waited alongside his sister inside the open doors.

"Mr. Gardiner. I'm happy to see you here tonight along with your esteemed wife and niece." He bowed and Elizabeth used the moment of their introductions to gird herself. Darcy looked uncommonly attractive in his blue coat and silver adornments. With his sister next to him in a matching pale blue dress, they looked like angels descended to Earth for this meager gathering.

Elizabeth's fingers trembled around her fan as his dark eyes fell upon her like a two ton weight. "Miss Bennet. My sister tells me you deserve congratulations for your accomplishment. I understand Mr. Anderson is publishing a book you authored."

"Yes, I've been honored by his support," she said. What did he mean by that little smirk? Was he mocking her? Implying she was selling herself to him for a bit of fame?

His eyes crinkled at the corners. "Then congratulations, Miss Bennet. You two must be very happy for your niece," he said, smoothly turning to Mr. and Mrs. Gardiner.

"We're very proud and happy," Mrs. Gardiner said, pleasure rolling off her in waves. "Elizabeth is finally receiving the recognition she deserves after so long working toward it."

"I didn't realize you were so prodigious," Darcy said, tapping his lips while she flushed when his hooded gaze turned to her. "Of course, I did find you searching the library one time at Netherfield, so I should have guessed."

I was your pet, so why would you learn anything about me? The words burned on her tongue, and she turned to her aunt and uncle before she could say something she regretted. "We shouldn't hold up the line anymore."

"Of course, we can converse more later," Mr. Darcy said, infuriating her plan to ignore him.

"Please make yourself comfortable in the sitting room," Miss Darcy said, her smile as radiant as ever.

That hadn't been terrible, Elizabeth thought while she followed her aunt and uncle away into the sitting room. She'd be very pleased with the night if that was the extent of her interaction with Darcy.

They had left on such bad terms that she had never expected they would meet again. After she denied Darcy treating her like his pet dolly, he shouldn't want to see her again—or at least that was what she thought. So the invitation was confusing, as was Darcy's greeting.

She shook away the confusion. No, it must have been Georgianna's idea to invite her and the Gardiners. The greeting was unusual, but it wasn't as if Darcy couldn't play a role for one brief interaction. He would still resent her for throwing his gift—she sneered internally—back in his face.

Elizabeth accepted a glass of champagne and stole a sip of it as she stepped into the sitting room. Chairs and couches had been arranged for maximum conversation, the pocket doors pulled open so guests could flow from the sitting room into the next room where someone played a lively song on the piano. Elizabeth, who did not recognize a single face, smiled blandly when people glanced her way, her attention so wholly centered on leaving as soon as possible that the air around her did not invite conversation.

"There you are, Lizzy. Why, you looked very forbidding when I approached, I almost didn't recognize you." Mrs. Gardiner stood at her side and sipped on a small glass of sherry while she took in the room. "Your uncle is in his element, of course."

"I see that. His conversational skills rival the greatest host in the country."

"We should start holding more parties," Mrs. Gardiner said, watching her husband mingle thoughtfully. "It would be beneficial for the business, certainly. If only it wasn't such a bother!"

"If my uncle doesn't push for it, then I wouldn't concern yourself. Perhaps he enjoys these parties so much because he doesn't have to endure the pain of preparation."

"Or the cost," Mrs. Gardiner said, and they broke out into giggles. Mr. Gardiner, who by no means was a miser, detested excess and extravagance. It was one reason why he did not get along well with his younger sister.

Miss Darcy approached in a flurry of blue like a fairy descending from her perch in a garden. "I was ever so excited to receive your book from Mr. Anderson. I hope it wouldn't be a bother if you signed my copy?"

Elizabeth softened at the woman. She truly was an angel—why did she have such an awful brother? "Of course, I'd be happy to."

Miss Darcy glowed. "Perhaps we can even read your book at the next bookclub! You'll come, of course? To hear the author's own thoughts would be wonderful."

Mrs. Gardiner took the glass of sherry a nearby servant offered. "In a few weeks, you won't be here, so it's better to visit while you can, Lizzy."

Miss Darcy turned to Elizabeth, her eyebrows drawing down and her lips parting. "You're leaving London, Miss Bennet?"

"I'm going to visit my sister and family," she said. "It's been some time."

Miss Darcy's disappointment was palpable, but she still

managed to look happy for Elizabeth. "Oh, that's nice. I suppose they've missed you."

"I know I've missed them terribly," Elizabeth said. Whether her family missed her was another matter. At least she could count on Jane's support.

No, there were two people she could count on, she thought, her mind turning to the letter sitting inside her desk at the Gardiner's house. And maybe with her newfound success, though still in its infancy, she might win some love from her mother, too.

AFTER DRINKS AND DINNER, the games began in earnest with card games, dancing, and smoking rooms enjoyed by the party. The hostess led the games with gentle earnestness which endeared her to everyone, and Elizabeth was thoroughly smitten by the younger woman's grace and manners. However, she was in no mood for games, and she joined a small group departing the sitting room for a tour of the Darcy's art collection. The gallery was located at the rear of the townhome and Darcy led them through it, his manners surprisingly cordial as he explained the works and their artists.

Elizabeth stayed at the back of the group, as far away from the gentleman as she could be, and turned to leave as soon as Darcy gave the guests leave to peruse the gallery as they liked. She was nearly successful, too, until she felt a hand on her elbow.

She spun around and met Darcy's burning gaze.

"I thought we might speak privately for a moment."

She pulled her arm out of his grip. "Mr. Darcy, that's not—"

"Merely to say our goodbyes, Miss Elizabeth. That is all. Don't we owe ourselves that much?"

Elizabeth sighed. A glance around the hall showed there were only a few people left after viewing the gallery. Her aunt and uncle weren't in sight either. They could easily sneak out with no one the wiser.

She nodded to Darcy and he led her down the hall, back toward the front of the townhome, before stopping by a door tucked by the stairs. A servant was stationed by the door and Darcy nodded to him.

"Make sure we aren't bothered."

The servant held Darcy's gaze. "Yes, sir."

That eased her nerves too, and she quickly followed Darcy into his study. He closed the door behind them while she moved further into the room, her attention drawn to the shelves lining the walls, filled from floor to ceiling with books. A thick rug stretched across the room, protecting the wood flooring and softening the masculinity of the dark wood desk and chairs by the fireplace. In the middle of the room, two wingback chairs provided either a comfortable place for conversation or for reading. Elizabeth could easily imagine Darcy opening the window and letting the air in while he read one of these weighty tomes on agriculture or economics.

"Lizzy."

His voice was closer than she expected, nearly right behind her, and she tensed.

14

"Lizzy."

She turned. Already her skin buzzed with his nearness. A traitor to her heart, it yearned to erase the distance between them, meld herself to him lean, strong body.

What a ridiculous idea.

"We shouldn't linger. Whatever you desire to say, please do so quickly."

"You're right," Darcy said, reaching out. His hand paused before he touched her arm and then he dropped it back to his side. "I apologize. I thought of what you said and... I've come to realize my failings."

The shutters on his eyes were open for once, shining light on the pain in his eyes.

"Your failings?" She couldn't imagine Darcy pondering such a thing, not with how proud and aloof he was, how confident he was in his righteousness. Elizabeth could not get over how vulnerable he seemed in this moment. Surely it was a lie?

Her doubt must've come out in her voice because

Darcy's stiff posture sagged. "Yes, my failings, of which there are many. Truthfully, they have been there from the beginning of our relationship. The fool that I am, I didn't take this—you, us—as something significant. And now it is too late. You're returning to Hertfordshire, aren't you?"

Elizabeth couldn't fathom what she was hearing. Shaking herself free of confusion, she focused on the only thing that made sense. "How did you… your sister?"

He shook his head with a bitter smile. "Even in a crowded room, you draw my attention."

"Well." She cleared her throat, not knowing how to respond to that confession. "I'm returning in a few weeks."

"For good?"

"I don't believe so. My father's illness is not progressing, but there's little hope of improvement either. I hope to see him and restore the bonds with my family."

"You don't sound certain of your return."

"Perhaps my mother will want me home again," she said, tucking away the pain of the words and forcing a bittersweet smile. "I've at least made headways with my reputation, so I won't lower my face in front of them."

"You've nothing to be ashamed of."

"I have plenty—" He cut off her denial when he placed his hand on her cheek.

"There is no shame between us," he said. "I won't allow it. Our start may not have been perfect in society's eyes, but it was honest to who we are."

Elizabeth gripped his wrist and drew it away from her cheek. The intimacy of it, no matter how much her skin warmed at his touch, couldn't be acceptable going forward.

"We've hardly acted respectably," she said.

"Which doesn't mean I've ever disrespected you. Not consciously, at least."

She stared up at him. His eyes made her recall her recent dream, his dark gaze capturing a tenderness that made him seem unreal, like they were back in that dreamworld with a question hanging between them.

What do you want?

She forced her face away. "It's not as if that matters now, Mr. Darcy. This time, we will truly be only acquaintances going forward."

"We cannot even be friends?"

"No—at least not yet."

"Even if I'm ready to give you what you want?"

Her lungs squeezed. *What do I want?*

She had no time to move away when he clasped her hands between his larger ones. His expression was plaintive, open and bared, and once she saw him, it was impossible to look away.

"I understand now," he said, squeezing her hands. "I understand how a proud woman like you would read my intentions wrong. To you, what I did was an insult, but I never intended that. My motivation has never been to cause you pain, yet that's what happened." His released her only to slide his hand over her cheek, settling with his thumb on her lip, his touch gentle and his gaze tender. "I hurt you, Lizzy, but you shouldn't run away."

She couldn't look away from the man before her. A man stripping his soul open for her viewing pleasure. So proud and noble, baring himself before her with honesty almost brutal to watch.

"Darcy," she began.

His hand dropped to her shoulder. "I'm going to do something foul."

"What do you mean?"

Darcy searched her eyes, and she found herself looking at a stranger. "You'll forgive me, won't you?"

"That depends," she said, a tiny smile drawn out of her. He seemed so serious even though he made no sense. Her smile fell away when his dark gaze remained troubled, the shadows of the room casting his expression in harsh lines.

"You'll forgive me," he repeated, almost to himself. "After all, you must…"

She tried to back away and hit the bookshelf. "What—?"

The door opened. "Mr. Darcy, are you in here?"

Her aunt's nervous voice drifted in. "I'm not sure he is…"

Cold froze her insides. Her aunt and uncle. Her relations were at the door and Darcy grabbed Elizabeth, wrapping his arm around her back and dragging her into an embrace. Elizabeth felt nothing of his lips on hers. Heard nothing over the buzzing in her ears… except for muffled footsteps drawing to a stop.

Saw only Darcy's eyes, open, shuttered. Empty of devotion, but victorious.

Victorious because he finally had bested her.

Bound her.

BOUND BY DARCY
BOOK THREE

I

A WAVE OF FEAR OVERTOOK ELIZABETH. SHE SAW THE SHOCK and anger on the faces of her aunt and uncle. Time seemed to pause as the air thickened, charged with the tension that rolled off them in waves. And then, it happened—her aunt's sharp, "Lizzy!" sliced through the air like a blade, and Elizabeth realized she had no chance of escaping unscathed from their seething rage. She closed her eyes and braced for their wrath.

Instead, Darcy released Elizabeth and faced her aunt and uncle with a smile worthy of the stage. "It was presumptuous of me, but I couldn't restrain my joy. Elizabeth—Miss Bennet agreed to become my wife." His smile grew when he looked at Elizabeth, frozen to the spot. "I am the happiest man alive."

Mrs. Gardiner gasped in surprise, her eyes widening with joy as she looked back and forth between the two of them. "Really, Lizzy? Is it true?"

Elizabeth couldn't form a word. No one would expect this reputable, wealthy man who moved along with the best of men to lie with a mouth full of spun sugar. Affection filled his eyes as he looked at his supposed fiancé. The Gardiners exclaimed in delight, with Mrs. Gardiner even shedding tears of joy and Mr. Gardiner offering his congratulations. While they were properly conservative, a kiss between an engaged couple was still deemed pure in their estimation.

Mr. Gardiner tugged at the lapels of his jacket, harrumphing while as his cheeks reddened with the pleasure of an excellent match for his niece. With a playful shake of his finger, he said, "I will overlook this out of love for my niece, but I won't be so kind in the future."

"Of course. I apologize for any slight to yourself or your niece," Darcy said with a low bow. Mr. Gardiner's pride at being treated to such respect by a man as esteemed as Darcy made his entire face light up. Darcy rose. "It will not happen again. Might we all enjoy a celebratory drink in honor of this moment?"

"Should we invite your sister?" Mrs. Gardiner asked.

"I'll go request her presence," Darcy said with a fond look at Elizabeth.

Their discussion, the clatter of glasses, the door opening. More exclamations, congratulations, and loud chatter. The wash of it was like a buzzing noise in her brain. Everything was all so… very… far away.

"I never even suspected," Mrs. Gardiner whispered, tweaking her elbow. Elizabeth responded with a shaky smile, finding a small glass clutched in her hands. The burn of alcohol singed her nose.

How did it come to be there? How was she here?

Was it too late to change the course of this awful night?

She met Darcy's eyes over the rim of his glass of port. *You'll forgive me,* he said.

Elizabeth turned away.

"Is there some reason you won't look at me?"

She wouldn't look at him? *After the farce which had just taken place, that* was what he was concerned about? She glanced toward the door, their relatives having left briefly. Mr. Gardiner wanted to call their carriage after the satisfactory night. Mrs. Gardiner had asked Georgiana to borrow a novel and left with her, giving Elizabeth a wink. Furious, she spat out, "Pray tell, does it offend you?"

"A little," he said, his glass clinking against the top of his desk when he set it down. "We only have a moment before your relatives return. Won't you speak civilly to me?"

She turned to the door. "I don't have anything to say."

"I find that hard to believe from you."

She paused, her hand landing on the cold metal doorknob. "You don't understand me at all."

And then she walked away, her footsteps being muffled by the silence in the room, leaving behind the man who had betrayed her.

2
SOME TIME BEFORE...

The name his steward announced to him jolted Darcy out of the world of Pemberley as seen through its ledgers and into London again. "Who did you say had arrived?"

"It's Mr. Anderson," the steward answered. "He's come to visit the young miss."

What did he want with Darcy's sister?

Darcy's eyes narrowed. "Bring him here first, please."

The steward bowed and retreated. Darcy drummed his fingers on the desk, glancing at the clock on the mantle, wondering about this social visit from an acquaintance his sister had little in common with. It was good Georgiana was engaged with her music practice, so if Anderson proved to be a nuisance, he could turn him away.

However, the likelihood of him turning away the gentleman expanded as he called up his recent disappointment with Elizabeth, and how he attributed most of it to the flatteries of this false gentleman. A gentleman who would put his wife to work was no gentleman in Darcy's view. He only wished she were here now.

See, Elizabeth—while he charms you, he preys on my little sister. Who is the better man again?

The steward returned shortly, and Darcy schooled his bitter expression while the guest was shown inside his study.

Mr. Anderson greeted him with a smile. "I didn't realize you were here. Your servant initially claimed you were out."

"When I learned it was you, I was curious." Darcy gestured to the chair across from his desk. He did not reveal why he was turning away all guests, and Mr. Anderson was discreet enough not to enquire as he sat down. The chair groaned under Darcy's back when he leaned back, clasping his hands in front of him while he looked at the man who desired to be his rival. "What brings you here today?"

Mr. Anderson held up a package. "My newest acquisition. It is fresh from the binders, and I believed your sister would be interested, so I brought it as a gift. I'm gifting several more to other ladies of my acquaintance this week."

"So you propose to make my sister part of your marketing scheme?"

Barking a laugh, he responded, "How cruel you are! Miss Darcy expressed an interest in the happenings of my humble business, so I thought to myself, 'who better to gift a new volume?'"

"Well, there is no doubt that she loves books," Darcy said begrudgingly. He couldn't fault the logic, and his experience of Anderson told him he was an honorable gentleman, so he didn't see any reason to make a spectacle of the man. "Who is the author?"

Mr. Anderson's flinch was small, but Darcy was not fooled.

"Miss Bennet, actually. She inked a contract for three volumes and, based on our initial assessment, I can see us doing business together for a long time."

"That is…" Unexpected. Shocking. "Good news," he finished softly. He studied the book in Anderson's hand and abruptly decided. "My sister doesn't like her music practice to be disturbed. I will give her the book and your regards, Mr. Anderson."

Darcy waited until he heard the front door shut behind Anderson before he picked up the package left on his desk. Feeling a pinprick of something like guilt, because he had not been truly aware of Elizabeth's devotion to the written word, he opened the package and ran his finger over the cover.

He did not mean to read it, initially, but he found himself looking up sometime later when the door to his study opened. Darcy blinked, realizing the room had grown dark with the passing of the day.

Georgiana stood before his desk with a quizzical expression. "Are you coming to dinner, Fitzwilliam?"

A glance at his clock showed him it was half-past five, when they usually had dinner. They were both of the mind it was better to wake early, so they arranged dinners for earlier in the evening.

"Yes, I apologize. I hope you did not wait for me long."

"It's so unusual for you to be late, so I stepped out after only a few minutes." Georgiana rounded his desk with the ease of being his favored, beloved sister and tilted her head at the book in his lap. "What are you reading?"

"It is Elizabeth—that is, Miss Elizabeth Bennet's novel."

Georgiana's eyes rounded in surprise. "She wrote a novel? How exciting! And it has kept you here past the dinner hour, therefore it must be good."

"It's quite entertaining," he agreed.

Georgiana studied the book with increased interest, blue

eyes gleaming. "She's had it professionally bound, too. What a magnificent gift she's given you."

He winced. "Actually, Mr. Anderson dropped off the book for you; he's recently signed Miss Bennet to his publishing house as an author. Knowing you are friends, he wished to give you the gift—and I rudely intercepted it. Forgive me."

She laughed lightly. "As long as you let me read it after you finish it, you are forgiven." She eyed him as he pressed a bookmark into the pages and closed the book. "So it is merely entertaining?" she prodded.

"Read it yourself. I do not wish to spoil you."

"How unlike you," she said. "You usually give me a hint of your feelings on the author's description of people or upon the plots or the language. Do you not have anything to say?"

"I have much to say. In fact, it is unique to Miss Bennet. You will understand once you read it."

"My curiosity knows no bounds!"

Darcy finished the book directly after dinner and passed it to his sister without a word in the drawing room afterward. She immediately opened it and he settled into the comfortable, quiet atmosphere with his drink of choice and pondered how foolish he had been.

At its heart, Elizabeth's novel was about love. Love between two people who, for various reasons, had determined that they were not fit to receive or give love. The brilliance of her characters, their illogical reasonings, and their support of their choices were described in an intelligent, diverting manner so each character was both charming and refreshing. There were fools within the novel, and they were foolish indeed with their attitudes and boorish manners, not recognizing the effect their uncouth actions had on the people around them.

She painted broad strokes of the countryside, town, and even of the seaside in such a way that the reader's mind could draw up the portrait she painted.

He laughed with the characters and at them, in turn. He cringed at their missteps and the consequences of their actions. Finally he rejoiced with the progress, though no consummation yet, of the main characters' love.

She had so expertly weaved together her story and characters that by the time he put down the book, he was already fraught with anticipation of how their story would continue in the next. How would they overcome the obstacles in their way to recognize they were meant to be together?

As he read on and on, he could almost imagine Elizabeth sitting beside him, telling him the story herself. With her ingenious turn of phrase, her entertaining characters surely drawn from her life in Hertfordshire—among others, he recognized pompous Sir William Lucas and the ever calm, always smiling Jane Bingley. They were so vivid and written so lovingly, it was impossible to deny Elizabeth had a deep fondness for them.

As well, the themes she weaved in these black and white pages spoke to him, revealing the mysteries of her mind to him in a way conversation likely never could. Her assessments of the *ton* and London were witty and charmingly insulting, but brought to mind a person who thought she could never fit in with the society crowd. The theories of love put forth the idea that it was all or nothing, and only character prevailed, with no middle ground for favorable traits like wealth, station, or reputation.

The opinions that she spoke about love and society brought him back to long before in the autumn, when he had not only obsessed over her body, but her mind and her spirit. Once, he had been attracted not to her pleasing figure alone, but to her turn of speech within a conversation, with her pert, charming responses to provocation and intimidation from Miss Bingley and others, and in her conversational duels with himself.

He had forgotten that, but now it all came together at once. What a fool he was.

How long had he been in love with Elizabeth Bennet?

How long had he been foolishly ignoring his own heart as he stubbornly insisted on a mere physical relationship? Now, through his actions alone, he had ruined every hope of securing her affections. If she ever held an affection for Darcy, surely his own actions had stamped it out like a spark upon the carpet.

"Fitzwilliam? Is everything well?"

Darcy broke from his reverie to see his sister staring at him from her chair. The book in her lap was half finished and the candle beside him was nearly a stub.

"I was in thought," he said, shifting and finding his body stiff with stillness.

"You have a dreary expression," she said. "How can I help you, brother?"

Darcy sighed. He could not deny his sister anything, including a light to his innermost worries. "I've come to realize the error of my ways, my dear sister."

"Is there some way I can help?"

"I fear not. I fear that I have, by my own accord, placed myself in an untenable position. There is no moving forward."

Georgiana closed her book, keeping a finger between the pages to mark her spot. "If it's you, Fitzwilliam, I cannot believe that. I say that not as your sister who loves you in every way, but from an objective standpoint. I've never known you not to overcome every obstacle placed in your path."

"I question your objectivity, then," he said with a small snort. "No, indeed, I have created a hopeless mess that cannot be corrected. There is no overcoming it because I have lost the opportunity to do so."

Georgiana stood and came to his side, placing her hand on his shoulder. It spoke to the hopelessness of his expression and voice that it moved her enough to provide him with physical comfort. "You will think of something. A mess can always be cleaned up with a towel once you roll up your sleeves, as you told me when I was a child."

"Are you telling me I should get a towel?"

"I'm sure you already would've if it were that easy. But you will think of something. You always do."

3

She smoothed her hand over the letter, wrinkled from handling. Tracing her father's neat writing on the outside, she breathed it in. Though it had been away from home for a while, she imagined she could still scent the faint aroma of home: the musty library, the lavender from the garden wafting through the window. If she shut her eyes, she could easily conjure the feeling of being there again, her dad's bony fingers clutching hers, his grumbles about this and that echoing through the air, and sweet music from Mary's piano playing drifting in from another room.

"I miss you," she whispered.

The letter did not contain much. A few lines thanking her for assisting Mr. Laurence, and to send any more letters through the attorney. The final line described his hope that she would come home soon.

He said nothing of her letters home. Pages upon pages she had sent, detailing her days in London, her pride in her work, her homesickness. The fact that he said nothing of her working, not even sardonically, was unusual.

"Lizzy, dear? Mr. Darcy's here to talk about the wedding. Oh, you're writing home?"

"I was about to," she said, pulling down the lid to her writing desk and hiding the mess behind its screen.

"Then you'll have much to tell them. Your mother will be overjoyed by the news. It appears Mr. Darcy's even obtained a special license already—isn't that marvelous? He's certainly well connected."

"I'm not surprised," she muttered, turning away. "I need to brush my hair. Can you entertain him for a few minutes, please?"

"Of course." Footsteps crossed the room and Mrs. Gardiner squeezed Elizabeth's shoulders. "Everything is working in your favour, my sweet Lizzy. Your book, now this. It's like a fairytale, isn't it?"

"A fairytale," she repeated numbly.

Mrs. Gardiner hummed and stepped away. "I'll leave you to it."

Elizabeth reopened the desk when the door closed behind her aunt with a soft click. She pushed away her father's letter, the bound correspondence with Jane, and reached for a small book of poetry she'd slipped near the back. The pages fell open at a touch, the binding old and worn by years of handling.

A small, pressed flower, nearly dried, sat tucked among the pages. It hadn't been so long ago Mr. Anderson had given her the bouquet. She'd clipped one daisy and preserved it, a record of the day she'd achieved her dream. It was still soft under the pad of her finger, wrinkled with age, its floral scent escaping the pages when she opened the book.

Eventually, she set the book aside and closed the desk, locking it away. Then she dried her eyes and went downstairs to greet her fiance.

"You're quiet."

"Hm? Oh, just enjoying the weather."

"You'll have a better view from the townhome," Mrs. Gardiner said. "That lovely little wilderness in the heart of town. You'll have to invite me over for tea often so we can compare."

"Right. Yes, of course."

"Lizzy?" Mrs. Gardiner set her teacup down with a gentle clatter. "Is everything alright? You haven't spoken much since your engagement. Have you changed your mind?"

Yes! Elizabeth wanted to shout. Yes, I've changed my mind. Don't let him take me. Don't let him lock me away—

She swallowed that all down. The shock of her aunt and uncle's faces as Darcy pulled away, his touch still tingling on her lips. The mortification, the distrust growing in their eyes. The breaking of her reputation in front of her beloved aunt and uncle—

Elizabeth closed her eyes. When she opened them, she smiled. "I'm just a little melancholy, I suppose. Everything's changing."

No, this time, she would take responsibility. She wouldn't cause a scene, not with her beloved aunt and uncle, who had opened their arms to her at her lowest point. At least if they thought she was happy, then it could help repay them for their kindness to her. She had not been an obedient daughter, but she *would* be a good niece. She wouldn't embarrass them.

Mrs. Gardiner softened. "I imagine it's all very sudden. I didn't suspect Mr. Darcy would move this quickly either. He must care for you very much."

"Right," she sighed, looking out the window again. Darcy was all smiles in front of her relations, never improper, a perfect fiance who neither over-flattered nor underappreciated her dear aunt and uncle. Mrs. Gardiner was practically smitten; all thoughts of Mr. Anderson had disappeared under this warm charm Darcy conjured for them.

Mrs. Gardiner brought Elizabeth's thoughts back to the moment. "It didn't come as a surprise that Mr. Darcy wanted to keep the wedding ceremony intimate. He is an introvert, and I know you don't care about a big, flashy event. However, there is still time to extend an invitation to your family if you would like. At least Jane should be here."

"No, it's fine. It would be rushed if I did it now, and I'm certain Jane's busy with taking care of father. It would only be a bother."

"It wouldn't be a bother to Jane," Mrs. Gardiner said firmly.

"It's fine as it is," Elizabeth said, heat stinging her eyes. *Let it go*, she pleaded. *Please let it go.*

Mrs. Gardiner's brows furrowed, her hand falling to her lap in an aborted motion, as if she'd wanted to reach out to Elizabeth. "Has something happened between you and Jane? Are you having an argument?"

"No, nothing like that. Jane is as sweet and loving as ever. I just… it's all such a fuss, isn't it?" She sighed and placed her forgotten tea down. "I think I'll go up. Mr. Davies wrote and I need to send a message back about the bookclub meeting."

It was the same week as her wedding, so she would need to cancel her attendance. She would be busy with a fitting that day for a new wardrobe, courtesy of Mr. Gardiner. She couldn't let him down, not when he was so keen to participate in some way towards the union. So far, Darcy had taken over all expenses, including the wedding breakfast, and Mr. Gardiner was itching to contribute in some manner.

"I hope it can be rearranged for a later date," Mrs. Gardiner said. "Get some rest too, Lizzy. Don't overwork yourself."

"I won't," she said, smiling at her aunt's warmth, though it did not touch the cold fist squeezing her heart.

Elizabeth returned to her room and sat at her writing desk. A deep despair settled within her as she realized she was mourning the loss of her freedom while at the same time preparing to marry the most desired man in the country. Each breath she took felt like a broken promise.

A few weeks ago, Elizabeth might have been carried away by the delicious thrill of Darcy's proposal. Her acceptance would bring forth a giddy, girlish laugh and a light-hearted leap into his arms, which he might not expect. Now, she felt no urge to leap except from a very tall cliff—dragging Darcy behind her.

Dresses, jewelry, or sentimental mutterings from her aunt and uncle could not quell the anger and resentment. They rejoiced. She brooded.

Elizabeth turned to the one thing she could rely on: paper and a pen with a newly filled inkwell.

She may not become a literary success with only one novel series on the shelves, and Darcy might never allow her to pursue success in the field she loved, but no one could stop her writing from her heart.

Elizabeth wrote.

4

When Miss Darcy called one morning and learned Elizabeth would soon go to the dressmaker to order her new wardrobe, Elizabeth could not find it in her heart to turn away the girl's round, hopeful eyes and invited her along. "She will be your sister, after all," Mrs. Gardiner said approvingly when she heard of the outing, "and it will give me time to arrange my surprise for you myself."

Elizabeth insisted otherwise. "There is no need for surprises or gifts. You and my uncle have done so very much for me already."

Mrs. Gardiner merely tapped the side of her nose with a mysterious smile. "I'll be the one to decide that, my dear niece."

Thus, Elizabeth rode in the Darcy's carriage with her future sister and Ms. Chapman, Georgiana's companion, to one of the most sought after dressmakers in London.

"I am surprised they could fit you in on such short notice," Georgiana said. "A few acquaintances of mine have been waiting for weeks for their appointment."

"My uncle seems to collect favors wherever he goes because of his business in trade. He supplies many of the fabrics for the tailors and dressmakers in town."

"How fortunate!" Georgiana exclaimed.

Whether she felt as enthusiastic about her future sister-in-law's close connection to trade, her face did not reveal it. Georgiana, Elizabeth decided, was a difficult character to understand. On the surface, she seemed good-natured, though afflicted with a shyness that made starting a discussion with her painful. However, knowing her background and her relationship to Darcy, Elizabeth wondered if that was all there was to the beautiful young woman who accompanied her. After all, Darcy had not turned out to be the gentleman she believed him to be, either. What did that say about his sister?

When they arrived at the fashionable shop, the dressmaker informed her that only a few items would be available in the next few days, including the gown she would wear for her wedding. "I would deliver the rest the week after," she assured Elizabeth with noticeable hesitation.

"That timeframe is acceptable to me," Elizabeth said, noting with some alarm that the dressmaker seemed to be almost nervous and exceedingly courteous toward Elizabeth. Was it because Georgiana Darcy was beside her?

Or perhaps it was due to her own person? Now that she was to be Mrs. Darcy soon, would others pamper her with this deferential service? Regardless, at the moment, she simply wished to be done with the appointment, and so she did not question it further.

Georgiana and her companion assisted Elizabeth in selecting the items that were most stylish, although Elizabeth leaned more frequently toward Georgiana's opinions, shyly provided though they were. Ms. Chapman's constant need to classify fabrics and styles as appropriate or inappropriate struck a nerve with Elizabeth. Georgiana herself seemed unaffected by it, as if she had long resigned herself to this facet of Ms. Chapman's personality.

I suppose she'll look forward to the day when she no longer needs her companion. Perhaps that is why Georgiana is so eager to see this marriage come to fruition, because then I will become her companion and chaperone.

However, if Georgiana did not enjoy Ms. Chapman's companionship, why continue to engage her? It stymied Elizabeth, because she knew Darcy would not put up with such impertinent behavior from those by his side.

Elizabeth gained an opportunity to learn more about her future sister when Ms. Chapman, weary from standing nearby for so long, retired to a nearby sitting area to rest, leaving Georgiana in Elizabeth's care.

As if she'd been merely waiting for the moment, Georgiana turned to Elizabeth. "Miss Bennet, I had something I wished to give you today, which was the main reason for my calling upon you without notice." With great trembling, Georgiana pulled out a small, pink velvet pouch and handed it to Elizabeth. "It is a token of my affection, and an expression of my sincerity that we will get along as sisters and friends in the future."

Elizabeth carefully opened the pouch to reveal a pair of teardrop diamond earrings that spilled out into her hand. It was a princely gift, and Elizabeth's first instinct was to reject them, feeling unworthy of such generosity. But Georgiana spoke and silenced her protests.

"They were my mother's," she said, her face softening with a smile. "She would have loved to be here today, and I'm certain she would agree that they will look amazing on you."

Elizabeth was deeply touched. "I'm honored, Miss Darcy," she murmured, her voice thick with emotion. "I will treasure them forever."

"When my brother's letters spoke of his great admiration and respect for you, I suspected this day would come. It was always my dearest wish he marry for affection to someone who recognizes how great he is," Georgiana said to Elizabeth's continued surprise. "I'm grateful he found you and that we will be sisters. Please call me Georgiana, as my friends do."

Elizabeth tucked away the knowledge of Darcy's letters to ponder over another time. Instead, she focused her smile on Georgiana. "Regardless of marriage, we will be great friends, I know it, so you must call me Elizabeth or Lizzy."

"I cannot begin to express how happy I am to become your sister!"

Georgiana's delighted smile held no ulterior motives, and Elizabeth put away all misgivings she had about Georgiana's temperament and spirit. She could not let Darcy's actions taint the perfect angel that his sister undoubtedly was.

With this newfound confidence that at least one part of her future would be bright with Georgiana's presence, Elizabeth and her companions left the dressmakers with a flurry of boxes and goodbyes. Their errand complete, they sought to return to Gracechurch Street, but the sight of two fashionably dressed ladies approaching made them pause. Two familiar ladies—Miss Caroline Bingley and her sister, Mrs. Hurst.

The former's expression paled upon catching sight of Elizabeth and Georgiana while the latter's expression warmed into a bright smile. Miss Bingley quickly arranged her features into a more becoming expression and greeted the two women with a fondness that Elizabeth was not accustomed to.

"How lovely to see you both. We've only just heard the good news, Miss Bennet, and it appears you are closer to your future sister already."

"Yes, I've been blessed with a new friend and sister," Elizabeth agreed, smiling at the blushing Georgiana.

"Please accept our congratulations, Miss Bennet. I do hope we can become closer, seeing as we are all related through marriage now."

So that was the reason for Miss Bingley's revised attitude toward Elizabeth. As she could not catch Mr. Darcy herself, she had resigned herself to accepting the connection through marriage between Elizabeth's sister and Mr Bingley. A family like theirs could not risk losing the substantial benefits of a connection to the Darcy's, Elizabeth realized.

The foursome quickly bid their goodbyes and parted. "I suppose that is not to be unexpected," she murmured to herself when she settled on the carriage bench.

"I'm sorry?" Georgiana asked.

"It is nothing," she said. "I'm merely woolgathering."

Soon Elizabeth could expect all manner of false smiles like Miss Bingley's. How many others would approach her hoping to capitalize on her marriage to Mr. Darcy? The prospect seemed tiring, but amusing. Undoubtedly, many people would see Elizabeth as someone easily influenced by rank or status, given her background. Elizabeth, not tempted by false flattery or friendships, did not plan to become an easy target for their schemes.

5

THE WEDDING DAY DREW CLOSER DESPITE ELIZABETH'S prayers otherwise. Her room and the house seemed to be in constant disarray or commotion as Mrs. Gardiner rearranged the rooms to her liking for visitors and invested frugally in new carpets and drapes for the guest room. Elizabeth did not comment on this, but she thought it queer since it was not as if Elizabeth's marriage would follow with Darcy and Georgiana moving into Gracechurch Street.

However, she had so many things to do on her own that she quickly forgot it until two days before the wedding, when an exclamation downstairs lifted her from her latest novel. A familiar voice drifting upstairs caught her interest. "But it cannot be," she muttered.

Elizabeth hastily tidied herself and then ran to her bedroom door and threw it open. With one less obstacle in the path, she heard clearly from downstairs, her dear sister's voice.

Elizabeth couldn't contain her exclamation of happiness when she ran downstairs and saw her sister still in the doorway, accepting Mrs. Gardiner's profuse greetings. Mr. Bingley was behind her, his hat still in his hand, and he caught sight of Elizabeth on the stairs first and issued a hearty greeting. Jane beamed at Elizabeth and all sense of decorum left them both; they embraced at the bottom of the stairs, squealing with happiness at seeing each other after their long time apart.

"Forgive my nieces their enthusiasm," Mrs. Gardiner said with a laugh.

Charles' pleasure at the scene could not be contained. His grin stretched wide across his face. "I've not seen my wife in such spirits in a long time. It pleases me."

Elizabeth pulled back from Jane only far enough to squeeze her sister's face in both hands. "But what are you doing here?"

"My aunt Gardiner invited us," she said. "But I am surprised that it was not *you*, Lizzy."

Elizabeth had the grace to blush when Jane clasped her hands in both of hers. "It is not that I did not want to invite you, but it seemed selfish of me to pine for my sister when I know you are comfortably settled at Netherfield and close to our father."

"Papa is doing well enough, and the estate can spare us for a few weeks. I couldn't miss my dear sister's wedding!"

It took her a few moments to compose herself. Thankfully, Jane diverted the others' attention while Elizabeth dabbed her eyes, and Mrs. Gardiner ushered her guests into the sitting room.

Elizabeth's composure was badly cracked, and she swiped under her eyes again before following them. Jane patted the sofa next to her and the conversation flowed to the young couple's journey into town, the recent changes at the estate, and matters of idle gossip about the residents of

Hertfordshire. After about an hour, Mrs. Gardiner suggested the young couple and Elizabeth enjoy the fine day by taking a walk to the local park. Charles latched onto the scheme and the women dressed while the young Gardiner children joined them. Mrs. Gardiner promised to use the time well to attend to personal matters, and the house quickly emptied.

Elizabeth felt at peace beside her sister despite all the fraught tension within their family and the enormous shadow of Darcy looming over them. Charles took charge of the children at the park, leading them away while Jane and Elizabeth settled on a bench. They both smiled while watching Charles play with the children nearby, his boisterous nature matching the children's perfectly.

In the comfortable silence left between them, Jane reached over and covered Elizabeth's hand with her own. "You haven't revealed much in your letters about your marriage. It almost leads me to believe it's not a joyous occasion. Can you tell me now what is going on?"

Elizabeth felt as if tears were ready to spring to her eyes at any moment in recent days. She sniffed now and commanded her eyes to dry up. "Oh, Jane. I really don't want to talk about it. It's such an entangled web of confusion I can barely comprehend it, much less explain it to you. Please forgive me."

"But are you unhappy? Is it because of Charles' disagreement with Mr. Darcy? Because I want to make sure you know that we are still just as delighted for you, if not more so."

"They had a falling out? I had no idea!"

Jane nodded, her lips in a sad line as she glanced at her husband. "Charles felt betrayed when Mr. Darcy left so hurriedly, without any explanation. Apparently Charles believed Mr. Darcy disapproved of him marrying me, since it happened shortly after Charles asked for my hand."

Elizabeth recalled what Darcy said. He had given his reason for leaving Netherfield to Elizabeth, and it had been because of Mr. Bennet's threats to reveal him as a dishonorable man who assaulted his daughter. This was a great shame, that this misunderstanding had lost Darcy a seemingly close friendship. Even if she despised him, she could still be sympathetic.

"That's not the case at all. He asked after the both of you with great fondness when I first met him in London some weeks ago. Whatever ill feelings there are between them were not caused by your marriage."

"That is good to hear, at least. I would despair to be a carrier of friction between them." Jane squeezed her hands. "However, I must confess I did not believe it to be the case in the first place. There is something I must confide to you, sister, and I'm only sorry it has taken me this long to gather the courage to do so."

"Oh, Jane, your complexion looks terrible! Whatever can it be?" She squeezed her sister's hands, worry gnawing at her stomach.

A tear fell down Jane's cheek. "It is I who told our father what I knew when you asked to leave Hertfordshire. You must understand, I kept secret your visits to Mr. Darcy because you are my dearest sister, despite my misgivings of such a relationship, but when I witnessed your bruises and your distress that fateful morning, I could not hold my tongue any longer—!"

"My bruises? What do you mean?" But Elizabeth's mind was quickly working out the answer itself. That fateful morning was the day Mr. Collins accosted her, and she'd continued on to the secret meeting with Darcy regardless, despite her shock, leading toward her own falling out with Darcy when he first introduced the idea of being his mistress.

But something struck her. "You knew of my meetings with Darcy?"

Jane colored. "I did. You must understand, I never meant to pry into a part of your life in which I was not expressly invited, but it was impossible not to notice. It was not as if I realized it all at once, but little by little the strange changes you exhibited formed into a suspicion."

"But how did you know? I did not believe anything about my manner had changed at all." That her sister had suspected Elizabeth in the first place mortified her. What had given her away?

"At first, it was merely seeing you turn quiet. You would gaze out the window with such an expression I had never encountered before. Then you started sighing—"

"Sighing!" Her cheeks turned pink.

"Like Lydia or Kitty over their favourite officers," Jane said with a small giggle. "I could not believe it at first, but it was true. You were lovesick, and the only question left was who put that look on my dear sister's face. I turned my mind over it for days before I realised it was Mr. Darcy. You had stopped criticising him when the opportunity arose with our mother. When his name crossed her lips, you would tense, as if you were holding yourself back from speaking up—and I wondered why that was, unless your feelings about the gentleman had changed, and you did not wish to admit it."

Elizabeth could only shake her head. "You are truly astute. Here I believed myself above notice, and yet you knew nearly all along!" She looked down at her lap, unable to meet her sister's gaze any longer. "But may I ask how you knew I was meeting with him?"

It was better to have the whole truth now than to wonder, though she hated bringing up the topic herself. She feared what Jane thought about her and her horrible, wanton actions.

"Your bearing, your manner… something about you changed. It was as if you had settled into yourself. Forgive me for saying so, but you had this smile that spoke of secrets, and they grew when you had spent the morning out of doors. So one day I followed you outside merely to see which direction you walked and found you setting out towards Netherfield. All my suspicions were confirmed then."

"I cannot imagine you being so sneaky!" Elizabeth forced herself out of her misery to tease her older sister, which did the trick of making Jane's sad expression brighten. "Oh," she sighed, leaning into her sister's side, "I was terrible. Why did you not give me an earful if you knew all about it?"

"I would never pry into your intimate feelings, nor scold you for them. If it is you, Lizzy, I trust you to be reasonable and level-headed and not put yourself into danger."

Which meant Jane did not realize that Elizabeth *had* put herself into danger. Well, perhaps there was one secret which Elizabeth could keep to herself.

"So tell me what you meant about the morning Papa let me leave Longbourn," Elizabeth said. "You spoke to him, didn't you?"

Jane's wide blue eyes once again shimmered with tears. "There were bruises on your wrists, Lizzy. You were so distraught, crying into your pillow after our mother intercepted you inside. I could not help but think something terrible happened—and to you, no less! I took what I knew to Papa because I understood then that we could not let you become tangled up with such a dangerous man! To put bruises on you…" Jane sucked in a shaky breath. "Lizzy, are you certain you wish to marry him?"

"Oh…" So all this time Jane had believed Darcy had hurt her, when the truth was much worse!

At the same time, Elizabeth did *not* want to marry Darcy, but for a very different reason.

She swallowed the bubble of hot tears at the back of her throat. "Jane, I must relieve your fears on one point. Mr. Darcy never harmed me. Indeed, he has always seen to my comfort." That, she could not lie about, though she might despise the man. He was not always be gentle, but he was no monster.

Jane paled. "Then who… surely, not Mama—"

"No, our mother would not ever raise a hand to us, not even to me. Jane, I must tell you that it was our cousin, Mr. Collins, who put me in such distress. He encountered me when I was leaving Longbourn secretly, and he attempted to… oh, I do not wish to speak of it!"

Even now, these months later, she could not form the horrible words. Jane lost all color as she stared at Elizabeth, and she squeezed Elizabeth's hands so hard that a whimper of pain escaped her.

"And to think I believed him to be an honorable man of the cloth!"

"I assure you, his wickedness knows no bounds."

"Oh, Lizzy, I do not mean to sound as if I doubt you, because you know I do not," Jane rushed on to say. "It is only I am shocked at such a revelation for I came here to talk you out of marrying Mr. Darcy, and now it turns out I have very much maligned his character! And to father too, which I cannot help but think that my foolish misconception has delayed your happiness with that gentleman. If not for me, you could have secured your happiness months ago. I cannot apologise enough."

"There is no apology I need from you, sister. Truthfully, without your intervention, I may never have come to London and found validation in myself."

"Then please allow me to speak from the heart and allow me to inform you how happy I am that you are marrying your fine, honourable Mr. Darcy at long last." Jane threw her arms around Elizabeth. "It is a great relief that you shall be settled with a gentleman who matches you in temperament and character."

Elizabeth closed her eyes, glad her sister couldn't see her expression.

6

"A NOTE HAS ARRIVED FOR YOU, SIR."

"Thank you," he said, accepting it. His steward bowed and left the room.

Georgiana, busy with her embroidery—a rare activity for her, though she seemed to be improving steadily—looked at him curiously to see what had interrupted their quiet morning together.

"It's a letter from Charles," he said in surprise, the words slipping out before he could consciously think of them.

"Mr. Bingley?"

"He says he's in town, residing in Cheapside for the moment with his wife's relatives."

"With the Gardiner's?"

"Yes, and he hopes I do not mind if he attends the ceremony. He wishes to visit me today, if possible."

It was just past the breakfast hour. From what Darcy knew of Charles, his old friend rarely rose before noon because of his custom of staying up late. His marriage to

Mrs. Bingley must have altered him into a man who would wake with the sunrise.

Darcy felt a sharp pain in his chest as he read Charles' handwriting, improved since their last correspondence, yet still containing a measure of recklessness. Months had passed since Darcy last sent a letter, but never receiving a response, he was convinced their friendship was over. He had given up all hope.

A response was soon dispatched, and it was within the hour that Mr. Bingley himself arrived on the doorstep. His greeting was as hearty and boisterous as usual, and his smiles genuine as he congratulated Darcy on his upcoming nuptials.

"Thank you for receiving me today."

"How could I not? Your note was actually readable, and I was so curious as to your change that I could do nothing else."

"I knew you would comment upon that!" Bingley grinned as he sat in front of the window. From the music room, Georgiana's piano practice continued. "You can thank Jane for my improvement. With her beside me, it allows me a little more patience in these matters, although long correspondence is still a tiresome affair. I would have come sooner, but we were involved in so many projects and improvements upon the estate that I could not reasonably leave."

Excuse or not, at least it gave them both some grace.

Bingley's hands fumbled in his lap before he reached for the tea the staff had put out. "I cannot say that I was convinced you would welcome me if I came," he admitted.

"Pardon?" Darcy said. "What gave you that idea?"

"Well, it was something Caroline said, to be exact. Your departure from Hertfordshire was on the tail end of my proposal to Jane. She speculated that might have something to do with it."

Darcy's lips twisted and bitterness flooded his response. "I imagine she had other motives to say such a thing to you. That is not the case at all. It was a personal matter which unexpectedly brought me back to London."

Bingley shook his head with a wry smile. "I should know better than to listen to Caroline."

"You should," he said.

"Luckily, I now have Jane's advice to rely upon, and she has never steered me wrong. You should see her with the staff, Darcy. They love their mistress, and so do the tenants. She is everything I could have hoped for in a wife."

"That is pleasing to hear," he said. "Your note said you were staying with her relatives for the time being. When do you plan to return to Netherfield?"

"We originally planned to stay for two weeks, but Jane has had little chance to enjoy the society in town, so I thought to remedy that. We may extend our stay longer, provided she enjoys town."

"I'm sure she will not find it to her dissatisfaction. If you like, you are always welcome to stay here at the townhome if lodging with the Gardiner's proves burdensome for them."

Bingley lit up. "I may take that under consideration, but I would not wish to disturb your honeymoon with my dear sister Elizabeth and earn her sharp tongue."

The notion made him smile. "I'm sure Elizabeth would find much joy in being close to her sister, but whether you stay here or there is up to you."

"The Gardiners are lovely people. I've found some commonalities with Mr. Gardiner, who displays expert knowledge of the fabric trade. It is no wonder he is well respected within town. Other than that, most of the day yesterday was spent speaking about the wedding," he said with a knowing smile Darcy's way.

"Has Elizabeth… No, it is nothing."

Bingley leaned forward at the first sign of Darcy's reluctance. "What is it? Are you feeling nervous? As a married man myself, I can share some advice, if you like."

"No, I do not feel nervous. If anything, I am eager to see it through," he said, which made Bingley brighten into a knowing grin. "However, Elizabeth's feelings are… muted, it seems. Has she said anything to you or your wife?"

Brow furrowed, Bingley thought a moment before shaking his head. "I cannot say I've paid too much attention, but I'm certain she is as excited as you are, Darcy."

"Yes," he said slowly. He could claim with some certainty himself that she was *not* as excited.

Darcy and Bingley visited for a quarter hour longer before Darcy realized his friend was fidgeting and glancing at the clock. "Do you wish to return to the Gardiners?" he asked.

"I daresay I should," Bingley said, looking relieved.

"Mrs. Bingley must like you to be by her side, given you are still newlyweds."

"I must say it is the opposite." Bingley blushed. "Jane easily seems able to go through the day without seeing me, but I fear it is impossible for me. Nothing makes my heart swell more than her smile, so I often find excuses to return to her throughout the day, no matter how busy it is."

"I'm surprised. It must make the day even busier with those constant disruptions for you both."

Bingley's grin turned into a grimace. "I am shameless, aren't I?"

"You are in love," Darcy said. "And I daresay your wife

enjoys the disruptions as much as you, or else she would have pointed out this behaviour already."

"What a good way to look at it!" he exclaimed.

Darcy stood as his guest did. He tried to sound confident, but the slight tremble in his voice gave away his nerves. "Would you mind if I accompanied you back to Gracechurch Street?"

Luckily, Bingley didn't seem to notice. "Of course. The Gardiners will not mind, and I'm certain Elizabeth will not either. Her and Jane were busy finishing the flowers this morning. Like Jane, she may appreciate the disruption," he added, nudging Darcy with his elbow.

"I'll go tell Georgiana," Darcy said, his mood much grimmer than his friend's.

He detoured to his bedroom and picked up the box he'd left on his nightstand since he found the set. Whatever he had to do to return to Elizabeth's good graces, he would do, but this particular gift was no sacrifice for him. It was perfect for Elizabeth.

He tucked away the box and made his plans known to Georgiana before he joined Bingley in the foyer. Together they made the quick trip back to Gracechurch Street, Bingley's smile growing with each block that brought them closer to his lovely wife. Darcy, meanwhile, tensed with every moment that his reunion with Elizabeth drew closer.

You will forgive me, he had told her. And she would, once she saw how Darcy would throw himself into making it so. But until then, he was vulnerable without their marriage contract settled.

Only one more day until he could finally call her Mrs. Darcy.

The past few times Darcy had visited Gracechurch Street after their engagement, Elizabeth's attitude toward him bordered on rude. She would sit with them, listen to her aunt or uncle with polite smiles, and grow cold whenever her eyes flicked to Darcy. Whatever plans were made, she desired limited input. She did not put forth her own opinions, only agreed to whatever modest choices Mrs. Gardiner suggested, as if she could not be bothered to be a bride.

Therefore, he was not surprised when he stepped into the room behind Bingley and heard his fiance say, "I have no preference."

"You usually have the most to say about these silk flowers," he heard Jane say before the group recognized the gentlemen's entrance.

The talk continued for some minutes with the women—Mrs. Gardiner and Jane—settling matters between them when Elizabeth offered no opinions of her own. They must have assumed her to be the most relaxed bride in the country, but to Darcy, her attitude only made clear to him how much distance she put between herself and the wedding.

Elizabeth met his eyes while her relations continued their discussions around her. She did not want this wedding, not in the least, but no one could see that except him.

Bingley cleared his throat when there was a lull in the conversation. His expression eager, he asked, "Could you ladies use a break? I would not mind stretching my legs and enjoying the day for a bit."

"Oh, I did not even realize the time," Mrs. Gardiner said, glancing at the clock on a nearby table. "You four should go for a walk and not waste this pretty day."

"That sounds a wonderful idea to me," Jane said with a wistful glance at Elizabeth.

Elizabeth noted it with a frown before she sighed. "Yes, what a shame it would be to waste this wonderful weather."

The two couples got ready for their departure. Darcy

waited outside while they did so, the bustle of the ladies finding gloves and bonnets in the background while he took deep, clearing breaths. So she found the marriage distasteful still—he had no hope of changing her mind, but at least now he had the chance to improve her understanding before the ceremony. Optimism felt silly to him, but he could not repress it.

Bingley and Jane walked down the steps together with Elizabeth trailing after them, her expression guarded. Darcy held his arm out to her. "Shall we walk together?"

"I suppose," she said, not sounding happy about it while she took his arm. He was glad her voice was low and didn't attract her sister's attention to her tight, unhappy expression.

They followed Bingley and Jane down Gracechurch Street, Elizabeth's hand on his arm like a leaden weight on his chest.

"You were right," he said, causing her to look at him in surprise. "The weather is too nice to stay inside."

She looked away, her lips in a firm line of distaste. Awkward silence stretched between them. Ahead, Bingley was speaking animatedly to Jane, who freely shared smiles toward her husband. *One day, perhaps,* he thought ruefully, the woman on his arm silent and frowning.

The short walk was filled with the sounds of birdsong, chatter from the happy couple who turned to include Darcy and Elizabeth in their conversation, and the uncomfortable silence between him and the woman who despised him. The park was surely pretty, but Darcy did not see a single flower or shrub. It could have been the King's own garden and he would not see anything beyond the unhappy woman beside him.

Darcy slowed his steps so a greater distance grew between them and the other couple. Bingley and Jane wandered on toward a small pond, unaware as they were wrapped up in one another—or perhaps deliberately giving them space—and he took his chance and turned to Elizabeth.

"Miss Bennet… Elizabeth," he said, forcing his tongue to work. "Elizabeth, I do not expect to earn your trust back so quickly after what I have done to secure your hand. Nor do I expect presents will do the work of honest contriteness. However," he said, his voice dropping as he removed the box from his jacket and handed it to her. "This is a gift to show my regard. It is nothing in comparison to my happiness that you will stand by me tomorrow on our wedding day."

Flecks of gold shone in her wide, dark eyes when she took the box, staring at it with her lips parted. Almost as if afraid to touch it, to accept anything tainted by *him*.

Darcy swallowed the hurt and waited until she opened the lid to say, "Georgiana told me she gifted you my mother's earrings. This necklace and bracelet are part of the matching set. It was my mother's most cherished set, a gift given to her from my father on their wedding day."

Darcy could see Elizabeth was not wholly unaffected by the gift. Her fingers trembled when she touched the teardrop diamonds that graced the necklace and fell off the bracelet's delicate silver chain. However, before he could grow too confident, she looked up with narrowed eyes.

"My forgiveness will not be won so easily, Darcy. The bridge between us is a large one and I will not lie to you and tell you that it can be traversed with presents."

"I'm fully aware of it." If he wanted a woman who would be content with dresses and jewels, he would be wed long ago. It was *Elizabeth* he wanted. He did not resent her honesty, and he felt compelled to speak his own feelings as well. "But I will not stop reaching out."

Elizabeth's lip trembled, and his fists clenched at his sides. *He* put that look there.

"This still makes no sense to me," she said. "After all, I don't even know why your mind changed. Days after you desire me to be your mistress, you push for marriage."

"That was a mistake," Darcy said at once. He sucked in a breath. It was time to reveal the truth. "The depths of my feelings for you were unknown to me." He scoffed and dropped his head. "No, that is not fully the truth." No matter how bad it looked, he wanted to tell her the truth. He could not go any lower in her eyes, so what was one more? He sighed and looked into her dark, curious eyes again. "I did not *wish* to see how much my affection for you impacted me, yet it did at every turn. Did you know that I hired a private investigator to search for you before I met you again?"

Elizabeth's eyes widened. "You did not!"

"I did," he said, touching her elbow, unable to hold back the desire to touch her but not wanting to frighten her. She stared up at him, searching his expression with confusion and he sighed. "And every time he informed me he could not find a trace of Elizabeth Bennet of Hertfordshire, my frustrations grew. It is to *my* folly that I did not recognize that my frustrations were because I had lost someone precious to me."

"You searched for me?" She still didn't seem to know how to absorb this information.

"I did. I dreamed about you most nights, Elizabeth," he said, making her flinch and suck in a surprised breath. "It is my own stubborn pride that got in my way. I hold you in the utmost regard. You are the handsomest woman of my acquaintance and my admiration of you grows daily the more I see your wits, charm, and sweet manners."

Elizabeth looked away and swiped at her eyes. "It is not

kind of you to make me cry," she said with a wet laugh. "I feel like I have been crying too much lately."

His heart swelled. "I'm sorry to make you cry. I never wish to hurt you again, and I promise upon everything I hold dear that it will never happen again. You will have a steadfast, loyal husband from tomorrow onward."

She radiated nervous energy, darting anxious glances at him between staring at the box in her hands. "I still don't know if I can forgive you," she said, her voice a whisper. Then, with her breath escaping her in a rush, she said, "But I will at least accept the sincerity of your words for now."

Darcy's determination boiled to the forefront of his mind. Her forgiveness would be a matter of time, a *when* not an *if*. Darcy would not rest until this woman was his, mind and body. Too long he had neglected her mind. He wouldn't make that mistake again.

Elizabeth glanced at where Bingley and Jane were loitering by the pond, still obviously giving them space. "Darcy… may we have a longer discussion tomorrow after the ceremony? I wish to clear up matters between us."

"Yes," he said, aware of how fortunate he was to have a woman like Elizabeth willing to marry him. He held out his hand. "Until then, will you allow me to escort you?"

"Very well," she murmured, and let him settle her hand on his elbow.

7

Elizabeth traced her finger along the edge of the box. If it was a bribe, it truly was an excellent one. "I'm still angry at you, and no amount of gifts will resolve it," she said into the silence. Charles and Jane were still beside the pond, her brother-in-law speaking animatedly while Jane laughed.

"I understand. Be angry with me as long as you wish."

"How understanding of you."

He took her restless huff in stride. "But I did not hope to calm your anger with my gift. My only desire is to recognize you as my future wife and companion of my life."

And Elizabeth didn't know how to respond beyond the flutter in her heart which she refused to voice. An unsettling, unshakeable hope. Darcy's gift today and, combined with his sister's friendship, made her resentment tangle with said hope for the future.

A hope she shouldn't have, given how this all began.

"Would you join me now, Lizzy? I have the settlement papers." Elizabeth put aside her sewing and rose, returning

Jane's small smile. It was nice to put aside her musings for the moment and return to the present.

Charles set aside his book. Given he'd been flipping back and forth through the advanced farming techniques listlessly, he appeared to be grateful for the reprieve. "May I come? Knowing Darcy, I expect it's all in order, but I might be able to offer adjustments since I'm familiar with his holdings."

"Please, join us," she said when Mr. Gardiner waited. They followed Mr. Gardiner into his study where he sat them down and went over the settlement items line by line.

Elizabeth made several noises. Charles, while raising his eyebrows at some point, nodded.

"Very generous," Mr. Gardiner finished.

Charles said, "I agree. I cannot think of anything to improve it."

Elizabeth untangled her tongue. "Heaven forbid if my mother was here. Please, I beg of you, do not inform her—she will undoubtedly pester you for details and this… it's…"

"I understand," Mr. Gardiner said with a glance at Charles, who nodded. "What of your aunt and elder sister?"

"I don't mind them knowing," she said, staring at her knees because she was still stunned. Could he claim *this* wasn't a bribe? Generous was an understatement. Multiple properties with attached income, substantial consideration for the first son and other sons, a specific, equal inheritance for all female heirs.

"He has provided for all your earthly needs—and more."

Elizabeth once believed that Darcy would take her as a mistress and place her in a gilded cage. She'd fought against it with every fibre of her being; she would suffocate and die under such restrictions. No matter how pretty the cage, she couldn't accept it.

But this cage… Elizabeth would be wealthy in her own right if she managed her resources well.

"There are no flaws, no traps, in the agreement?"

Mr. Gardiner chuckled. "I'm amused by your wording. No, there are no traps; a few penalties in the event you are infertile, but those are common in most every contract, and the provisions remain. For instance, it does not affect the holdings he'll transfer to you, though the rights to the properties revert to the Darcy blood family upon your death if an heir is not mutually selected by you both. It's much more than I expected."

"That is Darcy for you," Charles said with a chuckle. "May I have more of this scotch, Mr. Gardiner? It's quite good."

"Call me Edward, please." Mr. Gardiner did the honors of topping off his glass and settled down in his seat again. "You say this is common for Darcy?"

"Common, no. He is not so generous with everyone. But his friends, his family—he takes good care of them. He cherishes those he can find a connection with. He's given me great advice over the years, plenty of advice that would have tempted other people to take advantage of me when I was naïve to the ways of managing money." He peered into his glass with a fond smile. "I can truthfully say I have no better friend than him, and I'm glad we've renewed our acquaintance—and now we will be brothers, thanks to Lizzy."

Mr Gardiner studied her expression before he chuckled. "Perhaps you should have a small touch of the scotch too, Lizzy dear."

When they received the news of the fortune that had befallen Elizabeth, Mrs Gardiner took it as due course for Darcy should pamper her niece, while any of Jane's infinitesimal worries about the match faded away. "What a good man he is!" she cried.

Mr. Gardiner settled back into the seat beside his wife with a rosy glow not wholly blamed on his second glass of scotch. "An inauspicious start, certainly, but my worries are entirely cured."

"And you never need worry about your children!" Charles said. The drink had darkened his color, and soon after Jane ushered her smiling, happy husband to bed with a wry look over her shoulder at Elizabeth.

Elizabeth sat back, closing her eyes, the stiff drink impressing on her the idea of Darcy's sharp features alongside her own curly hair.

Her thoughts remained unsettled, her heart in turmoil, up to the morning of the wedding. The only writing she did, instead of dedicating herself to the edits of the next volume of her series, were scribbled notes of thanks to those who sent her letters of congratulations. She spent more time on her letter to Charlotte, but not much. She felt as if she spent too long at her writing desk, she might put to paper the complicated emotions besieging her—dread, regret, along with a healthy dose of curiosity and hope. The feelings were too tender to commit to reality yet, she decided. She would sit with them until they settled. Until then, Elizabeth threw herself into wedding preparations with a vigour that so far had eluded her.

The morning of the wedding came.

Elizabeth's feelings remained unsettled, but she devoted herself to at least pretending to a calm she only halfheartedly felt. Jane and Mrs. Gardiner shared concerned looks all morning while last-minute preparations were made and the carriage Darcy sent filled with flowers and decorations, but they trusted Elizabeth to come to them if need be. She packed herself away into the carriage with a quiet resolve, and the wedding would've proceeded in the same manner of unsettled nerves until Lady Catherine's arrival shoved Elizabeth back into reality.

8

Lady Catherine de Bourgh was a woman of mythical proportions in Elizabeth's memory, cultivated by Mr. Collins' episodic rhapsodies about his patroness. Now she loomed over the ceremony with all the aging bearing of a queen and the eyes of a demon. The happy couple had been in the beginning of the ceremony when a terrific commotion from the front door made the guests and Elizabeth look around in alarm.

Darcy, Elizabeth would recall later, merely looked resigned while he turned to his greying aunt who stood in the doorway of the sitting room like a giant silver spider blocking the path.

"I decree this marriage is a sham."

"Pardon?" Mrs. Gardiner stood alongside her husband, grabbing hold of Mr. Gardiner's arm. "Whatever can you mean?"

Behind his mistress, squat Mr. Collins lurked like a toad in a swamp, peering out from behind her with bulbous, bulging eyes. Lady Catherine drew herself up to her considerable bearing, hawkish face sneering down at Elizabeth and her family.

"Elizabeth Bennet is a woman of no consequence, lacking any extraordinary charm, beauty, or connection. Indeed, her own cousin admitted to me she is well versed in wicked charms and enticements, giving me authority to end this farce."

The room hushed. Elizabeth froze. This couldn't be happening—

But no, she was still here, under the scrutiny of her friends and family. An unpleasant tingle burned across the back of her neck while time stretched, moments turned to minutes, hours. Her vision wavered at the edges, her head light, wobbly. Each pair of shocked, horrified eyes stacked another awful weight to the piercing pressure on her chest.

Wicked charms and enticements. The words rebounded in her brain. Her aunt's face was a horrified white. Mr. Gardiner had turned a muddy red, while beside him Jane shook and Charles opened and closed his mouth, and there was Mr. Davies beside Georgiana and her humiliation could not be more complete.

Elizabeth wobbled, a moment away from sliding to the floor, before she forced strength into her legs. "I refused to be spoken to in such a way by a stranger who has not been introduced to me."

Lady Catherine stiffened. "*You* dare? Do you not know to whom you speak?"

"As I said before, we have not been introduced."

Darcy released one of her hands and took a half step toward his aunt, as if to block her from a blow from Lady Catherine's gleaming black cane. "Aunt—"

"I am Lady Catherine, the widow of Sir Lewis de Bourgh, the sister of Lady Anne, Fitzwilliam's mother. And with the birth of my daughter, it was my sister's dearest hope they would join our two houses in matrimony."

"Now you've said your piece, you may leave," Darcy said, breaking the silence. Darcy gently grasped her hands again, and he squeezed them now.

She ignored her nephew. "Now do you recognize your error, young lady?"

It was the sight of Mr. Collins toadying up behind his patroness which made Elizabeth see red. If she was wicked, then what was he?

"Why should I give consequence to you?" she said, stepping up to Darcy's side, her voice bitter and sharp. "Why should I when you cannot give myself or my family a modicum of respect? If you had objections, there were plenty of ways to express them; you could have sought privacy with your nephew, written a letter, or even approached me. Instead you have decided to grandstand over the moment, so no, I do not give you any consequence."

Darcy made a noise, but she refused to look at him. Let him contradict her loudly like his aunt if he wishes to. She wouldn't let him intimidate her in silence.

But he said nothing, only drawing her behind him again as Lady Catherine sucked in a breath like Elizabeth had gutted her.

Her eyes blazed with the fires of the self-righteous. "You will never be recognized by Darcy's family! Is that what you want?"

"You shall not speak for me." Colonel Fitzwilliam spoke up, drawing the room's attention to him. He bore it well, hands clasped before him, his disappointment palpable. "I have found Miss Bennet—my apologies—Mrs. Darcy, a pleasant woman who does not deserve such censure."

If her nephew had slapped her, she could not have taken

more offence. "And what of what she said to me? Will you allow her to speak to me this way?" she demanded, turning on Darcy.

Darcy's eyes were flat and colder than his chilly voice. "It was fairer than what I would have said. You've overstayed your welcome, Lady Catherine. You've intruded into my home without invitation, disrespected my wife, and brought that creature into my presence when I informed him not a six-month ago to never let me set eyes on him again." Everyone in the room heard his indrawn breath.

If Lady Catherine could hear at all, it was only the sound of her own voice. "My revelations—"

"Have revealed nothing. You have only exposed yourself. Elizabeth is perfect in every respect." He turned to Elizabeth, his curling lip softening along with the look in his eyes. Her chest tightened for a new reason as he spoke directly to her. "Her character is above reproach. Her relations are both charming and respectable—I look forward to their company in the future. There is no one else for me, and it's to my discredit that I have wasted so much time before this day arrived."

The whole room was still. Elizabeth couldn't look away. Sincerity shone in the eyes that had once entrapped her on a lonely road. A man who'd enraptured her with those sweet lips, with arms that held her and fingers that traced her face.

She had spent so long with her feelings muffled, underwater, she had forgotten clarity like this existed.

He held her gaze a moment more before he turned to his aunt. "I've allowed you to darken the day long enough, and I won't allow you another opportunity. Richard."

"Yes," Col. Fitzwilliam said, stepping up.

"Be gone from my house, Lady Catherine, and do not expect any invitations from me in the future, for even if Elizabeth forgives you, I will not. That is the end of it. Show her to the door—and her parson, too. I'll give you one last piece of advice, Lady Catherine. Beware the character of those close to you."

The glare Darcy singed Mr. Collins, sending him stumbling back a step to escape the flames. "S-Sir!"

"Lady Catherine," Col. Fitzwilliam said and took the elderly woman's arm. Lady Catherine made a noise, but three large servants came in and ushered the party out of the house.

Darcy turned to Elizabeth with his aunt's outraged gasps echoing in the hall. "Shall we continue or do you need a moment?"

The uproar of the wedding ceremony ended on a lighter note. The wedding breakfast was lovely overall. The townhome emptied of guests after Jane pulled Elizabeth into a relieved, happy hug. Georgiana left with her cousin to stay with the Earl of Matlock for a brief period to give the newlyweds their peace. Eventually, it was only Darcy and Elizabeth standing in the foyer of the townhome, looking at each other.

A long moment stretched between them and her gaze dipped to his mouth. When she forced her eyes up, she saw his own attention was preoccupied with her lips. Her face warmed. Would he…? Should she encourage such intimacy so soon? She couldn't deny seeing him stand up to his formidable aunt had nearly made her swoon.

Footsteps made Darcy's eyes flick over her head.

"Ah, right, Mrs. Fletcher." He cleared his throat when a plump woman with neatly combed grey hair stepped up to them in an unobtrusive, neat manner. "This is the housekeeper, Mrs. Fletcher. I should have introduced you earlier."

The woman gave her a closed-lip smile, hazel eyes sparkling. "I should like to give you a tour whenever you are ready, Mrs. Darcy," she said with an inclination of her head.

A flush crept across his cheeks. "I will take Mrs. Darcy on the tour." The tips of his ears turned red when he looked at Elizabeth. "If you don't mind, that is."

"Can we meet afterwards?" she asked Mrs. Fletcher. "I would like to get acquainted as soon as possible." Mrs. Fletcher would be a key figure in her life going forward, after all.

"Of course. I'll have some refreshments made while I wait."

Mrs. Fletcher's footsteps echoed on the floor until she reached the hallway where the long rugs swallowed the noise. When the sound faded, Darcy's throat contracted and then he offered her his hand. It was a stark contrast to the competent man in front of their guests earlier. This man was not so confident before her. He seemed almost shy.

"May I?"

Elizabeth placed her hand in his. His hand was warm and twitched when she curled her fingers around his palm.

The last time she had taken this tour, she'd been one of a handful of privileged guests. Now she was the mistress of this property, of *several* properties, which was still hard to wrap her mind around. But that memorable night had led her to this moment now, wife of the universally respected Fitzwilliam Darcy, wife of the man who'd forced her into this marriage and then stood up for her to his own family… perhaps Darcy was simply impossible to understand.

Darcy paused outside his study door. "And this is my…"

"Study, I know." She smiled at his suddenly nervous

expression. "This is a bit different from the last tour you gave me," she said.

He winced. "Can we forget that foolishness of mine? I dwell on it too much as it is."

Perhaps this was not the time to tease him, especially after the trials they passed through today. "Forgive me."

"I hope you can forgive me from now on."

"When you fight dragons for me, how could I not?" She squeezed his arm. "Let us think of the past only as it gives us happiness."

Darcy dipped his head. "With every day you prove how much I do not deserve you."

Yes, Darcy was simply impossible to understand.

ELIZABETH TOOK special care that night. Washing in a bath filled with herbs and scents. Perfume dabbed behind her wrists and ears. The next extravagance was the silk robe she donned, flowing down to her ankles and clinging to her wet skin. She let her hair fall down her back and arranged herself on the settee in her bedroom at the designated time he'd said they would meet. Nerves in the back of her throat, her body buzzed with anticipation. Their relationship might be fraught with tension in other areas, but *this* they were good at. Exceptionally good at.

Darcy called out to her, then opened the door. His gaze did not flicker from her face. "I took the liberty of stealing this book off your shelf earlier and brought my own copy. I'd hoped we could read together tonight."

Elizabeth, still in her artful, provocative arrangement on the settee, froze.

"Read? On our wedding night?"

Her cheeks were still flushed as Darcy cocked his head and said, "I don't see why not. We already know we are suitably matched."

Cold, sticky embarrassment hastened her to jerk her legs to the floor. "Right. Of-of course."

He shut the bedroom door behind him before crossing to her side, his calm manner doing nothing to temper her flaming face. "If it's acceptable, I'd like for us to get to know one another in other ways. Might I join you?"

"Go ahead." Elizabeth pulled a pillow into her lap, needing something to hide behind. She cleared her throat. "Ah, you've chosen the Merchant of Venice. I could never say no to Shakespeare."

The tiny smile he flashed when he sat made up for all the embarrassment—nearly. "I hoped that would be the case," he said, reaching for the drinks tray on the end table and pouring a glass. He paused, lifted the decanter, and she nodded. He poured another. "I've wanted to revisit it for some time."

She lifted the glass to her nose, burying her senses in the rich red while struggling to find her place again. As if nothing was amiss and this was any ordinary night. As if she wasn't swallowing bitter disappointment.

Darcy opened his book. "Shall I read to you some of my favourite passages?"

"Please," she said, at sea in this moment between them. Darcy leaned back, hooked his ankle over his knee, and began to read. His deep, melodious voice brought out the themes of, among others, wild justice and intolerance. Over time she sank into that deep voice, like a warm bath, and forgot her embarrassment.

A warm glow settled around them. Darcy even lounged, his head on her lap, provoking her laughter with his choice of passages and remarks. "You do voices very well," she told him, bold enough to run her fingers through his thick hair. "Never have I heard a more handsome Portia."

"A compliment to remember," he said in his dry way.

Eventually, they mutually agreed to read from their own books, and Elizabeth settled in for a night of exchanging words upon Shakespeare's work while they read. But when Darcy at once turned to the end of his book, her lips parted.

"Surely, you aren't beginning at the end!"

"Why not? The end is the whole point. You must know if a tale is worth your time."

"It is Shakespeare, of course it is."

"And does this opinion apply widely?"

"The *journey* is the point or else every book would be approximately ten pages long," she said, slumping against the back of the couch. Her husband was a heathen!

He didn't seem to care about the sacrilege. "But I have read *The Merchant of Venice* before, so why should I begin fresh?"

"Do you only read in one frame of mind? My moods are always different when I revisit a familiar novel. At one point I may be melancholy, thus focusing on the dreary weather captured in the pages. Other times I'm happy and content, thus allowing me warmer enjoyment of the heroes' supportive friends and family. One might reread a book ten times and find fresh pleasure an equal number of times."

Darcy said, "I think I will find fresh pleasure in Portia's love. *I feel too much thy blessing.* So, again I will return to the final pages."

She was helpless to him. "One cannot argue that," she said, and so it went until Elizabeth realised something *had* been consummated. Darcy did not touch her body, but her mind.

They read until they were both too tired to continue. The clock on the mantel read past two o'clock in the morning and she hid a yawn in her hand.

"Until tomorrow," Darcy said from the doorway.

"Are you sure you don't wish to stay?" she asked, gesturing to her bed.

He shook his head. "I will be up again in a few hours. I don't wish to disturb your rest. Thank you for tonight, Elizabeth."

"Lizzy," she said. "You once called me Lizzy."

With an incline of his head, he withdrew. Elizabeth forced her heavy limbs to climb into the large four poster, her large and *empty* bed. And how cold it was. He'd taken the warmth from her room, too.

Despite it all, Elizabeth fell asleep in moments. She slept well, with peaceful dreams scattering into the depths of her mind as soon as her eyes opened.

She took care when dressing, asking her lady's maid to help her pick a new perfume and brushing her hair until it was a bright sheen. She told herself it was for her own benefit, but seeing Darcy's open approval when he happened upon her at the bottom of the stairs made her flush.

"You wore them," he said, and she felt the weight of his mother's necklace was nothing compared to the satisfied gleam in his eyes. Elizabeth let him escort her to the dining room for breakfast with a light heart.

They had only sat down adjacent to each other at the large table when Darcy's doorman entered. "The guests I told you about have returned, Mr. Darc."

"That's right. Show them in." He turned to Elizabeth. "Apparently Charles and your sister came very early this morning, but my people turned them away. I sent them a note hoping you would be awake by now."

Elizabeth frowned and placed her napkin on the table. "Why would they try to visit so early?"

But upon sight of Jane in the doorway of the dining room, she knew.

Her sister's expression was wan and pale as if she hadn't slept a wink all night. Elizabeth abandoned her chair and rushed to her sister's side.

"Oh, Lizzy," Jane sobbed, hugging her fiercely.

"What is the matter? Is it our father?"

9

They set out that day. The Bingley coach was already prepared and packed. Darcy and Elizabeth rode with them, bringing with them a light day's worth of clothing. Darcy's coach would follow the next day with the Gardiners and the rest of Darcy and Elizabeth's things.

Mrs. Bennet's letter had arrived in the dead of night. Elizabeth thought of how many hours her gentle-hearted sister must have suffered while Elizabeth and Darcy chuckled over Shakespeare, and was not surprised when Jane fell asleep against Bingley's shoulder not a quarter of an hour after they left London. Sometime later, Bingley rested his head atop Jane's and closed his shadowed eyes.

Somewhere in the trees, a crow called out. Elizabeth pressed her forehead into the cold window, gazing out at a world shaded in grey. Her father had been sick for nearly as long as she remembered, but he had still been the anchor for her love for her family. He taught Elizabeth her letters, stories, the rhythm of poetry, and the artful meandering of novels. He'd introduced her to a world outside the strange one inside their home, where Elizabeth never felt quite right or wanted by her mother.

In stories, she could be anyone; she could be an adventurer or an educated gentleman or a money lender or a king. Stores were her refuge and as she grew older, she realised that they also allowed him to escape the cage of his failing body and the shackles of marriage to a woman who insisted on more and more children in her quest for a Bennet heir.

Darcy reached over and touched her hand. "I do not know what kind of reception I will receive at your home," he said.

She lifted her head to look at him. "Nor the one that I will receive," she said.

He clasped her hand. "Regardless, it will not change my support. Lean on me as you will. I know this is a hard time, and I imagine it will grow even more difficult if your mother's letter about his condition is accurate."

"I can hope it is not truly. I hope she exaggerated, though I know it would be a dreadful inconvenience to you."

Darcy ran his thumb over her knuckles. "It wouldn't be an inconvenience. I cherish the opportunity to make right with your father, and I want you to have peace with your family."

"Thank you," she whispered. "Thank you for being here, and being so kind."

She leaned over and attempted to kiss him. Darcy drew back before she could. A glance showed her that Bingley and Jane were still sleeping, but it was not that which made him from frown.

"I don't need a reward for doing the right thing. I'm here to support you."

A smile pulled at her lips, the first smile she'd felt since

Jane's appearance at the townhome. "You think of my kiss as a reward?"

"Of course," he said with a confused look. He patted her hand. "You should rest while you can. I imagine the rest of the day will be long."

Elizabeth swallowed her disappointment—a kiss would've settled her nerves somewhat—and did as he bid.

HER MOTHER GREETED them with her usual charm. They heard her voice before the carriage rolled to a stop outside Longbourn.

"It's only the Bingleys! My dearest Jane, of course," Mrs. Bennet's voice could be heard while the gravel crunched under the wheels of the slowing carriage. "Lizzy has no love to spare for her poor mother and father now that she's rich beyond belief!"

A deep blush of humiliation rushed to her cheeks. The glass of the windows could not dim Mrs Bennet's loud and crystal-clear voice, and all three people in the carriage were wide awake to hear her. She kept her eyes averted from Darcy, but Jane's mortification was evident.

"Don't pay it any heed," Jane said with a quaver in her voice. "She's lashing out in her grief, Lizzy. If she knew you were in the carriage—"

"She would have said it louder," Elizabeth said. Jane winced. Beside her, Bingley shook his head, eyes closing as if he couldn't bear to witness what came next.

Unfortunately, Elizabeth could not close her eyes. They were wide open when the carriage stopped. Darcy grabbed the handle of the door, his expression like stone, a muscle jumping his jaw. When the driver opened the door, Darcy descended like a fearsome God to the sound of gasps from her mother and sisters on the gravel.

He bowed, every movement displaying cold, furious, disgust. With no other greeting, he turned and held his hand out to Elizabeth. She took it, something about his anger, contrasting with the gentle way he held her hand, settled her.

Elizabeth descended from the carriage, stealing a glance at her mother whose face had gone pale with shock. Elizabeth turned away from the woman to meet her sisters. "How good it is to see all of you," she said.

"I knew you would come," Lydia said. Lydia smirked at her sisters and nudged a suddenly bashful Kitty in the side. Her grin faltered when she saw Elizabeth's neck. Her eyes widened and she let out a gasp. "What gorgeous jewelry! Lord, he really *is* rich!"

"And you are the same as ever," Elizabeth said, shaking her head.

Mrs. Bennet sprang into action when Bingley and Jane descended from the carriage. Grabbing her eldest daughter's hands and pulling her into a hug, she exclaimed, "My dear. I knew you would come at once, but I expected you hours ago! I've been all aflutter, you would not even understand!"

Jane patted their mother on the back. "Well, we are here now and our uncle and aunt Gardiner will arrive tomorrow."

"Is Papa awake?" Elizabeth asked her sisters.

Hearing it, Mrs. Bennet turned and bustled over to her. "You should change and wash up. You must've had a difficult journey."

Elizabeth gave her mother a wan smile. "My father won't mind the dust and neither do I."

"Our belongings will arrive tomorrow with our coach," Darcy said stiffly. "Please forgive us."

Mrs. Bennet brightened. "That is no matter, no matter at

all, Mr. Darcy. You already know that you can find anything in Meryton, anything at all that you need." While Mrs. Bennet prattled on regarding sending a stablehand into Meryton for anything they might need overnight, Elizabeth slipped inside, Jane at her heels. "She acts like I married into the aristocracy," she said.

Jane sighed while they took their gloves off in the dark vestibule. "You can't fault our mother for being nervous. You must admit it was a very optimistic start."

Now out of her mother's presence, Elizabeth had leisure to decipher the emotions lodged in her throat. She would not call them optimistic by any means. An acidic bitterness instead coated her tongue and made the backs of her eyes sting. She couldn't forget, like Jane did, how her mother had lambasted her person before she realized Elizabeth was in the carriage.

Elizabeth moved forward, the familiar rooms stirring up her memories. At the forefront were the last memories she had of Longbourn. The loud screeches to get out, to never darken her door again until Elizabeth could be a good daughter. She eyed the dark wood bannister. Mrs. Bennet had breathed down Elizabeth's neck all the way down those stairs, making Elizabeth trip on the bottom step and her attempt to scramble away with her heavy overnight bag.

"It is no matter," Elizabeth said. "I am not here for her."

They reached the door to their father's study. Jane squeezed her elbow before she pushed the door open.

"He's not in good shape," said a voice behind them, making them turn.

Mary had followed them in unnoticed and she now hugged her Bible to her chest and adjusted her spectacles. The corners of her eyes were red, which was the most emotion Elizabeth could recall ever seeing her younger sister express since she slept in the nursery.

"I read to him every day," she said, stroking over the leather cover of the Bible before she looked up at Elizabeth somewhat tremulously.

"I'm glad you were here to comfort him."

"But you should have come sooner."

"I know," Elizabeth said. "But I couldn't."

"You could've," Mary said, "but you are here now. The doctor has placed him on a heavy dose of medicine, so please understand if he seems strange."

Elizabeth stepped away from the door and reached out for her sister. "Thank you for taking care of him."

"It's my duty," Mary said, blinking at her owlishly.

"And yet how often are Kitty and Lydia in here?" She squeezed Mary's shoulder. "You're a good daughter, and a great sister."

Those wide eyes blinked in confusion. "Lizzy, I just chastised you."

Elizabeth smiled. "Like a great sister does." She turned away while Mary remained bemused and followed Jane into her father's study.

The faint scent of dust tickled her nose, but the wretched stench of illness overwhelmed nearly everything. Jane strode to the window closest to her father's bed and threw it open.

Elizabeth took a cautious step toward the bed. Would he recognize her? Had he forgotten her? They were silly fears, but she had them all the same as she looked upon his frail form, barely a lump under the blankets.

She stepped up to her father's side. "It's Lizzy and Jane," she murmured, studying her father's papery skin. "Papa?"

Mr. Bennet stirred. Cloudy blue eyes, brilliant and sharp, opened and blindly searched the room. "Lizzy?"

"Here, Papa." Elizabeth gripped his hand, bony knuckles under her palm. "I'm here now."

"Lizzy," he murmured. His eyes closed without falling upon her once. His breaths evened out and he slipped back into sleep.

Jane stood watching over her shoulder. She sniffled. "I'll leave you," she said quietly. "I'll go see to our mother now. Do you want any refreshments?"

Elizabeth shook her head. Her throat was too thick to speak, saltwater and pain and memory choking her. Jane tiptoed out of the room and the door shut behind her with the soft snick. Then it was only Elizabeth's voice breaking the silence. "You've always been my anchor, you and Jane. I don't know what I'll do without you, Papa. It's only home when *you're* here."

10

THEY SAT TO SUPPER. MRS. BENNET MADE A FUSS REGARDING the two extra plates she had not accounted for, but this did not stop her badgering Mr. Darcy into taking the best cut of venison. Lydia and Kitty enlightened their sisters about the latest happenings in the neighborhood, reminding Elizabeth once again how young they were. They even bemoaned their bad luck they could not go to Brighton for even a fortnight to see their recently departed friends in the regiment. Lydia even dared to ask Jane to intercede on their behalf with their mother.

Mrs. Bennet, however, sternly shut down this line of conversation, pointing out their father's condition and how they must be near at home for him. "Besides," Mrs. Bennet added, "undoubtedly you'll have better prospects soon." She glanced toward Elizabeth.

"Can you pass the juice, please?" Elizabeth asked Lydia.

Lydia held it out, but didn't release it immediately, a sly look in her expression. "Lizzy... can you lend me some pin money?

"Now that you have so very much," Kitty said laughing.

Mrs. Bennet cleared her throat. "There's no doubt your sister will take care of you girls, especially now you are earning so very much with your books. Lizzy is a published author now, isn't that right?"

Never had a proud smile been directed her way from her mother's end of the table. Elizabeth stared for a moment, then shook her head like a horse clearing away the flies buzzing about. She refused to look at Darcy, afraid of what she would find in his expression. "I gave everything to Mr. Laurence to help find a way out of the entail," Elizabeth said. She poured her juice and took a polite sip. "I'm sure you too have pin money aplenty now that Jane and I are out of the house."

"You've always been so fussy," Lydia said, laughing. "Kitty, do you remember when Lizzy made us sign a note when we borrowed her pink velvet dress?"

"She made *you* sign it. I didn't borrow it."

Lydia waved this way with her fork. "Anyway it was a very ugly dress, though you claimed it took you a month to fashion the lace. Your expression when I told you I tore that silly lace! I've never laughed so hard in my life. Do you remember that, Lizzy?"

Elizabeth wished for something stronger than juice vividly.

Lydia's laugh brayed across the table. "It did not really tear Lizzy's dress, so you shouldn't look at me so, Jane. It was only my little joke since she made me sign that note for it and gave me so many dire warnings."

"There wasn't a speck of dirt on it, I'll grant you that, and now I can almost laugh at your little joke," Elizabeth said with a smile. Lydia wasn't a cruel sister. Just a thoughtless one.

"How nice it is to have you back… though the circumstances…" Mrs. Bennet trailed off, pain in her expression. Elizabeth braced herself for her mother to start wailing about her hardships or otherwise embarrass herself in front of Darcy. But after a moment, Mrs. Bennet pasted on a smile and turned to Darcy. "Would you like another helping of the venison?"

Later after their supper, Elizabeth returned to Mr. Bennet's study to sit with him before she went to bed. Mrs. Bennet followed her inside, bidding her other daughters a gentle goodnight before closing the door.

Elizabeth sat at her father's bedside, her hands folded in her lap. She was prepared to sit with her father all night, but the tension aching in her shoulders said it might be much less if her mother intended to stay, too. *As long as she is quiet and respectful, I'll be content*, she thought.

Mrs. Bennet came to the end of the bed and folded her arms, scowling at Elizabeth. "You must know that giving all your money to Mr. Laurence does this family no good. We all know that there is no way out of the entail."

"It is the best hope that we have," Elizabeth replied, confused.

"Regardless, we could have used that money. There is the farm and we have not been able to collect as much taxes as we hoped. The two tenants on the north side did not have a very good crop year. And your dear sisters have had to go with only two new dresses this season."

"We never had many new dresses," Elizabeth said. "At least Jane and I did not."

"Regardless, you should send your income home from now on. It can be spent better here on giving your sisters decent hope for the future."

"Mama," Lizzy sighed.

"You cannot be so cold hearted to your sisters. And your poor mother. How we have suffered and to know that it only enriched Mr. Laurence's pockets! This useless endeavor to escape the entail—"

"It is not useless. It is our home, as you have reminded us all countless times." Elizabeth stared at her mother, her mind working, her disappointment like ash on the back of her tongue. "If my sisters' pin money is not enough, well, they must make do as I did."

"What do you even need such a thing for?" Mrs. Bennet exclaimed.

"For whatever she likes," Mr. Darcy said.

Elizabeth stiffened. Watching her mother's expression, she saw her mother pale to the roots of her hair. She spun toward the doorway where Darcy stood, his arms folded, his stare thunderous.

"Madam," Darcy said with a venomous tongue, "if you have some concern with the ledgers and the available funds for your daughters, please feel free to ask for mine or Charles' assistance. We would happily assist you in budgeting the estate's finances going forward."

Mrs. Bennet's hand shook as she placed it on the footboard. "O-oh, no, I couldn't possibly…"

"Ah." Darcy nodded like a heron spearing a fish. "Forgive me for misunderstanding. The way you asked your daughter for her hard-earned publishing money made it seem like the estate was experiencing financial difficulties. I'm glad to hear that isn't the case." Darcy's gaze flicked to Elizabeth, his black eyes unreadable. "My wife needs rest, so it's best if we go up now."

"Right," Elizabeth said, standing. It was no use, she decided, with a longing look at her father's still sleeping form. "Goodnight, Papa," she whispered, and then rounded the bed to reach her husband's side.

"Mrs. Bennet," Darcy said with an incline of his head. He led Elizabeth into the corridor and to the stairs with the perfect, haughty manners of the upper crust.

"How do you stand it?"

Elizabeth pinched the bridge of her nose. So deep did her exasperation for her mother run, it took a moment to form words. Finally, dropping her hand with a sigh, she said, "It is easier some days."

"How long has she done this?"

"Done what?"

"Targeted you like this? Not a moment after you left the table did she seek you out to spew this nonsense, and your youngest sisters, I'm afraid to say, laughed and shared glances."

"Is that why you followed her?"

"I followed you," he said. "But I don't deny my curiosity. How long has she sought to use you, Lizzy?"

"From birth, I imagine," she said. Seeing his expression, she sighed. "Mostly it was apathy until Mr. Collins. Where before I could easily escape her bemoaning what a poor daughter she had, to be more interested in men's doings than my family's fortune, with Mr. Collins' arrival came demands."

"To marry him."

She nodded. "To secure our family's position. If she thought I could ever possibly snag a gentleman with a fortune, surely she would have pushed unlucky Mary into his path instead."

He frowned. "You're teasing, but you're also serious?"

"Unfortunately," she said, and her expression morphed into a small smile at his stricken expression. "I do not mind it because I know she won't change. It would be like asking a rainstorm to change. I must weather the storm however I can instead of focusing on what might have been."

"Think of me as your umbrella, then," he said. They had reached the door to the room they would share. He turned to her, clasping his hands gently around hers. "Allow me to help you weather the storms. If your mother bothers you again…"

"You cannot protect me from every dragon in the land, Mr. Darcy."

"I can and will," he said.

11

She sank into him when he led her to the bedroom and they sat on the window seat together. Her head on his shoulder, his arm around her back, he seemed to dare any dragon to come close to her again.

"Thank you for this," she said, her fingers tracing the outline of his ribs.

"Of course."

The softness of his eyes when she looked up at him could not be overstated. Longing tugged at her senses.

"How is your headache?" he asked. She'd claimed a mild one before dinner. It'd been so long ago, seemingly, she had forgotten about it.

"It wasn't much of one in the first place." She squeezed him tighter and rubbed her cheek against his shoulder.

He shifted out of her arms and stood. "I should leave you to rest, regardless. The past couple days have been hard on you. Charles should still be downstairs—it is too early for him to retire. I'll speak to him about the ledgers and hopefully that will appease your mother."

"I'm afraid you don't know my mother," she said.

Darcy pressed his hand to her shoulder. "Rest, Lizzy. I'll take care of this."

Elizabeth didn't recall falling asleep. She remembered changing into her nightgown and stretching out on the mattress, feeling as if it would be impossible to go to sleep. Darcy remained downstairs, and she would speak to him at a minimum before she fell into Morpheus' arms. The bed was empty beside her, and cold.

Now hands shook her and a familiar set of owlish eyes blinked down at her.

"Lizzy, Papa asked for you."

"Mary?"

"You must hurry - there's no telling how long his clarity will last."

Elizabeth scrambled to dress and followed her sister downstairs. Mary left her at the door to the study, giving her a small smile before she headed toward the music room. Elizabeth took a deep breath and went inside.

"I didn't expect it would take a deathbed request for you to return home."

"Oh, Papa," she said, rounding the end of the bed to reach aside. She gripped his knobby hands between hers, holding tight to the man who seemed almost revived. There was health in his cheeks and his eyes sparkled. Those were good signs, weren't they? "You only needed to ask and I would've been by your side."

"If only that were true. Why did you not return my letters?"

"You only wrote the one, Papa. No, there were two. One you sent to Mr. Laurence."

"Ah." Mr. Bennet closed his eyes. "I see what has happened."

"I'm afraid I don't."

He shook his head and opened his eyes, pinning her underneath those vibrant blue eyes which had fascinated her since childhood. "It doesn't matter. Tell me why you have come here with Mr. Darcy."

Elizabeth groaned under her breath. "Papa, Jane has told me about the misunderstanding. But that's all it was. Mr. Darcy and I... We began courting prior to my leaving Longbourn, but I never told Jane my secret. And when Mr. Collins accosted me one day, she thought the resulting bruises were from Mr. Darcy."

Mr. Bennet's forehead wrinkled. He shook his head several times. "Accosting? Mr. Collins assaulted you? I think you need to start from the beginning, Lizzy."

So Elizabeth did, keeping the particulars private so as not to stress her father unduly. Not that it helped. He clenched his hands so hard when she mentioned Mr. Collins assault of her person that her bones creaked under his hands.

"Why didn't you tell me?"

"I was given leave to go to London," she said. "I didn't wish to make more of it, to cause alarm and add a delay, potentially stay another night under the same roof as him. I also didn't know that Jane had told you about Mr. Darcy, so forgive me if we both kept secrets."

"You are always very good at reminding me of my failings," he said with a chuckle.

"I didn't mean any harm. I simply wanted to leave, Papa."

"Understood. But you are here now and married, to boot, so our bad actions are not as terrible as they might have seemed." He squeezed her hand. "So you do love him?"

They had shared only a kiss on their wedding day, and no intimacy beyond handholding last night. Was his pity for her greater than his desire? Would he never kiss her again? Hold her again? With no way to tell, Elizabeth could easily fall into anxiety. But with her father in front of her, waiting for an answer about her mysterious husband, she needed to focus on what was important.

"I wouldn't have married him otherwise, would I? And do you… Are you angry at her?"

"I could not be angry at my Jane. But that's not who you're talking about, is it?"

"Mama never gave you any of my letters, did she?"

"To think of you living at the sufferance of my brother and sister was hard enough. To read about it, as well… Perhaps she was attempting to protect me from my disappointment." He caught her eye and smiled, the wrinkles beside his eyes much deeper than she recalled from her days sitting at his knee. "You think I should blame her? I have much to think about these days. Assigning blame, letting my temper rule me — it seems so pointless."

Those long hours at his knee. The days they spent talking about everything and nothing. The shared glances over the dinner table when Sir William retold the tale of knighting while everyone ohhed and ahhed again.

She squeezed her father's hands. "Papa, I'll stay as long as you need me."

"What will your husband say of such a declaration? Or has he abandoned all sense when he married you—all of two days ago, I might add?"

She raised her eyebrows. "I'm insulted. Naturally, I married a man without sense. Who marries a sensible man in this day and age?"

Mr. Bennet laughed so hard he choked, and Elizabeth hurried to get him a cup of water, grinning.

"You didn't give him any of my letters?"

She found her mother in the drawing room, her feet up on a stool, the fire blazing in front of her. The thick curtains drawn over the windows muffled her sisters' voices outside. They walked in the garden, and she could faintly hear Charles' peppy voice remarking upon the late blooming roses. Mrs. Bennet sighed and lazily fanned her face with a new fan Elizabeth didn't recognize.

"Oh, Lizzy, now is not the time. I hardly slept at all and need to rest. Besides, did you leave your father alone to shout at me?"

"As much as I want to, I'm not shouting. As for father, Mary is sitting with him. Why, Mama? Why didn't you give him my letters, and why did you never send along his to me?" She rounded her mother's chair and stood before her, disappointment crushing her chest, the tears she'd hidden from Mr. Bennet finally prickling her eyes. "Why would you do such a thing? Why hide those things?"

Mrs. Bennet closed her eyes, a wrinkle forming in her brow. She shooed her away with her free hand. "I have a dreadful headache and you're blathering on about the past in such a manner. Can't you see that your mother needs rest? You've always been such an illogical creature."

"These past months I've been under the impression that my father didn't write, didn't care at all!" She threw her hands into the air and let them come down to slap against her thighs. "To find out now that he sent me letters all along is heartbreaking."

Mrs. Bennet snorted. She opened her eyes and shook her finger at Elizabeth. "What would you have done? You were too busy with your books, with your friends, with your Mr. Darcy. You did not care at all for your family or else you would've sent money."

"Should I have read your mind from a hundred miles away to know that you needed money? You cannot accuse me without admitting your own fault. You never wrote to me. Indeed, now I wonder, if Jane had not been in London already, would you have notified me of father's situation?"

Her mother sat up, placing her feet on the floor so she could better glare at Elizabeth. "And did I once receive a letter from you? You may rage at me all you want, you don't know how I suffered—nor did you ever care."

Elizabeth drew herself up, cold fury stiffening her muscles. "Your last words to me made it clear you would not welcome any letter." Then the fury went out of her, aggravation sinking into resignation. Her shoulders sagged and she pinched the bridge of her nose. "I'll leave you to rest. Obviously, nothing I say will change your mind. To believe I hoped for an apology…"

She stormed toward the door, her mother's indignation chasing her out. "An apology, hmph! As ungrateful as always —wait, wait, Lizzy!" Elizabeth came to a reluctant stop and turned around, her expression set in stern lines of aggravation. Her mother did not notice, but switched subjects with all the grace of a three-legged dog. "We must discuss our move to London. Your father's time is coming and we must decide on things for your sisters and me."

"London? You plan to…" She drew off. Of course, her

mother planned to go to London. While Hertfordshire society was acceptable, her mother always loudly regretted not having access to the London *ton*. Hertfordshire was not enough when the glamour and glitz of London was available.

And now it is, with me, Elizabeth thought and closed her eyes.

"Kitty and Lydia can share rooms, of course—I expect Lydia will be off the market soon enough once London meets her, so Kitty will have her own room in a short time. I *do* expect there is enough room for me to retire away from all the bustle of it," she added meaningfully. "A small sitting room would be just the thing. Eastern facing, preferably, but you know I'm not particular."

Said by a woman who would faint if there was a single piece of chopped green onion in her potatoes, who ordered the furniture moved around on a whim due to phantom drafts or too much sunlight (which was "definitely not present yesterday, I tell you!").

"You wish to live with me?" She couldn't fathom this. "Not Jane or…"

"Well, of course. Look how well you've done for yourself after such an inauspicious beginning. How I despaired when you threw aside Mr. Collins—as if you didn't care one whit about your family being thrown into the hedgerow when your father passes. But now you've a fine house in town and our future is set for life." Smirking as if it were her very own triumph, she cast a knowing eye on Elizabeth. "Besides, it is only fair you take care of me when it is I who sent you to my brother's house. If not for me, you mightn't have met Mr. Darcy at all! *Nor* your fancy publishing endeavour."

A cold, terrible knot grew in her chest. Suffocating, thick. She stared at her mother, the mother praising herself for all her good fortune earned from her worthless daughter. Her numb lips formed words her ears did not hear, but her tongue shaped them anyway.

"You did not send me to my aunt and uncle, Mama. You cast me out."

Mrs. Bennet waved her fan at her. "Regardless—"

"There is no regardless," Elizabeth said. "You do not get to claim victory over any part of my life, except perhaps my birth. My education, my manners, my philosophy—it has formed *despite* you. Despite every obstacle you put in my path, I excelled. You've no claim, Mama."

"What's all this, then? Rowing again? I told you, Kitty."

Lydia laughed as she entered the room with her older sister at her heels. She threw herself onto the settee across from her mother and Kitty sat beside her, the two of them sharing identical mischievous looks.

Then Lydia put her hand across her forehead, sighing. "It is dreadfully boring here. We hoped to go to town and buy some ribbons to cheer up our spirits. How about it, Lizzy? Mama surely won't let us go if you or Jane do not chaperone us, and Jane has already said no."

Mrs. Bennet looked immensely relieved by this plan. "What a wonderful idea, Lydia. Lizzy—"

Anger stung her cheeks. "The last thing I came to Longbourn to do is shop and fritter away my time in Meryton," Elizabeth said.

"Lizzy!" Lydia's wails chased Elizabeth out of the room. She did not stop, even when she heard her mother consoling the two young women with sentiments like, "Never you mind, I'm sure you can talk her 'round—"

Elizabeth gave a sharp shake of her head as she stormed away toward the back of the house. Sense was lacking in most of her family. *Why* she let herself be disappointed by them again and again… it was almost comical.

She paused outside the western facing sitting room. Darcy had asked to use it to complete his business he left unattended in London, and she could hear the scratch of his pen against parchment through the open door. She debated going inside, but eventually shook her head and moved on toward the dining room. Putting herself forward for another rejection would be too much right now when she was so sensitive and fragile. Better to leave him alone, then, and soothe her wounded pride. She would relieve Mary and sit with her father again.

12

He noticed something off about his wife before dinner. The sadness was still there in her eyes, the slow way her lips pulled into a smile. That was not it. That was to be expected. Yet there was something added to the mix of his wife's mannerisms he could not attribute to her father's condition.

"Do you need to rest more?"

Elizabeth shook her head and gave him a not-quite-smile over her shoulder, her lips thinned into a tight line. "I dozed earlier when I sat with my father."

"You sat with him all day today. How is he?"

The apothecary had given them an update after his afternoon visit, and the shadow in her eyes confirmed it. "Not well. Very little time is left."

The sitting room door opened. It was the younger sister, the one whose childish, spoiled attitude prickled at his nerves. "Mama says to call you to dinner!" she said before skipping away. A giggle echoed down the hall and her voice was not the least bit muffled when she said, "I won, Kitty!

They're only speaking. And you said they must be kissing. What a laugh!"

Darcy stifled a groan.

"Sorry," Elizabeth said, standing. Her gaze didn't meet his, and a flush marked her cheeks. "I'll speak to them."

"It's fine," he said, hoping to mollify her. It didn't. She still wouldn't look at him. He held out his elbow. "Dinner?"

The rest of the house were settling into their seats when they entered. Mr. Gardiner was absent. "He's sitting with your father," Mrs. Gardiner said when Elizabeth enquired after him, and patted the seat beside her.

It did not go unnoticed to Darcy how Mrs. Bennet pursed her lips when Darcy sat beside his wife instead of taking the open chair at her left as she had made him do the previous night. Nor did he fail to see his wife's anxiety as Mrs. Bennet launched into an interrogation of the table, but Mrs. Gardiner in particular, regarding the state of London's society. Darcy was forced to admit several times how little knowledge he had of society when Mrs. Bennet turned to him to verify various facts and gossip she'd read in the papers.

With how tense Elizabeth was each time Mrs. Bennet turned to him, Darcy's suspicions grew.

"Yes," she responded when they were alone in her room that night after dinner and he asked the question lurking in the back of his mind all night. "She wishes to come to London and… live with us."

"Is that what you want?" She gave him a plaintive look in reply. "I see. Is it ridiculous to expect Mr Collins to allow her and your sisters to remain here?"

"She does not expect it, and truthfully, I would not wish it upon my sisters," she said quietly, twisting her hands in her lap. "Excluding what he did to me, his views are… unreasonable, in most instances. Fordyce, for example."

He winced and ran his hand through his hair. "Perhaps that is what we should focus on. Charles and I briefly discussed logistics, but if there is a way to purchase the entail rights from Mr. Collins, your mother could live here without worry."

"Do you really think he would agree to a deal after your argument with Lady Catherine? He takes great pride in being her loyal servant."

"That is why I think Charles would be crucial. *He* is not objectionable. The only concern is funds." The ideas had been percolating in his head all day and now they coalesced into an actual plan. "I could provide them to Charles and mortgage the property in return."

"You shouldn't have to do this," Elizabeth said. "Between my aunts, Jane, myself…"

"Marital felicity in all three of those marriages could be broken." He saw her face. "I apologise. That was rude."

Elizabeth put her face in her hands, a choked laugh escaping. "No, you were quite right. And it is *four* marriages which may be ruined, considering my aunt in Meryton." Lifting her head, she gave him a bleak look. "Do you think it could really work?"

"If it does not, then we may consider opening Ramsgate for her use. There's plenty of society there, though it is much smaller than Bath, and your sisters may enjoy the sea bathing."

"You would do that?"

"It is *your* estate," he reminded her.

Elizabeth blinked at him and then colored. "I forgot."

"The ease in which you settle into a wealthy life," he said dryly.

"I must be if I'm forgetting whole houses," she said with a laugh. He liked that laugh and he liked how he had caused it.

"So we have two options. My preference is to simply purchase the entail. This home has been in your family for generations. I despise the thought of Longbourn leaving the hands of the family who cared for it all this time. I could not imagine such a fate on Pemberley."

Elizabeth patted the bed covers beside her with a sad, fond expression. "My father, as much as he used to grumble about this old place, feels very much the same."

"He was not the only one." At that moment, Darcy knew what he needed to do. "I'll go speak to Charles," he said, turning for the door.

"Tonight?" She lurched to her feet. Darcy paused, taking in her pale features and how weak she looked. How much had she eaten at dinner? Perhaps he could beg the housekeeper for a light snack.

"Yes," he said, watching her closely for her reaction. "Hopefully we can send a rider overnight to Collins. I know London will be no issue, but to Hunsford, I'm less certain. Time is of the essence—"

Elizabeth curled her hand around the bedpost. Her gaze dropped to the rug, then flicked up to him. "Because the law changes when my father passes?"

"It does, I'm afraid. It may become much more difficult to convince him to sell if he becomes master of Longbourn."

She snorted. "He seems like the type that would get a taste of power and never relinquish it."

"Well spoken," he said. Despite her humour, the exhaustion in her sagging shoulders made his voice soften. "Try to get some rest and don't wait for me."

Her head bobbed, a sad smile lifting the corners of her

lips. It didn't satisfy her. Something else was on his wife's mind. But he had time to investigate it later.

He left with her sad smile lingering in his mind like a poison mist infecting his concentration but, in the morning, even that sad smile disappeared because the worst had happened. Mr. Bennet had passed.

13

Moments seemed to last forever. The hours drained away. *Blink* and she was in the hall outside her father's study. *Blink.* Now walking outside beside Darcy with the harsh wind blistering her cheeks. *Blink.* Sitting beside the fire with warm tea seeping through thin china into her fingertips. How she travelled from place to place, Elizabeth did not know. The sun sank below the horizon on the first day of her father's passing and the silent space inside her, which had overtaken her soul, sighed.

"He's gone."

For the first time, she saw her mother. Her mother who had, despite all her caterwauling, took her husband's early death as a foregone conclusion. Now Mrs. Bennet looked *small*.

Small and broken and nothing like the mother Elizabeth remembered. For all her talk as if this was inevitable, the loss of her husband had hit Mrs. Bennet hard.

The complexities of her mother's personality was as inexplicable as Darcy's. Perhaps it was the human condition to have so many facets, like a bauble hanging in the sun with the reflection scattering in thousands of different directions.

And it was another facet of Elizabeth which could allow her to love her mother despite every pain and betrayal Mrs. Bennet inflicted upon her.

The family gathered. Her mother and sisters. The Phillips. The Gardiners and their children. Charles and Jane. Sitting beside her, Darcy shifted and his arm brushed hers. The comfort she felt expanded across the small sitting room and out into the world.

"Shouldn't we move to the front sitting room? It's cramped!"

Lydia's complaining mutter reached her and Elizabeth shook her head. "I like this." Darcy opened his hand beside her knee and she clasped it, and the silence that had pervaded her all day turned the corner.

However, as inevitable as the sundown, the peace in Longbourn could not last. However broken she was, Mrs. Bennet's plans only paused, and as the family started to file out of the sitting room, yawning and rubbing their eyes, Mrs. Bennet called for Elizabeth to see her to her room.

"My dear," she said, grabbing Elizabeth's arms and leaning on her as if she could not bear her own weight, "what are we to do? Whatever can we do?"

Elizabeth caught Darcy's frown as she escorted her mother out. She gave him a smile, small though it was, and hoped it would placate him.

She helped her mother limp into the hall towards the stairs. "Let's get you settled, Mama. It's been a long day."

The short walk to her mother's room was the warmest moment she'd shared with her mother in… years. Walking together, supporting her mother, she realised how small her mother was, frailer than her loud dramatics made her out to be. Which one was her real mother? Or was this another facet she'd never noticed, never having been close enough in her mother's confidence to observe.

However, as soon as Elizabeth closed her mother's bedroom door behind her, Mrs. Bennet straightened to her full height and turned on Elizabeth. "Have you spoken to him? What has he said? No, your expression says it all," she said, sighing.

"Mama," she began.

Mrs. Bennet grabbed her hands tight. "Tonight, Lizzy. You must speak with him tonight. Tell me you will, tell me you will not turn out your own mother and your three young sisters."

She ripped free of her mother's grip. "Do you truly think I'm so cruel? You paint a picture of a villainess when I have done nothing to earn such a cruel designation!"

"Oh, you are too sensitive! What am I expected to think when my second eldest did not invite her family to her wedding except to believe you are embarrassed of us, ashamed and—"

"You cast me out, Mama. I will not say more on this matter. Nor will I entertain any more discussion about moving to London—not tonight, at least."

"Lizzy!" Mrs. Bennet wailed.

"You and I are different in countless ways, but our commonality this day is that we both woke up and found a person dear to our hearts lost to us forever."

Mrs. Bennet buried her face in her hands and wailed loud enough to cause several relatives to come running down the hall, the sounds of their footsteps background noise while Mrs. Bennet lifted her head and met Elizabeth's eyes, chin wobbling. "You are so cruel to me. You don't know how much I suffer having a daughter like you!"

Elizabeth could say nothing to that, and left directly. After all, Mrs. Bennet was correct.

DARCY WAITED IN THE BEDROOM. He took one look at her face and held out his arms. Elizabeth did not hesitate to throw herself into his embrace, pressing her face into his chest. She would snatch greedily at what little comfort he had to give her.

His voice rumbled through his chest into her. "What did she say?"

"Only that I need to convince you to bring them to London." She swallowed the salty lump in her throat enclosed her eyes, his embrace more comfortable than her childhood home. "I have written books that will outlive me, but I cannot have a civil conversation with my mother. How is that logical?"

"I will take care of this." When she leaned back, startled, he shook his head at her expression. "It's my duty to protect you, and if that's from the people in this household, I will do so. I won't let her hurt you again."

"What a dragon slayer you are," she said, and tilted her chin, shyly glancing up at her husband. "Would thou allow your maiden a kiss before you take this quest?"

"Naturally," he said, and his soft smile made her stomach flutter and her knees go weak. Her eyes closed, and she reached up on tiptoe, mouth pursed…

Darcy pressed a soft kiss on her forehead and retreated. "I unfortunately have some correspondence to return in the morning, so it'll be some time before I come to bed. You won't mind the candles, will you?"

Elizabeth swallowed her heart and her disappointment.

"No, I don't mind." The sting to her pride was one too many for this terrible day. She turned away, pasting on a brave smile, and resolved herself to forget about asking for physical affection from her husband.

"What cruelties! You would send us away, your wife's poor daughters and mother. Long have we suffered with my husband's illness, squeezing every bit of use out of our resources so we might raise our girls properly. And for this to be the outcome! To send us away with no hope for prospects, to a squalor, no doubt—"

Mrs. Bennet had gone on in this fashion for some time after Darcy had arranged this meeting and issued his decree. He stayed still, though all he wanted to do was put his head in his hands.

"Now, sister, that is unfair," Mrs. Gardiner began. He'd asked Elizabeth's aunt to join this conversation and well he had, given she was the only other source of reason in this room. "We must listen to Mr. Darcy before judgement is made."

Darcy tried again. "Ramsgate is not a small estate, nor is it in an unfashionable part of the town. I assure you the house and grounds have been maintained, and you can live there comfortably with your daughters."

Mrs. Bennet's flush made him wonder if he should open the window. "With no prospects? There is hardly any society in Ramsgate! Mr. Darcy, you once mocked the society of Hertfordshire, yet you would happily send us away to become recluses!"

"Then you may remain here and hope for kindness from Mr. Collins," Darcy said coldly. "He will, undoubtedly, be happy to control your lives in a manner he sees fit. Knowing the man's lacking character, I would not put your daughters in his way, but I will not go against your wishes if you choose to remain here."

Mrs. Bennet's befuddlement remained. Darcy suspected the woman was used to her antics, those tears, wails, and cries for smelling salts—all of which she had done in the past quarter hour—put to use to serve her agenda. But he was not to be cowed by an unhappy mother, and though he'd held his tongue til now about her discourtesies and blatant mistreatment of Elizabeth, it was not long until the respect he had for Elizabeth failed against his desire to put in her place this woman who dared call herself Elizabeth's mother.

Mrs. Gardiner leaned forward to capture Mrs. Bennet's attention. "And while we would be happy to take on Mary, even Kitty, potentially, your brother and myself simply do not have the means to take you all in. Please think on this rationally, sister."

Mrs. Bennet snapped at her sister-in-law. "You fail to believe I have thought of this rationally! Boon as my daughters are to me, I'm left with three unmarried girls who lack decent prospects. In London, if we might not just stay for the season at least—" She turned her pleas upon Darcy again. "Jane tells me your sister is recently out. My girls can help her navigate through these troubled waters with ease!"

Darcy pinched the bridge of his nose. He was done. Done, and he would need to beg Elizabeth's forgiveness, but a quarter hour in the same room as Mrs. Bennet was an impossible, Herculean task.

"Ma'am, your priorities differ from mine. Rightfully, you seek to secure your daughters' futures."

Her expression relaxed into relief. "Yes! And thus London—!"

"Whereas my priority is my *wife*." Mrs. Bennet's lips flapped opened and closed and he glared to keep her silent. "After the unbearable way you have treated her the past few days, I would trust my wife to a pit of vipers before I allowed you to live under the same roof."

Paling, she sank against the back of her chair as if Darcy tried to strike her. Her chin wobbled as she looked to her sister. "My word! Do you hear how he mistreats me? His own mother-in-law, to whom he subjects to his scorn!" She attempted to rally, pulling herself up. "I may very well not be wealthy like you, Mr. Darcy, but I am still worth respect!"

"Until the point you attempt to stomp on myself and my wife, yes," Darcy said. He rose and straightened his jacket, irritation making his movements jerky. "It is either Ramsgate or here, Mrs. Bennet. I unfortunately cannot bear the repercussions if you come to the London townhouse, and since it seems you will not bend on that point, I will take my leave."

He bowed and strode out of the sitting room. Mr. Gardiner and Charles were walking along the hall toward him; they paused at the sight of him. Mr. Gardiner lifted his eyebrows and took out his watch.

"I knew I was running a little late, but is the conversation over already?"

"It is for me." Darcy shook his head in disgust as Mr. Gardiner's eyes widened. "She cannot be reasoned with, unfortunately."

"Ah." Mr. Gardiner grimaced. "She has been under stress for some time... please excuse her, Mr. Darcy. She doesn't mean to offend."

On the contrary, she didn't care who she offended. Darcy held that thought and looked to Bingley. "I have informed her that Ramsgate is available. However, she insists on residing with us in London, which I cannot abide. Just so you both are aware, I will be convincing Elizabeth to leave as soon as our duties here are complete. She has been at Elizabeth's throat this whole time, and my wife needs peace and rest."

"Do I?"

Elizabeth appeared at the end of the corridor and walked up to him with a fractured smile. Still, she didn't hesitate to slide her arm through his and tuck herself against his side. For that, he was immensely grateful. Some of his irritation melted away.

The door behind Darcy opened and released a frazzled Mrs. Gardiner. He'd never seen the polite, sociable woman in such a state, but that was what a quarter hour of Mrs. Bennet could do to one person.

"Did you have any luck?" Darcy asked, suspecting the answer.

She shook her head slowly, a sad gleam in her eyes. "I fear we may have to speak to Mary ourselves," she told her husband. "She refuses to listen to sense, and she is saying all manner of cruelties in her disappointment."

"I'm certain my name has arisen," Elizabeth sighed. Though she was smiling when Darcy looked at her, he didn't like it. Brittle, cracking.

Mrs. Gardiner looked down, shamefaced, before she straightened, focusing on the matter at hand. "Perhaps if you told her Ramsgate is your estate, she might look favorably upon the situation, having that security. Right now, she claims she fears Mr. Darcy throwing them onto the streets."

"She fears a great many untrue things," Elizabeth said. "She only desires London, my dear aunt. Telling her about Ramsgate will only open her to more jealousy, and at this point, I'm afraid to say my husband is right. I need peace. If my mother refuses Ramsgate, then there is nothing more to discuss."

It was with pride he noted how Elizabeth's shoulders straightened, how her sagging decline over the past few days had been polished into solid determination. He placed his hand atop hers, and her gaze flickered to him but she did not return his approving smile.

"If that's the case... I will respect that," Mr. Gardiner said. He shook his head in disbelief. "She has always been stubborn, but to place herself in this position while pitting herself against her daughter is beyond imagination. We will speak to her, and whatever she decides is up to her. However, we will offer Mary a place in our home. We fear her treatment will become much worse if left as it is."

"Netherfield remains open to Mrs. Bennet, naturally, though she's declined it so far," Bingley said, shuffling his feet. "If the worst comes to pass, they have a home there."

"You are a good man." Darcy nodded to his friend who looked cheered at this, though the prospect of taking in his mother-in-law had made him look rather green around the edges.

Elizabeth squeezed his arm. "We'll leave you to it," she told the rest of the party, and Darcy bid them goodbye and escorted his wife away while the others muttered and began the hardship of seeing to Mrs. Bennet.

14

"You haven't mentioned I overstepped yet."

That night, Darcy broke the silence as she readied for bed, something he hadn't done before. Usually he made any excuse to leave until enough time passed she ought to be finished and covered modestly by bedclothes and blankets. She looked at him now in the mirror's reflection, her brush half-risen to her shoulder.

"I already said you were correct to act as you did. Are you gloating now?"

Darcy's stiff shoulders loosened some at her teasing. "Whatever you want to do, I am at your service."

She stared at him then, at this man who would entreat her sincerely one moment and give her a cold shoulder the next. She distracted herself as she tidied her belongings on the vanity. "After the funeral, what are your plans?"

Her voice was distant even to her own ears. A wall between her and the reality where her father was gone. Darcy seemed to hear it and paused.

"There's no pressing business in London for me," he

said. "If your work can be done long distance, I thought we might go to Brighton, or perhaps Bath."

"I've no interest in a busy tourist destination. But the seaside would be nice."

"I did receive an invitation earlier in the year. Campton-on-Sea. Mr. Anderson asked me to invest at one point. It's a developing village in the south with some small society as I understand it. Does that sound amenable?"

The sea and fresh air—closing her eyes, she could already feel it ghosting against her cheeks. "It won't be an issue for you?"

"There's nothing that I cannot do by post." Darcy stepped forward and rested his hand on her shoulder. "What worries me is I cannot say the same for *your* responsibilities."

"I think it could be managed," she said after a moment's thought.

Darcy squeezed her shoulder. "If you even need to. You should take all the rest you need."

"If only Mr. Davies shared your feelings," she said. She'd received a letter that included a query regarding her second novel's edits alongside his condolences for her father. Her lips curled when she read it. Trust him to keep his priorities aligned with the publishing schedule.

Darcy grumbled something under his breath, scowling. "I can send my solicitor to remind him of your contract."

"My knight," she said. She turned her head away from the mirror before her reflection could reveal how happy his care made her. Clearing her throat, she said, "Mr. Anderson's little village sounds perfect—and Mr. Davies cannot complain since I *do* plan to work. Escaping the trappings of London and the countryside is all I desire."

"As you wish," Darcy said.

He held true to his word. As soon as the funeral rites

were over, Darcy arranged for their journey to Campton-on-Sea.

The weather remained mild all the way south when the salty air touched their upturned faces along with the pungent, sulphurous scent of the sea. Elizabeth found herself dreaming of the scent; seaweed and brine weaving through her subconscious. The skies were grey more often than not when she opened the shutters in her bedroom. Gardens, carefully tended and blooming in the heat, surrounded the small manor Darcy let. Elizabeth couldn't call the view from any room in the house less than charming.

A small staff was hired. Some looked at her in askance when she rearranged the small back sitting room for her own convenience; a larger writing desk situated before the doors that opened to the front gardens. They now seemed resigned to the oddity of their mistress who spent long hours sequestered away while she prepared for publication.

Elizabeth's mother had sent several letters in the past few weeks, the address on the front becoming increasingly more scrawling and unreadable. Elizabeth had not opened them. Her correspondence with Jane informed her of the circumstances at Longbourn instead. Apparently, Mrs. Bennet had barricaded herself in her room the very hour of Mr. Collins' arrival, leaving Charles and Mr. Phillips to navigate the changes Mr. Collins desired to implement. Cost-saving measures had promptly been put in place; now with only one girl on to care for the house, Kitty and Lydia were now attempting, with little success, to provide meals to the household. From Jane's report, Lydia had broken down approximately four times in the first week, much to Mr. Collins' consternation.

The shame of such a change in circumstances must have surely changed her mother's mind regarding the offer, but

Jane's letters assured her that Mrs. Bennet had not yet seen sense. Reading between the polite lines of her sister's tidy handwriting, Mrs. Bennet was still wailing over her misfortunes and her ungrateful daughter loud enough for the rest of the neighborhood to hear.

Mary had grabbed hold of the Gardiners' invitation to escape to London with both hands. Her letters to Elizabeth were full of undeniable happiness.

At least one member of her family was happy, certainly. Elizabeth bound her mother's unopened letters with a ribbon and tucked them in her desk. There was only a small part of her which protested at this point as she ignored her mother. Her mother's actions at Mr. Bennet's death had overridden most of Elizabeth's feelings of responsibility in that quarter. Now she only wished for the silence Mrs. Bennet had given her in London.

"Lizzy, what is your opinion? Shall I go with the blue or the white?"

Georgiana had taken advantage the lateness of the day to knock tentatively upon the door to Elizabeth's study. She now held out two handsome paste sets for Elizabeth's consideration, prompting Elizabeth's thoughtfulness as she looked from her young, hopeful sister to the jewelry.

"They both are very fine, and look marvelously well with your dress," Elizabeth said. "It's only a dinner at the Eastman's, so it can hardly be called an extravagant occasion. I therefore choose the white."

Georgiana looked between the white opal and the dazzling blue topaz set and nibbled her lip.

"What is it?" Elizabeth asked, softly because Georgiana did still shy away from Elizabeth sometimes although they'd been living together for several weeks now, her carriage from London arriving on the tail of Elizabeth and Darcy's. She liked to encourage the girl out of her shyness, which had inexplicably grown in the past week.

"I just thought the blue would bring out my eyes," Georgiana said with a flush.

"They would also compete with your eyes. Without a speck of other color, your eyes and your rosy cheeks will glow all the brighter. Trust me, it will be brilliant. Leave the topaz for a fancier party."

"Thank you," she said. "It's so nice I can easily have the opinion of someone I trust in these matters."

"As long as you do not hope for advice about the latest fashions of *ton*, I might be very helpful."

"You certainly are! Now I must finish getting ready," she said and hurried out the room. Moments later she heard her footsteps retreating upstairs, with much excitement for a mere dinner party.

Elizabeth had her own considerations to make as she got ready, closer to the evening and with little fanfare compared to her sister. Her dress was a simple blue silk with a matching fan. She wore her grandmother's pearl pins in her hair, and her reflection showed that she looked handsome enough.

"Will you wear these tonight, ma'am?"

Elizabeth looked over to where Trudy held open the case of her diamond set. The young maid looked excited over this prospect, her eyes gleaming dreamily as she admired the diamond set. "They're so pretty," she sighed.

Elizabeth's smile withered, and she took the case from Trudy and put it back in its place. "I think something else, my dear."

She could hardly stand to look at the case, much less the jewels inside. A visible sign of how she'd been accepted into the Darcy family, yet the reception from her husband remained as cold as the diamond. He had not touched her beyond how a close acquaintance would, and though he routinely took her on picnics or walks down to the rocky beach, it only magnified the distance growing between them each day.

Trudy sighed as she watched Elizabeth tuck away the case. "It seems like a waste to never wear them, ma'am."

Elizabeth picked up her old pearl and diamond set. Reliable and while not especially fashionable, entirely hers. "I've worn them enough. Can you help me put these on?"

"Would you like to dance, Mrs. Darcy?"

Elizabeth smiled demurely. "I wouldn't wish to put you out."

Eileen House had been decorated wonderfully for the event by Mrs. Eastman and approximately twenty families across the county filled the elegant manor. *Small society*, it wasn't, at least to Elizabeth's untrained eye. The ladies, dressed in flowing gowns of silk and satin, moved gracefully across the floor, their movements like a symphony of color and grace. The gentlemen, dressed in crisp tailcoats and polished shoes, led their partners through the starting steps of the dance with confidence and poise.

In front of where she stood beside the wall, Darcy swallowed this rejection with not a flicker crossing his expression. "Then a walk about the room? Or the gardens," he added. "Mrs. Eastman said they've manufactured a small waterfall in the northern garden."

"It's rather cool tonight," Elizabeth said as she tugged her shawl further up her shoulders. "Georgiana looks very happy, doesn't she?"

Darcy turned smoothly and looked out over the dance

floor. Georgiana danced across from a young man from the village, Mrs. Eastman's nephew. He was as shy in his admiration for her as Georgiana was in a conversation. They suited each other well. Darcy sniffed. "I suppose," he said.

She would rather have liked to walk in the gardens. Mrs Eastman had mentioned the waterfall when they had chatted earlier, striking Elizabeth's curiosity. The many candles aglow in the room along with the rather large guest list for a simple dinner party dampened the small hairs at her neck. She waved her fan idly while Darcy's attention was stirred away from her.

She was saved from further conversation or any more invitations by the appearance of Mr. Anderson in their midst.

He mopped his brow while he joined their small party, returning Darcy and Elizabeth's polite greetings in turn. "I've given my apologies to Mrs. Eastman for being so terribly late, but I fear it's not enough. I'll be loudly complimenting the party all night."

"Shame on you," Elizabeth said with a laugh. Mrs Eastman, in Elizabeth's short acquaintance with her, had an extraordinary way of browbeating whose manners insulted her. It would take some sufficient grovelling on Anderson's part to set her bad graces straight.

Anderson tucked away his handkerchief and produced his amiable manners. "Well, I might as well get to it at once. Mrs. Darcy, is your next set free?"

"I'm afraid I'm sitting out tonight." Anderson's expression went blotchy in surprise—or dismay that he would have to find other dancing partners to relieve their hostess's anger against him.

He nudged Darcy who looked stiff at this familiarity and grew tense at what Anderson said next. "Darcy, old fellow, I can't imagine why you'd let your beautiful wife sit out tonight when we all know she dances so well."

"I'm certain it's none of my business," Darcy murmured, looking away.

"Miss Darcy!" exclaimed Anderson when Georgiana joined them, thankfully at the most perfect time to forestall any awkwardness. He bowed gallantly to the young woman. "Has splendour enough been called down to grace your countenance."

"Has your publishing enterprise been inundated with terrible poetry?" Elizabeth said, making Georgiana giggle.

"What insults I have to endure to keep my favourite author on board," Anderson said with a stern glance at Elizabeth. "Miss Darcy, would you do me the honour of a dance, if this terrible poet is acceptable to your sister?"

Elizabeth looked him over critically. "I suppose," she said, noting with some amusement how tense Georgiana grew under Elizabeth's consideration. So. Perhaps there was something to all that commotion getting ready.

Darcy approached her side while she watched the couple remove themselves to the dance floor to join the line. Quietly, he said, "It wouldn't put me out to dance, if that thought prevents you. I would enjoy it very much, with you."

He seemed sincere enough, his expression faintly reproving, though she wasn't sure whether it was directed at himself, for allowing Elizabeth to think him reluctant, or at Elizabeth, for believing him put out at the idea of dancing with his wife.

Either way, she did not desire to puzzle it out. "When one exercises the mind too much during the day, sometimes the feet are reluctant at night." She smiled blandly and patted Darcy's arm. On the line, Georgiana was receiving envious looks from their neighbors about her good fortune—

Mr. Anderson was a decided catch in any society, but especially this small one. "Perhaps another time?" she asked, watching Anderson bow to Georgiana to signal the beginning of the dance.

Darcy agreed in his quiet manner and decided to go out to the gardens himself, spurning the idea of cards when Elizabeth suggested it. She watched his broad back disappear through the balcony doors that led to the gardens and released the breath she'd been holding since the carriage ride.

She couldn't give her husband any sense of obligation. Not towards her. Not when he must regret his spontaneous actions on that fateful night the Gardiners found them. He had done so much for her, after all. She must respect that he wanted little else from her other than the outward signs of a happy wife.

Elizabeth had cut out the part of her which wanted more. She was happy as they were. She took a deep draft of her wine and set it down empty. Yes, she was very happy.

15

Darcy watched his hand as his pen moved across the page like a person outside of himself, a stranger watching another write. The majority of his attention was focused on the voices he could hear drifting through the open window which let beautiful golden sunlight enter his study on the east side of the manor. It was hard to concentrate on anything when he could hear the two ladies conversing, the notes of their soft voices floating on the wind to his ears.

It was the most he'd heard his wife speak since the night before. Darcy couldn't fathom it. He encouraged Elizabeth to dine with them, and they'd been on several picnics together and with Georgiana. He couldn't claim she was in a bad temper; her smiles were muted, her laughter rare, but that was to be expected, surely. But neither could he claim her melancholy was wholly related to her father's passing.

When he tried to broach the subject of her mother to Elizabeth, she'd responded with a frown of confusion and a slight shrug. "I'm not certain why we never developed a bond between mother and daughter, at least a less lopsided one. My respect for her has waned after years of disrespect bordering on malice, but the love due to her has not. I'll respond to her letters in time, so you needn't worry."

That wasn't his worry, and he left the conversation unsettled. He lacked the words to explain the uneasy churn in his soul.

In all appearances, Elizabeth *appeared* fine. She spent her days in her study working. On occasion she would break and he could take her to the beach or to the village; more often than not, she spent her free time during the day with Georgiana. Her nights, she was an amiable companion for any activity, whether it was a quiet night with the windows open to the balmy breeze or a dinner party at one of their neighbor's homes. But it was the ghost of his wife who joined them, not the vibrant woman whom he'd married. Every hour another brick joined the wall between them. Darcy couldn't see how to reach across. And he couldn't be sure Elizabeth would grab his hand even if he did so. She might just offer him another of those sphinx-like smiles and walk away.

After the Eastman's dinner party, he hesitated on his approach. So far, Elizabeth acted as if nothing were wrong. *Too well,* he thought. It almost fooled him and made him wonder if he read too much into her silences. But even frightened of him as she'd been in London, Elizabeth hadn't turned down a dance. She was no coward. That she would do so now, when there was presumably *happiness* between them, troubled him deeply.

But what was he to do? Darcy pondered on it while the hours passed. Eventually, the ladies returned inside. Elizabeth to her work, while Georgiana drifted into the front sitting room where Darcy had arranged a new piano for her pleasure. Rich and full music filled the house moments later, each note woven together to create a lighthearted, lifting tapestry laid over each room it touched.

And Darcy could not hear his sister's music without wanting to share this feeling overflowing him. He rose and stepped free of his office. The door to the sitting room was open to the hall, freeing his sister's soft voice as she began to sing.

He turned toward Elizabeth's office and paused. Elizabeth stood in the doorway, staring at him. Her doe-like eyes held his, emotions stirring behind her surprise. Wonder and deep admiration there while her knuckles turned white on the doorframe.

He held out his hand there in the hall. "Shall we dance, Mrs. Darcy?"

She paused. The hesitation was there, the joy drawing back to be replaced with that infernal wariness.

He kept his hand held out, steady. "Dance with me, Lizzy."

Elizabeth moved forward in her graceful way and placed her hand in his. "I would like that," she murmured.

The heat of her hand, the shudder of her breath, the effortless manner in which she moved. Wholly appealing, breath-stealing, Darcy could not take his eyes off her. It was magic he let sweep him away, into the deep richness of her gaze, their bodies floating on a cloud.

Connection was at the heart of why he loved this woman. This woman had placed a hook into the deepest part of his soul and drawn it into her hands. Now she drew it forth with the feminine allure of her body. The stairs were right there; it would be but a moment to retreat upstairs and a few steps more to his bed which would look even more handsome with his wife spread out over the coverlet.

"Lizzy," he murmured, their bodies so close in the dance his lips brushed her hair. Below him, she sucked in a breath.

A throat clearing from the front of the hall made him jerk back. Elizabeth yanked away, turning her head but not before he saw her intense mortification. Taylor, the young footman, stood in the hall. "Ahem. I apologize, sir, ma'am. I was just passing through and heard a knock. It's Mr. Anderson here to see you."

Darcy cleared his throat. A glance at Elizabeth showed her flushed, but she squared her shoulders and gave Taylor a nod.

"Show him inside, please," she said. When Taylor nodded and disappeared toward the front, she turned to him with a small, bland smile. "He asked if he could come by for an update for Mr. Davies. I didn't expect him to come today."

The venom that poured through him shocked him with its deadliness. Dark jealousy he'd thought he'd tucked away turned out to only be coiled in shadow, waiting to strike. It gritted his jaw and hardened his heart. Darcy turned to the stairs he'd contemplated with a lusty eye only moments ago. Now he strode up them with his heels striking the wood, anything but indifferent to the woman he left below.

It was either retreat or admit he could not control his vicious urge to strike *him*.

DARCY WAS in a fury of thought after hours passed, including a dinner he sat through in utter silence and left not a scant quarter hour after he sat. To look upon her face, pale as it was, made his senses roil in protest.

Something was terribly wrong.

He trusted Elizabeth unconditionally. She was an honest, loyal woman. If she would help her mother despite all the pain that woman had put her through, she would not turn away from Darcy's affections so easily. Therefore, Darcy did not believe for one instant that Anderson posed a threat to him.

But something obviously *did*, and Darcy determined that today he would find out what.

He received the perfect opportunity after dinner. He heard footsteps as someone passed his study and he stood, quickly crossed to the door, and opened it to peek out. Georgiana, her hand trailing on the bannister, hummed softly to herself as she ascended the stairs. To her bedroom, then, leaving Elizabeth alone.

He dithered only an instant. It was unlikely she would retire to bed so early herself. Unlike Georgiana, whose habits saw her rise hours before dawn, Elizabeth preferred a more reasonable hour. Darcy straightened his jacket, checked his reflection in the mirror above the mantle to ensure he was orderly, and then swiftly left his study to find his wife.

Tonight he would have his answers.

Darcy did not rush. He was not in a hurry. He may've been *swift*, but that in no way called for an accusation of being hasty. Darcy tugged on the reins of his control and held them firmly in his grasp, knowing the last thing he desired Elizabeth to see was her husband a worried, tense mess, wringing his hands like some fishwife. No. A wife needed a husband who was in control, and Darcy was a master of control.

Except where Lizzy is concerned, his mind whispered to him. He shoved the thought down.

A maid was waiting outside the sitting room's open doors. He nodded to her and murmured, "Leave us, please."

She bobbed a quick curtsy and left. Darcy tugged once more at the ends of his waistcoat, declared himself as tidy as he'd been half a minute ago, and entered the sitting room.

The furniture was elegantly upholstered in shades of cream and gold, with plump cushions providing comfort and sophistication, and Elizabeth looked like a vision straight from a master artist's brush in the middle of the elegantly appointed room. The large bay window Elizabeth sat beside looked out onto the manicured gardens, allowing natural light to fill the space in the daytime; now the panes of glass reflected candlelight. There weren't enough candles lit around her to illuminate her book. He could tell since she was squinting a little, her brow furrowed with a small frown turning down her soft pink lips.

His mother would have chastised her for reading too late into the evening. Smiling slightly at the memory of his mother doing the very same thing to him when he was a boy, he drew the pocket doors closed. Elizabeth lifted her head at the noise, blinking at him like an owl caught in a sunbeam.

"What are you reading this evening?"

"Another of the novels Mr. Anderson gave us," Elizabeth said. She paused. When he gave her no reaction, despite the embarrassment that stung him at the gentleman's name, the stiffness around her lips relaxed and she added, "This is one I haven't read before."

The first book she'd read of the little stack Anderson had dropped off for Elizabeth and Georgiana his first week arriving in Campton-on-Sea. Darcy didn't like the fellow, nor how coincidental his arrival seemed on the tail of their arrival, but he did appreciate seeing Elizabeth and Georgiana reading and talking together about their books with frequency every evening. "What is it about?" he asked, drawing nearer. The curve of her neck drew his eye, the candlelight touching her silky flesh in a dreamy way, painting her gold.

"A group of social climbers and their endless scheming to marry into wealth and status."

"Ah, so London."

She smiled, so quickly he could've missed it if he hadn't been paying rapt attention. But he did catch it and he did remember now, with a startling pain in his chest, that he hadn't seen enough of her smiles recently. Not ones directed at him, anyway.

"You're very right," she said. "It is rather like being there, especially because the author takes every opportunity to make his characters as witless and shallow as possible. I should like to say I'm surprised it was published, but I'm afraid I cannot."

"A severe judgement indeed," he said, sitting down on the settee next to her. The way her eyes darted to the closed door made him regret his jealous fit. That lack of control had lost her trust in him. He would need to earn it back, or else he would be stuck in this pit of uncertainty, without a rope, and not knowing how far he needed to climb.

"You left dinner early," she said, her gaze flicking to his before darting away.

"I did," he murmured. To be in her company, to smell the sweet jasmine of her perfume mixed with the salty tang coming in through the cracked window, was a heady affair. To be *alone* without his sister or her family or even a single member of staff... he cleared his throat and looked away. This might be dangerous to his control in other ways too. "I forgot a piece of correspondence. If I don't have it sent in the morning, it will be late to Pemberley."

"Ah." She nodded, relief crossing her expression. Foul guilt twisted in his gut at how he'd acted earlier. A jealous husband was not what she deserved. Her hands spasmed around her book and she looked down, away from him. "Well. I should probably—"

"Stay," Darcy said. He knew she would offer excuses, find some way to retreat from him again as she'd been doing since they arrived. It was time to put his foot down, to uncover the truth of matters as they stood between them.

Startled like a rabbit spotting the fox, she stared at him for a moment before ducking her head. "Al-alright. Did you have something to say to me?"

She's bracing herself, he realized with sudden foreboding like a knife to the back of his neck.

He turned on the settee to better see her face, the moment fraught with a tension that hovered over them like a falcon with its claws ready to seize its prey. Darcy searched her face, more sure than ever something was wrong, and yet still utterly clueless to what it could be.

"Is there something you're expecting?" he tested.

She blanched. "No," she whispered, shaking her head. Abruptly, she surged to her feet, stammering, "I really should retire."

Darcy grabbed her wrist before she could take more than a step away.

They stared at one another, her the rabbit and him the unwilling wolf. He softened his grip on her, unwilling to manhandle her. If she truly did not wish to speak to him… he would swallow his regret and agree, of course.

But first he had to try. "Will you keep up this running, or will you tell me what troubles you?" He rubbed his thumb over the delicate underside of her wrist while she trembled. "Believe me, if it is within my power to—"

Elizabeth shook her head, pulling her wrist out of his grip with a terribly wretched look.

"Please, Darcy. I don't—I can't stand this."

She backed away hastily when he stood. "Do you hate my presence so much?" he asked, his voice cool. If he had done something, upset her, and he couldn't repair it—his stomach clenched as slimy fear slid over his skin.

"*No.*" The vehemence of her response shocked them both. He saw her throat bob as she swallowed. More quietly, she said, "No. I don't hate you at all. Very much the opposite." Darcy drew in a breath, relief swelling his lungs, and then Elizabeth went on, fast, words running together as she struck out. "But I don't want to be rejected again. It's terrible and I-I understand you don't want that, not from me, but I cannot—I can't—" and she cut off with a choked sound as if stabbed.

If she had slapped him, he could not be more shocked. "Reject you? When have I done that?"

Fire roared in her gaze. "When have you *not*?" With a cutting gesture, she said, "Since our wedding night you have been the most determined husband in England to have nothing to do with your wife. You may sit beside me at dinner or breakfast, but attempt one kiss and you would disappear from the room like some bawdy magician's trick. It is unforgivable that I must put up with it and now must listen to this audacious tale of ignorance!"

And Darcy saw with frightening clarity how she may've made that assumption. Their wedding night when he'd first tested his restraint and saw her relax considerably toward him. But he'd made a considerable mistake to believe that she, a creature of vivacity and spirit, would be pacified by his most gentlemanly manners.

He closed his eyes. "I am sorry," he said, his voice ragged. "I am sorry, Lizzy. I can barely *think* straight when we are in the same room—I am a fool many times over. Believe me, if I'd known—"

Elizabeth's jaw clenched. "*If* you knew? I exhausted myself throwing myself at you, and now you apologize…" Breathing heavy, she shook her head. "The only thing I'm surprised of is that you haven't sought yet to annul this farce of a marriage."

"Farce?" He grabbed her wrist again when she attempted to spin toward the door. No doubt she would storm from the room with all the injured dignity due to her. *Annul?* The very idea made his blood run cold. "My heavens, Lizzy. If I'd known you thought this, I would've never let this misconception last!"

Her eyes glowed with challenge, her anger so great she fairly spat at him. "Then explain why you have ignored or turned your cheek at my every display of affection!"

"Because I wanted you to fall in *love* with me!" he snapped.

She stared at him. Glassy tears welled in her eyes, making her gaze shine.

"You terrible man," she whispered. "I *do*."

He searched her expression for any sign to the contrary, lightheaded and dizzy with relief and wonderment. All this time he'd told himself firmly that it might take a six-month or even a year to regain her trust, to prove his worth. Never in his wildest dreams had he imagined holding her respect again so soon.

"*Lizzy.*" Feeling choked him.

"I thought you regretted everything," she said, her voice just as strangled. A tear fell over the rim of her eyelid and raced over her cheek. Her chin wobbled. "I thought…

"I took advantage of your affection before. A gentleman,

I was not. I took advantage of your affection, resented you when you rightly dismissed my attempt to keep you in a fallen state, and tricked you into marriage, which feels like the least of my sins," he finished dryly. Another tear fell and his heart wrenched. What a bastard he was. Gently, he pulled her into his arms, cradling her with the tenderness and care she'd deserved from the beginning. "I only wanted to prove to you, and perhaps to myself, I was worthy of your love."

They held one another's gaze for a long, long moment. All the desire he'd pent up came racing to the fore, galloping away with his sense and control. Then she surged up, her fingers twisting in his hair, and he caught her.

The delicate end table was pushed out of the way and he had her there, right on the rug in front of the hearth, his trousers pushed down to his knees and her clinging to him like a strangling vine.

"Lizzy," he groaned, and was forced to bury his face in her neck or spend himself fruitlessly inside her in seconds.

She gasped to the heavens, chest heaving underneath him as if they'd run a mile. Inch by inch, he retook the field and won back his control. He lifted up with his arms braced to either side of her and admired the vision of his wife. The curls falling out of her tidy updo. A blush kissing the curve of her décolletage. Her lips bruised with his kisses.

She clutched at his shoulders with white-knuckled fingers and dug her heels into his backside. "Take me," she said. "Please, for the love of—"

Darcy surged forward. "I obey you, wife," he said as she thrashed underneath him. "I obey you, I obey you." The heat of her nearly suffocated him. He could not get enough, he could not breathe unless he was sheathed deep inside her, and his hips rolled back and came forward, sending her sliding upward on the rug, and him chasing her.

Now he had her, she would not escape.

"Ah, Darcy!" With a gasp, she slapped her hand over her mouth, her eyes wide over the edge of her fingers.

"No," he said, nipping at her jaw. "No, do not muffle your cries. Let me hear you. Let the world know how passionately I tend to my wife's needs."

Servants, neighbours, random sailors riding the waves of the sea—he minded not if her cries reached all their ears. As her cunt greedily clutched him, he begged for each wave of pleasure that rolled over her body in great, crashing waves and left him shaking and greatly affected in their wake.

Elizabeth was no passive princess. For every roll of his hips, she met Darcy. A siren's call answering every plea of his desire. Passion flooded their kisses, and need fueled the arch of her body to meet his thrusts. Her nails scored his back, and she came with a broken cry muffled in his cravat, and finally, finally, he followed her.

They rested together after this extraordinary explosion of love for several long minutes. Her heart thudded against his chest, almost as loud as his own heartbeat in his ears. Sweat made his clothes uncomfortable and itchy, and yet he did not want to move from the summery heat of their joined bodies. She caressed his side, sighing, and he pressed a kiss to her collarbone.

Her other hand was buried in his hair; her nails stroked over his scalp and he'd never felt so much like her pet before this. He enjoyed it immensely.

"Take me to bed," she said, and he did.

They barely made it to his handsomely styled bedroom before he was on her again like a savage beast. Their clothes became a tangle on the floor by the door and one stocking hung off her foot when he spread her out over the end of the mattress and feasted on her cries anew.

It took him back months to a season of lust when his days were filled with her bruising kisses and engulfing heat. When he first had her and realized her importance, though he was still oblivious to just how much he truly needed her. He had been stupid then, believing their affair could be temporary, and now he knew beyond a shadow of a doubt that she was a cornerstone of his soul.

Elizabeth met his urgency with her own, but she refused once more to let him control their liaison. She hooked her leg over his hip and then they were rolling and she rose up above him as his back hit the mattress like some kind of furious siren silencing her prey.

She sank down upon him and their mutual groans filled the room. His heartbeat thundered *tha-thump tha-thump* in his ears; every other sense was full of her. A drop of sweat sliding between her collarbones. The musky, feminine perfume of her pleasure growing thick. Her fingers curling against his stomach.

And she rode him.

Slow, so slow. Darcy could barely stand it. Every muscle in his body strained with the effort of holding back for her sake, Darcy watched rapt as she rode him. Forever, it seemed. The moonlight kissed her fine breasts and the soft curve of her stomach, framed by the red velvet bed hangings behind her. It gleamed in her eyes as she threw her head back, her fingers clenching on his thighs, her hair tickling his knees. *Goddess*, he thought. *I don't deserve this, but I have no guilt stealing every moment.*

"Oh, it feels…" Her voice broke. The slow roll of her hips was torturous. Darcy twisted his hands in the coverlet, veins on his forearms standing out as he controlled himself.

"Use me as you will," he gasped, watching this beautiful creature seek her pleasure with the greatest satisfaction. He would not interrupt this torture, and his mouth dropped open as she clenched around him, flaming, slick pleasure coating him. "F-fuck, Lizzy."

She clenched and shook and gasped and Darcy lost every fine edge of control. He grabbed her hips and rolled them, then rose above her and *finally finally* had his wicked way with her. The headboard hit the wall with each slow, hard thrust and he relished how it echoed with his heartbeat as he sent them both tumbling down, down.

"You wicked man," she murmured later when their blood finally cooled some. Darcy had thrown open the window to let in some cold air, though he regretted the loss of the delicious smell of their coupling. It hardened her nipples and pimpled her skin, yet she made no move to cover herself, merely lay across the bed like a starfish with her eyes closed.

Darcy grunted as he pulled the twisted blanket out from underneath him. He pulled it over them both before he slid into the cooling spot beside her.

"How so?" he asked with a kiss to her shoulder.

"We could've… been doing *that*… all this time…" She drew off sleepily.

He smiled. "I make poor decisions where you are concerned." At her faint stirring, he guessed the cause and continued, "It is not meant unkindly. Only, where you are the subject, I become the very fool I despise. Our liaison. My exposing us to your relatives and forcing a marriage. Once I came up with the idea, I should have known then it was not the right path. How may I make amends to you, Lizzy?"

She turned her head toward his. He couldn't see her

eyes, but he could hear the smile in her voice. "This is a good start."

He returned it, kissed her shoulder again. "Is it?"

"A rather good one."

"Good," he said, settling down beside her. She clasped the wrist of the arm he threw across her stomach. "I'm eager to make amends."

And so he was the next morning.

16

The morning was rapidly disappearing into a fine midday and Elizabeth could not complain, though she valiantly made the attempt.

"What of breakfast?" Even her voice was gone, now a husky rasp that seemed to stir Darcy's blood even as it embarrassed her. "Or lunch, now."

Darcy pulled her leg up and over his, enabling him to sink even deeper inside her. His chest was sticky with sweat and his flesh clung to her back, increasing the warmth of their bodies threefold, it seemed.

"I will feed you my cock now," he murmured, his gravelly voice in her ear powerful enough to make her clench around him. He pulled out and then pushed forward again, lubricated with her own arousal. "And I shall feast on you again," he continued and her eyes closed. "Then our bellies will both be full."

"It's difficult finding fault with that reasoning," she said.

"Impossible," he agreed.

And they didn't say much of anything for a time.

"How well you look this morning. Is the novel coming along then?"

"It's marvellous," she said, which made Mr. Anderson blink at her as he finished taking his seat in the small booth across from her. After a moment, he laughed and shook his head, and she supposed her reply was a tad too exuberant. Yet she couldn't help it, nor the smile pulling her lips apart. She could no more dim it than she could throw a blanket over the sun.

He took a sip of his coffee and placed it back down in its saucer with a tidy clink. "That's all very good then. Davies would shout the roof down if you so much as go to the beach one hour too many, with us on the second reprinting."

"I sent it off to London yesterday evening," she said. It was surprising how productive one could become when not beset by marital worries. She had call to be even more pleased about her increased industriousness when Mr. Anderson happily called for a fresh tray of biscuits to celebrate.

They were at the seaside inn where he'd arranged a private dining room for their conversation. It was a respectable room with a window showing a view of the tiny lane that ran down the length of the village and beyond that to the pier where several small boats were bobbing merrily in the waves.

A bell rang from somewhere in the distance, making Georgiana tilt her head beside Elizabeth. Georgiana had brought a book, but seemed less interested in it than the business being conducted here. She caught Elizabeth's eye and grinned shyly, ducking her head.

"A weight off my shoulders, I will tell you. The ladies in

ton begging information on the next novel sent me fleeing here, so they will be happy and I will be much happier," Mr. Anderson said with all his grace and good breeding. The dimple in his cheek deepened with his smile. "Then what is it I may do for you, Miss—Mrs. Darcy?"

"I actually have a proposal for your consideration." She paused, on the cusp of a path and understanding it would either lead her to success or to embarrassment. "I seek to invest in Campton-on-Sea with you and propose a subscription library to start."

To her delight—if an uneasy one—Mr. Anderson did not quibble or clarify. He didn't ask pointed questions about her husband's considerations of this endeavour. He looked straight into her eyes and he said, "What an idea! Of course, since you are creating quite a stir yourself in all the libraries of the country, it makes perfect sense. I have a planning meeting with some notable members of the community tomorrow. Would you be willing to join us?"

Elizabeth agreed to attend and Georgiana tentatively enquired what the gentleman proposed to change or improve, leading to a hearty discussion of Mr. Anderson's plans and what future he envisioned. It captivated Georgiana and satisfied Elizabeth. All of it echoed the investment proposal Darcy had provided to her, and she found herself pleased with every confirmation that this was an investment she could stand behind. She desired no great riches. Only to give back, in some small way, to this beautiful village that had helped heal her heart after her father's passing, and her marriage.

Georgiana looked thoughtful as they walked down the lane that led from the village to the manor. "That was… different from what I expected. I thought ladies were supposed to, erm—"

"Gossip and knit? Not to say those are not worthy endeavours," she added while Georgiana snickered, "but yet, I didn't find enough interest to subsume myself within it."

"I wonder if my brother will let *me* invest."

"Why shouldn't he? As long as you are aware of the risk and do not extend yourself past reason…"

"My brother must care for you greatly," Georgiana said with a wistful air. "Sometimes it feels as if I am simply the little sister he must shelter and protect—not that I resent his attention, certainly," she hurriedly added. "But I must confess I feel more like a burden than a person he can trust, like he does you."

"It is the calling of the eldest to look after the youngest. My own younger sisters probably believe the same as you, and perhaps it will be hard for me to see them as *equal* when they have not entirely expressed their maturity yet. After all, I've seen all their silliness. But I assure you, once you prove your understanding and knowledge, you will earn new respect from your brother. Our opinions are not set in stone, after all."

"That heartens me," Georgiana said but her lips were turned down in thought. "I fear my past actions won't endear me to him anytime soon."

Elizabeth giggled at her sister-in-law's far too serious expression. "I cannot imagine you have been any worse than *my* sisters."

Georgiana paled and drew her arms around herself. "Right," she whispered.

This curious reaction disturbed Elizabeth, but before she could probe—sensitively, of course—Georgiana in response, they reached the stone wall surrounding the manor. Georgiana grabbed her skirts and hurried forward, kicking up dust behind her. Surprised, Elizabeth let her go. In the months since their arrival here, they had become closer, but there were still some subjects Elizabeth would need to be sensitive of, it seemed.

Flowering vines crawling on the stone wall and bees buzzed industriously around their perfume. Ahead, she could hear the gate clanging and Georgiana greeting someone. She rounded the corner and saw Georgiana hurrying away up the garden path to the house while the postman spoke to a member of the staff.

"Sir," she said kindly when the gentleman greeted her with a tip of his hat.

Mr. Tremble held out two letters from her while the postman resumed his route. "Ma'am, he's brought two letters for you. Shall I bring them to your office?"

"I'll take them, thank you," she said, and accepted them. Georgiana had already retreated inside and Elizabeth looked down at the letters, recognizing her aunt Philip's hand on one while the other bore a hand that struck a chord with Elizabeth. She couldn't quite place it. Frowning slightly, she used her nail to open the envelope and unfolded the letter.

Within minutes, she was hurrying inside. "Mr. Darcy, where is he?" she asked the first servant she encountered.

The young woman looked startled. "In his study, ma'am."

Thanking the girl in a distracted manner, she rushed down the hall and barged into Darcy's study without knocking.

Darcy half-stood when he saw her expression. "What is the matter?" he asked, his hands on his desk as if he was prepared to jump over it to be by her side.

"My sister," Elizabeth said, gasping a little as if she had run the two miles here instead of a leisurely walk. She crossed the room and nearly sagged in relief when Darcy rounded the desk and came to her side, sliding his arm around her back. "Kitty wrote me. Something terrible…"

"Is anyone hurt?"

"Not – not that she says. Not physically. Oh, I'll have to disappoint Mr. Anderson. Darcy, they need me at Longbourn and I'm afraid I must go immediately."

"Tell me," Darcy said.

Elizabeth's hands trembled as she lifted the letter. "Kitty begged to come to us, *begged* me, Darcy." Her chin wobbled, and she stiffened her shoulders, pushing down the emotion to focus on what needed to happen. "She stated she didn't mind coming with or without Lydia as long as she could leave Longbourn. But Darcy, she would never ask to be separated from Lydia, not without cause. From this, I can only assume conditions are worse than even Jane knew, or else she would have insisted on my mother and sisters going to Netherfield. She provides no specifics—Kitty has always been a poor correspondent—but there is no doubt they are suffering from that alone."

"But your mother's letters have mentioned none of this?"

The heavy weight of dread which had grown immense in her stomach hardened into lead. "I haven't opened any of the letters except the first, and that I didn't read past the first line. My mother could have been crying for help all this time and—" She put her hand over her mouth, the burn behind her eyes breaking free and a tear spilling over her cheek. "Oh, I must go see!"

"I'll arrange the carriage and our things. Georgiana should go with the staff back to London in our absence; I don't favour her being days away in the event she needs us. Do not fret, my dear. We will see this through together." He squeezed her hands and brought them to his lips, kissing the tops of her knuckles. "Go read your letters and find out as much as you can, then pack."

"But this is my fault, Darcy. I shouldn't upend the household for this. What if I go to Netherfield and from there seek out Kitty—"

"If it involves that Collins character, consider it already done. I will be there—even a hurricane of chaos is worth it to keep you safe." His demeanour darkened, jaw clenched as he seethed. "I have no doubt Collins will attempt to bring some form of retribution, to stroke his bloated pride. He is the type of coward who takes pleasure from inflicting pain on others."

Relieved, she closed her eyes, but a mighty weight still gripped her in its claws. "I can't deny that I'm relieved you'll come," she muttered, turning her head so he couldn't see the shame on her face. "I must confess relief to the idea," she said. "Is it terrible that I'm afraid to face him again?"

"If you wish me to proceed alone, I will gladly—"

"I know," she whispered, her throat tight. "I know you would. But I must go and if you are there, at least I will not falter. Oh, Darcy, what if he…" She couldn't finish, the thought was too terrible.

He squeezed her. "Go. Read your letters and pack, Lizzy. We'll leave in the morning."

17

"Are you warm enough?" Darcy asked, straightening the blanket stretched across her lap.

"Yes," she said quietly. A blanket would not cure the chill which had settled in her bones yesterday. Her shoulders hunched, she rested her forehead against the side of the carriage, wishing the countryside would go by faster. In her hand was her sister's letter, crumpled and smudged with oils from Elizabeth's hand. She had worried at the problem all night, and now unpleasant exhaustion stung her eyelids.

"It's about an hour to the coaching inn. Will you be able to wait or do you need a rest?"

A two-day trip. Elizabeth sighed. "I can wait."

The weather turned colder the further north they travelled. A weight wrapped around Elizabeth's chest, squeezed when her thoughts attempted to stray from the plight of her sisters. At least her mother's letters had not described any torments, only the complaints Elizabeth had expected when she set aside the letters unopened. Her poor sisters; how could she have left them to suffer at the hands of that man?

If only she'd insisted! Now they were undoubtedly tormented by the foul man, tortured enough for Kitty to beg to be parted from her beloved little sister as long as she got *away*.

Elizabeth was a terrible daughter *and* a terrible sister.

An ache in the back of her throat prevented her from getting much rest. Despite how she resented the delay, she longed for a comfortable bed. Anything to escape this unsettled miasma of dread and worry.

"Come here," Darcy said, sounding as if he'd finally reached the end of his tether. He curled his arm around her and drew her away from the window, against his chest. Fingers carefully tilted her chin up. "All will be well. I will make it so."

"Oh, what would I do without you? All I've brought you are problems, and yet greedily I hold on to you."

Darcy huffed, but his rebuke was mild. "I didn't pledge devotion to you only when times are good."

She smiled slightly; in seconds, it faded. "If only I'd thought of my sisters before we left Longbourn. And I was so grateful to leave, too! Not once did the consequences occur to me."

"I have the same knowledge as you and thus the same guilt," Darcy said. "But we had to respect your mother's wishes, and it would have been an insult to take all her daughters away and leave her alone, would it not?"

"Don't be reasonable," Elizabeth sighed, leaning into him. "I can't stand it."

Darcy's fingers smoothed along her jaw, moved into her hair, a comforting and real weight. "Let me distract you," he murmured, and kissed her. She let out a quiet sigh as her body melted into his and felt the world around them start to slip away. His kisses were sweet and slow, and with each one she felt a little more of her tension unravel. Yielding was easy. She was so ready for distraction, and Darcy eager to give it, that she spent the remainder of the hour clinging to him, and she fell asleep at once as soon as she stretched out beside him in the inn's bed.

She dreamt of a homecoming, of the garden gate creaking open and her sisters running out with happy tears in their eyes. But she awoke to find that the road home seemed even longer than before; her heart was heavy in her chest when she remembered what waited for her. Darcy helped as much as he could, but there was only so much distraction her guilt-ridden heart would allow her.

When they finally reached Hertfordshire, it was with much trepidation that Elizabeth agreed to go to Netherfield first. "The more support we have when we collect your sisters, the better it will be for them," Darcy said, and Elizabeth reluctantly agreed.

"But she's said nothing to me!" Jane said when Elizabeth explained their sudden appearance at their door. Jane smoothed Kitty's letter flat and read it again in shock, her head shaking back and forth. "I was only there Saturday and she said nothing. Perhaps she is merely hoping for a change in scenery?"

"Was she *able* to speak comfortably to you?" Darcy bowed his head when Jane stared at him in rising dismay. "I apologise, Jane, but it may be that Mr. Collins's presence does not allow them to speak their feelings."

"I did see him listening at doors when he visited the first time," Elizabeth said sourly. The image of Mr. Collins skulking around the house and terrorizing her sisters was perfectly reasonable, in her opinion.

Jane's face had paled. She could imagine the realisation that her sisters hadn't felt safe enough to speak comfortably to her would hit dear, sweet Jane hard. Her hand shook as she held the letter back to Elizabeth. "We shall go at once then? But what do we do about Mother? She still insists she will not leave Longbourn unless it is to London, and our aunt Gardiner remains adamant that they cannot support her nor our sisters entirely. We have discussed letting a small house in London," she added, looking to Bingley, "but I'm afraid the expenses of maintaining two households may stretch us unreasonably. It would be better if she would agree to live here, but she will not."

Elizabeth and Darcy shared a look of understanding. It seemed the only solution was to discuss how they might all share the burden of supporting their family if everyone were to move to London. Elizabeth spoke first, offering up some ideas for small economies that could be made in both homes, forgoing her investment in Campton-on-Sea to support her mother and sisters. There would be little extravagance, not even on special occasions such as birthdays or holidays, and their sisters would need to be content with an economical wardrobe. Bingley nodded along with each point she made, then offered his own suggestions on ways they could stretch their funds further while still providing comfortable lodgings and food for both households. Jane gave her opinion on what services she thought they could outsource so that they would not have to pay full-time wages for servants, such as hiring local women to do the laundry or tasking the local boys with helping keep up.

But Darcy did not nod along. He looked grave, and his expression grew more and more stern as he listened.

"Longbourn belongs to the Bennet line. What we need is a solution to Mr. Collins's presence. We must buy him off. It is the only way."

"It is what we planned to do before your father passed," Bingley said gently in the face of his wife's surprise.

"You planned to do that?" Jane reached out to grab her husband's hand, tears in her eyes. He hugged her and she sniffled. "I never knew. Oh, Charles! How I wish my father could have known you for the man you are!" Pulling back from her husband, she smiled tearily at Darcy. "And you too, of course, Mr. Darcy."

"I cannot wait any longer," Elizabeth said, standing. She had ignored the tea tray Jane had ordered brought into the sitting room for them. She was gritty and tired from travel, but her body refused to relax until she set eyes upon her sisters and saw them unharmed. "We should go."

"At once," Jane agreed, standing and reaching out for Elizabeth. She grabbed hold of her sister's hand and squeezed. They would get through this. Together.

Of course Darcy was right to insist we come here first, Elizabeth thought as the group walked outside to the Darcy's carriage which was ready for the short trip to Longbourn. She leant against his side as she waited beside him while Bingley handed Jane inside the carriage and closed her eyes.

"Thank you," she whispered. "I don't know how I would have managed without your help."

He pressed a kiss to the top of her head. "Anything, my dear."

SHE WONDERED what kind of state their house would be in. Mr. Collins had already let go the majority of their staff and set her sisters to work they were unaccustomed to. Jane had described the work: in addition to cooking all the meals, they were to perform chores like laundry, preparing the fires, and gardening. Activities her sisters would have no idea how to perform, much less well.

"Economy is all well and good, but they are young ladies unaccustomed to such work," Bingley said, tsking as they discussed the altered situation at Longbourn while the carriage rocked back and forth around them. "I tried to explain to the fellow how any young lady faced with such chores would flounder, and it didn't look good for their respectability if they were marked with signs of hard work, but he wouldn't listen. Lady Catherine de Bourgh had given him strict instructions, he said."

Darcy sunk deeper into his seat, frowning. Elizabeth watched him with an unease she couldn't name. "You think Lady Catherine has much to do with the changes at Longbourn?"

He sighed heavily. "I fear as much. She would undoubtedly have shared all her ideas to bring Longbourn up to her expectations and given her anger at our union… I expect her advice was not well-spirited."

Elizabeth tensed, her anxiety rising. "Do you think she knew what she suggested was unreasonable?"

Darcy nodded, his jaw tight and eyes darkening further with each passing moment. "I can only assume that even if those suggestions seemed easy enough for such a proud lady as herself in theory, it likely didn't occur to her that servants would be needed for such tasks in practice—even if it did function against the estate's funds."

He shook his head and ran a hand through his hair before continuing: "But I wouldn't put it past Lady Catherine to believe your sisters could manage the work without assistance—and worse still, no doubt if they were seen struggling with it or if their appearance began to reflect hard labor, she wouldn't care."

The stale air made her nose wrinkle. Dust gathered on the baseboards and a musty smell hung in the air. It felt abandoned though she could hear the sound of voices—loud with an undercurrent of anger and resentment—coming from the kitchen.

"He will be arriving tomorrow and you will be on your best behaviour, young lady. Mr. Stonewort is a discerning gentleman and he will *not* accept any of your foolishness, understand?"

Lydia's furious voice cut off Mr. Collins' speech. "I don't see why I shouldn't act as I want! *I* don't want to marry some fussy parson like you, especially if all he does is make me *work* all day and night long with my hands burnt and broken from—"

"As master of this house, you will respect my—"

Elizabeth had heard enough. Heedless of Darcy's hand slipping off her shoulder, she hurried for the kitchen. Mr. Collins's face was red with fury and his eyes seemed ready to burst with anger and indignation as he glared at her sister. Lydia stood tall and hearty despite her rather drab muslin gown, surely nothing Elizabeth recognized from her sister's wardrobe. Her cheeks were suffused with colour and her lips pressed together in a thin line, her expression a mixture of anger and tears she would not let fall. Elizabeth stopped in the doorway right when Mr. Collins did something very stupid.

He raised his hand.

"Don't you dare!"

Elizabeth dashed forward, throwing herself between the squat, toad-like man and her sister before any blow could land. Surely it looked silly from an outsider's perspective; Lydia had outgrown Elizabeth last year, and towered above her now. But the urge to protect her little sister overwhelmed her like icy ocean spray. She pushed Lydia back towards the countertop.

Mr. Collins sputtered at her, his eyes gone wide. "Y-you! How *dare* you step foot where you are not welcome!"

"Are we not welcome? That is surprising news, to forbid a daughter from visiting her mother and sisters on no pretext," Darcy said coolly from the doorway. "And I daresay you should lower that hand, or else one might believe you think to strike my wife."

Mr. Collins paled, and he snatched his hand back as if Darcy had tried to whip said appendage. "Mr. D-Darcy! I did not expect you. For-forgive me. It has been a rather trying day as we prepare for—"

"He plans to sell me off like we're at the market, and the man is one foot in the grave already at one-and-sixty!" Lydia cried. She clung to Elizabeth and her distress must have been great, because she burst into tears as she had not done since she was in the nursery. "Oh, Lizzy, he won't let us go to any assemblies or even any dinner parties. And look at my poor hands! What man will take me for a wife now?"

Lydia's hands were indeed in terrible condition. Broken and cracked, the skin peeling off in long stripes. Elizabeth stared at them in horror before lifting her gaze to meet Mr. Collins's.

He stumbled back a step. "Some sacrifices must be made. The st-state of the finances didn't provide enough for the upkeep of the house.. Your father, God have mercy upon his soul—"

"We saw a new coach outside—I recall a serviceable one remained here when we left," Darcy said with a voice as cool as an icicle poised above the back of one's neck.

Mr. Collins looked ill. "A gentleman must have a respectable conveyance, of course. Surely you would understand that…" Darcy's glower darkened and Mr. Collins gulped. He looked around the room, at Bingley holding Jane's shoulders behind Darcy, to Elizabeth still cradling her sister and glowering at him, and his Adam's apple bobbed. "A gentleman…" he tried, but his quavering voice apparently refused to go on any further.

Contrary to this, Elizabeth's voice was hard as steel. "Why is my sister injured? And where is Kitty?"

Lydia furiously answered. "He sold off all our nicest dresses and made us cook and do laundry. The soap hurt our hands but he only told us to stop crying. And when Kitty tried to leave for our aunt Phillips', he dragged her to the attic!"

"My goodness—!" Jane exclaimed. "Charles!"

Bingley caught Jane's hand before she could hurry off toward the stairs. "Of course. At once. Darcy?"

"I'll watch him," Darcy said, watching Mr. Collins as the man trembled and stuttered out something incomprehensible but that sounded like 'my house to do as I please.' Darcy said, "Lizzy, come out of there. Go to your mother. I need to *speak* to Mr. Collins now. We have much to discuss, don't we?"

Mr. Collins fumbled out a handkerchief and mopped at the sweat beading his temple. He didn't look at Elizabeth again; he didn't dare to with Darcy's icy stare pinning him down.

Elizabeth nodded. She was in no position to speak to Mr. Collins when her soul demanded she make him hurt as much as her sisters did. Turning her back on him, she urged Lydia to come along, and the two left under Darcy's protective eye.

Elizabeth turned to her sister as soon as they were far enough away from the kitchen. Behind her, she could hear

Darcy's cold tones start—on the path to setting Mr. Collins straight, she expected.

"Let's get you washed up. We'll go out to the pump and later boil some water—"

Lydia was already shaking her head, pulling her hands out of Elizabeth's. "We should go see Mama and Kitty. Kitty'll be so relieved, I tell you. Mr. Collins was all set to marry *her*."

"No!" Elizabeth gasped. But she should have foreseen it. There was no better way to cement his grip on Longbourn than to marry a Bennet. Poor Kitty. "We'll take you all to London if we have to," she promised. Lydia just looked tired. Elizabeth chivvied her toward the stairs, worried and not a little anxious by her gregarious sister's altered personality. "Why didn't you tell anyone? Kitty wrote me, but if you had told me sooner, I would have come even sooner to put a stop to this!"

"I couldn't leave Mama," Lydia said simply. "She's been so unreasonable. We begged and begged her to move to Netherfield, but there's no convincing her. You *will* talk to her, won't you?"

"I will," Elizabeth said. She squeezed Lydia's shoulders. "I'm so proud of you, Lydia."

Lydia offered a tired laugh in response to this. "That's a lark. He wasn't so bad until that old cow wrote and told him to put us to work. If I *ever* have to touch his smelly shirts again, it will be too soon!"

Jane and Bingley had retrieved Kitty from the attic. The younger girl saw Elizabeth and Lydia and burst into fresh tears. Elizabeth caught her awkwardly when she threw herself forward to hug them both. "Oh, I'm ever so happy you came for us," she cried. "Thank you, thank you! Shall I go and pack?" she added as she pulled back, sniffling while she looked between Jane and Elizabeth. "Lydia swears she will not come—"

"And I won't—or at least I wouldn't, before," Lydia. "Not unless Mama came with us. But now…" The thought of marrying someone so unsuitable, vastly older than her age, obviously put matters into perspective for the young woman, who bit her lip.

Elizabeth looked between them. "How is she? What has she said about all of this?"

"Oh, you know Mama," Lydia said while Kitty accepted Jane's handkerchief and dabbed at her splotchy cheeks.

Elizabeth and Jane exchanged a glance, and Elizabeth sighed, wishing there was someone else to take charge but knowing there wasn't unless she wanted to drag Darcy upstairs away from the *true* issue. Her mother was a decidedly smaller issue, in comparison. "We shall see what Mr. Darcy can do," she said. "In the meantime, we should not get our mother's hopes up."

A look of understanding crossed Jane's face, and she turned to Bingley. "We will be fine," she said, while he softened at the hand she pressed to his shoulder. "Go assist Mr. Darcy. This is something we must handle."

Bingley went and then Jane turned to their youngest sisters. "You've both been through much. Rest would—"

"I'm not missing this," Lydia said and marched down the hall to their mother's room. Elizabeth and Jane turned to Kitty, who shrugged and followed Lydia, locking their arms together before stepping inside without knocking. Elizabeth groaned. *Sisters.*

Jane squeezed her elbow as she passed. "That's decided then, I suppose. Coming?"

And though it was like her shoes had turned into lead

weights she had to drag forward, she followed her sisters into her mother's bedroom.

Elizabeth watched her youngest sisters with a heavy heart as they entered their mother's room before she turned to see what had become of her mother. Hill had been Mrs. Bennet's faithful champion and companion, but in her absence, along with Mrs. Bennet's self-imposed confinement, her appearance had deteriorated drastically. However, Mrs. Bennet had always had extraordinarily good health, according to the same professionals who visited Mr. Bennet, so Elizabeth was consoled that though her mother may look bedraggled and tired where she lay stretched out across the bed, she was still as healthy as ever.

Jane stepped to the side of the bed tentatively, her voice softening as she spoke to her mother. "Mama," she said gently, trying not to disturb their mother's rest.

"So. You've finally come."

The rasp was not directed at Kitty and Lydia, who'd squeezed in together in the same seat beside Mrs. Bennet's tall bed, nor was it directed at Jane who stood tentatively at the foot of the bed. Mrs. Bennet saw past all her other daughters when she cracked open her eyes to stare balefully at Elizabeth.

"Yes, I'm here," she said, forcing herself to step inside and close the door. She turned back to her mother and clasped her hands before her. "How are you?"

"In fine form, naturally. Look at me, Lizzy. How do you think I feel with that odious man picking apart my home and my daughter who I fed at my own breast turning her back on her own blood!" The arm Mrs. Bennet was waving about in her impassioned speech dropped to the mattress beside her. "Really," she huffed.

"I'll accept *'fine'* as an answer," Elizabeth muttered,

coming forward reluctantly. Steeling herself, she slid into the spot beside Jane and met her mother's bitter gaze. Her sisters' health and happiness mattered more than petty resentments, and she told herself that even as her mother opened her mouth for a new barrage.

"You could at least make an effort to oblige me! It isn't as if I am asking you to move Heaven and Earth. Just that you set us up in London, as I know all the right people who can help secure a suitable match for Lydia and Kitty."

Elizabeth glanced over at Jane, finding her taken aback by their mother's attitude. Clearly, she had expected Mrs. Bennet's ire to be directed at Mr. Collins, not Elizabeth. Elizabeth wasn't surprised, and a part of her hurt anew seeing her sister's expression fall in disappointment.

Taking a deep breath, Elizabeth mustered all her courage and spoke firmly yet respectfully. "Mr. Darcy and Mr. Bingley are hopefully arranging it so Mr. Collins will be leaving Longbourn. However, if that cannot happen, we must discuss our options, with an eye toward ensuring Kitty and Lydia's safety and wellbeing."

Jane furrowed her brow as she looked at their mother. "Mama, did you know what Mr. Collins was doing? Surely you spoke to her?" she added, looking to their young sisters.

While Kitty was occupied dabbing at her cheeks with a stained handkerchief, Lydia opened her mouth. Mrs. Bennet swiftly cut her off. "And what was I supposed to do? Put you out, Jane, when you are but a newlywed and should be focused on giving Mr. Bingley an heir, or should I have inconvenienced my sister? You know I loathe being an inconvenience!"

Elizabeth could not believe her ears. "Inconvenience! It is not an inconvenience to ensure your daughters are treated like respectable gentlewomen. Look at Lydia's hands, Mama!"

"And whose fault is that? If *you* had not turned your back on us—"

"The fault is Mr. Collins', of course," Elizabeth snapped. "But it also the fault of the guardian who failed to see to their basic needs for health and happiness. No, Jane, I will not hush. Look at them. Kitty was locked in the *attic*, and I will not be silent."

"It is just as I have always said. Ungrateful girl!"

"Perhaps it is best I am, because look at the ones devoted to you!" She gestured to her dirty, injured sisters. "You have failed them in every way a mother can," she said, and perhaps seeing her youngest huddled, smudged with dirt and cobwebs in Kitty's case and Lydia soot stained, finally penetrated the fog of her selfish pity. Mrs. Bennet's gaze softened for a split second before she turned back to scowl at Elizabeth, but that split second was enough.

Elizabeth's resolve broke. Her mother knew, she *knew* what miseries her daughters were suffering, and yet she did not care enough to even make the attempt to cure it. All because she valued entering the London drawing rooms and social circles as Darcy's mother-in-law above her daughters. Which made Elizabeth realise that whatever love she claimed for her daughters, it wasn't deep enough to overcome her own larger self-interest.

It wasn't only Elizabeth, either. Even her favourite daughter—and there was no doubt Lydia was her favourite —was of lesser standing in Mrs. Bennet's eyes.

To say the truth shocked her was an understatement.

"Stop," she said when Mrs. Bennet's mouth opened to no doubt sow more discord. She held up her hand and took a deep breath, praying for patience. "What I do from this point forward will be for my sisters, not you, because your actions have demonstrated that my sisters need more care than you can afford to offer."

"Lizzy," Jane murmured, and Elizabeth looked at her and found her not disapproving, only cautious. Kitty was staring at Elizabeth with dawning hope in her eyes, and that was the worst part.

Mrs. Bennet gasped. "What is the meaning of this? Lydia, Kitty, don't just sit there, tell her how put upon by my troubles—oh, the tremblings, the flutterings I've suffered, so that I can sleep neither night nor day!"

Neither girl looked at their mother. Kitty's lips were pressed in a tight white line. For all Lydia's gumption when she declared she'd stay with their mother, this blatant, *calculated* disinterest struck like Mr. Collins never could. Lydia's hands were fisted in her lap and she didn't look at Elizabeth, didn't look at anyone, only stared at her knees.

Elizabeth looked at their faces and swallowed salty regret. She never should've assumed they would be fine with Mr. Collins in the house. She'd had too much trust in her mother, and that was a lesson her sisters had to pay in her stead. "Look what your stubbornness has got you, Mother: the lifelong trauma your two youngest must now live with for the rest of their lives while you, you, sat up here and bemoaned your comforts! You will either stay here or you will go to whichever of our relatives will have you, but either way, Kitty and Lydia will be under *my* care, not yours, as you've seen fit to throw away your opportunity to be their mother!"

"How–how could you let her speak to me like this? Jane! Jane, dear, you saw too how terrible my condition was—"

But the final Bennet daughter in the room had finally lost their rosy perspective, at least where it concerned her mother, and she turned to their younger sisters. "Come along. Let us go clean up and see what damage is done."

"Come back!" Mrs. Bennet cried. "After all I have done for you. Lydia, look at me! Lydia, you know I could do nothing to that insufferable man. *Lydia!*"

Elizabeth put her hand on Lydia's shoulder when the girl passed her, and their mother's cries followed her out.

18

"My dear, how plump and happy your cheeks are!"

"Aunt!" Elizabeth said, squirming slightly away from Mrs. Gardiner's hands which squeezed her cheeks.

Mrs. Gardiner sniffed in approval as she released Elizabeth and turned to Kitty and Lydia. "The sea air did you all three good. You even have a bit of sunburn on your nose, Lydia! And you said you should never suffer because of a lack of a bonnet," she said, tsking, and Lydia blushed and loudly disputed this spin on events, and claimed Campton-on-Sea was simply too hot and bright for her fair, delicate skin.

"And it has nothing to do with your constant forgetting of your parasol," Elizabeth said, to Lydia's further consternation. After a few minutes, however, and with the arrival of Mary along with their small cousins, Lydia was back in good humour, settling herself down in the corner with her sisters and cousins to gossip and make merry.

Elizabeth broke away and followed Mrs. Gardiner to the spot by the front window. So long ago they had sat here with

Mrs. Gardiner happily speaking about her expectations for Elizabeth's future. Believing her aunt then had been impossible, but now, after

"We depart for Pemberley in a fortnight. It means missing most of the season, but truthfully, some time away is what we all need. Georgiana grows tired of London anyway."

"Oh, does she? Poor dear. She didn't say so when she invited me to visit. Though she did seem lonely, I suppose."

"It has more to do with Darcy's choice of companion, I suppose," Elizabeth said. "At least Ms. Chapman cannot come to Pemberley, and I'll work on Darcy in the meantime to find someone more suitable."

Which wouldn't be a hardship, she thought with a private smile as she poured tea for them both. Darcy's irritation after a day in her presence made it obvious he disliked the woman, and he would probably seek out a suitable position in another family for her as soon as they left London. Ms. Chapman was as convinced of her rightness as a bird was convinced it could fly. She made it hard to like her, but the prospect of *convincing* her perfectly willing husband to find her another position made Elizabeth grateful to the unpleasant woman.

"Your uncle and I have already begin daydreaming about our trip for Christmas," Mrs. Gardiner said. "It's lucky you married someone so close to Lambton that I may visit old friends—if you weren't such a happy couple, I might think you married him for my benefit," she said, laughing. Elizabeth concealed her smile, looking away, only to hear Mrs. Gardiner delicately clear her throat. "May I ask," she began, her brow furrowed as if this was the last topic she wished to discuss, "no one's said, but will your mother be invited?"

"She has been," Elizabeth said, pursing her lips while she sipped her tea.

Mrs. Gardiner winced at her expression. "I suppose she didn't reply well to that."

"Barred the whole village from Longbourn for a week, Jane said, and didn't even go to the dinner arranged for Sir William's birthday, though she'd looked forward to it." Elizabeth sighed. "It's terrible to *feel* like I should be more responsible for her state than I am. Sometimes I feel like her condition is my fault, and then I remember what she did, and my sympathies wither again. Am I strange?"

"No," Mrs. Gardiner said slowly. "Fanny has suffered much as a caretaker to your father, and she did the best she could by you girls, but she keenly knew what joys of society she'd missed and bitterly lamented them. I can sympathise with her while at the same time understanding that does not give her the right to hurt others as she had, and continues to do. All I can hope for is that she still has that tender spark of compassion that drew your father to her, and for which my husband speaks so fondly about, and hope she rekindles it. We both do." She sat her tea down and looked over to the other Bennet girls, a small, fond smile forming. "In the meantime, we'll take good care of her daughters."

Elizabeth followed her eye and knew it was true. Her sisters were whole, healthy, and moving forward. And Elizabeth and Jane had both learned hard truths about themselves, and about their family. Elizabeth had learned not to ignore an issue simply because tackling it was too difficult, or seemed insurmountable—something she would apply to her own marriage, too, going forward.

Meanwhile Jane had learned a bitter, unfortunate fact about their mother's character which could not be explained away. Jane's disillusionment was not something she wished for, and Elizabeth would've gladly given her the gift of ignorance, but Jane was recovering too, reviving some of her rosy optimism as the days went on.

Lydia and Kitty, as generally happy young ladies were wont to do, rebounded beautifully, and had spent the time since leaving Longbourn giggling about the eligible gentlemen in Campton-on-Sea, sunbathing, and generally creating good-humoured gaiety around them. Darcy pronounced them promising, as long as they kept them away from officers. Why he included Georgiana in this pronouncement, she wasn't sure, but she didn't fault his good sense.

And Mr. Collins, once Darcy and Bingley propelled him bodily into his new coach while Mr. Collins whimpered about informing his former patroness, learned some harsh truths of his own. While travelling back to the home he'd left in Hunsford, his coach had been set upon. His shaken driver claimed they'd been overtaken by a pressgang, and spun a far-fetched tale about the former parson shouting in fright when he recognized the gentleman leading them—for he was a gentleman, the driver insisted, and he led the gang with all the presence of a military commander. No one thought any pressgang would do their dirty deeds that far into the countryside, and the driver was given a pint and sent on his way while everyone shook their heads. Anyway, far-fetched though it was, Mr. Collins hadn't filed a countersuit against Darcy's claim on some Longbourn mortgages in the courts, and the estate eventually ended up back within the Bennet line, safe for future generations. Colonel Fitzwilliam had come for supper just last evening to celebrate.

Kitty had once wondered what had happened to Mr. Collins. Lydia had shared a glance with Elizabeth, before Lydia shrugged and said, "La, who cares? Let us go to the shore today and watch the ships."

Regularly travelling with Kitty and Lydia was still something Elizabeth was still adjusting to. They were giggly and full of nonsense, and it took some courage for a sane, sober person to willingly enter a carriage with them. If he could have, Darcy would have travelled the whole way from the seaside to London with his hands clamped over his ears.

Elizabeth was still recovering from the short trip from Cheapside to the townhome while she took down her hair in the silence of her bedroom. The house was quiet; Georgiana had retired from her music room to join Elizabeth's sisters for tea. She had heard the faint echo of them chattering together until she closed the door of her bedroom. While she unclasped her earrings, the door opened behind her and their voices painted the silence again before the door closed.

"Hello, dear," she said, looking at the reflection of the man coming closer over her shoulder. "Did they chase you from your study?"

He shook his head with a slight huff of laughter. "Having a full house full of people has been quite the experience, I must say."

"Especially when you're outnumbered." She leaned back into his hands when they slid over her shoulders. "How was your day, love?"

"Better now," he said, bending down to press his lips to her cheek. Twinkling eyes held hers in the reflection and she once again thanked her good luck to have married such a devastatingly handsome man. Even more so when he dipped his head, nipping at her ear, then the pulse point high on her neck. "My love," he murmured as she grew warm in the wake of his affection, "I missed you. Are you undressing?"

"Changing," she corrected primly, and focused on unclasping her other earring. "It's almost time for dinner."

His hand lifted to the pins in her hair. Slowly, he pulled out one, sending a curl tumbling over her shoulder. "I can arrange it in our room," he said, lust shimmering between them.

"*My* room," she said. She caught his gaze in the mirror and tilted her head, eyebrows lifted. "Unless you are inviting yourself to it?"

Darcy's reflection smirked at her. "If I said I am?" he said, lowering his head to press a warm kiss with a hint of teeth to the juncture of her neck and shoulder. He pulled another pin free and a lazy curl of desire uncoiled in her breast. "What would you say?"

Her eyes half-lidded. "Mm. I wouldn't resist."

"I'll give you all the privacy you need," he said, pulling her up and helping her take the last of the pins out of her hair. When her hair curled freely down her back, he drew her into him, his embrace the right sort of temptation. "But your nights"—his lips grazed hers, once, twice, watering the bud of desire in her breast—"are wholly mine."

Tangling her fingers in his hair, she smiled up at him. "And yours mine."

"Naturally," he growled, and lifted her atop her vanity table. Her brush and pins scattering to the floor, their hands eager to yank and tug at each other's clothes, they collided together into a familiar, beautiful madness.

His cravat was only halfway free when he notched himself at her entrance and surged forward without warning, one stroke making them both gasp and freeze. The back of her head hit the mirror, and the spell broke. Darcy fell atop her breasts, licking and sucking, and she hooked her legs about him and hunted the divine friction she needed.

"Ah, don't stop," she whimpered, but Darcy was already pulling free, turning her, sending a hatpin off her vanity while she slammed her hands down atop the wood top and met his eyes in the mirror. He thrust, and her eyes closed, her lips parting.

"There you are, just like our first time. Don't you remember?" He impatiently tugged down the shoulder of her rumpled dress, baring the skin to his demanding mouth. Eyes dark with lust met hers in the mirror and he thrust again, harder, making her hips bump into the wood. "Remember?"

"Yes." It was a whimper, even as her core squeezed tight around him.

Darcy groaned, and his pace began to increase. "Better this time," he rumbled, watching her greedily, his hand clamping down on the back of her neck and making her go taut all over. His grin was savage as his hips snapped forward. "So much better."

Forced to keep watching their reflections surge together, reliving the moment twice over, Elizabeth's body was overrun with the pleasure of giving herself completely over to Darcy.

"Tell me, wife. Tell me what you want."

"Darcy—!"

The blush burned under her skin though she knew it had been coming. Every night he said some variation of this, made this demand for her to say something that made her insides squirm and her core clutch at him. He rolled his hips, pinning her against the vanity, and slammed his free hand over hers as he bent over her back.

"Say it," he said, black gaze a brand on her flesh.

"Put a babe in me," she whispered.

Darcy hissed, his fingers tangling with hers, the sounds of their rough coupling filling the room. Her backside hurt with each furious demand from her husband's hips, her core clenching around him when he ground hard and deep. Elizabeth lost control. Blackness swirled at the edges of her vision. Her head dropped, her thighs shaking, only Darcy's arm snaking under her waist keeping her upright.

"I'll see you heavy with our child," he said into her hair when several moments had passed. Elizabeth's heart was still hammering behind her closed eyes. His hand brushed over her stomach. "See your belly round and your breasts grow ready to nurture our heir. I'm having dreams, you know."

Dreams like the ones he'd told her about, dreams of them together before they were married. Eyes still closed, she let him pull her back against his chest, her hands lifting to clasp the arms that encircled her waist, bound to him heart and soul. "Can you tell me about them?" she said before a yawn escaped her.

Darcy carried her to bed and did so.

A tiny flame was growing inside her with each heartbeat. Elizabeth pondered on whether she should tell him… well, she'd tell him soon enough. When she was certain. When he didn't look so sweet, she thought sleepily while her husband expanded on his dreams of two dark-haired girls.

EPILOGUE

FOUR YEARS LATER

"Care-careful there—oh, she is pretending she cannot hear me again, isn't she?"

Elizabeth sighed as she watched Eleanor run across the lawn with her head upturned toward the pink silk kite flying merrily over her head against the pale blue sky. Beside Elizabeth, Darcy placed his hand on her back and chuckled.

"I believe so. As stubborn as us both, I'm afraid."

"To think such an unruly child is *your* offspring! Mrs. Reynolds reminds me daily how perfect you were as a child, and here is your daughter who cannot keep her dresses clean for a quarter of an hour."

She looked up at her husband and found him staring with quiet pride after their daughter, who indeed did have grass stains on the knees of her gold dress. Elizabeth heard stories about Darcy's frequent visits to the nursery throughout the day and wondered how he got *any* work done. Of course, Elizabeth herself slipped away from her writing desk to peek in on her apple cheeked Eleanor with enough frequency to fill Mr. Davies's latest letter with rebukes to keep to his publishing schedule.

"Perhaps this one will be a more respectable Darcy child," she said, placing a hand on her growing belly.

Darcy's chest expanded and a dimpled smile flashed over his face. "I expect Eleanor would see to that."

Once again, Elizabeth sighed, though her lips twitched as she watched their little girl shouting indecipherable nonsense up ahead. "I expect so."

He turned to her and covered her hand with his. The light in his eyes hadn't faded since the birth of their daughter and they only grew warmer with the announcement of their second. "My love," he said, tangling their fingers together. "I would be happy with a nursery full of Eleanors, as I know you would. Little Bennet or Helen will have the most loving elder sister in the world, and the best mother a child can want."

She tilted her chin up and he didn't resist the invitation for a kiss. "And the finest father, too," she said against his lips. Elizabeth couldn't imagine being any happier.

ABOUT THE AUTHOR

Emma is a married, happy mother of one living in the Southern United States. Her hobbies include spoiling her two cats and writing steamy romance novels. She loves dabbling in all kinds of romance genres, especially historical and paranormal, and writes fiction under several pen names.